An

Rachel Dove is a tutor and romance/rom-com author from West Yorkshire, in the UK. She lives with her husband and two sons, and dreams of a life where housework is done by fairies and she can have as many pets as she wants. When she is not writing or reading she can be found dreaming of her next research trip away with the family.

CHRISTMAS MIRACLE ON THEIR DOORSTEP

ANN McINTOSH

SINGLE MUM'S MISTLETOE KISS

RACHEL DOVE

MILLS & BOON

First published in Great Britain 2022
by Mills & Boon, an imprint of HarperCollins*Publishers* Ltd,
1 London Bridge Street, London, SE1 9GF

www.harpercollins.co.uk

HarperCollins*Publishers*
1st Floor, Watermarque Building,
Ringsend Road, Dublin 4, Ireland

Christmas Miracle on Their Doorstep © 2022 Harlequin Enterprises ULC

Special thanks and acknowledgement are given to Ann McIntosh
for her contribution to the Carey Cove Midwives miniseries.

Single Mum's Mistletoe Kiss © 2022 Harlequin Enterprises ULC

Special thanks and acknowledgement are given to Rachel Dove
for her contribution to the Carey Cove Midwives miniseries.

ISBN: 978-0-263-30143-4

11/22

CHRISTMAS MIRACLE ON THEIR DOORSTEP

ANN McINTOSH

MILLS & BOON

For Mary-Eve, who loves Christmas romances best.
Thank you for your friendship and support!

CHAPTER ONE

NYA ADEMI TOOK OFF her seldom-used reading glasses and blinked rapidly. Normally she didn't have to put them on immediately on arriving at work but waited until the afternoon, after a day particularly heavy with paperwork. But this morning she'd woken up with scratchy eyes and gummy lashes, as though she'd been crying during the night. Unable to go back to sleep, she'd come into work at a ridiculously early hour.

She couldn't remember her dreams but it was possible, of course, that she'd shed a few tears. After all, the day before had been an emotional one, although she wouldn't classify it as sad, really. There had been times when she'd even laughed.

Like when the wind had pushed her along the pavement, and she'd clutched the shiny balloons by their strings so they wouldn't blow away in the blustery autumn weather. She'd been using her body to shield the flowers in her other hand, worried all the petals would be blown off if she didn't protect them. It would have been ridiculous to arrive with just a bunch of stems, rather than the bouquet of lovely red roses.

The thought of it happening had made Nya snort, knowing Jim would find such an eventuality infinitely amusing. She could so easily picture him doubled over, his deep barks of laughter echoing through the air.

'Just stems,' she'd imagined him wheezing, tears gathering in his gorgeous brown eyes and laugh lines turning his face into a landscape of mirth. 'Not one flower left, after that heap of dosh you spent on them.'

She'd giggled, then, and had still been chuckling to herself as she'd turned into the cemetery then made her way to his grave.

Now, pinching the bridge of her nose, she allowed a sensation of unreality to wash over her.

Jim's fiftieth birthday.

His being gone for almost twenty years.

Although Jim was always in her heart, most days she was fine—going on with her life with a smile—but even now waves of grief and loss could bowl her over. No longer as fresh as they once were, but heartbreaking just the same.

Yesterday, however, had been planned and she'd expected to feel far worse than she actually had. She never went to Jim's grave on Remembrance Day. On November eleventh she went to the cenotaph here in Carey Cove to pay her respects to all the men and women who'd served. Jim's day was always December first.

His birthday.

And enough time had passed that she didn't need to go every year, so now she kept her trips to Andover to milestones. His fortieth, and forty-fifth. Yesterday, his fiftieth.

During her time there, alone beside his grave, she thought about him in a way she didn't allow herself to the rest of the time.

Remembering his smile, his laughter and tenderness. The way he'd cared so deeply about her and his family. About the plans they'd made, oh, so long ago now. Sometimes she'd even allow herself to slip into a fantasy where he hadn't been killed in combat, and those plans had miraculously come to fruition.

Perhaps it wasn't surprising, then, that while she hadn't really felt sad yesterday, the agony of loss had crept up on her last night, while she slept.

Pushing her glasses up on her nose, she determinedly forced her attention back to the schedule she'd been working on. As Head Midwife of the Carey Cove cottage hospital, she had to evenly distribute the workload, which just now took some fancy footwork. She had a newish midwife—Kiara—who was working out well, and a trainee—Lorna—who needed her supervision. With another midwife—Marnie—out on maternity leave, and her replacement delayed for another two weeks, Nya had to juggle to keep the midwifery centre and maternity ward running efficiently.

When someone knocked on her office door, it was almost a relief to be interrupted, but she was surprised when her mother, rather than one of her co-workers, came in.

It was at moments like this, when she saw her mother unexpectedly, that she realised why one of her friends from nursing school had compared Mum to an *orisa*. With her wonderfully straight-backed posture and dark skin beautifully set off by her intricate green, gold, and red headwrap—a *gele* today—she looked the epitome of an African goddess.

While Nya had inherited her mother's smooth complexion and plump, curvy figure, she knew she didn't have the older lady's regal bearing.

'Mum. What are you doing here so early?' she asked, glancing at her watch as she went around her desk to kiss her mother's cheek. 'It's just gone six.'

'I was on my way to Penzance for the textile seminar but wanted to see you,' her mother replied, in her usual crisp tones. 'I stopped by your cottage and realised you weren't home, so came here. You really should lock the front door when you're here alone this early.'

Nya wrinkled her nose.

'This is Carey Cove, Mum. Not exactly a dangerous place.'

Iona's raised eyebrows spoke volumes, but she didn't pursue the discussion. Instead she said, 'I wanted to show you this.'

She'd been unbuttoning her hunter-green coat as she spoke and, when she opened it, Nya gasped, then clapped as she saw her mother's sweater.

'You got it finished,' she exclaimed. 'It's lovely!'

Mum smiled, glancing down at the garment in question. 'Just in time, too.'

Iona had been working on a new knitting pattern, using two African fabrics—*aso oke* and *kente*—as the inspiration. Nya knew just how much work she'd put into trying to get it finished in time for the special presentation at the university, given by a visiting expert on African textiles and weaving.

'Now I want one,' she said.

Mum laughed and shook her head. 'You know how bad I am at writing patterns, but if you want to look at my notes and try for yourself...'

Nya couldn't help giggling at the thought. Mum's handwriting—normally perfectly legible—somehow turned to chicken-scratch when she was designing a new knitting pattern, and that fact was a longstanding joke between them.

'I'd need an interpreter to do that,' Nya replied, still laughing.

Mum clicked her tongue, as though in disapproval, but was still smiling as she sat down in the visitor's chair. Then her smile faded and Nya was the recipient of a sharp, penetrating look, along with a nod of her head towards Nya's chair on the other side of the desk. It reminded her why Iona Bradford's university students had been terrified of their professor of English literature and African studies. Retirement hadn't softened that steely look.

Taking the less than subtle hint, Nya went back around to her own chair and sat down, wondering what to expect. One never knew with Mum.

Raising a hand to touch her *gele*, Mum asked, 'How did yesterday go?'

Nya hadn't said she was going to the cemetery, but wasn't surprised that Mum guessed where she'd been. What did surprise her was that her mother had brought it up. For the last five years, ever since they'd argued about Nya's apparently unwillingness to get involved in another relationship, they'd avoided talking about Jim.

'I don't mind if you've decided not to have children, even though I feel you'd make a marvellous mother,' Mum had said back then. 'But you've locked yourself—your heart—away, and it's not healthy.'

That Mum had spoken about Jim, and Nya's trip to the cemetery, now felt a little like a minefield.

'It was good. Even had a bit of a giggle.'

As Nya told her mother about the flowers, and what she thought Jim would have said, her mother nodded.

'I can imagine his reaction too,' she replied, a small smile pulling at the corner of her lips. 'He did have an amazing, if quirky, sense of humour. Such a zest for life. I don't think he was afraid of anything.' She hesitated, as though about to say something more, then glanced at her watch. 'Well, I must get going or I'll be late for the seminar.'

Nya rounded the desk again to receive her mother's goodbye kiss, and another of those penetrating looks. 'I've been invited by the bursar to stay on after the seminar and have dinner with the faculty and Dr Agyapong, but I can come back instead and meet you at The Dolphin, if you like.'

Nya gave her mother another hug, and said, 'Of course not, Mum. I'm behind on my paperwork here, so it's probably best I stay late this evening and get it done. We'll have our usual dinner next week.'

Not exactly true, about the paperwork, since although she had been behind, she was almost completely caught up now. But her mother's visit, and the fact she'd asked about the trip to the cemetery, had Nya on high alert, sensing there was something more Mum wanted to say, but hadn't. It was probably better to let a few days go by before they had that talk, whatever it entailed.

The last thing Nya wanted was to argue with Mum again.

Hopefully, by the time her mother came back to Carey Cove, she'd turn her mind to Christmas, and the small mountain of half-finished gifts still in her yarn bag. Iona kept a small bedsit in Penzance, as well as a cottage in Carey Cove, splitting her time between the two. Often once she got to Penzance and started socialising with friends and old co-workers, she ended up staying a few days.

After walking her mother out to the vestibule and going back into her office, Nya couldn't help thinking back on the conversation—and the long-ago argument too.

She'd never been able to understand Mum's attitude.

It was as though she'd completely forgotten the fact she never remarried after Nya's father died. Why, then, was it so difficult to understand her daughter's choices? They'd both mourned, long and hard, and turned to their professions as a source of solace and meaning.

Nya hadn't had the chance to have the babies Jim and she had talked about, but helping other women bring healthy children into the world gave her the greatest satisfaction.

Besides, she thought as she pulled her chair closer to her desk again, even if she were interested in a relationship, it wasn't as though Carey Cove was overrun with eligible men. And she hadn't come back here in the hopes of finding love in her childhood village—just peace and a modicum of happiness.

She'd achieved that, and more, she reminded herself stoutly, pulling the schedule closer.

And she was absolutely content.

Dr Theo Turner drove through the still-quiet streets of Carey Cove, trying to jolly himself out of his sour mood. The world seemed intent on making him miserable just now, and although the last year and a half had been extremely difficult, he refused to allow unhappiness to become habitual.

Hard not to, though, when everything felt so incredibly unsettled and he was trying—and failing—to adapt to a new normal.

One where he lived the life of a divorced man, battling loneliness by working as hard as possible, and even considered leaving Carey Cove—a place he loved, but no longer felt he belonged.

A light mist lay over the picturesque village, giving the landscape a ghostly air. As he approached the main road, he saw a car go past towards Penzance, and recognised Iona Bradford by her colourful headscarf, but was too far away to wave. Once he got to the centre of the village, he glimpsed Avis Mitchell on the green, training one of her German shepherds.

She glanced up as he passed, but didn't acknowledge him.

Colin Duncan was making his way towards his small shop and post office. The older man waved and smiled, and Theo lifted a hand in return, yet found himself wondering if Colin's greeting came from friendliness, or just familiarity.

Strange to have such thoughts when he'd lived in Carey Cove for twenty years—had felt completely comfortable up until Femi, in the midst of an argument, had accused him of being a visitor in his own home.

'You come and go as you please. Spend more time in Falmouth with your patients than at home with your wife and children. TJ and Gillian hardly know you, much less the people here in Carey Cove. You might as well set up house in the blasted hospital. You probably enjoy being with your co-workers best anyway.'

Highly unfair, he'd thought at the time, and still did. Yes, his profession made a lot of demands on his time. Mothers and babies didn't adhere to schedules when they went into distress—a fact he'd explained to his children as soon as he thought they were old enough to understand.

Femi had taken exception to that too, accusing him of trying to avoid his responsibilities by sloughing all the daily graft off on her, and getting the children onboard with it. Pointing out it had been her decision to give up her clinical psychology practice and become a stay-at-home mum hadn't gained him any brownie points. And his suggestion that she hire help so it didn't all fall on her only caused another row.

But he'd been determined to give his children everything he hadn't had as a child.

Stability.

A father who was a responsible member of society and could provide them with whatever they needed.

And he'd also done his best to be there for them as much as possible. They'd had uninterrupted days out, family holidays, and he'd spent umpteen hours on the touchline of rugby games, at piano recitals, and all their other activities. Intellectually he knew, despite what Femi intimated, that his relationship with his children was solid, but the seeds of doubt she'd planted had flourished.

He now felt a stranger in his own life.

Usually by now, at the beginning of December, he'd be getting excited about Christmas. Planning surprises for his children, even though they were both grown—Gillian already out of university and working in London, TJ in his second to last year at Cambridge. Thinking about getting a tree, and taking dedicated time off to decorate it and the cottage.

Femi had put paid to any enthusiasm he might have had, by the expedient method of shutting him out of the holiday festivities with his children.

'Devi and I are having a big family get-together,' she'd said on the phone last night. 'I've already told the children that they're expected on the twenty-third, and that they're to stay as long as they like. Gillian said she's due back at work on the twenty-seventh, but TJ will stay until it's time to go back to uni.'

Theo's heart had sunk, and he'd been trying to find the right way to express his disappointment when Femi had continued, in the acidic tone he knew all too well.

'Please don't harass the children about coming to see

you. It will just upset them. Besides, I'm sure you're glad, since that lets you spend as much time as you want at St Isolde's and you don't have to think about anything but yourself and your patients.'

He hadn't told her that the powers-that-be had forced him to take time off, since he'd been working non-stop for the last eighteen months. Femi was, in his opinion, having more than enough fun at his expense.

And he hated feeling so bitter about it all.

Even the sight of the holiday decorations all along the streets and in shop windows did nothing to buoy his spirits. In fact, they seemed to mock his dreariness and make it worse.

At least he had his office at Carey House, where he could go and hide out and, unless he told them he was there, no one would notice. After all, only if there was a patient on site would anyone be at the cottage hospital this early, and he didn't plan to go near the maternity ward. Staying alone in the house one more day could potentially drive him insane. On his office computer were at least six months' worth of medical journals and studies he wanted to read but hadn't had time to get to. They would keep his brain busy, hopefully stopping these depressing thoughts from bombarding him all day.

Once on the hospital grounds, he drove around to the side of the building and parked before climbing out and retrieving his briefcase from the rear seat.

Still deep in thought, he approached the front door, keys in hand, ready to let himself in, when he spied something on the doorstep and hesitated for a moment.

It looked like a long package of some kind, covered

with a blanket, and as he strode closer his heart rate picked up. As soon as he got to the door, he put his briefcase down on the stone step, and bent to lift the edge of the blanket.

From the basket beneath, a pair of unfocused blue eyes blinked up at him, as though trying to figure out who he was. And then, almost in slow motion, the baby's little face grew wrinkled as he or she began to cry.

CHAPTER TWO

IT WAS STILL too early for Hazel to be in to take up her post at Reception, so when Nya heard the front door of the hospital rattle, she got up to see who it was. While it wasn't unusual for them to have an expectant mother come in at all hours in labour, the midwife on call for that night would usually already have been alerted to attend. As far as she knew, that hadn't happened.

And was that the cry of a baby echoing down the corridor?

Not knowing what to think, Nya increased her pace, turning the corner into the reception area and stopping short at the sight of Theo Turner seemingly struggling to close the door behind himself.

Not surprising, since he had a basket, his briefcase and keys in hand—and a swaddled, crying baby in the crook of one arm.

The incongruity of it kept her frozen in place for a moment. Long enough for the obstetrician to turn to face her, and when their eyes met her heart did a funny little stutter, causing a rush of heat to her face.

She'd always thought Theo was handsome. He had

the type of understated good looks that caused most women to give him at least a second look, and a quiet charm that nonetheless lit up whatever room he was in.

But since they'd met, on her return to Carey Cove, he'd always been Theo, Femi's husband, an intrinsic part of a couple she knew well, so completely out of bounds in every way. To suddenly find herself aware—as if for the first time—of his good looks, and self-conscious in his presence, was shocking.

Then there was no time to wonder about her strange reaction to her old friend, as she rushed forward to relieve him of the basket and briefcase.

'Theo, what on earth…?' she asked, as she put the items down on Hazel's desk, and then instinctively reached for the baby, holding and shushing while Theo took off his coat. The slight weight in her arms, the scrunched little face, fat tears running down pinkened cheeks, all tugged at her heart.

'The baby was on the doorstep,' he replied. Before Nya knew what he intended, he'd plucked the infant from her arms and was heading towards one of the examination rooms, leaving Nya to trot to be able to keep up with his long strides. 'I don't know how long he or she's been out there.'

'Couldn't be more than ten minutes or so,' she told him, turning on the light over the examination table where he'd laid the baby, who was now wailing lustily. 'My mum left about fifteen minutes ago, and I let her out the front. Believe me, neither of us would have ignored a basket on the doorstep.'

The quick smile Theo sent her lit up his oft solemn

face and caused a little fan of laugh lines to appear at
the corner of each eye. Fighting another wave of heat
rushing to her face, Nya looked down at the baby so as
not to stare at his lips. But then she found herself watching his hands as he un-swaddled the squirming infant,
and this time her own hands tingled, and the warmth
spread through her belly.

'I glimpsed Iona when I was driving here, and I have
no doubt what you say is true,' he replied, amusement
still lingering in his voice even as it dropped to a low
croon. 'There's no way super-midwife Nya wouldn't
have seen you, is there, sweetheart?'

Obviously he was talking to the baby, but Nya
couldn't help the little hitch of her breath.

What on earth was happening to her?

Taking herself in hand, Nya turned her thoughts to
the practicality of the situation, just as Theo got the
blanket undone, revealing the warm pink pyjamas beneath.

'Unless your mama is one of those people who don't
go by tradition, I'm guessing you're a little girl,' he continued, in that same low, sing-song voice she'd heard
him use with babies before. 'And you're in need of a
clean nappy.'

Thankful for something to do, Nya rushed to the supply cupboard and retrieved a clean nappy, along with a
blanket and baby wipes.

'How is her babygrow?' she asked, poised to dash
off to find one to fit.

'Still dry,' Theo replied, as he took the wipe she offered him and efficiently cleaned up the little girl's bum.

'She looks to be about a week old—don't you, sweet-heart? Do you recognise her?'

'No.' Nya shook her head, running a finger over the little clenched fist closest to her, and then over the wisps of light brown hair on the baby's pate. 'I'm sure she wasn't born here. I'll start a file on her, if you'll take weight and measurements, and then call Social Services.'

'She seems to be in good health,' Theo sing-songed as he replaced the pyjamas, adroitly managing to do it with a minimum of fuss. 'And Mama wrapped you up nice and warmly, so there's no hint of hypothermia.'

'I wonder what her poor mum is going through,' Nya murmured. 'She must have thought this her only option.'

'Yes,' Theo said as he gently lifted the now gurgling baby onto his shoulder. 'And brought her to a place where she knew her little one would be safe and well taken care of.'

How like him not to judge the baby's mother, Nya thought as she assembled the appropriate forms and went over to the weighing station, where Theo waited. He probably felt the way she did, that everyone deserved the benefit of the doubt. With some of the horror stories they'd heard and seen, the mother probably had done the very best she could by bringing the baby to their doorstep.

'Oh,' she said, staring down at the clipboard in her hand. 'What should we call her? I refuse to put "Baby Jane Smith" on this form.'

'Well, I should hope not,' Theo replied, amusement

once more vibrating in his voice. 'She's too beautiful for a name like that.'

'That's it,' Nya said, unable to stop a little giggle of glee from breaking through. 'How about Hope? As her name, I mean?'

'Perfect,' he replied. 'Especially at this time of year.'

And Nya couldn't help her little thrill of satisfaction at his agreement.

As they worked together examining Hope, Theo relayed the information he gathered to Nya in the same sweet croon as before, and Nya had to force herself to concentrate. Although they'd worked together in the past, and she'd heard him speak to babies this way before, for some reason today she found it unreasonably adorable.

There was something about a man with hands as large as Theo's so tenderly handling a week-or-so-old baby that just made Nya's heart melt too.

She shook her head, bringing herself up short. Maybe this was an after-effect of her mother's visit, or just her own thoughts earlier, but this was no time to let her mind wander this way.

'If you can manage by yourself for a while, I'll run down to my office and call Caroline at Social Services. We need to get Hope a safe place to stay until they can find her mum.'

Theo sent her a glance that had her heart racing and stumbling over itself. Then he turned that dark, twinkling gaze back to the baby, who was once more safely ensconced in his arms.

'Of course we can manage. I think I'm quite quali-
fied to take care of Hope for however long it takes.'

'Brilliant,' Nya said, tearing herself away from his
and Hope's side with more difficulty than she liked,
and heading out of the door. Then a thought struck her,
and she turned back to ask, 'What are you doing here,
anyway? I heard you were on holiday.'

The slight smile on his face faded, and his eyes grew
guarded as he looked back up at her to give a negligible
shrug of one shoulder. 'I thought I was coming in to do
some paperwork, but it turns out I was really here to
rescue this little darling—wasn't I, Hope?'

And since his somewhat dismissive tone came
through clearly despite that special baby voice, Nya
turned away without another word.

But it stung, all the same. They'd been friends for
years, but she knew Theo had been avoiding her since
his divorce and she couldn't help wondering why he'd
turned so cool. Surely he didn't think she'd hit on him,
as she'd heard some of the other women in the village had? Or perhaps it was the fact that she and Femi,
while not good friends, had been more than acquain-
tances—going to lunch on occasion, or out to the pub
of an evening.

She'd thought it best to give Theo space, hoping that
in time he'd realise she was, if not on his side, particularly, then still a friend, but it seemed he wanted nothing to do with her, at all.

And if that was what Theo wanted, then that was
what he'd get. As soon as they got Hope appropriately
situated, Nya would make sure to keep her distance.

Probably for the best, with these strange emotions he'd stirred in her today!

Theo watched Nya walk away and found himself watching the sway of her hips with far more interest than he should. Somehow, this morning, he'd been aware of her in a new, disquieting way.

The gleam in her warm brown eyes.

Her gentleness as she touched baby Hope, and swept her narrow, lovely fingers over the baby's hair.

The fresh scent rising from her hair as she leant close to him, and the smooth, dark curve of her cheek, seen in three-quarter profile as she smiled.

All of those, plus that infectious giggle she always seemed to try to suppress, had filled him with the kind of joy he'd begun to think he might never feel again.

Then he'd thrown back up all the barriers she'd so easily slipped behind.

At some point he'd have to apologise. It had become instinctive, this need to keep a new distance between himself and other people. Much easier than trying to gauge who was still a friend, and who was looking askance. Realising the village grapevine had been hard at work, and people were probably talking about how he'd been forcibly sent on holiday, had caused him to treat her coolly.

Yet, he knew he was being unfair to Nya, who was the nicest, most caring person he knew. He'd often wondered how it was some lucky man hadn't snatched her up long ago, even knowing perhaps it would be impossible for any man to have a chance to do so. Everyone knew she was still in love with her husband, although it must be close to twenty years since he'd died.

Theo believed in everlasting love, so thought he understood her hesitance.

It was a shame though. Nya had so much to give and would have been a phenomenal mother.

And, he realised, he was thinking about all this so as to be able to ignore the fact that he'd hurt her feelings.

'I was a heel, wasn't I, Hope?' he asked the little girl, who was staring up at him and sucking on one hand. 'We should go find Auntie Nya, and apologise, shouldn't we? Or I should, at any rate.'

But he found himself reluctant to go after Nya. She'd so easily stirred something deep within. The kind of longing he had no business feeling.

He'd always considered her a friend, and to even for a moment wonder what it would be like to touch her, maybe even kiss her, threw him into confusion.

However, they had to work together just now, to make sure Hope got the care she needed, and, after a deep breath and a quick kiss on Hope's forearm, he made his way to Nya's office.

She was still on the phone, glancing up quickly at him as he came in her door and gesturing to the chair on the other side of her desk with her chin.

'Certainly,' she said into the receiver. 'Of course we can. Keep me informed. Thank you.'

Putting down the receiver with her habitual brisk movements, she took off her square, black-framed glasses and rubbed the side of her index finger across one eye.

'Caroline says they're run off their feet at the moment, but she'll start trying to find Hope a foster family. She'll also advise the police about you finding her, and they'll probably be by later to take our statements. In the meantime, she's asked if we can take care of Hope here.'

Hope made a little sound, and Theo looked down. The infant had fallen asleep, her fist still in her mouth, and the sweet innocence of her tugged hard at Theo's heart.

'Well,' he said, without thinking it through. 'Since I don't have anything planned for the day, why don't I take care of her until Caroline finds a suitable placement?'

Nya's face lit up, and her lush lips curled into one of her warm smiles.

'That would be brilliant,' she said, leaning back in her chair and swinging it from side to side slightly. 'I know the midwives coming on duty shortly would be willing to keep an eye on her, but unfortunately we're a bit short-staffed, and there are no patients in the maternity ward right now. If you're willing to keep an eye on her, when she's awake you can give her the physical contact she needs.'

Hope stirred against his chest, and Theo glanced down at her again, shifting her to a more comfortable position. The infant sighed, and snuggled in closer, and he couldn't help smiling down at her.

When he raised his gaze to Nya, there was a look in her eyes that froze him in place, and had his heart pounding.

Then she turned away, as though looking out of the

door, and said, 'That'll be Hazel coming in. Let's go tell her what's going on, so she doesn't have a conniption when the bobbies turn up at the door.'

Before he could even move, she was out of her seat— heading for the corridor—and it took him a moment to regain his equilibrium and follow her to Reception.

CHAPTER THREE

IT SEEMED AS though every midwife, doctor, and even a few patients wanted to see Hope for themselves, and it took for ever for Nya to get Theo and the baby comfortably ensconced in his office.

'What a darling,' Sophie French cooed. 'Wait until I tell Roman about this. He'll be gobsmacked.'

'I heard best wishes are in order? Have you and Roman set a date?' Theo smiled at the midwife, who turned a beguiling shade of pink in the cheeks.

'It's all so new, we haven't got to that stage yet. You'll come to the engagement party on Christmas Eve, won't you?'

Nya saw the change in Theo. Although he was still smiling, his eyes looked sad, and she thought he seemed to retreat a little.

'I'm not sure where I'll be,' he replied. 'But if I'm here, I'll certainly come.'

And that seemed to satisfy Sophie.

When Nya suggested Theo put Hope down for her nap in the small nursery attached to the maternity ward, he immediately nixed that idea.

'We'll both be more comfortable in my office,' he said, his gaze pinned to Hope, who was still sleeping soundly in his arms. 'I'm just along from the staff room, so when she wakes up and is hungry, I don't have far to go to get her bottle.'

'If you need a break, just call down and let me know,' she told him, once they'd arranged a crib, and everything else he needed, to hand. She'd decided that, until she got these strange impulses she was experiencing around him under control, it was best to give him a wide berth.

But even so, it was hard to walk away, and she found herself stopping at the door for one last look.

Theo seemed almost mesmerised by the baby in his arms—still standing beside the crib, holding her, looking down with the tenderest expression on his face. Nya's heart seemed to expand as it raced, sending a warm, intimate sensation out into her bloodstream, until she thought she'd simply melt away.

Then, as Theo gently set Hope down in the crib, Nya slipped out of the room, before he could notice her still watching him.

But she had to stop and take a deep breath, blinking against the moisture in her eyes, before she could go back to work.

And even though she'd decided to make herself scarce until after Social Services had collected Hope, she found herself drawn back to Theo's office over and over during the day.

Making sure both of them had everything they needed.

Taking Theo lunch when he insisted he didn't need

anyone to take over Hope's care so he could go and get some.

Popping in and demanding a turn at feeding Hope when she found him just sitting down to give her a bottle.

'I'm beginning to think you don't trust me to take care of her,' Theo said, as he reluctantly relinquished the infant to Nya.

'Of course I trust you,' she replied, settling on the comfortable chair he had for visitors. 'But why should you have all the fun while I'm slogging away at work?'

That earned her a huff of laughter, and a warm glance that made her turn her gaze swiftly back to the baby in her arms.

When he looked at her like that, she wanted to shiver in reaction. Not a *bad* shiver, but the kind that had her thinking thoughts that weren't only untoward, but also wouldn't lead anywhere.

Hope twisted her head, losing the nipple for a moment, and let out a little squeak of dismay. Nya angled the bottle into place again. 'There you go, sweetheart. It's right here.'

She'd cared for hundreds, if not thousands, of babies during her time as a midwife, but there was something extra special about Hope. Perhaps it was the knowledge that the little mite was—to all intents and purposes— alone in the world that touched Nya and created the ache in her heart.

So focused was she on the baby that when Theo spoke, it was a little startling.

'I owe you an apology,' he said, in a tone that sounded

both reluctant and a little defensive, as though he wasn't sure of the advisability of having the conversation.

After a swift look at his unsmiling face, Nya kept her attention on Hope, who was still happily sucking on her bottle.

'I can't think of why,' she replied, keeping her voice level with effort, as her heart did a silly double-time thump.

'I was short with you earlier—when you mentioned my being on holiday. I just...'

When his voice faded, she risked another glance his way, but found his gaze fixed on the baby in her arms, rather than on her.

'You just, what?' she asked softly, aching to see him so solemn and sad.

'I was angry when they put me on leave, and when you mentioned it, I realised that word must have got around, and that anger came back.' His lids lifted, and Nya could see the pain and uncertainty reflected in his eyes.

'We were told that you wouldn't be on call until the new year, Theo, so that's how I knew. I thought perhaps you were taking a much-deserved break and were heading off for somewhere warm and fun for a week or so.' She risked a little giggle. 'I was a bit jealous.'

One side of his mouth twisted up in an abbreviated smile that immediately faded again. 'No, I wasn't given a choice.'

She'd known him long enough to know that couldn't have sat well. But she'd also watched him overworking himself since the divorce.

'Just as well,' she rebutted mildly. 'If you had been given a choice, you wouldn't have taken it, and it's been ages since you've had any time off. Sometimes other people actually do know what's best for you.'

He got up abruptly, and walked over to the window, staring out, one hand raised to brace against the frame.

How had she never really noticed how long and strong his fingers were, until today? He really had lovely hands.

'I suppose you're right,' he said, but it didn't sound as though he were really agreeing, rather just saying what he thought she wanted to hear. 'But I don't like being forced.'

'Of course not,' she replied briskly. 'But we've all watched you working yourself into the ground, or at least seeming to. But you've been through a lot over the last eighteen months. Perhaps it's time to take a break and take stock—figure out what's best for you. Think of it in that light, and maybe it won't sting as much.'

Theo nodded, his gaze still trained out of the window, and Nya saw his chest rise on a deep breath and then, after a beat, fall again. When he turned and paced back to his chair, his expression caused a cold spot to bloom in her chest.

'That's something I've been doing, almost obsessively over the last few months,' he admitted, his deep voice almost distant, as though he was talking more to himself than to her. 'And some days I feel as though I don't belong here any more.'

The cold spot spread so rapidly Nya shivered from the onslaught of ice through her veins. And there was nothing calm or gentle about her tone when she snapped, 'What kind of nonsense talk is that?'

Hope stirred, and Nya looked down in time to see her tongue the nipple from her mouth. As the bottle was almost empty anyway, Nya shifted the infant onto her shoulder and began to rub her back.

Meeting Theo's gaze across the desk, she fixed him with the stern glare she gave recalcitrant husbands or nosy mothers-in-law, and said, 'Explain to me what on earth you're talking about.'

The look he gave her was rueful, but solemn.

'Ever since the divorce, I've felt as though my life no longer fits. That I don't really belong here in Carey Cove any more.' His lips firmed into a line, and then he shook his head. 'Femi always said I was hardly here anyway, and rattling around the cottage by myself... I just don't know where I need or want to be at the moment.'

Now *that* she understood, and she nodded, sadness replacing whatever that cold wash of emotion had been.

'When Jim died, I couldn't stay in Andover because the memories were too hard to bear. So, I came back here, because this was where I felt safe and at home.' Unsure of whether she was expressing herself as well as she wanted to, she shook her head. 'What I mean to say is, divorce is hard, and you're entitled to grieve for as long as you want, or need to. And if getting over it— or on with a happier life—means starting afresh, I can certainly understand that impulse. But to say you don't know if you belong here? I think that's a step too far.'

Theo leaned back in his chair, his eyes fixed to her face as he said, 'Why do you think so?'

'You're an integral part of our community, and not just because you're a respected doctor. You've lived here for twenty years, and there isn't one person who hasn't turned to you—relied on you—at some point or another. I've never heard a bad word said about you by anyone. Not even Mrs. Prentiss, and you know she dislikes almost everyone.'

That brought a touch of a smile to his lips, and Nya felt her shoulders relax.

'I try to stay on Gwenda Prentiss's good side, because she scares me,' he said dryly. Then he shrugged. 'Truthfully, this has always felt like home to me, from the first time I came to Carey House on a consult. I went back to Falmouth and told Femi I'd found where I'd like to live, and once she saw the village, she agreed it would be the ideal place to raise the children. Unfortunately, her love affair with Carey Cove didn't last. She found village life boring.' Again, a little hesitation, before he added, 'Found me and the life we were living boring.'

Deep and dangerous waters here, Nya thought, glad of the interruption when Hope let out a burp almost too big for her little body, which made both adults laugh.

'Not very ladylike, Miss Hope,' Nya said, but her mind was racing with how to respond to what Theo had said.

There was always the option to simply ignore it— change the subject to something less inflammatory— but that wasn't what a friend would do. But, despite them being divorced, was it wise to say anything that could be construed as critical of Femi?

How would that even be helpful?

Yet, Theo looked so solemn and hurt, there was no way she couldn't say what she thought. He was her friend and needed her support.

And maybe even a little of the clarity someone outside the situation could bring.

'I think,' she said slowly, then paused, searching for the right words. 'I think you need to look forward rather than back, and recognise that we're all responsible for our own happiness.'

There, that was fairly neutral, wasn't it? But Theo's eyes sharpened.

'Why do you say that?'

Trust Theo not to want to leave well enough alone, and want clarification.

Once more Nya was left picking her words carefully.

'I just think that sometimes we have to take a good look at where we are in life, and what it is we want, then make it happen. It's not up to anyone else to make us happy, you know?'

Theo opened his mouth, as though about to ask her for more details, but thankfully just then the telephone rang, and he answered. From his side of the conversation, she realised the police had arrived to take their statements, and there was no more time for the discussion.

There was no way she'd tell him that, in her opinion, Femi had made no effort to integrate into village life, and if she'd been bored and unhappy, it was mostly her own fault. The other woman had had a stable marriage, two lovely children, and the ability to do almost anything she'd wanted to make her life more fulfilled. But instead of taking whatever steps necessary, she'd chosen to blame her husband for her discontent.

Years before, when the children had got older and more independent, Femi had once more complained about boredom, and about giving up her career in psychology.

'Why don't you set up a part-time consultancy at Carey House?' Nya had suggested. 'When we need to refer patients for counselling, we have to send them to Penzance or Falmouth. It would be wonderful to have someone on hand here instead.'

They often had mothers—both expectant and postpartum—who needed professional help to work through their issues, sometimes quite urgently too.

Femi had shrugged and frowned, half-heartedly saying, 'Yeah, sure, I'll consider it, but I always want to be on hand, in case one of the children needs me.'

Nya had been forced to bite her tongue at that. Oh, she completely understood that being a stay-at-home mum was a full-time job, but Femi seemed to have forgotten how often she took off to London to shop and visit. It showed she had lots of time to herself, to do whatever she wanted.

And, of course, nothing came of Nya's suggestion.

No. Femi had seemed determined to be unhappy in Carey Cove, and perhaps in her marriage, which made it difficult for Nya to be as sympathetic towards the other woman as she would have liked.

Especially now, when it was apparent how badly Theo had been affected by the end of his marriage, to the point where he was considering leaving Carey Cove.

Just the thought made Nya in turns angry and sad, but if that was what he needed to get over Femi and move on with his life, then all she could do was be sympathetic.

Even if what she wanted was to force him to stay, although just how that would be achieved, she had no idea.

And why that was so important to her own happiness was unfathomable.

CHAPTER FOUR

AFTER NYA GAVE her statement to the constable who attended to take the report, she went back to work, leaving Theo to finish up. Once the constable departed, Theo checked on Hope, making sure she was still sleeping, then walked over to look out of his office window.

The view out over the small side garden of Carey House and down to the harbour beyond was one of his favourites and he found himself appreciating it even more than usual.

After talking with Nya, he felt a little lighter, a bit better about life.

He'd been avoiding her since the end of his marriage, and he wondered why.

He should have known she wouldn't blame him, or treat him any differently, and he now admitted how he'd allowed his guilt and doubts about himself to cloud his decisions.

It was a relief to suddenly feel less weighed down by circumstances—a little more optimistic about the future.

Hope made a sound in her sleep, and he found himself looking over his shoulder at her, and smiling.

Having her to tend to had also helped to elevate his mood. He'd helped to birth and handled so many babies, including his own children, but that sense of falling in love with each infant never waned. It was their total innocence, and the knowledge that here was a new life just beginning, that always touched his heart.

Watching Nya feed her had filled him with warmth. It was obvious she felt the same way about Hope that he did—that although they were in the infant's life for just a short time, they would do whatever necessary to protect and nurture her.

Hopefully the police would find her mother or father quickly, and the reunion would be a safe and success-ful one. No one deserved to feel alone and abandoned.

Those kinds of scars were difficult to heal.

Why that made him think of Nya, he didn't want to contemplate, so he went back to his desk and pulled up the next journal he wanted to read. With one more quick glance at the sleeping baby, he turned his attention to his computer screen, and lost himself in a study about the effect of influenza during pregnancy.

When a soft knock came on his door, and Hope stirred, Theo was surprised to realise the afternoon was almost gone. He wasn't terribly surprised to see Nya come in, but there was an air of suppressed excite-ment about her that had him looking at her closely as he picked Hope up.

'I heard from Caroline, at Social Services,' she said, and he couldn't help noticing how her eyes sparkled, and she was smiling. 'They're having a very difficult time finding a fosterer to take Hope.'

'Oh?' He gave her a sideways glance as she came up beside him to watch him change Hope's nappy.

'She explained that there had been a fall-off of people volunteering to foster over the past two years. And at this time of the year, with Christmas so close, it's even harder than usual to find a foster parent at short notice.'

Theo didn't even think about it. As he turned to face Nya, Hope in his arms, he said, 'I'll foster her. For at least as long as I'm on leave from the hospital. That'll give them a chance to find her mother, or a permanent fosterer.'

'Oh…' Nya exhaled, and her smile faded away. It was as though she deflated right in front of his eyes.

'What is it?' he asked, resting a hand on her arm when she would have stepped aside, and holding her gaze.

'Oh, it's just that…'

When she hesitated, Theo joggled her arm. 'Tell me.'

Her eyes glittered, and he realised it was tears making them gleam.

'Well, I was planning to foster Hope myself.'

She was holding herself stiffly, and tried to look unconcerned, but although the moisture had disappeared from her eyes, he could easily see she was still upset and trying not to show it.

'Here.' He motioned for her to take Hope from him, and Nya didn't hesitate. In a trice she had the infant snuggled close. 'Sit down, and let's discuss this.'

'I don't know that there's anything to talk about,' she said as she walked to the armchair and subsided into it. 'You're actually a better choice than I am. I can't take holidays now, because I have a trainee, a new midwife, and we're one midwife short too. You fostering Hope makes far more sense.'

She was right, but seeing Nya's tender expression as she looked down at a relaxed and cooing Hope, he knew not fostering the baby would be a huge disappointment to his friend.

'We could share the position as Hope's fosterers,' he said, again without giving it any thought, but he knew he'd made the best suggestion when her face lit up.

'I'd love that. If you don't mind? I can have her at night, and you can look after her during the day, while I'm working.'

Time to tread gently here. Knowing Nya's strength of will, he didn't want to put her back up.

'Are you sure you'll be able to get enough sleep, if you have her at night?'

Nya hardly spared him a glance.

'Single mums do it all the time. I'll be fine. Besides, I rarely sleep more than four or five hours a night.'

'I didn't know that.'

That brought her head up, and she gave him a wide grin. 'You've only known me for twenty years. Normally, you'd only get that type of information after twenty-five. This constitutes special circumstances.'

He couldn't help chuckling, and it occurred to him that he hadn't laughed as much in ages as he had today.

'So, is it that you don't go to bed until late, or do you wake up extremely early?'

'It depends. Sometimes, if I've had a particularly

hard day, I'll go to bed early—by ten. Otherwise, I'm up until at least midnight.'

Theo nodded. 'I'm something of a night owl myself,' he admitted. 'But if you find yourself getting sleep deprived, just let me know and I'll take Hope for a night or two.'

'I'll have some days off during the time leading up to Christmas, and I can catch up on sleep then.'

She was smiling again—almost glowing—and Theo couldn't take his eyes off her face.

'That's settled, then,' he said, earning another of her wide grins. 'I'll call Caroline and let her know what we've decided—that we'll share the care of Hope until at least the end of the year. I'm sure she'll have a mountain of paperwork she'll need us to fill out.'

'Normally the last thing I want to do,' Nya said, smiling at Hope and stroking one chubby baby cheek with the backs of her fingers. 'But I'll gladly do it for you, sweetheart.'

And the warmth that filled Theo's chest felt so good, he ignored the little voice in the back of his mind, telling him to be careful of what he was getting into.

That one round of heartache was more than enough, and he was definitely courting another.

By the time they'd got all the legal details dealt with, it was getting late, so Theo said he'd call down to The Dolphin and ask the publican Davy Trewelyn to send dinner up for them.

'Lovely,' she told him, casting an eye over the pile of nappies, babygrows, wipes, and other necessaries, ticking things off the list in her head. 'By the time you get home, you won't want to have to cook.'

'And you won't have time to,' he replied in that low sing-song voice that let her know he was talking to Hope rather than her. 'Right, Hope?'

'Tomorrow I'll get a car seat for her on my lunch-time,' she said. 'Thankfully Marnie said she wasn't planning to take Violet anywhere tomorrow, and we could borrow hers tonight. And the carrycot from the nursery here will do as a place for her to sleep tonight too, but it will make sense for both of us to have one, rather than have to take it back and forth.'

'Don't worry about that,' Theo told her. 'Give me a list and I'll order everything online tonight for one-day delivery.'

'You don't have to—'

Theo held up his hand and shook his head.

'Just let me buy my girl some things, please? I want to.'

It was on the tip of her tongue to warn him not to get attached—that this was a temporary situation—but he looked so happy and appealing, Nya kept the thought to herself.

Besides, she was having just as hard a time reminding herself of that fact too.

Since she'd walked to work that morning, after they'd eaten they packed everything into Theo's car, and he drove her and Hope to her cottage. Nya had used the app on her phone to turn on some lights at home, including her outdoor Christmas lights, and as they drew up she cast a critical eye over the modest display.

'I need more decorations outside, I think,' she said to Theo as he switched off the engine. 'Somehow each year I end up doing less than the year before. Or I suddenly can't find strings of lights I was sure I had and get frustrated.'

'It looks lovely,' he replied as he opened his door. 'Very cheery indeed.'

'Have you put up your decorations yet?' she asked, opening her door as well so as to swing her legs out.

'No. I haven't got around to it.'

If voices could have a 'keep out' sign attached, Theo's did just then. The way his voice cooled had her wondering if there was more to the story than just not having time to deal with the holidays yet.

Going into the cottage in front of him, carrying Hope in the borrowed car seat, she directed him where to put the packages. Then she bustled about, putting supplies away in an orderly way, so she knew where to find them.

'Who knew that one tiny baby could need so many things?' she said, stifling a giggle. 'I never thought I'd need more counter space in my lifetime.'

Theo smiled and shook his head. 'It does look like a lot, doesn't it?'

Hope chose that moment to awaken, and before Nya could go to her, Theo was there, lifting her from the carrier, checking whether it was a nappy change or feeding time again.

Nya stayed where she was, watching him, wondering why her heartbeat was suddenly so erratic, and tingles were firing along her spine at the sight of the pair.

Then she gave herself a mental shake.

It had been an emotional day—at least for her. And now she had the wonderful prospect of taking care of Hope for a month or so, until a permanent fosterer or her parents could be found, to look forward to. No wonder she was feeling a little gooey on the inside at the sight of a handsome man holding a tiny baby.

Almost any woman would, wouldn't they?

Theo was almost finished changing Hope's nappy, and although Nya was assailed with the wish that he didn't have to go, she forced herself to say, 'We have to remember to put the car-seat base into my car, so I have it for the morning. What time should I bring Hope over to you?'

He sent her a glance over his shoulder and shrugged. 'Whenever you get there will be fine. I'm usually up early to go for a run, but if I know you're coming before eight, I'll stay home.'

Suddenly the image of him in running attire popped into her head, sending a rush of heat out through her veins, and it took a moment to get her brain back into working order.

'No…no. Go for your run. My first appointment is at nine, so I'll bring her by at about eight-fifteen.'

All too soon he was handing her Hope and taking her car keys so as to transfer the car-seat base, and then coming back in to take his leave.

Hope was starting to fuss a bit, ready for her next feed, so Theo didn't linger.

'See you both in the morning,' he said, before bending to kiss the top of Hope's head.

Then, before Nya realised what was happening, his lips—warm and firm, yet wonderfully soft—were on her cheek, seeming to linger on her skin for an eon, before he straightened.

Something in his eyes had her heart galloping along like a runaway horse, and all she could do was stare up at him, until he suddenly swung around and headed for the door.

Finding her voice, she called, 'Night,' and got a wave in return.

Then he was gone.

As she was warming Hope's bottle, Nya thought back on the day and the roller coaster of emotions she'd been on.

Jim, and Mum, and Hope, and Theo. Each played a role. But Nya's head kept taking her back to that moment when she'd seen Theo come through the door at Carey House, and the way her body had reacted.

It was just *Theo*, after all. Long-time friend and co-worker.

A man obviously struggling with everything life had thrown at him over the last couple of years.

Someone she wanted to see happy again, instead of so often stern and sad.

Hope spat out the nipple, then rooted about for it again, making Nya giggle. It seemed the baby's favourite trick.

'There you go,' she said, lining it up for her again, making encouraging noises as the infant went back to her bottle.

Once upon a time, so long ago now it seemed just

a dream, she and Jim had talked about the children they hoped to have. Two boys, he'd insisted, so they'd have each other to torment and fight with, and at least three girls.

When she'd laughingly asked him why three, Jim had said, 'Because then they can take turns looking after me when I'm in my dotage, and when one gets tired of my tricks, she can send me off to the next.'

She'd agreed, even as she'd shaken her head at the thought. Five children were too many, in her book, but since all that childbearing had then been in the future, it had been easy to go along with him.

And of course, none of that had happened.

When she'd lost Jim, the thought of children had been put aside. She couldn't envision herself parenting with anyone other than him—had never even really tried to find another relationship. He had been one of a kind, but when she'd said as much to her mother, Iona had shaken her head and given Nya a stern look.

'Each of us is one of a kind, and different. If you spend your time trying to find another Jim, you're going to be sorely disappointed. Look for—find—another one-of-a-kind man who will love you differently, but just as much. You deserve that.'

'I don't want anyone else,' she'd replied, which had led to that heated discussion between them. And the unspoken agreement not to speak about it any more that Mum had broken earlier in the day.

A welter of emotions washed through her as she rocked Hope and let her thoughts wander where they would, seeking some kind of peace and clarity, both of which proved elusive.

'Oh, Jim,' she whispered finally, shaking her head. 'How I miss you still.'

But that night, after she got Hope settled and climbed into her own bed, it was Theo Turner's face that floated up into her mind and followed her into slumber.

CHAPTER FIVE

JUST BEFORE DAWN next morning, Theo pounded along the narrow lanes surrounding his home, determinedly getting the exercise he knew he needed but despised having to get. Every time he went for a run, it reminded him of his age and the swift passage of time.

When he was young, he'd played football and been a keen cricketer, but once he'd got to university he'd stopped playing regularly because he could no longer commit to a team schedule. Yet, although that was many years ago, he still considered those team sports the only exercise worth doing.

Running or jogging was rather boring, and really gave him far too much time to think.

And no matter what he started thinking about, he ended up on one subject.

Nya.

Her warm smile and gorgeous, soft skin that suddenly, after all these years, made his fingers tingle with the urge to touch.

The tenderness she showed to Hope. Her gentleness as she stroked over the baby's head or cheek.

He was used to her brisk common sense, the way she always made him feel heard and appreciated, but noticing these other, far more personal things had his brain spinning.

Was this just another side effect of the life changes he'd gone through?

He'd be the first to admit he'd been terribly lonely. While he'd always thought it was his responsibility, not only to support and encourage his children, but also prepare them for adulthood, it had been a wrench when they'd left home. And once they had, the cracks in his marriage had widened until there was no way to traverse them.

When Femi had left, it had been almost a relief. A surcease of the constant arguments interspersed with cold silences.

At first the peace had been soothing, but then the emptiness of the cottage and his apartment in Falmouth had begun to register.

And the peaceful feeling had drained away, making him not want to go home after work.

Last night, as he'd looked around Nya's cosy living room, decorated for Christmas, he'd realised just how cold and sterile his own place was. Nya's personality was obvious everywhere—her warmth and humour clear in the colourful decorative items, the festive baubles—and, strangely, he'd felt his attraction to her go up a notch. It all had made him want to pull her to sit down on the sofa beside him, cuddle her and Hope close to his side, and find a kind of sweet oblivion.

Of course, he had done no such thing.

While there had been a couple of times yesterday he'd caught Nya looking at him in a way that made his heart race, there was no way to know exactly what she was thinking. Suspecting he wasn't alone in this new awareness didn't make it so, no matter how the idea interested him.

No doubt that was why, as he got to the next crossroads and looped back, he got a little spurt of additional energy as he realised Nya would be dropping Hope off soon.

Trying to distract himself, he went over the list of things he'd accomplished the night before.

Ordered probably more things for Hope than she'd ever need, but he'd been enjoying himself so much that he'd ended up deciding on gifts for TJ and Gillian too.

That had led him to think about what Nya had said about people being responsible for their own happiness, and admit to himself that he was allowing the past to shadow the present. Calling his children had seemed appropriate then, and their conversations had further soothed his soul.

'Since I'm stuck here until the day before Christmas Eve finishing this collaborative project, I was hoping to come down to Carey Cove between Christmas and New Year,' TJ had said. 'But only if it's no bother.'

'It will never be a bother for you to come home, whenever you want,' Theo said, surprised but trying not to show it. 'But I thought you were spending the hols with your mum.'

There was a pause, and then his son said, 'Yeah,

I said I would, but I wanted to figure out if you'd be around, should I decide to come down to see you.'

Theo knew his son well, and could put two and two together. Femi would never outright lie to their children, but she was expert at hinting at things, leaving them open to interpretation. Just as she'd hinted to Theo that the children had no interest in spending the holiday with him, she probably did the same to them by insinuating Theo had no time for them.

'Oh, I'm not going anywhere,' he replied, feeling more cheerful than he had in ages.

Gillian had apologised for not having enough time off to visit, adding that she was spending the following Christmas in Carey Cove, no matter what.

Intellectually he knew his children loved him, but hearing evidence of it made all the difference in the world.

And when he'd told them about Hope, and his offer to co-foster her with Nya, they'd expressed their approval, although Gillian had teased, 'What, Dad? Didn't think you could manage a baby all on your own?'

'Shut it, you,' he'd replied, as Gillian had hooted with laughter. 'I offered, but Nya looked so disappointed— because she'd wanted to foster the baby herself—that I suggested we share.'

'Ah, I see,' she'd replied slowly. 'Well, that's good, then.'

But when he'd asked her to elaborate, she'd brushed him off and changed the subject, leaving him wondering whether his children would be pleased or annoyed if he got involved with Nya.

And there he went again, thinking about Nya as he jogged up the driveway towards his door.

But if he was hoping for some indication that she'd felt the same rush of interest as he had the day before, he was quickly disillusioned.

She was her usual brisk, bustling self when she dropped Hope off, but even more so, since she whirled through his front hall like a tornado, depositing supplies. Bringing him up to speed about how the baby had slept, and how often she'd fed, as she transferred the car-seat base to his car. And then, after kissing the top of Hope's head, she headed right back out of the door, leaving him feeling as though he'd been run over by a small but determined lorry.

'Well,' he murmured to Hope, watching Nya's car turn onto the road. 'That'll teach me to misinterpret things, won't it?'

And Hope made a sound that he swore was half amused, half sympathetic, and he couldn't help laughing, even though there was no mistaking his disappointment.

Nya found herself speeding away from Theo's house and eased off the accelerator. She was flustered, just from seeing him, catching a hint of his fresh, soapy scent. It had made her imagine him in the shower after his run, his body slick with water, the suds running down a stark contrast to the darkness of his skin.

The fantasy caused a rush of desire she was desperate to hide from Theo, and the best way was to retreat behind her work persona. But even then she wasn't sure she'd been completely successful, since her heart was racing and she felt slightly breathless by the time she got back into her car.

'Get a hold on yourself, Nya,' she muttered, turning the car into the driveway of Carey House. 'You don't have to see him again until the end of the day.'

But her heart did another of those silly lurches at the thought, and she still felt off-kilter as she went inside.

Thankfully it was home-visit day, and having Lorna the trainee midwife with her forced Nya to keep her mind on work and off Theo Turner.

At least until they got to Marnie's to check on her and baby Violet.

'So tell me everything,' Marnie said as Nya supervised Lorna's wellness check of Violet. 'About Theo finding a baby on the doorstep of Carey House, and how both of you are taking care of her. I didn't have time to chat when I dropped the car seat off with you yesterday, but now I want to hear the entire story.'

Just hearing Theo's name made Nya start, and that gained her a surprised glance from Lorna.

'Oh…er…' Nya stopped talking to say to Lorna, 'Remember to make notes as you go along. Don't try to commit anything to memory. Well-kept records will aid parents and medical practitioners alike going forward.'

'Yes, Mrs Ademi—I mean Nya,' Lorna said, obviously remembering that Nya insisted they be on a first-name basis. As she then turned her attention to noting Violet's length and weight, saying them out loud, she thankfully gave Nya a chance to recover her equilibrium.

But she knew Marnie had noticed her reaction, and it

took all her focus to smile and tell the younger woman about Hope. Even then, Nya concentrated on telling Marnie about the evening before, when the baby was with her, rather than the rest of the day when Theo had shared the responsibility.

Then, once Lorna was finished with Violet, Nya pulled her into the conversation and, to her relief, Marnie turned her attention to the young trainee, grilling her about her plans. While they chatted, Nya held Violet, who was just a few weeks older than Hope. It came to mind how, once upon a time, she'd dreamed of raising her children alongside those of her friends, but of course that wasn't to be.

If Hope were to stay in Carey Cove—stay with Nya—she would grow up with Violet and have a built-in best friend and pseudo cousin.

Over the years she'd come to accept her childless state, and it was no longer a source of pain. However, today she felt a pang as she reminded herself that her custody of Hope was only temporary. Even if they didn't find her mother, Social Services would find a permanent fosterer, and that was all there was to it.

But it was surprisingly easy to drift off into a fantasy where she and Theo were together, raising Hope. Living together, sleeping together…

'Isn't that right, Nya?'

It was only when Marnie nudged her that Nya realised she'd missed the entire conversation, and heat rushed to her already warm face.

'Umm… What?'

Marnie's eyes narrowed, and she looked as though

she was about to say something, but then she glanced Lorna's way, and just shook her head, saying, 'Never mind. What else do you ladies have on the schedule today?'

Taking the reprieve in both hands, Nya smiled, replying, 'Why? Are you missing the hustle and bustle already?'

'I am, in a way,' she said with a laugh. 'But I'm enjoying my new job too much to leave it just yet.' Violet chose that moment to start to fuss, and Nya handed her back to her mum with a grin, as Marnie tacked on, 'No matter how demanding my new employer is.'

Lorna and she left not long after that, heading back to the clinic.

As they drove along, Lorna said, 'That layette set you made for Violet is lovely, Mrs Ademi—I mean, Nya. Where did you get the pattern?'

Nya glanced at the young woman as she replied, 'From my mother, who has a huge collection. Do you knit?'

'A little,' Lorna admitted. 'But I get frustrated, I'm that slow. I'm far better at crochet.'

'We have a fibre arts group here in the village, if you're interested. We usually get together once a month to chat, share patterns, drink tea or wine or, if you're Mrs Haymore, a vodka martini.'

'Oh!' Lorna sat up straighter and Nya knew the trainee was looking at her. 'I noticed the postbox topper outside the village shop, and the tree on the green wrapped to look like an angel. Did one of you make them?'

Nya tapped the side of her nose, grinning. 'The first rule of yarn bombing is—'

'Don't talk about yarn bombing,' they finished together, and they were laughing as she turned back into the drive at Carey House.

Nya was telling Lorna more about the club and some of the projects they'd done over the years as they walked into Reception and saw a little crowd of people around Hazel's desk. And in the midst of them, Theo, holding Hope.

It was impossible to ignore the way her heart flipped, and then started galloping. Thankfully Theo hadn't noticed her yet, so Nya had the chance to both feast her eyes and also compose herself. Yet, the latter was difficult.

Theo looked so handsome, so comfortable and proud holding Hope and showing her off to the midwives, patients and Hazel that Nya almost couldn't stand it.

Just once it would be nice to see Theo unkempt, or as frazzled as Nya felt just looking at him. Oh, she knew just how very human he was, but just now, with this new awareness of him sending carnal shivers through her body, she wished he'd put a foot wrong in some way. Maybe that would break the spell.

Then, as she hesitated just inside the door, Theo looked up and saw her, and his smile just about knocked her over.

Suddenly there was a flurry of motion, as all the midwives with patients escorted them away, and the others vanished too, as though Nya were poison. It happened so quickly it was almost cartoonish, and between her rush of pleasure at seeing Theo's smile and her amusement a giggle broke through before she could stop it.

Who knew she was scary enough to have that kind of effect on people? Luckily Theo didn't seem to feel the same way, because he was walking towards her, that gorgeous smile still in place.

'There you are. We came to ask you to join us for lunch.'

'I'd love to,' she said instinctively, but then added, 'But Hope's too young to be going to the pub. In fact, she shouldn't be around so many people yet. We don't know anything about the circumstances of her birth, her health, or her mother's. We don't even know if she was born in a hospital.'

Theo nodded, not losing his smile. 'Yes, I fended everyone off as best I could. And I thought we could order out and either eat in my office here, or at my house.' Before she could reply, he held up his hand, continuing, 'I know you've been doing home visits, and Hazel said you usually bring lunch from home, but I doubt you had time to make much of anything this morning.'

Nya was very aware of Hazel sitting at her desk, no doubt listening intently to their conversation, and was glad when the phone rang, and she had to answer.

'I'd love to,' she said again, 'but—'

'Nya, Dr Turner.' Hazel was always unflappable, but Nya recognised the note of urgency in her voice and swung around. 'Liz McDermott is suffering excruciating back pain. Her husband wants to know what to do.'

'Tell him to bring her in, immediately.'

It was Theo who answered, and Hazel nodded, tak-

ing her hand away from the receiver to tell Kyle Mc-
Dermott what had been said.

Turning to Theo, Nya said, 'Placental abruption,'
making it a statement, rather than a question. Liz had
been under Theo's care for the last two months, closely
monitored since the partial abruption had first been diagnosed. Liz had been on bed-rest and was almost full
term now, but the danger to both mother and baby if the
abruption had progressed was still very real. 'I'll prepare for ultrasound, and the delivery room.'

'Contact Roman too,' Theo said, striding across the
room. 'We may need to airlift Liz to St Isolde's for an
emergency C-section, depending on what we find.'

It was all hands on deck then.

Hazel took charge of Hope, while Nya found Lorna
in the staff room, and had her assist in setting up the
ultrasound machine, and laying out everything they'd
need, including instruments for a caesarean, just in case.

'I'm sure you remember from your classes that placental abruption is when the placenta begins to de-
tach from the uterine wall.' Nya brought Lorna up to
speed as they worked, so her trainee would be prepared
by the time the patient was brought in. 'Liz McDermott, a twenty-six-year-old first-time mother, came in
two months ago for a routine check-up, and reported
light, intermittent vaginal bleeding. She was thirty-
one weeks along. Our GP, Dr Wilde, diagnosed the
abruptio placentae and referred Mrs McDermott to
Dr Turner. Dr Turner recommended bed-rest, and both
Mr and Mrs McDermott were given a list of symptoms
to look out for.'

As she spoke she was mentally double-checking the room, making sure Theo would have everything to hand if and when needed.

Then came the sound of voices down the corridor, Liz's shrill with fear, and Theo's soothing tones.

With one last look around, Nya turned to Lorna, who looked a little worried. No wonder. This was Lorna's first placement, and she'd been honest about her lack of experience.

Nya smiled, and bumped the younger woman with her elbow.

'You'll be fine. Just follow Dr Turner's lead. And get the door.'

CHAPTER SIX

THEO'S EXAMINATION AND the ultrasound determined that Liz's abruption had grown larger.

'I'm going to induce labour, Liz. It's time to get this little fellow out.'

'All right,' she said, looking terrified and hanging onto her husband's hand so tightly his fingertips were turning white. 'Is the baby doing well?'

'We're monitoring him carefully,' Nya told her. 'Don't worry.'

After Theo had administered the oxytocin, he took Nya aside.

'Have Hazel call and get Roman on his way here. I want to make sure that if there are any complications after delivery, Liz and her son will be on the way to St Isolde's for treatment as soon as possible.'

Nya nodded, and slipped from the room to do as told. The chances of haemorrhage and clotting issues after an abruption were high, and although the baby was near term, he might still have issues with his lungs.

Liz's labour started in earnest not too long after, and in quick time her son was born. Just then Nya heard the distinctive *wump-wump-wump* of the helicopter's rotors, as Roman brought the aircraft in for a landing in the field behind the hospital.

Baby McDermott gave a weak wail as Nya placed him briefly on his mother's chest, and both parents cried with relief at seeing him.

Then she had to break up the tender scene, taking the infant for a quick check of his Apgar score, glad that Theo had arranged for transport.

'Seven on the Apgar,' she told Theo quietly. 'With a one on the A, G, and R.'

He nodded tersely. 'I'm going with them to Falmouth. Let's get them ready for transport.'

After a flurry of activity, soon Roman was wheeling mother and baby to the helicopter, Theo walking alongside the gurney, holding Liz's hand.

As the helicopter rose into the afternoon sky, Lorna sighed.

'Think they'll be all right, Nya?'

Putting an arm around the younger woman's shoulders, Nya gave her a brief hug.

'There are no guarantees, but I think so. Beside the fact that St Isolde's is a first-class hospital, Dr Turner is one of the best obstetric consultants around.'

Making their way back into the hospital, they parted company—Lorna going off to salvage what she could of her long-abandoned lunch, and Nya to go and collect Hope.

'Oh, do let me keep her here with me.' Hazel, always so motherly, was clearly enjoying the task of babysitter. 'I haven't had a baby to cuddle for ages. Besides, you're still on shift, aren't you?'

Nya laughed, and waggled her fingers in a *give it here* motion.

'I don't often pull rank, but what's the use of being Head of Midwifery if I can't occasionally skive off to take care of my foster baby? If anyone needs me, I'll be in my office. And if there's another emergency, I'll bring her back to you.'

With an exaggerated sigh, Hazel handed Hope over, and Nya set off for her office, going via the staff room to collect the container of salad she'd thrown together that morning.

Hope was awake, but not fussing. Nya checked her nappy anyway, and settled her in her carrycot before tucking into her lunch.

Thank goodness today was Saturday, and senior midwife Sophie was on call for Sunday, while Nya took the next two days off. That meant Nya had time to take care of Hope and still get some of her usual chores done. She'd been meaning to tell Theo she'd keep Hope tomorrow and the next day, so he didn't need to worry, but, somehow, she hadn't got around to it.

And she knew why.

Until she could figure out what these feelings and reactions she was having whenever he was around were, she was determined to minimise contact. Yet, wouldn't that mean telling him not to worry about taking care of the baby for the next two days, so there was no need to see him? Instead of doing that this morning, when she'd thought of it, she'd blithely gone on with her day.

After all, she could easily have texted him after she'd dropped Hope off…

Tearing her thoughts away from that particular conundrum, she pulled out her phone and brought up the app she used to make her to-do lists.

The last one she'd made a couple of days ago still had a number of chores on it, and she quickly picked out the ones she deemed most important. Laundry. Finishing the ruana she was knitting for her mother, and the last of the lap blankets she was planning to donate to the care home in Penzance. Putting up the last of the decorations in the cottage and finding time to deal with her super-secret project.

Then there were new items to add.

A layette set for Hope.

Maybe a gift for Theo?

Leaning back in her chair, she gave that some thought.

Since she'd never given him a Christmas gift before, except for once when she drew his name for the work Secret Santa, wouldn't doing so now seem strange?

Yet, at the same time, they were friends of long standing, and co-fosterers now too. Wouldn't *not* giving him a gift seem even stranger?

Should she invite him to spend Christmas and Kwanzaa with her, Mum and Hope? She had no idea what his plans were, or if he'd even be interested in coming to her cottage on the day. Maybe he was thinking of having Hope to himself, unless TJ and Gillian were coming down to spend the holidays with him?

She'd have to ask him, and that was all there was to

it, since that was the only way to find out. Adding asking him his plans to her list didn't solve the question of the gift though, and Nya didn't like not having her ducks in a row.

'Don't be daft, Nya,' she scolded herself, rubbing her temple. 'Ask him about his plans, *then* decide about the gift.'

But there was no way to avoid the knowledge that she hoped he'd want to spend the day with her. With them, she corrected, even as she grimaced and admitted she'd got it right the first time.

She wanted to spend time with him, even as she dreaded it too. Whatever was happening with her, she knew it was one-sided and, if she were smart, she'd never let Theo figure out how her feelings towards him were morphing.

It was probably just a temporary thing—an anomaly brought on by the time of the year, and the shared experience of caring for Hope.

Besides, there was no telling whether Hope would still be with them at Christmas time, she reminded herself firmly. The social worker had intimated that unless they found the baby's parents, she probably would be, but Nya knew she had to brace herself for whatever came.

In the past, the first part of December had always been an off time for her. Jim's birthday, coupled with the Christmas festivities rushing towards her, had often made her feel off-kilter. It had taken a number of years after his death for her to genuinely enjoy the holiday season again. He'd loved it so. Insisting on dressing as

Santa Claus and handing out gifts at the base party, even though it took pounds of stuffing to achieve the proper dimensions. Buying his mum and dad the very best gifts he could afford, and watching with such joy when they opened them.

Showering her with presents too, even when she scolded him for spending so much of his money. He'd just laugh, and pick her up to spin her around until she was dizzy, threatening not to stop until she admitted she liked them. Making her laugh so hard, as she clung to his neck, that tears rolled down her cheeks.

Such a zest for life.

Mum's words came back to her, lingered in her mind, as she closed the app, and picked back up her fork.

Loving Jim had taught her to enjoy whatever came her way.

Losing him had taught her nothing lasted for ever, and it was wise not to get too invested in anyone.

All things, especially good things, came to an end.

And, for once, she was glad to have her phone ring in the midst of her lunch, since it put paid to her muddled, somewhat maudlin thoughts.

'Hello. Nya Ademi,' she said briskly into the phone.

'Hi, it's Caroline Harker. I was just calling to see how things were going with baby Hope, and to tell you I've made an appointment with the paediatrician on staff with us to have a look at her next Tuesday. Will you be able to take her to Penzance then?'

'Of course. Just tell me the time, and either I or Dr Turner will make sure she's there.'

By the time she'd got off the phone, having taken all

the details, and despite what she'd said to Hazel, it was time to get back to work.

Luckily the afternoon wasn't particularly busy, but what with Nya supervising Lorna and seeing patients, Hope spent more time with Hazel than Nya would have liked. All the comings and goings around the reception area made it a less than optimal environment for such a young baby, even though Hazel made sure to keep everyone at bay.

Except herself, of course.

'She's such a little darling, isn't she?' she cooed, as she once more reluctantly handed Hope over to Nya at the end of the day. 'Such a good baby too.'

'She is,' Nya agreed as she strapped Hope into the car seat in preparation for the trip home. Unfortunately, the base was still in Theo's car, and the keys were presumably in his pocket. Luckily, Nya's cottage wasn't too far, and she'd decided to walk home rather than risk driving with the untethered carrier. 'She really only cries when she's hungry or needs a fresh nappy. Otherwise, she's just as happy as can be.'

'My youngest seemed to never stop crying,' Hazel said with a laugh. 'Came out wailing like a banshee and didn't stop until she turned twenty or so.'

'I'll make sure to tell her you said that the next time I see her,' Nya replied, trying to make it sound like a threat, even though she couldn't help giggling. 'I'm sure she'd enjoy hearing it.'

'Oh, she'd give me an earful, for sure. Off with you, before you get me into trouble.'

Although still early it was dark outside, but the

streetlights were on, and although it had drizzled earlier and a light mist hung in the air, the walk home wasn't unpleasant. Most of the cottages visible from the street were festooned with lights, and here and there a Christmas tree twinkled behind the windows. Nya took a deep breath of crisp air, grateful that the day was coming to a close, and she had two days of loving up on Hope to look forward to without interruption.

Drat it. She still hadn't texted Theo about that.

Shrugging to herself, she decided to do it after she'd got home, and settled Hope for the night.

As though on cue, as soon as she got to her door, Hope stirred, and let out an exploratory cry, which Nya now recognised as the preamble to her *I'm hungry... feed me now* wail.

'Just a few minutes,' she said, giggling as she got the door open. 'Your timing is impeccable.'

This was, she thought a while later, her new favourite time of day. Hope was fed and bathed, exuding that sweet, heart-melting baby scent as Nya held her on her shoulder and rocked her to sleep. She couldn't remember a more peaceful time, or one that made her feel as though she were exactly where she was supposed to be. So much so that it took a great deal of determination to finally get up and take Hope to her cot, and put her down to sleep.

Wandering back out into the living room, Nya stood still for a moment, contemplating whether to bother eating or not. Really, she didn't feel like cooking, and crackers and cheese didn't appeal. As though in objection to the thought, her stomach rumbled.

'Crackers and cheese it is, then,' she said aloud, heading for the kitchen.

Then headlights swung across the glass pane at the front of the house, and she paused. The sound of the car's engine shutting off had her walking to peep out through the window, in time to see Theo getting out of the vehicle.

Even as her heart did that ridiculous thing it had taken to doing whenever she saw him, Nya was trying to reason with herself, and get her breathing under control.

He must have just stopped by to bring the car-seat base. That was all.

She stepped back from the window, giving herself just a few seconds before opening the door.

Theo indeed had the base for the car seat in one hand, and in the other was a paper sack.

'Sorry for leaving you without use of the seat,' he said, with one of those heart-melting smiles. Holding up the sack, he continued, 'I brought dinner, as a peace offering.'

'Not necessary,' she replied, stepping back so he could come in. 'But gratefully received. I was just about to have crackers and cheese, not wanting to bother cooking.'

'Not the most nutritious way to end the day, but I completely understand. I've had a few nights like that myself.'

Funny how her perfectly adequate home, with its open living and dining room combination, suddenly seemed to shrink when Theo entered. He took up all the space, and apparently more than his fair share of the air, since Nya still had to fight to catch a deep breath.

'I'll get cutlery,' she said, for the sake of something to say. 'Sit down.'

Setting the bag down on the dining table, he started taking out containers, and Nya's stomach rumbled again at the heavenly scents suddenly filling the air.

'I wasn't sure what you'd like, but I stopped at the Ethiopian place in Penzance, since I know their food is always good.'

Nya felt a giggle rising in her throat, and bit it back.

'You must have been talking to my mum. She loves that restaurant.'

She was coming back out of the kitchen as she spoke, and saw his head tilt slightly, before he replied, 'You know, I think it was Iona who told me about it, months ago.'

'I'm not surprised. She'd eat there every night if she could. How are Liz and her son?'

Theo was unwrapping a foil packet, those lovely hands deftly opening it without tearing either the covering or the injera within.

'She's stable and should make a full recovery. We needed to cauterise and give her blood, and little Nicolas will be in the NICU at least until tomorrow, to make sure his lungs are functioning properly.'

'Yum,' she said, as he opened a container and the familiar scent made her mouth water. '*Doro wat*. My favourite.'

Theo smiled, and she had to look away.

'Many kinds of *wat*,' he said. 'Since I wanted to make sure there was something you'd be happy to eat.'

They used the plates, but the cutlery remained pristine as they both ate in Ethiopian style—tearing off pieces of injera and using the bits to scoop up mouthfuls of the various stews.

Conversation was restricted to requests to pass each other dishes, as they both ate hungrily. When they were finished, Nya got up to put away the leftovers, while Theo asked to look in on Hope.

'Of course. Last door at the end of the hall.'

And she turned towards the kitchen, not wanting him to see how the thought of having him in her bedroom made her face feel as though it were on fire.

All she could hope was that by the time she went to bed, there'd be no trace of Theo's distinctive scent lingering there, to bedevil her dreams!

CHAPTER SEVEN

NYA'S BEDROOM WAS something of a surprise, and yet very much like her. Bright and cheerful, eclectic yet quite traditional when it came to the furniture and patterns.

Somehow, knowing how Afro-centric her mother was, Theo had half expected the décor to lean in that direction. But, rather, William Morris-esque curtains, mid-century modern furniture, and pops of colour proclaimed that Nya's style was whatever she happened to like, rather than a set pattern.

He liked it. A lot.

Even though entering into what was her private space also gave him more of those untoward thoughts he was continually battling whenever they were together. His eyes gravitated towards her neatly made bed, and he quickly jerked them away, looking instead at the cot.

Hope was fast asleep, and hadn't even stirred when he turned on the light. Going to stand over her, Theo touched her cheek, then her tightly curled fist, with one finger. How tiny and vulnerable she looked and was.

His heart ached each time he thought about what might become of her.

Even if they found her mother, would the woman be fit to take back her baby, or would Hope end up one of the hundreds of children entering the foster system? Staying in it until they aged out. Never knowing a truly loving home.

A part of him wanted to rail at the thought. To swear it would never happen on his watch. Yet, he knew, in this case, he had no real power over the situation. Whatever was to happen, he'd have to wait and see.

Knowing there were no answers to be found tonight, he bent to press a kiss to Hope's hair, and turned to leave the room.

A picture on the bedside table caught his eye, and he paused, staring at it.

This, then, was Nya's husband, James. Jim, she'd always called him, the few times she'd spoken of him in Theo's presence.

A tall, well-built man, broad of shoulders and thick of neck. Obviously in perfect physical shape, if this full-body shot was anything to go by. Dressed in his army uniform, he could have been an overawing sight, except for the absolute delight on his face as he grinned at the camera.

Nya usually gave one of her delicious little giggles when she talked about him. He was, she'd once said, a man who never seemed to have a bad day. He brought joy and laughter with him wherever he went.

Why looking at the picture made Theo's chest tighten was inexplicable, and when he turned away to exit the room, he couldn't help glancing back once more, before he turned off the light.

Trying hard to battle a sudden surge of resentment against a man simply because he was loved so deeply, and for so long.

'Still sleeping peacefully?' Nya asked as Theo walked back into the living room, having paused in the hall to compose himself.

'Like the little angel she is,' he replied, wondering why he was so reluctant to say goodnight and go home. Of course, it was because he had nothing to rush home *for*, did he?

'Sit down. Can I offer you a cuppa? Or a drink?'

Suddenly relieved that she wasn't kicking him out just yet, he opted for a cup of tea. When he moved back towards the dining table, she waved him towards the fireplace instead.

'Can you put a match to that for me? It's getting cool in here, and a fire will make sure Hope doesn't get a chill.'

'Funny how things have changed over the years, isn't it? Before the 1990s, the norm was cover baby with a blanket, put her on her stomach, and leave all her stuffed toys in the crib with her. Nowadays, it's dress baby warmly and put her to sleep on her back with nothing whatsoever in the crib.'

Nya made a little sound of assent in her throat.

'Everything changes, especially in light of new research. How are Gillian and TJ? Are they coming for Christmas?'

He didn't look up from the fireplace, glad she wouldn't be able to read his expression.

'Not this year.' He hesitated, and then decided he might as well tell her the rest. 'I don't know if you heard, but Femi got married a couple of months ago. She and her new husband are having a big family get-together, and TJ and Gillian will be going to that.'

Nya didn't comment right away, but he heard the rattle of teacups and pot as she walked back into the room.

Putting the tray down on the occasional table in front of the love-seat, she sat down, and he thought he could feel her gaze on him, making a little shiver run down his spine.

'I didn't know about her marriage.' Thank goodness there was no sympathy in her tone, just a deeply contemplative note. 'I tried to reach out to her a few times since she left, but she never replied, so I stopped. Well, if you don't have any plans, you can spend Christmas with Mum and me. And Hope, of course, if she's still here.'

Her thoughtfulness made him smile, and feel able to get up and face her, instead of hiding.

'I'd like that. Especially if Hope is still in our care. It'll be her first Christmas, and she deserves a good one.'

The fractional tightening of the skin around her eyes was the only indication of anything untoward, since her mouth was still smiling, but he knew how she felt. He didn't want to contemplate giving up Hope either, although he knew they'd have to, eventually.

Wanting to take Nya's mind off the subject, he heard

himself say, 'You know, when I think back on all the holidays I missed with my children, I really regret it now. I let my work consume me, to their detriment.'

Her eyes widened. 'But surely you don't believe that's true?'

'It is true.' Sitting down beside her on the love-seat, he turned slightly so he was facing her, his arm along the back. It wasn't the largest couch in the world, and he was suddenly aware of the heat of her leg against his, the proximity of her hair to his hand.

If he could have shifted away without it being obvious, he probably would have, but since that wasn't an option, he held still.

'Why do you think so, Theo?'

When she looked at him like that, with that clear-sighted gaze, he felt as though he would tell her anything she wanted to know.

Even his deepest shame.

'I know it's true, because I lived it. I was so determined to make sure they had everything they needed—stability, financial security, someone showing them how to be a productive citizen of the world—that I sacrificed my home life.'

She tilted her head. 'But those things are important. Why should you feel guilty about providing them?'

'Yes, they are important, and I know that because it's the complete opposite to how I grew up. My father was a shiftless bastard, who rarely worked. And when he did get a job, he spent all his money drinking and gambling. I promised myself I'd never turn out that way, and worked hard to make sure of it.'

Even to his ears his voice sounded choppy—uneven—but he couldn't stop the spate of words.

'That I'd never endanger my family by putting my pleasures before their needs. But there's a line between being successful and letting that success be everything in your life, and I crossed it.'

Nya's lips pursed, and when she leaned forward to pour the tea, he wished he could see her face.

'And what's your relationship with them like now?'

'Good,' he said, surprised at what he thought was a change of subject. 'I spoke to them just last night. TJ wants to come and visit between Christmas and New Year, if he can manage it. The engineering degree he's taking at Cambridge is intensive, but his marks have been amazing.'

'And Gillian?'

He couldn't stop the smile that took over his face as he took the proffered cup from Nya's hand.

'She's doing brilliantly. She's working for a fertility clinic in London as a researcher, but I think she may opt to go back to school to become a doctor eventually.'

Nya took a sip of tea, her eyes downcast. Then, when she lowered the cup and turned to look at him, he was surprised at the tenderness in her gaze.

'Theo, stop being so darn hard on yourself. You've helped to raise two wonderful young people, who love and admire you. Can't you give yourself credit for that?' Before he could respond, she raised her hand to stop him, and a soft smile tipped the edges of her mouth. 'I don't know if you realise, but my father died when I was eleven, and Mum raised me by herself. Now, you think you're driven? I wager my mum would run circles around you in that respect. She was determined to get a professorship, and was always studying and writing books to make that happen. Then it was getting the university to create an African studies course. She was determined and focused but, at the same time, she was raising me. It wasn't always a successful combination.'

She was smiling, but he felt his heart clench. He wanted to know how that had affected her, but the words stuck in his throat, fear of what she might say keeping them there.

Nya took another sip of her tea, then reached to put the cup down, before she continued.

'Yes, there were times when I resented her not being at home, or was hurt when she'd missed a special occasion at school, but I also always knew she was *there*. Available to me if I needed her. And she was the very, very best role model I could have ever had. She taught me that if you want something, you have to work hard for it, and sacrifice too, if that's what was necessary.

'Your children know you're there for them. They watched you work hard and strive to make their lives comfortable—to give them the opportunities they're enjoying now. I know I saw you at rugby matches, and at concerts in the hall when they were performing. If you were as much of an absentee father as you seemed to think, you wouldn't have bothered with any of that, so cut yourself some slack.'

Her words, coupled with that sweet, gentle look in her eyes, made his heart swell, and then begin to race.

Unable to resist, he touched her cheek with the back of his hand, and almost groaned at the softness of her skin.

He wanted to thank her, to tell her how much he'd needed to hear what she'd said. How suddenly free he felt, as though she'd let loose a rope that had been slowly squeezing the life out of him, allowing him—for the first time in months—to take a deep, cleansing breath.

But none of those words emerged from his mouth, because by then he was too busy kissing her, and all thoughts of talking fled.

Nya didn't move, as Theo's lips touched down on hers, but her immobility lasted only for a moment. Then her arms went up around his neck, and she was pulling him closer, deepening the kiss herself, as need exploded out into every vein and muscle in her body.

She'd tried so hard not to imagine what it would be like to kiss Theo, but now she had to acknowledge that no matter what she might have come up with, it would never have been enough.

His lips were softer than she'd have imagined.

Their firmness and mastery couldn't have been dreamt up accurately.

The first sweep of his tongue across the seam of her mouth was hotter, slicker, more arousing than any fantasy could ever be.

Was this what they meant when they talked about melting into someone's arms? It felt like it, as her skin grew hot and so sensitive that when Theo's hand curved around her nape, it sent energy surging into her trembling belly.

He gentled the pressure on her mouth fractionally, sucking on her lower lip, nipping at it with his teeth, and there was no stopping her moan of desire.

Then the kiss turned wild, a frantic tangle of tongues, as their breath rushed and her heart beat so hard and fast, she could hear it in her ears.

He leaned forward, tilting her back against the arm of the love-seat, and she didn't resist, wanting to know where this was going. Wanting to feel the hard press of his body against hers.

Wanting him in a way she'd never wanted before.

And then, a shrill wail rent the air, and they both froze.

Instinctively, Nya's hands fell to Theo's heaving chest and pushed. Immediately he pulled back, his arms falling from around her, leaving her suddenly cold. And as she stumbled to her feet, she realised she was shaking from head to toes.

Theo's hand came up, as though to steady her, and she sidestepped out of reach. She should say something—make a pithy comment or something trite—but nothing sensible came to mind, so she did the only thing she could think of.

She fled to the bedroom to scoop up the crying infant and hug her close.

'You're okay, sweetie. There's a good girl,' she crooned, hearing the wavering in her voice. Her tension must have transmitted itself to Hope, since the little girl stiffened and cried harder, rather than relaxing the way she usually would.

Taking deep breaths, Nya rocked Hope, trying to

get her own heart rate down. It wasn't time for a feed yet, so once Hope calmed a little, Nya quickly laid her down and changed her nappy.

Hope stopped crying, and Nya was contemplating if she had the nerve to go back into the living room, when she heard the unmistakable sound of her front door closing and knew Theo had slipped away.

Blowing out a long, hard breath, she plunked down on the end of her bed, putting Hope on her shoulder in her favourite position for falling asleep.

She'd kissed Theo.

Theo!

And not just kissed him but enjoyed it in a way that left her shaken and aroused, aching for the type of physical contact she hadn't had—or wanted—in ages.

Closing her eyes, she relived the moments, imagined it continuing, becoming more intimate.

Theo's hands and mouth exploring her body, touching and slipping, increasing her need until it reached fever-pitch...

Pulling her thoughts back from where they'd so wantonly taken her was far too difficult, but Nya knew she couldn't afford to let them stray too far along that path.

None of this was or could be real. Theo was going through a difficult time, and no matter who objected, or thought she should move on, her heart belonged to Jim, and no one else.

Theo and her being thrown into close proximity because of their shared care of Hope, at this particular time in their lives, had created an anomalous situation. Once things went back to normal, they'd both be left considering what on earth they'd been thinking, kissing like that.

It was wrong—for both of them—but as she lay down on her bed, still cuddling Hope and looking at Jim's picture, she wondered why it felt so very right all the same.

CHAPTER EIGHT

IT WASN'T UNTIL the next morning that Nya remembered she hadn't spoken to Theo about not having Hope that day or the next. She was dithering between calling and texting him when her phone rang, and her heart tumbled over itself before she realised it was her mother calling.

'Morning, Mum,' she said, hoping her breathlessness wouldn't be too apparent. 'How was the seminar?'

'It was lovely, but what's this I hear about you fostering a baby?'

Trust her mother to come straight to the point, once the minimum of niceties was out of the way. Nya couldn't help giggling.

'So, you already heard. That'll teach you to go haring off to Penzance and leave me to my own devices.'

Her mother's snort spoke volumes.

'Tell me everything, from the beginning. I've only got dribs and drabs through the grapevine.'

Nya did as she was told, outlining for her mum all that had happened the last two days, trying to make it all sound quite normal and banal. Yet, each time she had to say Theo's name, her heart missed a beat, and she was worried it affected her tone of voice.

A fear that seemed to be borne out when, after she was finished, her mother asked, 'So, you and Theo are sharing custody of little Hope? That's...interesting.'

'No, Mum,' Nya quickly interjected. When heard that way it sounded too intimate, as though they were creating a family together. 'We're temporary co-fosterers. Just until they either find her mother or can arrange for a permanent foster situation.'

Nya could usually interpret the sounds her mother made, but this time she didn't even want to.

'Well, I'm looking forward to meeting Hope soon. From what you've said, she'll be with us through Christmas, yes? Have you asked Theo to join us?'

'Yes. Unless they find Hope's mum, she'll be with us until the new year. I told the social worker I'd keep her at least that long, so they didn't have to fuss about finding a fosterer before then. And, yes, I did invite Theo to join us.'

Why did that last bit feel like making a concession?

'Good. And please invite him to our Kwanzaa celebrations too.'

'I'll tell him about it, Mum.' Nya glanced at her watch. If she didn't contact Theo soon, he might turn up on her doorstep. 'But I have to go. I think I hear Hope stirring.'

'When do I get to meet her?'

Just her luck that this morning, when she was eager to get off the phone, Mum wanted a bit of a chat.

'She's only a week or so old, so I'm trying to limit

her exposure to new people for a little while more. But you're family, so why don't you let me know when you're free, and I'll bring her by?'

'This afternoon will be wonderful,' Mum said promptly. 'Come for tea. I'll wear a mask when I'm holding the baby.'

Nya shook her head, but couldn't help smiling. It was impossible to get annoyed with her mother's high-handed ways, simply because she saw it for what it was—a way to navigate a world that hadn't always been kind. Iona had built a no-nonsense persona to not just ensure she got what she wanted, but also as a barrier against disappointment.

'Oh,' Iona continued, before Nya could respond to the invitation. 'Bring Theo with you. I always enjoy his company.'

Then she hung up.

Theo.

Without time to consider whether to text or call, she brought up his number and pressed call.

And heard his phone ringing outside her door.

Darn it. Too late.

A soft knock sounded just as he answered, and she could hear the laughter in his voice as he said, 'Hullo. Fancy letting me in?'

'Let me think about it,' she replied, feeling a bit silly as she patted her hair like a schoolgirl getting ready to see her crush.

She tried to pull herself together, but his soft chuckle sent a shiver through her, and she felt even giddier as he said, 'I brought gifts.'

'Are you Greek?'

'Not the last time I checked. And I don't have any horses with me.'

Opening the door, she shook her head. 'You better not have. My back garden isn't that big, and it's a little early to be buying Hope a pony.'

His grin made her heart soar as he bent to pick up the pile of boxes at his feet, and she stepped back to let him in.

'Oh, I don't know. It's something to think about.'

He put down the boxes, then promptly turned and went back outside for more. Nya watched him, torn between amusement and that silly, flustered sensation.

'You might not have bought her a pony, but this looks like a pony's weight in things. What is all this?'

'Just a few things I thought Hope needed.' He looked so ridiculously pleased with himself, Nya's heart—already doing little somersaults—absolutely melted. 'I found a car seat that comes with two bases, so we can each have one in our car, and give Marnie back hers. Then there are blankets, bibs, babygrows, towels…'

He was pulling things out of boxes as he spoke, and Nya put a hand over her mouth to stifle the giggle rising in her throat. Theo paused and skewered her with a look.

'Why do you always do that?' he asked, gesturing to her hand. 'Muffle your laughter?'

She didn't think anyone had ever noticed that habit she had, and it made her feel a bit self-conscious. But not wanting him to know, she wrinkled her nose and replied, 'It's silly, the way I laugh. I sound like a twelve-year-old, rather than a mature woman.'

Theo's eyes narrowed. 'Whoever told you that is a twit. I love the way you laugh. Every time I hear it, it makes me smile.'

Heat rushed to her face, and Nya turned away so he wouldn't see how his words affected her.

She'd been teased about her laugh since secondary school, and had actively started trying to hold it back in nursing school. Once she'd started rising in her job, she'd felt it undermined her authority and really tamped it down.

Pretending to survey the stack of boxes, she said, 'It's a good thing it's wash day for me. All of this lot— barring the car seat, of course—will need to be sanitised before we can use them.' More in control now, she glanced over at him, and made sure not to get snagged by his gaze again. 'I had planned to tell you that you didn't have to come and get Hope today. That I'd be happy to do the Sunday/Monday shift, since I'm off tomorrow too.'

'Oh, no, you don't.' He sounded amused, but there was a hint of steel in his voice too. 'You're not depriving me of Hope's company, and yourself of a chance to get some well-deserved rest.'

'I don't mind. She's so good, and I have some chores to do here, and then I promised Mum to take Hope around to see her, so if you have things to do—'

'The only thing I have to do is take care of Hope.' He sounded so firm Nya knew he wasn't budging. 'So, if you want me to just hang about here until it's time to go to your mum's, I can do that too. That way if you want to nap or just not have to stop whatever it is you're doing, I'm here keeping things under control.'

If she made a fuss about it, he'd surmise their kiss the night before had changed their relationship, and Nya wasn't willing to have that happen. So, although everything inside was screaming that she shouldn't spend any more time with Theo than was absolutely necessary, she gave in.

Throwing her hands up, she huffed. 'Okay, then. Have you had breakfast?'

Both of them couldn't fit comfortably in her little kitchen, so it would be a good way to put a little distance between them.

'I had a protein shake.'

Trying to get back the teasing atmosphere they'd achieved when he'd just arrived, she said, 'Is that how you keep your schoolgirl figure?'

Theo actually looked shame-faced, as he replied, 'Actually, the truth is that I'm a terrible cook. Really terrible.'

She couldn't suppress her giggles, but found breath enough to say, 'I very much doubt that's true. You're far too competent a human being not to be able to boil an egg and make some toast.'

Which led him into a hilarious story about burning a meal on the outdoor grill, making Nya laugh until tears filled her eyes.

But it was the sense of relief that things were back to the way they were—before his divorce, and definitely before that kiss—that made her light-hearted.

* * *

Having spent most of the previous night reliving their kiss, and trying to figure what, if anything to do about it, Theo had come to the conclusion that it was an anomaly best left unremarked.

At least, he assumed that was what it was for Nya. And her determined effort to get rid of him at first, and then to keep the atmosphere light when he made it plain he wasn't going, seemed to bear it out.

She wanted him to know she wasn't interested in him physically, but still wanted to be his friend, for which he was overwhelmingly grateful.

As for how he viewed their kiss...

That was where things became far less clear-cut.

Not only had holding her felt amazing, and kissing her been mind-blowingly arousing, but it had all felt... somehow...

Right.

As though somewhere in his subconscious he'd been waiting for the chance to hold Nya, taste her lips, know what it felt like to be touched by those soft, capable hands.

Which was absurd.

He'd taken his marriage vows seriously. It had never, ever occurred to him to be unfaithful by look or thought. So he was quite sure he'd never thought of Nya that way, at all. Yet, there was no mistaking the sheer delight he'd experienced the night before.

Which had brought a rush of guilt and confusion that had kept him up, pacing the house late into the night.

Since his marriage fell apart, both friends and family

members had urged him to start dating, but he hadn't been interested. His whole persona had been built on focus and stability—being responsible and committed to whatever he was involved in. While mentally he accepted his failure to hold his family together, emotionally it was difficult to break the chains. Dating had felt like cheating—an attitude he knew would eventually hold him back, but hadn't seemed something to worry too much about in the short term.

And his response to even that brief intimacy with Nya showed he was right. Even if there hadn't been the issue of Nya being his friend, and seemingly determined not to get involved with anyone, he wasn't ready either.

Maybe, like her, he'd never be.

Which made her attitude and reception this morning something to be thankful for. It felt as though he'd lost so much over the last eighteen months, it would be devastating to lose Nya's friendship too.

Leaning on her kitchen doorframe, he kept their conversation light, even though he was hyper-aware of her every move as she bustled about making breakfast. When he heard Hope stir, he went to get her, before Nya had a chance to do more than look up.

The one thing he was determined to do today was make sure Nya had all the help she needed, whether she wanted it or not.

After changing the baby, he took her into the kitchen to find that her bottle was already in the warmer.

'I could have done that,' he said.

Nya gave a little snort and rolled her eyes. 'I was already in here and I know where everything is. It would have been silly to make Hope wait while you fumbled around, when it took me all of two seconds.'

'Do you hear how she talks to me, Hope?' He turned the infant, who was making unhappy sounds but not yet crying, so they were face to face, her little body easily fitting between his hands. Hope's gaze seemed to focus on his, enthralling him totally. 'You'd think she'd be nicer to us, wouldn't you?'

He glanced up in time to see Nya's nose go up in the air. 'I'm always nice. Don't you be turning my baby against me.'

For Theo time seemed to slow, almost stop. The way she said it, the ease of the atmosphere, was like home. Home the way he'd always dreamed it could be, but never actually was.

Then he pushed the thought away.

He and Nya had always had a bantering relationship, both at work and in social situations. There was nothing new or strange about this morning, except that there was precious Hope added to the mix.

And, considering the way he'd been avoiding Nya since the divorce, having the infant throw them together, reigniting their old friendship, made it all extra precious.

Best not to make too much more of it.

So he went back to teasing, as he fed Hope and ate his breakfast, feigning annoyance when Nya, in turn, twitted him about his ability to do both at the same time.

The day flew along, but with an effortless flow Theo found entirely enjoyable. He'd bought a knapsack-type carrier, and put Hope in it so he could help Nya hang clothes on the line in the backyard. They'd had a spate of nice, sunny weather, cool enough to need a light jacket, but the wind, which had been blustery over the last few days had died down.

In the same vein as before, Nya said, 'Well, you're a champion washer man. You obviously know your way around a clothes line.'

She was so easy to talk to, he found himself explaining, 'My mum worked two or three jobs when we were young so, being the oldest, I had to figure out how to keep things going at home when she wasn't around.'

Nya sent him a questioning look. 'Had your father left, and she'd become a single mum?'

'No.' Even after all these years, he couldn't keep the derision out of his voice. 'She would probably have been better off if she had been. My father wasn't interested in doing anything around the house, although he hardly worked. Mum kept the trains running mostly by herself in those days.'

She was silent for a moment, and then asked, 'I remember meeting her once, about five years ago. She lives in America, doesn't she? I don't remember meeting your father, though.'

Harder now, but he didn't feel the need to retreat from the conversation the way he usually would.

'Yes, Mum lives in San Francisco with her second husband—an American she met when he was stationed at the embassy here, but the last time she visited she was on her own. I have no idea if Dad is alive or not.

He divorced Mum just about the time I started uni, and never looked back.'

'I'm sorry.' It sounded as if she was, although he appreciated the brisk way she said it. 'That must have been hard on you all.'

He paused, the clothes peg in his hand hovering above the line, and waited for the anger, but somehow when it came it was more subdued than usual.

'I think it was more of a relief than anything else.' The words came slowly, and it felt somehow *good* to say them. 'I know Mum was hurt by it, because she'd tried so hard, and stuck it out no matter how difficult it became. But I thought it was the best thing that could have happened. The situation was wearing her down, you know? Making her old before her time. She's a lot happier now.'

Nya made a little sound of acknowledgement in her throat. 'It's so heartbreaking, watching someone you love go through the tough times, and there's nothing you can do to make it better.'

The way she said it was like putting a full stop at the end of a sentence, and Theo was more than happy to change the subject thereafter, asking her what time she was due at her mother's.

'She likes to have tea at four, and you're invited, if you'd like to come.'

It was on the tip of his tongue to refuse, but instead he instinctively said, 'I'd like that.'

Then wondered what that sideways glance she gave him meant.

'I have something to do afterwards, but it's a secret. Can I count on you not to say anything?'

Intrigued, he said, 'Of course. What is it you're up to?'

There came that lovely giggle, and a teasing, arched-brow look.

'You'll see. Later.'

And no amount of prying could get it out of her.

CHAPTER NINE

NYA KNEW SHE'D be a fool not to be worried about going to her mother's house with Theo. Mum was an astute observer, who far too often noticed things other people missed, and didn't hesitate to comment. Yet, to her surprise, Mum said nothing untoward, and seemed too wrapped up with Hope to perhaps notice the change in her daughter.

And Nya was sure there must be some outward signs of the turmoil raging inside.

Oh, she thought she did a good job pretending the easy relationship she'd always had with Theo was unchanged, but she knew it was just a façade. Her heightened awareness of him, and the way her gaze was constantly drawn back to him, made her self-conscious. She spent much of the visit trying to find anywhere else to look, rather than at him, and with her fingers fisted, so as not to touch him in passing.

Telling herself it was just the after-effects of their kiss the night before didn't help. In fact, it made it worse, because it brought their embrace back to mind, and caused crazy waves of heat to rush from her torso into her face.

But somehow she got through tea with a smile on her face, and when Mum suggested they bring Hope to visit again the following day, did her best to dodge the invitation.

'Theo will have Hope tomorrow, Mum,' she said, knowing she was contradicting what she'd said to Theo earlier, about being willing to take care of the infant the next day herself. 'And I'm sure he has other plans.'

'I don't actually.' Theo smiled, looking so adorable with Hope nestled against his chest in the carrier, Nya could hardly stand it. 'I just planned to hang about. Maybe tutor Hope on the finer points of football while we watch a match or two that I've missed today.'

'In that case, definitely bring her back here,' Mum said, the laughter in her eyes belying the acerbic tone of her voice. 'I'll have to counteract that with a discussion about Beowulf and the beauty of Old English literature.'

Theo laughed as he bent to kiss Iona's cheek, and Nya shook her head at the two of them, although she couldn't help laughing too.

'That was nice,' Theo said as they set off walking back to Nya's cottage. 'I really like your mother a lot. She's always interesting.'

Nya laughed, only just stopping herself from muffling the sound with her hand. 'You mean colourful?'

Theo's eyes glinted with laughter. 'She is that, but no, that's not what I meant.' His lips pursed for a moment, as though he was trying to find the right words. 'Iona always struck me as the type of person who doesn't give her trust or friendship easily, but once you've earned it, it's immovable. That's something I can appreciate.'

'You're rather like that too,' she said, although the realisation surprised her in a way. 'But without Mum's sharp edges.'

Theo shrugged one shoulder, tipping his head back to look up at the moon, which was waxing and, although not yet full, lit up the lane. His profile was rendered sharp by the play of light and shadows, and as Christmas lights flashed colours across his dark skin, she found him heartbreakingly handsome.

'I learned to be careful of people, to recognise that not everyone will have my best interests at heart. But, at the same time, I actually like most of the folks I meet. I'm just not willing to let everyone into my inner circle.'

She nodded, hearing the self-reflection in his words, appreciating his candour.

'Mum's life hasn't always been easy,' she replied. 'And I think that's another thing you have in common too.'

He slanted her a look from beneath lowered lids, his lips twisting slightly, before relaxing into a smile again.

'Maybe. I'd never really been one to self-analyse, but for the last year I feel as though it's almost all I've done, when I'm not working. And I still don't have any answers.'

They were at the corner of the high street now, and she stopped him with a hand on his arm, unable to resist touching him.

Just in sympathy, she told herself, as she would have done at any time at all during their long friendship.

'Sometimes you have to accept there aren't any easy answers, and sometimes no answers at all.' Then, because the air around them felt too heavy, and she was fighting the urge to tug him close and kiss him again, she let go of his arm, and said, 'Are you ready for our secret mission?'

His teeth flashed as he grinned. 'What are you up to?'

'Come this way, and you'll see.'

When she turned up the road, away from her cottage, he followed. There were a few people on the high street, and from the sounds of it The Dolphin pub was full, but the farther they got from it, the quieter it became.

'Are we going to the hospital?' he asked.

'Shush,' she said, looking around as they approached the postbox near the entrance to Carey House. 'We're stopping here.'

'What are you up to?' He spoke quietly, as though her surreptitious behaviour had infected him.

'You'll see.'

The postbox topper was the first she'd ever crocheted, and she was quite proud of it. She'd created a retro winter scene of a pond partially ringed by trees, with couples in Victorian costumes skating on the surface. Around the edge she'd attached holiday-themed ornaments that dangled down on ribbons.

Definitely over the top, but hopefully worth the effort.

Pulling it out of the bag, she carefully fitted it over the top of the box, heaving a sigh of relief when it actually fitted properly, and the trees and figures stood up without drooping.

When she stepped back to look at it, Theo was close by her side, and when he put an arm around her shoulder, she couldn't bring herself to move away.

'That's beautiful.' He sounded enthralled. 'And impressive. But why...?'

'Let's get out of here,' she replied. 'I can't be seen in the vicinity. I'll explain later.'

Then, setting a brisk pace, but trying not to look too conspicuous, she led the way back towards home.

'It's called yarn bombing,' she said, once they were far enough away, and there was no one around. 'It's a type of street art, not illegal, but sometimes frowned on by the powers that be. The ladies of our fibre arts group have been doing it for a few years. You must have seen some of our work around the place.'

'I have, and always thought they brought a bright spot to the streets. Why would it be frowned on?'

'Well, it's sometimes seen as a nuisance—not as bad as graffiti, but in the same vein. Usually, though, they leave it up for a while, especially when it's close to Remembrance Day, and the artwork is military or poppy themed. As long as it isn't impeding the public in some way, the council here in Carey Cove doesn't seem to mind.'

'So, why all the cloak and dagger, then?'

He was laughing at her, a bit, but she liked that better than the solemn and stern Theo she'd been used to seeing recently.

'Well, half the fun is in leaving everyone guessing who actually did it. This time, no one will think it's me.'

'Why not?'

They were turning into her driveway then, and she knew, suddenly, she didn't want the night to end just yet. Without looking at him, she said, 'Because I'm known as a knitter, not a crocheter.'

He chuckled softly, the sound tickling down her spine, making her shiver. 'You know I don't have a clue what the difference is, right? But I'll take your word for it, and promise not to spill your secret.'

'Thank you.' At the door now, before she lost her nerve, she said, 'I'm going to bathe Hope when I go in. Would you like to help?'

'I would,' he said, in a calm tone that nonetheless sent a little shiver along her spine. 'Thank you.'

'You're welcome.' Her fingers felt a little unsteady as she fitted the key into the door, and she took a deep, silent breath to get them under control. Hopefully she wouldn't eventually regret the invitation, but just then, as they walked into her living room, all she felt was elated.

Nya turned on her Christmas tree, bathing the house in twinkling lights, reminding Theo of how very sterile his own home looked.

'I should put up some decorations,' he said as Nya helped get Hope out of the carrier. 'Every time I see yours I think so, then I just forget about it.'

'And get a Christmas tree.' Nya laughed up at him,

her dark eyes sparkling. 'Do it for Hope, if you won't do it for yourself.'

'Of course,' he replied, laughing with her. Feeling ridiculously happy to be with her and Hope, and invited to participate in the evening ritual. 'I'm sure Hope will appreciate a tree.'

It wasn't until they were at the kitchen sink, Hope kicking her little legs on the counter while he undressed her, that Theo realised the close quarters he'd be in with Nya during the bath.

Too close, he thought, as his arm brushed the side of Nya's breast and his breath hitched momentarily in his chest.

Steady on.

But even while concentrating on undressing the squirming Hope, his awareness of Nya kept growing.

A soft scent he recognised as purely her own.

The sight of her capable hands as they moved to turn the water on and off and gather the supplies closer to the sink.

Her body's warmth, which seemed to reach out to him.

And every time their bodies touched, a bloom of heat spread from the spot, until his entire body vibrated with warmth.

Desire.

'Here we go,' Nya said gently, reaching over to pick up Hope so as to place her on the rubber sink liner. Hope's eyes opened wide for a moment when she was submerged in the water, and then her little legs and arms started waving back and forth. 'Oh, you love your baths, don't you, sweetie?'

He didn't know exactly what the emotion was that overtook him, but the backs of his eyes prickled, and his voice came out a little roughly when he said, 'I'll hold her for you, and you wash.'

'Thank you.'

They fell into a rhythm that only served to increase the sense of intimacy enveloping them in Theo's mind. Working together to wash Hope's hair, both of them leaning close, so from the corner of his eye he could see the smooth curve of Nya's cheek. He searched for a topic of conversation that would put some emotional distance between them, and decided it would help to remind himself of Nya's unavailability. Maybe that would dissipate this growing longing tightening his muscles and making him light-headed.

'May I ask you a very personal question?' he asked, not really sure whether he wanted her to answer yes or no.

'Of course,' she replied, still in that sing-song voice she used with Hope, but he saw the way she shot him a quick sideways glance. 'Anything.'

'Why did you never remarry?'

The hand wielding the washcloth paused for an instant, and then resumed its gentle stroking.

'Do you know, I don't think anyone has asked me that so bluntly before.'

'I'm sorry,' he said quickly, but she shook her head.

'Don't be. It's better than people just assuming they know and giving me unsolicited opinions.' She was quiet for a beat, and then continued, 'The short answer is that I never found anyone who made me *want* to get married again.'

'And the long answer?'

'Could you sit her up, just a little, for me, please?' He did as she asked, holding Hope up so Nya could wash the little back easier. 'The long answer is that when Jim died, I was so devastated it took me two years to think about him without crying. He'd always warned me that with him being in the army the possibility of his death in action was very real, but I was too young, too inexperienced to believe it would happen. And staying in Andover was too painful. I'd see a uniform in the distance, and my heart would leap, and then break again when it hit me that it wasn't Jim.'

'Would never again be Jim.'

She paused, leaving Theo wondering if that was all she would say, but then she sighed, and shook her head slightly.

'Coming back to Carey Cove was an effort to seek comfort. Being closer to Mum, seeing familiar faces and visiting old haunts helped me heal, but it was never meant to be permanent. I always thought at some point I'd be "ready".' She put down the washcloth and used soapy fingers to do air quotes. 'Then I'd leave again and move on with my life. But somehow months turned to years, comfort turned to comfortable, and when my career was going so well, it felt like a sign, and I put any other plans aside.'

'So it wasn't that you consciously decided not to

marry again—just that the opportunity never presented itself?'

'Something like that.' The little snort she gave wasn't quite laughter, but it was close. 'Carey Cove isn't crawling with eligible men, and the times I go to Falmouth or Penzance, it's not to party or go to clubs. I've dated a little over the years, but that brings me right back to where I started—with not finding anyone who could make me feel even a fraction of what I felt for Jim.'

He'd been right. This was a subject that helped get his head back on straight.

Obviously, Nya had been so intensely in love with her husband that no one had ever been able to compete. He'd even heard Hazel mention that December first was Jim's birthday, which was why Nya had taken the day off. Probably to visit his grave.

Realistically, who could compete with a man who would, in Nya's mind, always remain young, full of joy and life?

Nya had turned aside to pick up the towel she'd placed close to hand, and Theo let out a silent breath, keeping his focus on Hope, who looked relaxed and sleepy after her bath.

Here was someone whose life he could make a real difference in, even if it were for just a short time. And he needed to remember it was all for a little while— that no matter how homey and lovely being with Nya and Hope felt, it wouldn't last.

Remembering that was the only way to save himself from further heartbreak, and he was determined to do just that.

Yet there was no mistaking the tender ache around his heart as he watched Nya wrap Hope in the towel. Telling himself it would be wise to leave to return to his own life didn't work, and it was only when Nya went towards her bedroom with Hope that he realised he couldn't stay a moment more.

The intimacy of going into that room with Nya, to be under the laughing stare of her beloved husband, felt like too much to bear just then.

Even so, it took considerable strength of will to make his goodbyes, and leave the lovely warmth of the cottage behind.

CHAPTER TEN

NYA FELT THAT life was settling into a dangerous routine, but there was nothing she could do to change it—even had she wanted to.

Both she and Theo had taken on the responsibility of caring for Hope, and if that brought them together in a way Nya knew was dangerous to her peace of mind, what was she to do?

Over the following days Theo would appear at her door in the mornings and, depending on what each of them had planned, either picked up Hope or came with Nya to Carey House. Each lunchtime he would appear, either with a meal from the pub that they'd share at Nya's desk or with a picnic if the weather looked nice enough for Hope to be outside.

In the evenings, he lingered at Nya's cottage, helping her to feed and bathe Hope and invariably having dinner too. Some nights he seemed reluctant to leave, and Nya could understand that. Living alone, after being used to having his family around him, had to be difficult.

Making sure not to sit on the love-seat with him again—not because she didn't want to invite his kisses, but because she worried she'd grab and kiss *him*—Nya would take out her knitting.

And that was when she had to forcefully remind herself how temporary all of this was. It felt so cosy and natural to have him there. They drank tea and discussed everything from world affairs to the doings around Carey Cove—like how Don Mitchell had fallen from a ladder while putting up more decorations.

'I'm quite sure he was trying to outdo Kiara's display,' Nya told Theo with a shake of her head. 'But all he's accomplished is a broken leg and worrying his family. You know their daughter, Tara, is heavily pregnant, and I heard she's insisting on coming from Milton Keynes to check on her dad.'

'Poor Avis must be beside herself,' he replied. 'Now she'll not only have Don and the kennels to worry about, but Tara too.'

So like him to be concerned about others. Moments like that just intensified Nya's sense of him belonging in her cottage. In her life. By the third night, she almost found herself asking if he were ready for bed, as though he lived there, rather than had his own place to go to.

On the Tuesday, Nya took a few hours off, and they travelled together to Penzance to take Hope to her doctor's appointment.

'All seems well,' Dr Miller told them, after a comprehensive examination. 'She's a bit on the smaller end of the height and weight scale, but not as though she was premature. You mentioned that over the last couple of days she's been a bit stuffy, but her chest sounds clear. Because we don't have any information on her mother, birth, or first days of life, I'd suggest keeping a sharp eye for any infections or illness. Otherwise, it seems as though, between you, you're doing a marvellous job.'

She hadn't been able to stop herself from grinning over at Theo, and when he grinned back, she was once more struck with the sense of family, and of rightness.

Dangerous indeed, she reminded herself later that night as she lay in bed, and even looking at Jim's picture didn't make the feeling fade.

'You look like a couple,' her mum said, thankfully quietly into Nya's ear, as they were all together for the lighting of the village Christmas tree later in the week.

Nya thought about laughing but, realising she couldn't manage to make it sound natural, she gave her mother a stern look instead, and a shake of the head.

'We're just friends, Mum. You know that. Please don't do anything to make it awkward.'

That earned her a twist of her mother's lips, and one of her high-handed glares. 'I would never do anything inappropriate, Nya. I just made an observation.'

And, thankfully, Mum left it at that, although Nya was sure there was lots more she really wanted to say.

The night was surprisingly warm and dry, and the village green was filled with people. Davy and Darleen Trewelyn from The Dolphin Inn had set up a tent where they were dispensing mulled wine, hot chocolate and cider. Across the way, Kiara's amazing Christmas display eclipsed every other attempt at decorations, and all the children lined up to have their pictures taken in Santa's sleigh.

Hope, snug in the carrier against Nya's chest, was

awake and chewing on one fist, and Theo, who had gone to get them all drinks, was making his way slowly back towards them. Every few steps, someone would stop him for a chat, and Nya smiled to see how relaxed he looked.

How happy.

Even with her mother's words still ringing in her ears, warning her again that she was getting into deep waters, Nya couldn't help wishing that she'd been the one to bring that smile to his face.

Finally getting to them, Theo said, 'Sorry it took so long. Hopefully your drinks aren't cold.'

He handed Iona her mulled wine first, and then stepped close to Nya. So close that his arm rested against hers, and when he bent his head, he could speak right into her ear.

'There's a spirited, almost combative discussion happening near the tent regarding who put up the postbox cover near Carey House.'

He sounded so amused Nya had to laugh too, as she took her hot chocolate from his hand. 'Did they mention anyone you know?'

'Several people, but not you.'

She laughed again, a little breathlessly now, because having him this close seemed to steal the air from her lungs.

'I'm pleased to hear it.'

Someone called out to him, and Theo straightened and turned to answer. Nya was still smiling when she met her mother's gaze, and Iona's lifted eyebrows seemed to clearly say, *Really? Just friends?*

All Nya could do was throw her mum a narrow-eyed glare and turn away, hoping that the heat filling her cheeks wasn't obvious.

The tree was lit, amidst cheers, and a round of carols was sung with gusto. At Theo's insistence, they made their way over to Kiara's display and climbed onto the sleigh to have their picture taken with Hope, Mum standing at the side, beaming.

When Hope began to fuss, Nya said, 'Time to head home, I think. She's been a doll but it's getting too chilly for her to be out much longer, especially with that snuffy nose of hers.'

'I'm going to stay a bit longer,' Mum said. 'Lisa has been wanting to start a book club over the winter, and I promised I'd give her some suggestions.'

'Okay, Mum.' Nya leaned in for her mother's kiss, and wasn't surprised when, after kissing her daughter's cheek, Iona pressed her lips to the top of Hope's head too.

As Mum walked away, Nya turned to Theo to say, 'You can stay too, if you like. We'll be fine walking back alone.'

Theo snorted, and didn't bother to reply, unless you considered slinging an arm around her shoulders and guiding her away from the crowd an answer.

'Actually, I wanted to ask you a favour,' he said, when they were on the pavement and heading towards her cottage.

'What is it?'

His arm was still around her shoulders, and although she thought she should pull away, she couldn't bring herself to do so. It just felt so good.

'I still haven't put up my decorations. If I offer you dinner tomorrow evening, would you be willing to help? I'll be the first to say decorating isn't my forte.'

'Sure,' she replied, trying to match his casual tone, but inside already looking forward to it. 'Instead of you bringing Hope to me, I'll come over to yours after work.'

'Excellent. I promise not to cook for you.'

'Thank you,' she teased. 'I appreciate that.'

When his hand cupped the back of her neck, she swore his palm heated her nape, even through her coat collar and light scarf.

'If you don't behave,' he growled, 'I'll be forced to break out my grill.'

She had to swallow against her suddenly dry throat and fight a threatening shiver, forcing herself to maintain the casual banter.

'Oh, no! Anything but that!'

And somehow she kept the jovial atmosphere going all the way to her front door. When she unlocked the door and stepped inside, she was surprised to realise Theo had stopped on the threshold.

'Aren't you coming in?' she asked, as she looked down to unbuckle the carrier, and then eased Hope out. When she looked up, the expression on Theo's face made her freeze, the breath catching in her throat.

Then he looked down for a moment, and said, 'Not tonight. I'm going to head home.' With a smile that didn't quite reach his eyes, along with a wave of his fingers, he turned away to stride off into the night.

Just as well, she thought a little shakily as she closed the door behind him. If he'd stayed, she might have been tempted to kiss him again, and she couldn't afford to go down that road.

Not if she wanted to maintain their friendship, her pride and sanity.

Theo knew if he'd gone back into that warm, cosy cottage with Nya and Hope, spent another evening with them, as though they were family, he wouldn't be able to resist.

Resist the draw of Nya's smile, her shining gaze, her lush, sassy mouth.

The urge to pretend he could belong again and start over.

Walking away had been a wrench, but necessary, so as not to make a fool of himself, and risk the friendship he had with Nya. Yet, the following morning, as he looked out of his kitchen window at the light drizzle, he still regretted doing it, and wondered if inviting her over this evening was wise too.

He wanted her, with an intensity he found difficult to comprehend and was still trying to come to terms with and understand.

Was it just a case of rebound on his part?

Loneliness?

A result of his long sexual drought?

Or was there something more there? An emotional connection that went beyond that all-important friendship?

Until he could figure that out, he wouldn't chance losing the relationship they did have, on a whim.

And, even if there was something more on his side, would Nya ever be willing to explore it?

She'd always seemed happy—content—with her life. Safely ensconced behind the bastion of her widowhood. Remembering a love that would never age, or change, or wither.

In a strange and stupid way, he envied her that unwavering emotion.

The love that was trapped in amber for all time, never to disintegrate.

That never had to be questioned or held onto, so it wouldn't slip away.

When his phone rang, still lost in thought, he picked it up without looking at the screen.

'Theo.' The sound of Nya's brisk voice made his heart start to race. 'I'm sorry to call so early, but can you come and pick up Hope at Carey House?'

'Is there a problem?'

'Hazel just called to let me know she's not feeling well and won't be in today. We have a full schedule, so I have to go in as soon as possible to try to keep everything flowing smoothly.'

'I'll be there in thirty minutes, at the outside.'

'Thank you. I have to run.'

He was already halfway to his bedroom when she hung up, and it took him only a few minutes to change and be on his way.

It turned into one of those days that consisted of putting out one fire after another at the hospital. Theo was glad that, once he got there, he decided to just stay, rather than take Hope back to his house.

'I've asked Lorna to fill in on Reception,' Nya told him, looking totally calm, although the pulse at the base of her neck was thumping. 'But she's totally out of her depth. I'd ask Sophie to keep an eye, but she's off doing home visits, and I need Kiara to see to patients. And I just got a call about a mum who's fallen. A neighbour is bringing her in. I may have to ask you to consult, but then I don't know who will look after Hope.'

'Hey.' He put a hand on her shoulder. 'We'll figure it out.'

She nodded tersely, and went off to supervise her domain.

'Your auntie Nya's not having a good day,' he said to Hope, who kicked her legs in response.

And it got more muddled, as poor Lorna got some files confused, and Nya was trying to sort that out when Carla Nixon—the mum who'd fallen—came in.

Since Lucas Wilde was in with a patient, Nya asked Theo to examine her.

Luckily Hope was napping, and could be safely left with Lorna for a short time, while Nya came in to assist.

As it turned out, Carla had been alone at home when, on her way to the kitchen, she'd passed out. Luckily her neighbour had come by just after and found her. Frightened for both herself and her baby, she'd called through, and was told to come in.

'Syncope—or fainting—isn't uncommon during pregnancy,' Theo said to the young mother-to-be, before explaining to her about the effects of hormones and increased blood flow coupled with the relaxation of blood vessels. 'I want you to take your time when you stand up, in particular, since that can cause a rush of blood away from the brain.'

Checking her chart, he continued, 'I also want you to make a note of any other instances of dizziness and tell your midwife when next you see her. If there are any other worrying signs, I'm going to make a note on your records that you see your assigned obstetrician.'

After Carla had left, while he was making notes in the computer and Nya was sanitising the room before the next patient, she said, 'You're worried about the possible effects of her syncope?'

'There have been studies that seem to indicate that there may be a correlation between syncope and future medical issues for both mother and baby,' he said. 'While it's not conclusive, and there's no way to know if syncope is a symptom or causation, I always tell patients to advise their practitioners, especially if it happens often. In the past, women have been told it's normal to get light-headed or faint during pregnancy, but I don't subscribe to that way of thinking. Any physical symptoms should be documented.'

'Agreed,' she said, before bustling off again, no doubt to make sure Lorna hadn't set the computer system on fire in her absence.

By the end of the day, Theo could see how tired Nya looked and, taking her aside, he said, 'Listen, you don't have to come by this evening. In fact, why don't you let me keep Hope overnight, so you can get an uninterrupted night's sleep?'

'Don't be silly,' she scoffed. 'I'm fine. Besides, we can't have everyone saying you're turning into Scrooge.

Your house is the only one without any decorations visible. It's time to remedy that. I just need a few minutes to speak to Lorna before I can leave.' She gave him a rueful smile, adding, 'I might have been a little abrupt with her today, and want to make sure she knows it wasn't her fault.'

'That's fine,' he said, thinking how wonderfully she managed her staff, making everyone feel comfortable and special. 'There's no rush.'

And as she walked away he once more asked himself if it really was wise to have her over to his house, but was honest enough to admit he didn't care whether it was or not.

He was looking forward to it too much.

CHAPTER ELEVEN

NYA WOKE UP, disorientated and confused.

She was in bed, almost fully clothed—just her shoes missing—but in a room she didn't recognise.

And...

She sat up abruptly.

Where was Hope?

She scrambled to get up, her brain whirring, trying to figure out how she'd slept through the night feedings.

Then it came to her, as she found her shoes neatly placed beside the bed and saw her handbag on the dresser.

She was at Theo's house.

'Oh, Lordy,' she groaned to herself, as she ran her fingers through her hair the best she could, trying to remember what, exactly, had happened the night before.

Theo had insisted on driving her and Hope to his house, stopping on the way to pick up some of The Dolphin Inn's famous fish sandwiches for dinner. Once here, they'd eaten first, and then set about decorating.

Theo had called a halt when Hope had started grizzling for her supper, but when Nya had said, 'I'll get her bottle ready,' Theo had objected.

'Just sit with her, and I'll get it.' He'd given her a cheeky smile, adding, 'I know where everything is.'

'Throwing my words back at me, are you?' she'd asked, putting her nose in the air, even as she'd settled into a corner of his couch, cradling Hope.

'Whenever I get the chance,' he'd called back, from the kitchen.

She'd handed Hope over to him some time thereafter, and recalled doing a teenager-like swoon over just how precious Theo always looked feeding the infant, and then...

Nothing.

Obviously she must have fallen asleep, and he'd carried her to bed.

That thought made her stop with her hand on the doorknob, heat working its way through her torso and up into her face.

Why was it that she regretted not remembering *that* bit of the evening?

She nipped out into the hallway and could hear Theo's voice in the distance—that sweet, crooning tone he used with Hope—before she went into the bathroom to wash her face.

Ridiculous to feel so nervous, she thought, staring at her reflection for a long moment. It wasn't as though they'd slept together.

Taking a deep breath, berating herself a bit for being silly, she opened the bathroom door and made her way into the living room. Stepping quietly into the doorway, she paused, her heart melting at the sight of Hope lying on a play mat on the floor. Theo was sitting cross-legged beside her, singing softly along with the tune playing on the mobile above her head.

Maybe she made a sound, or he'd been listening for her, but Theo looked up before Nya had a chance to get her emotions under control, and he froze.

Was it her imagination, or did his gaze turn hot for an instant, before it was veiled, and he smiled?

'Good morning.' His voice sounded normal, and he glanced down at Hope, giving Nya a chance to catch an elusive breath. 'I hope we didn't wake you.'

'You definitely didn't,' she said tartly. 'Why'd you let me sleep like that, and make you get up with Hope in the night?'

He shrugged slightly, one finger caught securely in Hope's little fist, his thumb stroking over the back of the infant's hand.

'You were exhausted. There's tea on the hob, or coffee in the cupboard, if you prefer.'

Nya huffed, but his concern for her warmed her straight through, nonetheless.

'At least let me make breakfast.'

Theo laughed, shaking his head. 'If you can find anything in there worth cooking. I told you, I'm rubbish in the kitchen. Why don't you let me take you out for a meal?'

Nya was already looking through the cupboards, and, despite his protestations, had a menu in mind. Clearly when Femi had moved out, she'd left all or most of the tinned goods behind, and there was a loaf of bread in the box, which she determined wasn't too old.

'No need. Breakfast will be ready in a jiff.'

'You must be a miracle worker,' Theo said, his amusement clear.

'I can teach you to cook, if you like,' she replied absently. Then, realising what she'd offered, and how it might sound, added, 'You *can* teach old dogs new tricks.'

'Did you hear what she said to me, Hope? She called me old.'

And having reset the casual, teasing tone she felt most comfortable with around him, Nya set about making them a meal.

Clearly, with no one to corral his paperwork, Theo had spread it out over the dining table.

'Do you mind if I move some of these things so we can sit here?' she asked, tapping a pile.

'Not at all. There are place mats in the drawer behind you, if you want them.'

Nya shifted a couple of piles of paperwork, but when she picked the third one up, a couple of sheets fell to the floor. Bending, she picked them up and glanced at them, then went still as she realised what they were.

Property sales brochures. One for a house for sale in Luton, another in Chelmsford.

She remembered Theo had spoken about feeling as though he didn't fit in any more, but she hadn't really taken it seriously. In her mind Theo and Carey Cove were synonymous.

Was he really thinking of moving away? Giving up working at both the cottage hospital and St Isolde's too?

She wanted to ask, but the words stuck in her throat. Looking across at him, she allowed herself the luxury of taking him in, fully. Of acknowledging how handsome he was, how much he meant to her, and just how desperately she didn't want him to leave.

Yet hadn't she made the same type of big change when she left Andover and came to Carey Cove? It was impossible not to understand why he might feel the need to go somewhere new, where the past wouldn't keep rearing its head, keeping him in a state of perpetual mourning.

So, instead of bringing it up, she carefully put the brochures back under some other papers and tried to pretend she hadn't seen them.

But although she tried to act normally, the ache around her heart wouldn't go away.

'What are your plans for the day?' Theo asked as they were finishing up breakfast. 'I thought we could go for a drive along the coast, if you'd like.'

Torn, she stared down at her plate for a moment, pretending interest in her last bite of salmon and toast. One part of her wanted to spend as much time with Theo and Hope as possible, knowing this lovely idyll would soon end, but the other part—the wounded heart of her—needed some time alone.

'Although Kiara has been doing so well since she came, I try to stay close to home when she's on call at the hospital, in case she needs me.' That much was true, although Kiara knew she could also call on Sophie, or any of the others if necessary. 'Besides, I have all my usual chores to get done too.'

'Okay,' he said easily, as though it made no difference to him. 'I'll drop you at the clinic to get your car, and probably just come back here with Hope, then.'

No offer to stay and hang about at her cottage, which was how they'd spent the previous Sunday, which, she told herself stoutly, was fine by her. Hadn't she just decided she needed time to get her head around the thought of Theo leaving?

Before she could answer, his phone rang, and he got up to answer it.

From his end of the conversation, she realised he was needed at the hospital, so she quickly gathered up their breakfast things and took them into the kitchen to wash up.

'That was Kiara,' he said, after he hung up. 'Roman's on his way to pick up Molly Chalmers from Scilly. Her husband called to say he was worried about her, and Kiara dispatched the helicopter right away.'

Familiar with Molly, who had type one diabetes, Nya nodded in agreement. 'That was a good call.'

Theo was across the room when he stopped, 'What about Hope?'

'Don't worry,' Nya told him. 'I'll keep her as long as you need.'

He thanked her and rushed off to change. Nya went to where Hope was sleeping in her travel cot, and gently touched her hair, glad not to be going home alone.

Wondering how she was going to manage when they were both gone.

Then she set about collecting Hope's things, and making sure they were ready when Theo was.

Silly as it might be, she felt slightly surreptitious as she got out of his car at the clinic and transferred Hope into hers for the short drive home. It took everything she had not to look around to see if anyone had noticed the transfer, or that she was wearing the same clothing as the day before.

She'd heard about the 'walk of shame' but never thought she, at her age, would ever know what it felt like.

Her mother came by, bringing a tiny multicoloured hat she'd knitted for Hope, using a variation of the floral *aso oke* pattern she'd developed.

'Mum, it's gorgeous!' The rich pinks, purples, and yellow glowed like jewels.

'Hope needs something lovely, and I'm guessing you've been too busy to make her anything.'

'Not true,' Nya said, with feigned annoyance. 'I put your Christmas gift aside to make her a layette set. It's almost finished.'

'Good,' her mother promptly replied. 'Then you'll have time to get mine done before the day.' She sat on the couch and pulled a mask out of her pocket. After putting it on, she held out her arms for the baby.

'She's been a bit grizzly this morning,' Nya warned as she placed Hope in her mother's arms. 'Her nose is still stuffy, but it hasn't got any worse.'

'I'm sure we will be just fine,' Mum replied, with her usual assurance. 'Now, what's happening between you and Theo? I heard you spent the night at his house.'

'Mum.' She felt too raw to talk about it, and tried to infuse a *Stop it now* tone into her voice. 'All that happened was that I fell asleep on his couch.'

But her mother's raised eyebrows spoke of scepticism. 'I'm not suggesting your…involvement with Theodore is a bad thing,' Mum replied at her autocratic best. 'It's time you enjoyed some companionship. But I just thought I should warn you that he may still be on the rebound after his divorce.' When Nya started to reply, her mother's raised hand forestalled her. 'I just don't want to see you hurt, Nya.'

And, in the air between them, she heard the word 'again', although her mother hadn't said it.

Later that morning, after Mum had left, Theo called to say he was transferring Molly to St Isolde's by ambulance.

'I don't like how uncontrollable her diabetes has become,' he told Nya. 'And I've given the doctors there my opinion that they should do a caesarean as soon as possible.'

Surprised, Nya asked, 'You're not going with her?'

'No.' There was a bit of terseness in his tone, but then it softened. 'My locum is on hand, and I'll leave it to him. As soon as I'm squared away here, I'll come and get Hope.'

'Okay, but just a warning, she's been fussy all morning.'

'She is all right?'

'I think so,' Nya replied. 'No fever, and I haven't had to suction. Sometimes babies just want a bit more cuddling than usual.'

'She'll certainly get all she needs from me,' he said, in that fond, loving tone he so often used when talking about Hope. Then she heard him blow out a breath, and say, 'Hey, if you're not too busy, can we still go for that drive along the coast? I feel like getting out for a bit, and I'd love the company.'

Silly heart, to do that little stutter step, and Nya knew she should refuse, but in his voice she heard his continued annoyance at being sidelined at St Isolde's, even if it were for his own good.

And she found herself saying, 'Sure. I'll dress Hope warmly, since it looks like rain.'

The truth was, Theo didn't want to go home without Nya, even with Hope.

The night before, when he'd looked up and realised she'd fallen asleep curled up on his couch, the wave of need that swept him had rocked him back on his heels.

With her face softened with sleep, those all too knowing eyes veiled, she'd looked as soft and tender as the infant in his arms. Yet, there was no ignoring the lush curves and generous mouth that he longed to explore again.

He'd been reluctant to pick her up and carry her to bed, because he just knew that holding her that way would be torment. And it had been—sweet torment, and almost overwhelming temptation.

Nya had hardly stirred, just murmured under her breath as he'd picked her up, and snuggled her face into his neck, causing a cascade of gooseflesh over his skin.

Oh, how he'd wanted her just then.

And when he'd put her on the bed in the guest room, he'd stood looking down at her for a long moment, trying to work through the complex emotions battering him.

There'd been no answers forthcoming, and he'd swiftly removed her shoes, then left the room before he gave in to the desire to simply lie down beside her and pull her close.

Going back into the living room, he'd pulled up some of the house listings he'd saved on his computer and begun going through them again. He'd been playing with the idea of leaving Carey Cove for months, and now he knew doing so would be the right thing.

If being with Nya and Hope for one week could unsettle him this way, make him care so much, what would happen to him when it was all over?

When Carey Cove once more went from being a homey haven to a place of tormented memories?

Yet, there was a part of him that was determined to enjoy this found family as long as he could. And perhaps, in spending time with Nya, he would figure out that it wasn't the big emotional deal he was making it out to be.

He went to pick them up and couldn't help laughing in appreciation when he saw Hope's jaunty new hat.

'Iona's been hard at work, I see,' he said, and got a grin from Nya.

'Oh, you know her so well.'

He drove down towards Land's End, planning to circle around and back to Penzance for an early tea.

There was something a bit different in Nya's mood,

but it didn't make the day less enjoyable. In fact, she seemed more relaxed than she'd been that morning.

Which was surprising, once she said, 'I have to warn you: it's already being spread around the village that I spent the night at yours last night.'

Thankful that they'd stopped for dinner and he wasn't driving, he watched her face as he asked, 'How did you hear that?'

She snorted. 'Mum. When she came by this morning.'

'What do you want to do about this?'

Nya shrugged. 'Nothing. If anyone asks me, I'll tell the truth—that I fell asleep on your couch. It's not that big a deal, and no one's business, to boot.'

'It looks like, between us, Hope and I are ruining your stellar reputation,' he joked, only to have her turn those dark, somehow shadowed eyes his way.

And although she was smiling, he didn't believe her light-hearted tone when she replied, 'It's about time, don't you think? After all, all work and no play make for a dull life, right? And who wants to be known as boring?'

What on earth could he say to that?

'Anyone who calls you dull is an idiot,' he said, shaking his head.

She wrinkled her nose, rocking Hope back and forth against her bosom. 'I know myself, Theo. I work, knit, do a little gardening, volunteer occasionally. I haven't travelled much, or done anything exciting, and have no interest in going outside my comfort zone, really. If that's not the definition of boring, I don't know what is.'

It didn't sound boring to him, and he said so.

'We live in a time when everything is online and vis-ible—faraway places, exciting adventures, every mate-rial thing you can imagine. So many people get sucked into wanting more and more, often at the cost of their peace of mind.'

He stopped, wondering if somewhere along the line his ex-wife hadn't got sucked into that very trap. Then he mentally shrugged the thought away. Femi was no longer any of his concern.

'Contentment is difficult for most people to find,' he went on, smiling across at Nya, who had gone still, and was watching him with an intensity that held his gaze on hers. 'You've somehow found that—found a life that I think you've been happy living. There's nothing truly boring about that, is there?'

Her eyelids drooped, so he could no longer see the expression in her eyes, and just then the waiter came to ask if there was anything else they needed, and they somehow never resumed the conversation.

Leaving Theo wondering if she agreed with his as-sessment or not.

CHAPTER TWELVE

THEO THOUGHT SHE was content and comfortable.

If anyone had said that just a week or so ago, she might even have happily agreed, but today she felt neither of those emotions.

Instead, she felt restless and needy, and discontented with everything.

She'd thought she'd come to terms with all the things in life she'd never have, yet in Theo and Hope's company her prior choices—and loss—were more painful.

Coming to terms with never being a mother, or having someone who loved her the way Jim would have, had been hard. At some point she'd thought she had, but now she was forced to admit that dream hadn't really died.

Or maybe you had to actually hold something in your hands, feel the emotional heartbeat of it, to *really* know what you were missing.

Sitting across the table from Theo, with Hope a sweet weight against her chest, Nya knew *this* was what she wanted.

What she *craved*.

What she would only have for a short—far too short—time.

Family, in all its incarnations.

Soul-soothing companionship.

Love shared, without restriction.

But none of that was meant to be—at least not for much longer—and so she swallowed the bitter sense of lost time and forlorn dreams, putting it all aside. Not wanting Theo to sense her disquiet.

From somewhere deep inside, from the place where all her fears and pain lived, she found the strength she needed to make small talk with him while they drove back towards Carey Cove. It was moments like this, as she sensed the day coming to an end, that she longed, more than ever, to extend their time together.

When she looked back on this period of having this unusual little family, she wanted as many wonderful memories as she could hold in her mind.

Dusk was falling as they drove back into Carey Cove, and Nya leaned her head back against the seat, watching the final rays of the sun touching the western sky. As they went over the little hill outside the village, Carey House came into view, and Nya sat up.

'What on earth...?'

The parking area was full, and an ambulance stood outside the patient entrance, making Nya wonder if it was there to collect a patient, or drop one off.

'That doesn't look good, does it?'

Theo slowed the car as he spoke, and Nya leaned forward so as to see better.

'No, it doesn't. It looks as though Hazel's still there too, and she should have gone home ages ago.'

The car picked up speed again, continuing down the road towards the hospital entrance. Sophie was in charge today, and probably had everything under control, but even so Nya couldn't help worrying.

'Theo, do you mind—?'

Before she'd even finished, Theo had turned on the indicator, and was slowing to make the turn into the hospital driveway.

'How did you know what I was going to ask?' When she glanced at him, he was smiling in that sly, sexy way he had. 'I thought you'd have just kept going.'

'Just so you could spend the rest of the evening stewing and wondering what was going on here?' he asked as he found a spot to park. 'Or jump on the phone before we even got home?'

Even as worried as she was, Nya couldn't help laughing as she reached for the door handle.

'When did you get to know me this well?'

Theo didn't reply to her question, but said, 'Go on in. I'll bring Hope.'

How like him to be so understanding, Nya thought as she hurried into the reception area.

Hazel looked up almost fearfully when she heard the door open.

'Oh, thank goodness,' the receptionist said on recognising Nya. 'I thought it was another patient coming in. Did Sophie call you?'

'No,' Nya replied. 'I was passing by and saw all the vehicles. What's going on?'

'Five expectant mothers turned up, one after another, over the last fifteen minutes. One came by ambulance from St Buryan, where she was on holiday. Then Margie Landry, Velma Jones, and Karin Howell came in, one after the other.'

The latter three women were all mums-to-be who Nya knew were due or overdue, so she wasn't terribly surprised, except for the fact they all decided to go into labour at the same time!

'And the fifth?'

Hazel lowered her voice, although it was just the two of them in the room.

'Tara Mitchell-Powers. Avis's daughter. She's not due for another month, but Avis is convinced she's in labour, so she brought her in.'

Just then the door opened, and Theo came in—baby Hope's carry seat in one hand, holding the door with the other, his phone tucked between shoulder and chin. For a moment Nya froze, thrown back in time to the day he'd first found Hope on the doorstep, and Nya had first felt that surge of attraction towards him.

Was it really only days ago, although it felt as if a lifetime had passed?

'I'm actually just stepping into the hospital now, Avis. Yes, I'll come right up.'

Nya pulled herself together to ask, 'Avis called you about Tara?'

'Yes. I've never heard her in such a state.' Everyone knew Avis Mitchell was the quintessential unflappable, no-nonsense type. 'She said she wouldn't feel comfortable unless I examined Tara.'

'Well, it's her only child, and first grandchild. I'm not surprised.'

Theo nodded. 'Me neither. Do you mind taking care of Hope for a while?'

He was talking to Nya, but Hazel jumped in before she could answer.

'I don't mind at all.'

Nya gave the receptionist a laughing look.

'It's way past time for you to be going home. Artie will wonder where you are and send out a search party.'

'I already told him I was staying late,' Hazel replied, taking the seat out of Theo's hand. 'And I'm sure Dr Theo would be happy for your help, since it's all hands on deck up there.'

Still chuckling, Nya gave in, and followed Theo to the stairs, explaining what was happening to him as they made their way to the labour ward.

Once there, Nya paused, and took in the sight of more relatives and friends than they were used to having to accommodate. The entire waiting room was filled to capacity. Standing room only.

As soon as Avis saw them, she came rushing towards them.

'Oh, Theo. I'm so glad you're here.' Avis pretty much collapsed into his arms. 'I don't trust anyone but you.'

'There, there.' Theo patted Avis on the back, his expression solicitous—his tone calming. 'You stay here while I examine Tara, so we can see what's going on.'

As he walked towards the nurses' station, Nya at his side, Sophie came out of one of the labour rooms, and her face lit up when she saw them.

Coming close, she whispered, 'Thank goodness you're both here. We're stretched to breaking, and Avis has been having a conniption. When she told me she was going to call Dr Turner, I'm afraid I was a little sharp with her—saying she should go ahead, although her daughter is having Braxton Hicks contractions and seems in perfectly good nick.'

'Avis has a lot on her plate just now,' Nya told the younger woman gently, but she also gave Sophie's arm a commiserating squeeze. She knew only too well how frustrating it could be in their line of work. 'How are the other mums doing?'

Theo had gone to wash up, while Sophie gave Nya a quick rundown.

'Velma Jones just delivered. Baby and mum doing perfectly well. Margie Landry's labour isn't progressing quickly, but baby isn't in any distress, and Karin Howell is at seven centimetres dilation. It's the visitor that came in by ambulance I'm most worried about.'

Nya took the chart Sophie held out to her, and read the notes, as Sophie continued, 'Brittney Henderson, thirty-three, second child, only thirty-six weeks along, no history of premature labour. She was visiting relatives when she started having what she thought were Braxton Hicks contractions. When she noticed some spotting, her aunt called for an ambulance, since she didn't want to take any chances.'

'Good for her,' Nya said, absently, still reading Sophie's notes. The patient's contractions were seven minutes apart, and the ultrasound had shown the baby was transverse.

'If Theo has a chance after he checks on Tara, I'd appreciate him taking a look at Mrs Henderson. I was going to wait a bit more before calling in the consulting obstetrician on duty, but, since he's here, I want his opinion on whether I should send her on to St Isolde's. I asked the ambulance to wait, and they agreed, unless they're needed elsewhere.'

'I'll let him know,' Nya said, realising she might have to rescue Theo from Avis. 'Let me go and see how he's getting on.'

After scrubbing her hands thoroughly, she made her way to the room Tara had been put in. Opening the door, she realised that Theo had obviously done what Sophie hadn't managed.

He'd calmed Avis down.

'So, I think the best thing is to go back to your mum and dad's and get some rest. If the contractions start again, move around—change position—and see if they go away. If you have any other symptoms, come back to Carey House.'

'You're sure she isn't in labour? She's been so stressed about Don, and travelled all the way from Milton Keynes…'

Well, perhaps not all the way calmed, although while Avis asked the question she was helping her daughter put on her shoes, obviously in preparation to leave.

'Oh, Mum,' Tara sighed, sounding more exasperated than worried. 'If Dr Turner says I'm fine, I believe him. You've always said what a wonderful doctor he is. Even asked me if I didn't want to come down here so he would be on hand in case there were any problems when I delivered.'

'I know. I know.' Avis gave both Theo and Nya wan smiles as Tara's silent husband helped his wife up off the bed. 'First grandbaby and all that, I suppose.'

'Totally understandable,' Theo said, with a smile, as they made their way out into the corridor. 'Take care, now.'

Then he looked down at Nya, and said, 'I just need to write up these notes, and then we can go.'

'Actually, Sophie was hoping you'd give her your opinion on another patient before you go. Brittney Henderson, a visitor that was brought in by ambulance. Sophie has the ambulance waiting, in case you think they should transport her on to St Isolde's.'

For the first time since she'd known him, Theo seemed to hesitate when asked for his professional input, but then he nodded, and said, 'Let me look at the file.'

That momentary pause, that expression of near annoyance, made Nya wonder what he was thinking, but before she could ask Theo was striding towards the nurses' station.

Theo tamped down the surprising spurt of irritation he'd felt as he wrote up the few notes on Tara's card. Nya waited patiently beside him, the chart for the patient she wanted him to see in hand.

Rather than stay at the hospital any longer, what he really wanted to do was take Nya and Hope home.

Help to feed and bathe the baby, then snuggle with

her as Nya's gentle voice read Hope a story, and the infant nodded off to sleep in his arms.

There was, in his mind, this constant *tick-tick-tick* of the time they'd have together slipping away, and he didn't want to miss a moment.

Yet, with all that was happening at Carey House, his conscience and professional pride wouldn't let him leave.

Taking the chart from Nya's hand, cognisant of how late it was getting, he reluctantly said, 'If you want to take Hope home, I can give you my keys. I can walk to your cottage when I'm finished here.'

Nya's smile did funny things to his insides. Made his heart skip a beat, and his stomach muscles tighten.

'Let's see what your opinion of the patient is before I go and try to pry Hope away from Hazel. She's already called her husband to tell him she'll be late home, so I don't think she's in a huge rush just yet.'

Just then, Sophie came over and announced, 'Karin's just about nine centimetres now, so I'm going back in to deliver her baby. Have you seen Mrs Henderson yet?'

'Just heading in there now,' Theo replied, his gaze on the file in his hand. 'Premature labour, thirty-six weeks... Did anyone come in with her?'

'Her aunt, who she was staying with.'

No dad in sight yet, then. Theo didn't ask any further questions, but was aware of Nya trailing after him as he set off for her room.

Brittney Henderson turned a narrow-eyed gaze their way as they entered, and the older woman sitting at her bedside straightened to add her own suspicious glare.

'Mrs Henderson, my name is Dr Theo Turner, and this is Head Midwife Nya Ademi. Midwife French asked me to examine you and determine what the best course of treatment should be.'

'She said I was in premature labour,' Mrs Henderson said, her tone as hard as her expression. But Theo noticed the gleam of tears in her eyes and wondered if it was the stress of her present situation alone making her want to cry. 'Does that mean the baby's coming now?'

'It may be, but I'd like to run a couple more tests to see exactly how far along you are.' Turning to the aunt, who was silently watching the exchange, he added, 'If you don't mind giving us some privacy for a few minutes?'

As Nya prepared the ultrasound machine, Theo tried to gently coax some additional information out of his patient. And, as it turned out, she was staying with her aunt because she'd had a massive row with her husband back in Norwich and decided to leave.

'I told him I wouldn't stand for his nonsense,' she said stoutly, but despite her best efforts her voice wavered just a little. 'So while he was at work, I took my son and came away to Aunt Ruth's. I never thought there'd be any problem for the baby.'

'Don't blame yourself,' Nya said softly. 'Babies come when they're ready, whether we are, or not.'

No mention of how stress and travelling at such a late stage in pregnancy could induce premature labour. Just comforting words and that gentle manner. Not that Theo would expect anything less. Nya was a born caretaker, with a huge heart and overwhelming compassion.

Just then she looked up and their gazes met, creating a cascade of emotions Theo wasn't sure how to categorise. All he knew was that being the focus of her regard just then, even for the brief moment before she turned back to their patient, filled him with warmth and longing.

And a visceral fear that he'd lost himself—his heart—at a time, and in a way, he could least afford, and didn't know how to deal with, at all.

CHAPTER THIRTEEN

LATER THAT NIGHT Nya lay in bed staring at the ceiling, thinking back on the day just gone and trying to relax enough to go to sleep.

Theo had administered drugs both to promote the development of the baby's lungs and slow Brittney Henderson's contractions, then sent her by ambulance to St Isolde's.

'Hopefully they won't have to do a caesarean section,' he'd told the patient as he'd carefully explained what he was doing. 'But do prepare yourself for the possibility.'

Nya had offered to call her husband, but after some consideration, Brittney had said she'd do it herself.

'Better I tell him,' she'd said, damp-eyed again. 'If he hears it from anyone else, it'll just make things worse.'

As it turned out, the Hendersons' argument hadn't been about anything important.

'Jamie says I've been a bit crazed this time around, and he's right,' Brittney had admitted. 'I don't remember being this emotional with my first. Or as stroppy.'

'Just like each baby is different, each pregnancy is too,' Theo had reassured her, and Nya had agreed.

'On top of the variance in hormones, there are all the external factors too. Changes in your home life, any financial difficulties that didn't exist when you were expecting your first can make a big difference too.'

Thus reassured, Brittney had been put back into the ambulance, and sent on to Falmouth.

Theo had written up his notes, and they'd collected Hope from Hazel, bringing her home just in time for her early evening feed.

Theo had stayed, helping Nya get Hope ready for bed as he so often did. Being next to him at the sink, hearing his every breath, feeling his warmth against her arm, inhaling his scent, had made the sensation of disgruntlement she'd experienced earlier return.

Why, she wondered, did life insist on giving her a taste of paradise, and then yanking it away? Giving her this brief, wonderful time with a man and a child, neither of whom would ever be hers?

Yet more of her mother's words of five years ago came back to her, reminding her she'd made a choice not to move on from Jim's death.

You've closed yourself off from life. From the opportunity to build a life with someone, have children of your own. One day you're going to look back and wonder what you were thinking, and why you let the chance of happiness pass you by.

Nya had been angry and hurt. Didn't Mum understand that losing Jim had meant giving all of that up, anyway? That for her own peace, she'd locked all of those urges away, and got on with her life as best she could?

Jim had been her soulmate. The one person who had made her feel truly alive in every sense.

His exuberance had been contagious. Growing up, she'd been solemn, studious, conscientious, because that was what she'd needed to be, especially after her father died.

Dad's death had left her floundering, all too aware of how capricious life could be, and when she'd met Jim, and he'd tried to sweep her off her feet, she'd resisted as long as she could.

How could she get involved with a man with such a dangerous job?

But Jim had got under her skin, and into her heart, and she'd lulled herself into believing nothing would go wrong. He'd made it easy to believe too.

'Safe as houses,' he'd said. 'If it wasn't, there wouldn't be so many old army veterans about, would there?'

Then he'd laughed that rich, booming laugh, and she'd just melted.

James Ademi could have made her believe anything, risk anything, give everything.

And she had—to her detriment.

When he'd died, he'd taken all her trust, her hopes with him, and left her nothing but fear, and the over-riding knowledge that she didn't dare risk loving again.

What she'd told Theo, about thinking she'd eventually leave Carey Cove and look for a more fulfilling life somewhere else had, she thought now, been a big fat fib.

She'd always been too afraid, even though she'd refused to admit it, even to herself.

Now, she had to face that fact, and acknowledge she was still too afraid to reach for what she now knew she wanted.

Theo, and Hope, for ever.

Oh, she knew Hope was just with her for a little while, and while that was heartbreaking in itself, she could bear it—just. All she wanted, in the final analysis, was for Hope to have the very best life possible, hopefully with her mother or father or, if that wasn't possible, with a wonderful family who'd raise her as their own.

But Theo? Theo was still hurting from his divorce, still trying to figure out how to move on, and once again Mum had hit the nail on the head.

If Nya let him know that she was interested in him, physically and emotionally, and it turned out to just be a rebound situation on his part, she'd be devastated again.

She wasn't the quickie affair type—that much she knew for sure.

And she couldn't risk wanting more.

Flopping over in bed, hugging a pillow, she considered her options.

In a week, the midwife hired to cover Marnie's maternity leave would be arriving, and, although it would stretch the team even further than they already were, Nya would take leave. Then she could tell Theo she would take over Hope's care on her own, limiting the amount of time they spent together.

Then, with a sigh, she realised that plan wouldn't work.

Theo was committed to Hope's care, and he was a

man who never walked away from responsibility. Even telling him she didn't need his help wouldn't stop him from helping anyway.

And the change being around Hope had wrought in Theo was too wonderful for Nya to risk interfering with it. He was smiling again. Seemed more alive—less solemn and sad. He needed Hope even more than the infant needed him.

No.

Nya would just have to deal with the emotional turmoil she'd brought on herself as best she could, until the situation resolved itself.

Until Hope was relocated.

Until Theo left Carey Cove and moved on with his life.

And she could go back to her safe, boring existence.

She'd left the Christmas lights on in the living room, and the colourful flashes of light illuminated the room enough to allow her to see Jim's picture. His glorious smile. The strong arms that had made her feel safe and treasured.

In a way, she thought she'd let him down. He'd had a zest for life, and an indefatigable spirit that had made each day with him a delight. If she'd wanted to honour his memory properly, she should have taken up skydiving, or rock climbing. Moved to the South Seas and become a pearl diver.

Instead, she'd run away from life.

And, as she finally fell asleep, she was wondering whether she'd ever feel content with her life again.

There was no way to know how long she'd slept when

she suddenly jerked awake and, without knowing why, immediately sat up.

A quick glance at her clock showed it was just gone midnight and, as she swung her legs out of bed, searching with her toes for her slippers, she was listening intently. Had someone been trying to break in?

Then, she heard it, and rushed to turn on the light.

Hope's breathing sounded wrong.

Laboured.

The cot was right beside the bed, and Nya was there, looking down at Hope in an instant.

The baby's chest was heaving and, as Nya watched, it stopped moving altogether.

Was that a blue tinge around her lips, too?

Quickly snatching her up with shaking hands, Nya ran for her phone.

Theo was still awake, poring over property listings, when his phone rang, making his heart skip a beat.

Calls after midnight were never a good thing.

And when he saw Nya's name on the screen, his heart rate went into gallop mode.

'Nya?'

'Hope's not breathing properly.' Her voice was shaky, uneven, and Theo was on his feet, already heading for the door, as she continued. 'I've already called an ambulance.'

'I'm on my way,' he said, snatching up his car keys and medical bag. 'What are her symptoms?'

Nya outlined them quickly, her voice getting steadier,

probably because now it was medical jargon, and her training was kicking in.

'I just don't understand. She's been a little off colour the last couple of days, with that slightly stuffy nose and being a bit fussy, but I've not noticed any other symptoms. How could this come on so quickly?'

He was in his car and put the phone on speaker as he started it up. 'I didn't notice anything either, Nya.' He was already kicking himself for that, but didn't want her beating herself up. 'We don't know what's happening, so don't start blaming yourself.'

It took only minutes for him to get to Nya's, and she was right there to open the door for him. Her drawn, grey-hued face made his heart clench, and his chest tightened when he saw Hope, limp in Nya's arms, her chest heaving with each breath.

'She's getting worse,' Nya said. 'Where do you want to examine her?'

'On the couch,' he said, setting down his medical bag and taking out his stethoscope. 'What's the ETA on the ambulance?'

She glanced at her watch. 'About five minutes, I think.'

He listened to Hope's chest, worried not just by the obvious pulmonary obstruction, but by the infant's lethargy.

'Get a bag ready for her,' he said, keeping his voice level with effort, wanting to give Nya something to concentrate on. 'And put on your clothes. If you go with her in the ambulance, I'll follow in my car.'

He heard her breath hitch, and then she rushed off

towards her room, leaving him and Hope alone in the living room.

Hope's face scrunched, as though she wanted to cry, but she didn't seem to have the strength.

'Come on,' he muttered, as though the ambulance driver could hear him telepathically. 'Come on.'

The swift onset of the infant's symptoms worried him.

Asthma? Bacterial or viral infection? Allergy?

As a doctor, all these questions were instinctive, but Theo really was only focused on Hope's breathing. He found himself inhaling, as if trying to give her more air by osmosis—the actions of a father, rather than a medical practitioner.

He was so glad Nya had called an ambulance. Right now, he was going on adrenaline, but he knew he wasn't fit to drive safely if he had to take Hope to Falmouth, and there was no time to call out Roman and the helicopter.

'Come on. Come *on*.'

Hope's cyanosis was getting worse.

He heard the sirens in the distance, and the rush of relief almost brought him to his knees. Nya came dashing out of her room, Hope's baby bag over her shoulder and a tote in her other hand, which she tossed down near the door.

She seemed to have got a better grip on her emotions, since her voice was steady when she said, 'Bring that bag with you when you come, please. I'll be staying with Hope for as long as necessary. I'll call Kiara when we get to Falmouth, and the paediatrician has looked at our baby.'

Flashing lights heralded the arrival of the ambulance, and Nya pulled the door open before the attendants were even out of the vehicle.

How many times had he put a patient into an ambulance and, although concerned, hadn't felt as though his entire world were shattered by it? Too many to count, really. But this time, as he stumbled over his words, telling the ambulance attendants what he'd observed, it took everything he had to let Hope go.

With brisk efficiency, Hope was taken to the ambulance and Nya paused only long enough to thrust her house keys into Theo's hand before she followed.

Then, siren going, the vehicle pulled away, leaving Theo standing in the driveway, watching it, until it disappeared.

'Theo!' The urgency of the voice coming from behind him had him spinning around. 'Theo, what happened? Is it Nya? Hope?'

Iona, in a dressing gown and winter boots, her head wrapped in a silk scarf, her eyes wide and her voice frantic, came running towards him.

'It's Hope. She's developed a problem with her lungs.'

He tried to sound matter-of-fact, but the desperation he felt couldn't be masked, and the next thing he knew Iona was hugging him, tightly.

'She'll be all right, Theo. Keep the faith.'

Then she held his shoulders, and stepped back, so she was looking up into his face.

'Let me pack Nya a bag, and then you have to pull yourself together and go after them. They'll need you.'

'Yes,' he said. 'Yes.' But he remained rooted where he was, until Iona gave his shoulders a hard shake.

'Now, Theodore. Come on.'

That autocratic voice jerked him out of the shaking stupor he'd fallen into, and he snapped into action, following Iona into the house.

'Nya packed that tote,' he said.

'Poor baby.' Iona was giving it a go-through, and seemed to find the contents inadequate. 'Give me a moment.'

In what seemed like an age, but couldn't have been more than five minutes, he was in his car with Nya's repacked tote, plus another bag Iona tossed onto the back seat.

'Her knitting,' she said as she leaned in to kiss Theo's cheek. 'She'll need something to do with her hands. I'll lock up. And make sure you keep your mind on the road, Theo. There'll be time enough for worrying when you get there.'

But it was only as he was driving away, trying his best to keep within the speed limit, that Nya's words came back to him, and struck him like a blow to the chest...

Our baby.

And he had to blink against the tears that threatened to fill his eyes.

CHAPTER FOURTEEN

THE NEXT THREE days were some of the longest of Nya's life, and she didn't know how she would have got through them without Theo's calm strength.

'Severe bronchiolitis,' the paediatrician diagnosed. 'Without a history, it's difficult to say exactly why she was so susceptible, or why it presented with such rapid onset. Right now, we're making sure she remains oxygenated and hydrated.' He hesitated for a moment, glancing from Nya to Theo, then back again, before continuing, 'We're monitoring her oxygen levels and lung function carefully. Hopefully we won't have to intubate.'

It was only when she felt Theo's arm around her waist that Nya realised she'd sagged at the knees, joints made watery by the thought of just how very ill Hope was.

The hospital staff had Hope in a special cot, where she could receive humidified oxygen and a saline drip. It had taken everything Nya had inside not to cry the first time she was allowed into the room and saw Hope with the tubes and monitors attached to her tiny frame.

'It looks worse than it is, Mum,' the nurse said, patting Nya's arm.

How many times had she said something similar to a patient over all the years she'd worked as a nurse, without understanding just how devastating seeing a child that way was? Oh, she knew, intellectually, but now she was experiencing it with her heart, and it was almost too much to bear.

As she sat in the chair the nurse put for her next to Hope's cot, all Nya could do was stare at the baby, noting her pallor, the still laboured breathing. Occasionally glancing at the monitors to check her oxygen levels, heart rate and blood pressure, praying, *bargaining* for them to improve—willing Hope to get better.

Mum came each day, to offer her support and bring both Nya and Theo food. And the day after Hope had been admitted, Hazel had shown up during evening visiting hours. When Nya had hugged her, and thanked her for coming, the receptionist had burst into tears.

'You don't think she caught that virus from me, do you?' she'd sobbed, clinging to Nya. 'I would have never offered to take care of Hope if I knew I'd be exposing her to a virus.'

'I'm sure you didn't make her sick, Hazel. Viruses, like the one they think Hope has, take up to two weeks to incubate, so she was probably already infected when she came to us.'

Hazel's relief had been palpable, but neither that nor her misplaced guilt had truly penetrated Nya's mental fog.

It took everything she had just to put one foot in

front of the other. Everything inside her was focused on Hope, and each precious breath the baby took.

But she understood Hazel's guilt. Only too well. She'd known that a baby less than a month old, with an unknown history, should be protected. Now, she knew she hadn't done enough. That she'd possibly made things worse by her lack of care—exposing Hope to the clinic and a variety of people. Taking her out and about, when they should have kept her indoors.

Well, she was paying the price now, wasn't she?

She didn't need to look up to know when Theo came into the nursery. Somehow, over the last few days, she'd developed a type of radar attuned just to him. So, when he sat down beside her and reached for her hand, all she felt was relief as she curled her fingers around his.

'Your turn,' he said quietly, but with that hint of steel in his tone. 'Go and get something to eat.'

'I'm really not hungry.'

'Then at least go and walk around for a little. Get some fresh air. You'll be of no use to Hope if you collapse from hunger and exhaustion.'

They'd been allowed to stay past visiting hours for the last two nights, returning to Theo's Falmouth flat for a little while. Then, as soon as was feasible, they'd returned to the hospital to keep vigil.

Nya knew Theo was suffering too. It was there in his eyes, and in the deepening lines bracketing his mouth and creasing his forehead. There was also the fact that, as she lay in the guest bedroom at his flat, fitfully dozing, she could hear him quietly pacing back and forth in the living area. Knowing he too was unable to sleep through worry increased her own tension. That was the only other thing Nya felt—the need to make sure he was okay.

It was strange to have someone to support and be supported by. Yet, whenever she thought of getting up and joining him, she hesitated. The only things he asked of her was that she stay fed and hydrated and get some rest. If he knew she wasn't sleeping, he'd worry even more.

And now, not wanting to increase his stress levels, she gave in.

'I have my phone,' she said as she got up. 'Call me if there's any change.'

Theo had stood up too, and he squeezed Nya's fingers, tugging gently at her hand until she looked up at him.

'I will. Keep the faith, Nya. She'll get through this. *We'll* get through it.'

From what felt like the depths of her belly she dredged up a smile, although she knew it was a weak effort at best.

'Yes.'

But after she walked away what stayed with her, along with the fear of losing Hope, was the thought that his statement that they'd get through it was untrue.

In the final analysis there was no 'we'.

They were united now through their separate love of Hope, but once she was no longer in their lives, whatever this union between them was would also dissolve.

Theo would be moving on, hopefully to build a good new life for himself.

And just now Nya couldn't help being glad. Even if Hope pulled through, the entire situation had reiterated how fragile life was, and how much it hurt to think of losing someone else she loved...

Loved?

She meant Hope, right? Just Hope.

Her brain shied away from the thought that it was more than that.

There was too much on her plate right now to consider otherwise.

As Nya left the nursery Theo sank back into his chair and, being alone with the baby, allowed himself to rub his hands over his face, weariness weighing him down.

He was trying so hard to keep it all together for Nya, but inside he was falling apart, bit by bit, each day that Hope didn't improve.

Nya seemed to think, because he was a father, this was a situation he'd been in before—or that these were emotions he'd already experienced. But his son and daughter had been healthy children. The worst he, as a parent, had experienced was when Gillian broke her collarbone at eleven.

But this—watching Hope struggle to breathe, not even having the energy to cry properly when they suctioned her nasal passages—was something far different.

Heartbreaking.

Terrifying.

And seeing Nya struggle, that shell-shocked expression in her eyes, was even more devastating.

He couldn't recall a time when he'd felt more powerless.

Theo looked up at the light tap on the glass to see Iona outside looking in at him. With a jerk of her chin, she let it be known that she wanted to speak to him and, since the hospital was only letting Nya and him into the nursery, he got up to go and speak to her.

'Will you be in the room for a while?' he asked the nurse, who was checking Hope's lines and nappy. 'I shouldn't be gone long.'

'I'll be here until you get back, Dr Turner. Take your time.'

As Theo closed the nursery door behind himself, it came to him that Iona looked as if she had aged ten years over the last few days. There were stress lines at the corners of her eyes, and the skin of her face above her mask had lost its lustre, making it seem dull and pale.

'How is Hope?' she asked.

'Still the same.' He couldn't tell her that the doctors were taking about intubating—the words sticking in his throat.

'Oh, Theo.' Iona's eyes glistened, and he knew she was holding back tears. 'Isn't there any medication they can give her? Something more they can do to help?'

'They're doing all that they can, Iona.'

He said it gently, even though he wanted to shout. Ask if she didn't think he was monitoring Hope himself, making sure everything possible was being done. But he knew Iona was just as concerned as he and Nya were.

'Where is Nya?'

'I sent her to get something to eat, although I'm not sure she'll take my advice.'

Iona lifted her glasses and rubbed her eyes.

'Nya tends to retreat into herself when she's sad, or frightened.' Iona sighed and settled her glasses back in place. 'And she's had so much loss in her life, I can only imagine what's going on in her head.' She was staring straight into Theo's eyes, when she continued, 'I'm glad you're here, with her. You'll keep her from shutting down completely.'

Would he, though?

It felt as though, in this too, he was failing.

Nya was there, physically, but she had, as her mother said, retreated to the point where Theo felt there was an emotional chasm between them. When he reached out to her, trying to impart what strength he had to offer, there was no sign that she recognised or accepted it.

Once more he was left impotent to make things right—for Hope, or for Nya—and that failure cut him to the depths of his soul.

'Theo,' Iona said. 'Don't give up on her because she seems unreachable. All I ask is that you see her through whatever happens, as best you can.'

Before he could reply, he heard Nya's distinctive footsteps approaching, and he turned to watch her walk towards them.

How stiffly she held herself, as though relaxing even a little would cause her to fall apart. Seeing her like that made him want to take her in his arms and hold her close. Give her everything and anything he had, so as to make it all better, even though he knew it wouldn't really help.

'Mum. What're you doing here so late? Did you drive all the way from Carey Cove?'

'No, love.' Iona leaned forward and, holding her daughter's shoulders, pressed her cheek against Nya's. 'I've been staying in Penzance, to be a little closer. Have you eaten? Got any rest today?'

Nya looked as though she didn't know what those words meant, and she shook her head.

'I'm fine, Mum. I just took a little walk and got a cup of tea.'

Iona's chin came up, and she gave her daughter a stern look.

'Nya, you look dead on your feet. Go with Theo. Have some dinner and get some rest. You have to take care of yourself.'

'That's what Theo's been saying,' she replied, almost absently. 'But how can I leave her?'

'She's in the best of hands. You running yourself into the ground isn't going to help her. It's almost the end of visiting hours, so go. I'm sure they'll call you immediately, if there's any change.'

Theo found himself holding his breath, and when Nya looked at him, all he could do was nod, silently willing her to let him in, and let him take care of her.

Nya took a deep, shuddering breath and, as she released it, she nodded.

'Okay.'

Theo let out the breath he'd been holding.

'I'll tell the nurses what we're doing, and meet you downstairs,' he said, wanting Iona to walk Nya out, so she didn't have a chance to change her mind.

'Agreed,' Iona said briskly. 'Come, Nya.'

Now, at least, there was a plan to follow—some action to take.

Get Nya to eat, to get some rest.

Somehow, in some small way, help her relax.

He'd order some food and pick it up on the way home. Instead of sitting at the dining table, he'd turn on the gas fire and they'd eat in the living room, casually and comfortably.

Going downstairs, he found Nya and Iona in the lobby of the hospital. Outside, the grey, rainy day had morphed into a cool, damp, windy night. As he approached the two women, he saw the way Nya twisted the straps of her knitting bag between her fingers in a physical manifestation of her restless agony of spirit.

She'd carried the bag back and forth from the flat to the hospital, but rarely took her needlework out. There was a disconnected air about her, which now made sense in light of Iona's explanation of how Nya reacted to emotional pain by retreating into herself.

'Ready?' he asked as he joined them. 'Iona, will you have some supper with us?'

Perhaps with her mother there, Nya would actually eat something, rather than just pushing the food around her plate.

'No, thank you. I'm going to go back to Penzance, but I'll be back in the morning.'

She walked partway to Theo's car with them, and then veered off to go to her own.

Once they'd picked up the food and got back to the flat, Theo got Nya settled on the couch and the fire going. Taking off her shoes, she curled up in the corner of the sofa, and closed her eyes.

Making up two trays with their fish and chips, he carried them through to the other room.

'Here you go.'

Nya sat up, taking the tray from him.

'Thank you.' Placing the tray across her lap, she stared down at the food for a moment.

'I know you don't feel like eating,' he said gently. 'But you need to keep up your strength.'

Her gaze was surprisingly fierce when she looked up at him. 'I'm getting tired of being told that.'

He shrugged, not looking away. 'Then eat, and I won't say it again, this evening.'

And, after narrowing her eyes at him, she seemed to give in, and began to eat.

They'd finished, and Theo had taken the dishes into the kitchen, when he heard Nya sigh.

'I hate to admit it, but I needed that.'

'I'm glad you had some.' She'd eaten more than he'd expected. 'Would you like a cup of tea?'

'I would, thank you.'

He turned on the kettle and put out the cups. Then, before the water could boil, his phone rang. He didn't recognise the number, but his heart started racing anyway, as he answered, 'Theo Turner.'

Nya was somehow right there beside him, by the time the person on the other end of the line spoke.

'Dr Turner, Dr Porter asked me to call and let you know that baby Hope's fever has broken, and the mucus in her lungs has started to thin. She's not out of the woods just yet, but it appears she's on the mend.'

Theo had no idea what he said—whether he thanked the caller or not—but as he hung up the phone he was aware of his hand shaking, and the sensation of his head being about to float off his neck.

'What—?'

He didn't give Nya a chance to say anything more, but punched the air. 'Yes! Hope has turned the corner.'

'Oh!' Nya sagged at the knees, and Theo instinctively caught her around the waist and pulled her into his arms.

'Our baby's going to be okay,' he said, holding her close, feeling the way she trembled.

Her face lifted to his, shining with joy, her smile making his heart sing, and Theo could no longer resist.

With a groan of surrender, he kissed her.

CHAPTER FIFTEEN

THERE WAS NO time for thought, or for doubts.

As Theo's mouth captured hers Nya wrapped her arms around him, and kissed him back.

Her heart was racing, pounding as though trying to beat its way right out of her chest, but there was no fear. Just an overwhelming sense of relief and need more powerful than she'd ever expected to feel.

She pressed closer, her entire body heating, becoming so sensitised goosebumps broke out across her back and arms.

Theo moved, his arms tightening, as he swung her around and pressed her back against the cupboard.

Now the full, hard length of his body was on hers, and Nya shuddered. Surrounded by him, she dug her fingertips into his back, wanting to make sure he couldn't, wouldn't move away.

'Nya…'

His mouth had slipped from hers, down to her throat, and she arched her head back to give him full access.

He didn't hesitate.

Nipping, licking, sucking, he searched for and found

the spots that made her shiver, pulled little gasps and moans from her throat.

Desperate for the feel of his skin beneath her palms, she tugged at the back of his shirt until it came free of his trousers and plunged her hands beneath it. The sensation of gooseflesh rising beneath her fingers brought a rush of intense satisfaction.

Suddenly, Theo turned her again, and lifted her onto the counter. They were eye to eye now, and the heat in his gaze pushed her own arousal even higher. She tried to spread her thighs so he could stand between them, but her legs were tangled in her skirt, and Theo had other plans.

Holding her gaze, he pushed her cardigan off her shoulders, then down her arms, and Nya helped as best she could to get free of the garment. When his fingers grasped the hem of her blouse, his hands brushing the skin of her waist, she instinctively raised her arms.

It was off in a trice, and her bra followed immediately.

Stepping back half a pace, Theo held her hands out to the sides, and gave her now bare torso a long look, the tightness of his face telling her he liked what he was seeing.

'You're so beautiful.' Theo's voice was rough, and the sound of it brought her already tight nipples to even harder peaks.

She wanted to tell him to touch her, to do something to relieve the pleasure pressure building between her thighs, but her larynx didn't seem to want to work.

At least not until he released her hands to cup her

breasts, palms supporting the weight of them, thumbs sweeping across her nipples.

Then, oh, then she cried out his name, shocked at her own reaction, already on the brink of drowning in the rising tide of ecstasy.

'Come to my bed.' It was a growl of sound. 'I want to strip you down completely. Touch you, taste you—everywhere.'

'Yes.' It didn't even occur to her to hesitate. 'Yes.'

Picking her up off the counter, he strode through the flat and down the short hallway to his room. Nya clung to his neck, peppering it with kisses, tasting his skin, inhaling the scent she'd so come to love.

Laying her on his bed, he reached over to turn on the bedside light, his lower body not losing contact with hers. He was breathing as hard as she was, and she could feel his erection pressing against her belly. The knowledge that he was as desperate for this closeness as she was filled her with joy, and power.

Pulling him back down into her arms, she kissed him, hard, exulting when he groaned and kissed her back just as desperately.

Frantic, they rolled together, undressing each other, kissing and touching as the various bits of skin were revealed.

Then, suddenly, Theo rolled her onto her back, and trapped her there by throwing one hard thigh over her legs.

And, oh, with almost torturous slowness, he began to explore her body. Cupping her breasts, he swirled his tongue over them, nearing and then moving away from her nipples, over and over, until she stiffened and, panting with desperation, begged him to suck them.

When he complied, Nya cried out, wracked by shudders of delight.

Lost in the sensations, she twisted beneath Theo's weight, need building, rising so swiftly it threatened to overcome her, just from the blissful feeling of his mouth.

Theo slid lower, brushing his mouth across her belly, and Nya's breath caught in her chest. Shifting to the side, he used one hand to nudge her thighs apart, and Nya happily opened them to those seeking fingers.

It had been a long time since she'd felt this way, since she'd been touched so intimately, since she'd wanted culmination more than she wanted her next breath. So long that, when Theo's finger circled her clitoris, just once, she exploded into orgasm.

Her brain short-circuited. Stars danced behind her eyes. Her body shook and shook, the pleasure of it almost too much to bear.

'Nya.' Theo's forehead rested on her belly as he whispered her name. 'God, I feel as though I've been waiting for ever to touch you this way.'

It was how she felt too, but the after-effects of her orgasm made it impossible for her to do anything other than groan his name through a too-dry throat.

And Theo didn't give her a chance to recover, but slid even lower still, lifting her thighs so they draped over his shoulders. Needing to see what he was doing, Nya opened her eyes and looked down along her body to meet his dark, desire-hot gaze.

'I'm going to taste you now.' It was a statement, but he waited, as though to see if she'd object.

Her reply was to open her thighs wider in invitation, already anticipating with avid delight what that beautiful mouth would do to her equilibrium.

And Theo didn't disappoint. Instead, he took Nya to the heights of ecstasy—once, twice—until the room, the very world seemed to retreat, and it was just the two of them left.

'I want you now, Theo.' She didn't care that it sounded as though she was begging. In fact, she was. He'd brought her back to the edge of orgasm, kept her hovering there for several long moments.

She wanted to have him in every way possible.

And she didn't want to wait.

Wriggling out from beneath him, she angled her body so as to be able to swoop in for a kiss. Theo's hands were all over her, and she exulted in the way they rushed and pressed, as though wanting to explore and know every inch of her body.

Giving his shoulders a push, she got him over onto his back, and sat back on her heels to look down at him.

He was beautiful.

His body was long and sleekly muscular. The type of frame that made all his clothes look good, but that looked even better unclothed.

And he was obviously, wonderfully aroused.

By her.

Wanting *her*.

'If you keep looking at me like that, you're going to

make me lose control,' he said, in a raspy tone she'd never heard from him before, and immediately loved.

'I want you to,' she admitted, swinging her leg over his thighs. 'You've made me scream your name over and over. It's time I return the favour.'

And the way his face tightened, as she positioned herself over him, she thought there was a good chance she'd get her way.

Theo held his breath, his heart pounding, sweat breaking out on his forehead, as he watched Nya lower herself, taking him into her body.

It was the most erotic scene he'd ever beheld, and there was a part of his brain that almost refused to believe it was real.

But it must be. No dream could feel this good, could take him from aroused to desperate between one rushed breath and the next.

Nya had completely engulfed his penis, rocking her hips to take the last little bit, and it took every ounce of determination not to close his eyes. He wanted to watch her pleasure. Commit to memory the sight of Nya lost in an erotic spell they'd cast together.

She arched back, making her breasts rise, her dark, beaded nipples begging for his fingers, his lips. Putting his hands on the bed behind him for leverage, he sat up, and took first one nipple and then the other into his mouth, sucking and laving them with his tongue.

Then, as her body pulsed hard around his, he had to stop. He was already at risk of coming too soon, and he wanted this first time between them to be all for Nya.

She laughed—a breathless giggle that he thought was the most wonderful sound he'd ever heard—and said, 'Why did you stop?'

'You know why.' It was so hard to get the words out, he had to pause and catch his breath. 'You're making me crazy.'

She touched her nipples with just the tips of her fingers. 'That's my intent. To make you crazy.'

Beginning to move again, she rocked and swivelled, her breath coming faster and faster.

He was going to come, the orgasm rushing towards him with all the power of a freight train, and although Nya was obviously enjoying their coupling, she wasn't as close as he was. So, reaching up, he took one of her hands off her breast, and guided it to between her thighs.

Nya gave him a slumbrous look from beneath her lashes. 'You want me to touch myself?'

It had never occurred to him Nya would be such a frank, vocal lover, or that it would be such a turn-on.

'Yes,' he groaned. 'I need you to come for me, love. Please.'

There was no hesitation, and Theo went up on his elbow to watch as she did as he'd asked, watch her pleasure herself, her face growing tight and desperate. Hearing her cry out. Feeling her contract around him, catapulting him into his own orgasm, as she found hers.

Nya slumped over him and Theo reached up to pull her all the way down, wrapping her firmly in his arms.

She snuggled in so sweetly, and his emotions were so

overwhelming just then that the words *I love you* wanted to emerge from his lips and had to be bitten back.

This encounter could just be a result of Nya's relief that Hope was going to be okay and, if that was the case, Theo refused to put her on the spot.

Or open himself up to more pain.

'Mmm…' The sound was rife with satisfaction, and hearing it reignited Theo's desire.

If this turned out to be the only time they made love—although he fervently hoped it wouldn't be—he wanted to make it memorable.

Burned into her brain for ever.

Yet, she'd hardly slept in days. Was it greedy of him to want her again, already?

To expect her to want him again too?

'Can we do that again?'

It was as though she'd read his mind. Rolling over, so they were face to face, he asked, 'Now?'

Nya grinned, reaching between them to encircle his erection.

'I was going to say, "If you're up for it," but I already know you are.'

This time as they rolled around, while the passion was as hot as it had been before, it was mixed with laughter, and that made it even more precious.

And later, as he lay with Nya in his arms, he knew he'd never felt more content, refusing to let the fear niggling at the edges of his mind spoil the moment.

Nya stirred in the night, and Theo awoke to find he was spooning her, one of her breasts nestled in his hand as though it had been made to fit there. She started to ease away, and he tightened his grip.

'I need to go to the loo,' she said, with a giggle.

'Well, hurry back.'

With another giggle, she slipped out of bed, and he watched her shadowy form cross the room.

How was it that it had taken him so long to notice how sexy Nya was?

But it was a rhetorical question. He'd been married and had trained himself not to notice things like that. Was it horrible that right now, at this very moment, he was glad Femi had left him, since that act freed him to make love with Nya?

He didn't know and didn't care. Putting the thought from his mind, he waited in the dark until he heard Nya coming and threw back the covers for her so she could dive back into the warmth of his bed. Cocooning her in his arms once more, he was considering making love to her again, when sleep claimed him.

CHAPTER SIXTEEN

NYA WOKE UP the next morning ridiculously early, with memories of the night before flooding through her, stirring her libido anew. When she took stock and realised she was alone in the bed, she rolled over to stare up at the ceiling, taking note of muscles that usually didn't ache, but were making themselves felt today.

Had it really happened? Had she really made love with Theo? Not just made love, which seemed to suggest something inherently gentle and sweet, but pretty much held him down and had her wicked way with him?

And it had been bloody brilliant.

Earth-shaking, mind-shattering, ego-boosting, orgasm city.

And utterly stupid.

Stuffing the edge of a pillow into her mouth to muffle her manic, close to hysterical laughter, Nya let herself go for a moment, trying to release the tension.

Oh, it had been magical. She hadn't even known she could feel that way—that it was possible for her to be that insatiable. But yes, it was also the last thing she should have done.

She'd been warned about the pain she would be opening herself up to. And she'd warned herself as well.

There was no future for her and Theo, and giving in to the attraction was a *great* way to hasten and intensify the future heartbreak.

So now she was left trying to figure out just how to extricate herself from a situation she actually didn't want to get out of, but darn well knew she had to.

If last night had proven anything, it was that Theo Turner's brand of loving could very well be addictive, and she couldn't afford to get hooked. Falling for a man who obviously was still grieving the end of his marriage, and who was planning an escape from the one place Nya felt safe?

Absolute foolishness.

Just the thought of it made her heart race, and had sweat breaking out on her forehead, as the remnants of her post-coital glow drained away, leaving her scared and shaky.

It would be easy to tell herself it was just the relief of hearing Hope was going to be okay that had made her susceptible to Theo's kisses, but she knew she'd be lying. The very least she could do was be honest with herself.

She'd fallen for Theo, probably from the first time she'd seen him holding Hope. Maybe, a little voice whispered in the back of her mind, from before that—when he was still a part of 'Theo and Femi'. Although she would never have allowed herself to even think of him as anything other than a friend while he was married, she'd always had a special place in her heart for him.

His quiet charm. The way he lit up a room, and made others feel important. His tenderness to and care for his patients.

And now she knew he was also a skilful and considerate lover, which just made him seem far too perfect.

Although she knew exactly how she felt about him, there was no way in hell she was letting Theo know.

Sitting up in bed, she came to a decision.

If—when—he brought it up, she'd tell him it was the joy of hearing about Hope, coupled with her exhaustion, that had created the perfect storm. That she'd reacted instinctively, and wantonly, and while she didn't regret it, it wouldn't happen again.

Couldn't happen again…

Thus determined, she swung her feet to the floor, and took a deep breath, trying to slow her heart rate.

There were no sounds from outside and as she turned on the light beside the bed she wondered where Theo was.

Obviously he'd been up for a bit before her, and her sleep had been so deep, he'd been able to come and go in the room without waking her, since her clothes, neatly folded, were on a nearby chair.

They were a reminder of the night before, and Nya blushed to see them. Then she drew herself up.

She was a grown woman, not a teenager, even if being around Theo made her feel like one.

No. If she was going to get through the next few weeks, she was going to have to brazen it out—pretend a sophistication she didn't possess. She'd put on her undies and shirt and march out of the room as though this weren't the first time in too many years to count that a man had seen her naked. As though she couldn't care less and her heart weren't about to thump its way out of her chest.

Thus buoyed, she all but flung open the bedroom door, and was instantly deflated when she realised the flat rang with the kind of echoing silence that indicated it was empty.

Well, so much for sophistication.

Wandering farther into the room, she saw a note on the kitchen island and went to read it.

Theo had gone to get them breakfast.

Nya shook her head. Why on earth did the damn man have to be so perfect?

At least she didn't have to face him just yet, and could have a shower and be properly clothed by the time he got back.

But by the time she was finished getting ready he still wasn't back, and Nya was tired of feeling as though she was on tenterhooks. Calling the hospital to check on Hope's progress took up some of the time, but not enough to calm her down.

Suddenly, she remembered she hadn't called her mother to give her the good news about Hope, and since it was now late enough to do so without waking Mum up, she put through the call.

The happiness in Mum's voice mirrored Nya's own.

'Oh, thank goodness. You and Theo must be so relieved.'

'We are,' she replied, refusing to let her brain relive

exactly where that relief had led them. 'He's gone to get us some breakfast, and then we're going to the hospital.'

Mum's sigh spoke volumes. 'He's such a good man. Seeing him with that little girl just about melts my icy heart.'

Nya couldn't help laughing. 'Really, Mum? Well, you know he's single now. Maybe—'

'Ha. Just you stop right there. I'm rather hoping he'll melt *your* heart and get you to live again.'

If only you knew...

But there was no way she'd entertain that kind of conversation with her mother.

'Mum, I told you, we're—'

'Just friends. Yes, you've mentioned that ad nauseam. That hasn't stopped me from hoping.'

'Mum, it's not like that, so don't get your hopes up. In fact, between you and me, I think Theo is planning to leave Carey Cove, so even if there was something between us—which there isn't—it wouldn't be serious, anyway.'

Mum was quiet for so long, Nya was beginning to think the conversation was over, but then a sigh came down the line.

'Nya, why does everything have to be serious? Nothing is meant to last for ever. Sometimes you just need to enjoy the moments.'

It wasn't the first time they'd had this conversation, and Nya didn't really want to have it again.

Especially not now.

'All right, Mum. I'll think about what you're saying.'

Iona sighed again. 'I doubt it, love. Kiss Hope for me and let me know when she's coming home.'

'I will.' Just then she heard Theo's key in the door, and added, 'I have to go. I'll call again later and update you, when I know what's happening.'

Hanging up, she turned to face Theo, who was putting a couple of bags down on the counter, and had to forcibly push aside the urge to cross the room to him. Hold him tight. Kiss him.

Take him back to bed.

'Good morning,' he said, smiling, although his gaze was searching her face, as though trying to decide what her reaction to him would be. 'Sorry I was so long, but it seems I was just one of a long line of people trying to get fed. The café was terribly busy.'

Time to make it plain the night before was a one-off. She made her voice brisk, as though they were discussing a patient back at Carey House. 'It's fine. I haven't been up that long anyway.'

She saw his eyes narrow, and then he turned away to open the cupboard where the plates were kept.

'Come on, then,' he said. 'Let's eat, and then get to the hospital. I just spoke to Herman Porter, and he's prepared to release Hope later this morning.'

'Oh, how wonderful!'

'Yes,' he replied, but in an absent tone, as though his thoughts were elsewhere. Then he turned to face her again, and her heart did a flip at his expression. 'Nya—'

His phone rang, interrupting whatever it was he'd planned to say, and, with an impatient sound, he picked it up and answered.

'Theo Turner. Yes. What?' He turned and walked away from her, leaving Nya staring at his back. 'Where? Yes, I'm familiar with it. Yes. We'll come as soon as possible.'

For a few moments after he hung up, he stayed where he was, staring out of the window, then he faced her, his expression inscrutable.

'That was the police. They've found Hope's mother.'

And Nya felt as though the bottom dropped out of her world all over again.

'Where is she?' she asked as she sank down onto the nearest chair.

'At Longworth Hospital, in Truro. She came in and was diagnosed with a thrombotic pulmonary embolism, and eventually admitted she'd given birth three weeks ago. We've been asked to attend at the hospital with Hope.'

'But…'

There was no way to articulate the pain sitting like a band around her chest, stealing her breath.

Theo glanced at his watch.

'How soon can you be ready?'

Nya dug deep, reaching for and finding the professionalism and strength that had seen her through everything life had thrown her way.

After all, she'd known this day would come. Later, when she was back home, she'd break down but, for now, there were things that needed to be dealt with.

She got up, keeping her back straight and her chin up.

'I'm ready now. I think, since Hope hasn't been released yet, we should go back to Carey Cove and collect her things, then come back to pick her up. At least her mum will have whatever she needs for the time being.'

'Good idea.' He nodded towards the bags he'd just brought in. 'Do you mind eating while we're driving? I'd like to get on the road as soon as possible.'

'Of course.' Forcing her trembling legs to move, she walked blindly towards the guest room. 'I'll just get my things together.'

This, then, was how it all would end. The all too brief slice of happiness she'd found was about to disappear.

Another heartbreak had found her—and she wasn't sure she knew how to get over this one.

Theo watched Nya until she disappeared down the hallway, then turned away, scrubbing a hand over his face, which had gone numb as he'd spoken to the constable.

Even though, as a doctor, he'd experienced some events others would perhaps classify as unbelievable, he'd never really believed in miracles, until last night.

Holding Nya, he'd felt as though this Christmas he was being offered something as close to miraculous as he'd ever had.

A new beginning. A second-chance family. More joy than he'd felt in years.

But even then, he'd known it was just a fantasy, and Nya's reception this morning, along with Hope's mum reappearing, showed him he'd been right to think it couldn't last.

Had it only been less than two weeks since he'd found Hope on the doorstep at Carey House? He felt as though he'd lived a lifetime since then. A glorious, wonderful lifetime, where the pain and guilt and stress he'd been living with had melted away, and he'd felt renewed.

Somewhere along the line he'd forgotten being Hope's carer was only temporary. And last night, lost in ecstasy, he'd forgotten that Nya's heart wasn't his to win—that it had already been given, lock, stock, and barrel, and there was no space left in it for him.

How ironic to finally find a path forward, after feeling so lost and stuck, only to realise it had just been a mirage.

There was nothing he could do to make any of it less painful. Wishing they could go back to a week ago, reliving the days before Hope got ill, was fruitless. It was time to face reality and face his responsibility to both Hope and Nya—which was to let them go without a fuss.

'I'm ready.'

Nya sounded so cool and in control, Theo felt a spurt of anger, but he tamped it down. At least one of them was dealing well with the situation.

Without looking at her, he headed for the door, grabbing the bags of food and his car keys on the way.

'Let's go,' he said, knowing how terse he sounded, but unable to help it. 'It's going to be a long day.'

Long, and extremely painful.

CHAPTER SEVENTEEN

THEY MADE GOOD TIME, driving to Carey Cove and back to Falmouth to pick up Hope from St Isolde's, but to Nya it felt like an eternity, especially since the trip was a mostly silent one.

It was as though the knowledge they were giving Hope up had stripped Theo and her of all the intimacy they'd shared, and there was nothing at all left to say.

Nya felt heartsick, knowing she was losing his friendship as well. Surely it couldn't survive this latest blow.

Bad enough that she'd slept with him, but once they'd handed Hope over to Social Services and her mother, there was nothing left to bind them.

And she wouldn't try to use her love for him as a way to hold onto him. That wasn't her way. Far better to keep that to herself, rather than reveal it and make him uncomfortable.

'Why does everything have to be serious?'

Mum's question came back to her as they made the drive back to Falmouth after collecting Hope's clothes, toys, books, and other possessions.

She didn't have an answer.

For as long as she could remember, that was just how she was. The important things in life deserved to be given due consideration. Family, friends, her job. These were the things that meant the most to her, and she took them to heart.

If she didn't love Theo, then maybe she could suggest they sleep together until he left, but the reality was that if she didn't care about him, she wouldn't have slept with him at all. Even knowing he was going to desert her and Carey Cove hadn't been enough to stop her wanting him, although she wasn't one to court heartbreak.

In fact, up until this last week, she'd have classified herself as completely risk averse.

Hadn't life beaten up on her enough?

The thought made her snort.

Apparently not.

'Everything okay?'

Theo's question brought her out of her reverie.

'Yes.' Then, knowing she was being particularly terse, she added, 'Just a little sad at having to give up Hope so soon. I'd thought she'd be with us at least through Christmas.'

Theo's grunt was unintelligible, but she imagined he felt the way she did: that Christmas had completely lost its lustre.

Then she remembered that Theo's children weren't coming home for Christmas either, and sadness for him almost made her ask him to still spend the holiday with her and Mum. She quickly squelched that idea.

She wasn't strong enough to deal with that with any kind of equanimity.

The one bright spot in the day was seeing the vast improvement in Hope. Although she was still a bit congested, the infant's skin was once again pink, and her eyes were bright, rather than glazed with fever. Nya hugged her close, savouring these last moments of contact, trying not to think about them that way, but cognisant of the parting fast approaching.

Glancing up, she caught Theo looking at them, and her heart clenched. She recognised that stern distant persona. The one she'd seen fall away over the past days.

Unable to stand seeing him that way, she walked over to where he was standing with Dr Porter and held Hope out to him.

Theo hesitated, and she thought he was going to refuse to take the infant, but Hope proved irresistible.

'Come here, my sweetheart,' he said, in that voice that never failed to melt Nya's heart. And he carried her all the way down to the car, settling her into her seat, murmuring and crooning to her the entire way.

Then they were on their way to Truro.

'I wonder what they'd do,' Theo mused, 'if we took off for the Scottish border, like a pair of brigands stealing the princess away?'

Nya shook her head, too heavy-hearted to even laugh.

'I'm not sure, but I don't think I'm cut out for life on the lam.'

'I thought you might say something like that,' was all

he said in reply, before lapsing into silence once again for the rest of the drive.

Caroline Harker from Social Services was waiting for them at the hospital in Truro, and took them into a conference room when they arrived.

'Willow Carter is only sixteen,' she told them. 'When she discovered she was pregnant, she ran away from home, afraid of what her parents would say. The father was apparently a young sailor she'd met one night, and he was long gone by the time she realised about the baby. She had no prenatal medical care, and gave birth in a squat her cousin was living in. One of her friends told her about Carey House, and how kind everyone had been when her own mother gave birth there, so they got someone to drive them and left the baby there.'

'Poor little soul,' Nya said. 'What will happen now?'

'She's very confused, and frightened. We've offered her counselling and will make sure she and her baby are taken care of while she decides what she wants to do. If she ultimately decides she wants to put Hope into care, we'll make sure she gets placed in a good home.'

Nya wanted to ask how they planned to make sure that was the case, but bit the words back.

It was time to start disengaging, even though doing so was so painful she felt ill.

'I told Willow about you both, and she's asking to meet you.'

Nya looked at Theo, and they exchanged a long glance. She saw the same hesitance she felt mirrored in his eyes, but it seemed the right thing to agree.

'I'm willing,' she said, and saw Theo nod too.

Handing Hope over to the paediatric nurse tasked with taking her to the nursery felt like taking a knife to the stomach, but Nya reminded herself this wasn't the first loss she'd sustained.

And overcome.

Somehow that steadied her enough that she held back the threatening tears, but she had to turn away when Theo was saying goodbye to the infant. Seeing that would have broken her.

Nya wasn't sure what she was expecting of Hope's mother, but Willow Carter, sitting propped up in the hospital bed, looked so tiny and lost Nya couldn't help sympathising. A little slip of a girl, with big blue eyes, her complexion pallid because of her illness, she had the forlorn look of an abandoned fawn.

'I wanted to thank you,' she said, her gaze focused on where her fingers twisted in the sheets. 'Ms Harker told me you'd looked after the baby since I left her at the hospital.'

'We did,' Nya told her, reaching out to cover those restless fingers with her hand. 'She's beautiful, and so good. We called her Hope.'

Willow looked up at Nya with tears in her eyes.

'I don't know how to be a mum. I don't think I can do it. I don't want to do the wrong thing. I mean, I didn't even give her a name, before I gave her up.'

'Willow, I think you did what you thought best, and you have time to make a decision about both your future, and Hope's.' Theo's voice was soft, reassuring. 'Take Ms Harker up on her offer of counselling, and then make up your mind.'

Willow's tears were flowing, and Nya pulled some tissues out of the nearby box, and mopped at the young woman's cheeks, making soothing sounds.

'They called my mum, and she said she doesn't want to know. That if I was old enough to have a baby, I was old enough to make a life for myself.'

Nya clenched her teeth, so as not to say what she felt about a woman who'd desert her own daughter at a time like this.

The thought came to her, and before she thought it over, she said, 'Willow, if you'd like to come and spend Christmas with me and my mum, you just let Ms Harker know. We'd be happy to have you.' She gave Willow a smile. 'I'll warn you, though, that my mum celebrates Kwanzaa. Do you know what that is?'

'I do,' she said, a little spark of enthusiasm lighting her eyes. 'I read about it once. I thought that was only celebrated in America?'

'It started there, but it's spreading around the world. My mother was a professor of African studies, and that's how she learned about it. Then, the next thing I knew, we were celebrating it too.'

Nya had injected a disgruntled tone into her voice, and was pleased to see a smile tip the edges of Willow's lips.

'You'll like Mrs Ademi's mother,' Theo interjected. 'She wears the most amazing headdresses and jewellery she got from Africa.'

'She is a character,' Nya admitted. 'And when you first meet her, you'll think she's stiff and starchy, but once you get to know her, she's really very nice.'

'I… I'll think about it.' Willow didn't sound very sure, but at least now she didn't seem petrified. 'Thank you.'

'You take care of yourself and Hope,' Nya said, when they were leaving. 'And if you need anything, you tell Ms Harker to let me know, all right?'

'I will.' Willow hesitated, then said, 'Mrs Ademi, could I have a hug?'

'Of course.'

And, just like that, Nya was once more battling tears.

When they left Willow's room, as though in complete accord, they both turned towards the nursery, walking in silence to look in through the window.

The breath hitched in Nya's throat as she took one last look at the baby, who was thankfully sleeping in one of the cots. If she'd been awake and crying, Nya didn't think she'd be able to leave her.

'We should go.'

Theo's voice sounded gravelly, and Nya knew he was battling the same emotions inundating her, so she nodded, and made herself turn away, although leaving felt, oh, so wrong.

How could Nya seem so calm? Theo wondered. So collected, when he wanted to bellow at the top of his lungs, in turns angry and devastated by loss?

Of course, although she clearly loved Hope, she hadn't been building silly fantasies in her head about making a family with the three of them together, living happily ever after. No, Nya was far too sensible for that, whereas Theo knew himself to be the consummate stupid romantic.

The kind of man who fell in love with a woman, knowing full well she would never be his.

A modern-day Cyrano, although without the overly large nose.

Caroline Harker had already left the hospital, so there was no reason to linger. As they walked through the gaily decorated corridors, Theo tried to ignore all the signs of the season. There was no joyous anticipation any more. He was hollow with grief and loss.

Once more silence filled his car as they set off back to Carey Cove, and he couldn't think of one single topic of conversation to break it.

What he wanted was to ask Nya to come home with him, to be there, so they could share their pain, and hopefully mitigate it, but he knew she'd refuse. She'd made it clear that last night had been an aberration, not to be repeated, and there was no way he'd open himself up to more agony by courting her rejection.

When they got to Carey Cove, he could see the start of preparations for the Guise Ball on the green. The Christmas tree lights were on, and a few children capered around near it, playing tag. A couple walked hand in hand along the pavement, a little boy on a scooter racing ahead of them, and he realised it was Kiara, Lucas, and Harry.

A perfect little family scene.

Seeing them made his stomach clench painfully with jealousy.

All too soon, they were at Nya's door, and she was getting out.

As he was reaching for the doorhandle, she said, 'Don't bother getting out, Theo. I can manage.' She opened the back door and took out her bags, then, before she shut the door again, said, 'Enjoy the rest of your holidays.'

Watching her walk up her front path was so agonising Theo put the car into reverse and backed out of her driveway before she'd even got inside.

Getting home, he sat in his car for a few minutes, knowing he didn't want to go inside.

For all the lights and baubles, ornaments and the tree, it would be barren, cold and lonely without Nya and Hope.

Once upon a time, this house had been home. Not always a happy one, but still the place he looked forward to going back to.

That feeling was now gone. Instead, it was like a haunted mansion, peopled not with spirits but with the ghosts of happy times and lost loves. Now he understood what Nya had meant when she'd spoken about leaving Andover after Jim died. He didn't think there would be a day when he didn't see something here that reminded him of Nya, and of Hope.

It was time to move on. Find home, or at least some kind of peace, whatever that might look like, somewhere else.

Eventually, unable to put it off any more, he got out of the car. Letting himself into the house, he went into the kitchen to turn on the kettle. While waiting for it to boil, he leaned against the cabinet, thinking about Nya.

Wishing, cravenly, that he'd met her first, before she'd known Jim. Before she'd had a chance to give the other man her heart, and then bury it with him.

Because Theo had given her his, and now he had to contemplate what it would be like to move on without it.

Without her.

CHAPTER EIGHTEEN

HER HOME HAD always been her sanctuary. The one place where she knew she was safe, and happy. But as she turned on the lights on the Christmas tree, Nya knew it would never be the same.

She'd thought Theo's utilitarian flat in Falmouth, a place where he stayed only during emergencies at St Isolde's or if he was on call there, had seemed sterile and lifeless. Then, she'd thought it was because he'd made no effort to add any personal touches, opting strictly for function.

Yet here, surrounded by all her own personal items, pictures and art, the blankets she'd knitted and the ornaments she'd picked up over the years, she felt that same sense of emptiness. All the strength she'd gathered, so as to hold it together while they left Hope in Truro and Theo dropped her home, drained away, leaving her as hollow and lifeless as her cottage.

Sinking down onto the ground, she pressed the heels of her palms into her eye sockets, letting all the pain she'd been suppressing batter her in waves.

Just weeks ago, her life had seemed ideal. She had a

job she loved and was proud of doing, friends she could count on, her mother near at hand. She'd been content in the knowledge that she'd been loved passionately, had loved Jim in return, and been true to that love. Living in Carey Cove, delivering babies, had given her great satisfaction. It hadn't been perfect. What life was? But it had been *enough*.

Would she ever get that contentment back? Be peaceful in spirit? Happy and grateful for all she had, without this grinding agony over what she'd lost?

What *more* she'd lost.

It overwhelmed her, hammering away at her control, and the more she fought the agony, the harder it came at her, until she was gasping with the effort to hold in her tears.

But they wouldn't be denied, and she had to, for once, let them fall, sobbing as the pain kept striking through her.

She cried for Willow, little more than a baby herself, who'd given birth and was scared and confused. Just when she'd needed her mother, more than ever, she'd been heartbreakingly rejected.

And she cried for baby Hope, so sweet and good, whose future was uncertain.

For Theo. A man of such strength of character, such sensitivity and devotion, who'd been hurt in a way he didn't deserve.

Then for Jim, for the life they'd shared, and the one they'd never had a chance to live. For the children they'd both wanted, and the home they would have created to nurture them.

And even as she cried, she realised the truth.

Losing Jim hadn't just hurt. It had been the death of her hopes and dreams. The destruction of her future. There would be no children with Jim's gleaming, heavy-lidded eyes. No shouts of laughter over silly things that others couldn't understand. No more surprises prefaced with, 'I saw this, and thought of you.' No one who understood her sometimes better than she understood herself.

Over the years, even thinking about being with someone else had felt like a betrayal and had burdened her with guilt. It had been more comforting to lock her heart away and lean on Jim's memory. Mum had seen and tried to point it out, but Nya hadn't wanted to hear.

Besides, why love again when she already knew, all too well, that those you loved only left? Losing her father and then Jim had created an immense hole in her heart that had filled with fear.

But that hadn't stopped her from loving again, had it? Only stopped her from reaching for that love with both hands, too afraid to risk being hurt again.

Too cowardly.

The tears abated, bringing calm, and clarity.

She'd always love Jim, but he was gone, and had been for a long, long time. Because of the man he'd been—generous, full of life and laughter—he wouldn't have wanted her to lock her heart away the way she had. In fact, she thought he might be disappointed if he knew. He'd always been one to seize life and wring the most joy and pleasure out of it.

He'd have urged her to move on, to take all the love she had inside and give it away.

And Nya was almost positive he would have liked Theo, a lot.

Jim would have wanted her to take the chance to tell Theo how she felt, to risk rejection, in the hope that he would want her the way she wanted him. Loved her, the way she loved him.

She had no idea how Theo really felt about her— or whether he was ready for a relationship after his divorce. But she knew he'd touched her with tenderness and passion. And she'd seen how he looked at her when he thought she couldn't see, with the kind of longing that made her feel more feminine and sexier than she ever had before. And after all this time, without a doubt she could trust him with her friendship, trust him to tell her the truth, and, if he wanted it, trust him with her heart.

As for that last one, there was only one way to find out.

Gather her courage and tell him how she felt—without expectation. Simply because her honesty would allow them to salvage their friendship, if that was all he wanted from her.

Getting up, she went into the bathroom to wash her face, and in twenty minutes was in the car and on her way to Theo's house, her heart pounding like a bass drum.

Driving through Carey Cove, she was struck once more by how lovely the village was. With its stone and half-timbered buildings, the small, perfectly proportioned church and Georgian homes here and there, it was, in her mind, one of the most beautiful places she'd ever seen. Especially now, when everyone had taken the time to decorate for Christmas, and the village glowed with lights and festive ornaments.

Growing up here, she'd always taken it for granted. Not until she'd returned, heartsore and depressed, had she appreciated the benefits of living village life.

All the things other people complained about were the things she loved. Being instantly recognisable by name to everyone else. Having only one pub and one café, where you always knew exactly what they'd be serving. The camaraderie that brought everyone together in times of need, or simply to celebrate. Even the petty competitions that sometimes reared their heads: who made the best saffron buns, or most delicious ice cream, or had the freshest eggs.

Those, along with her work at Carey House, were the fabric and rhythm of her life.

Stopping the car near the turn-off up to the cottage hospital, where the main road dipped and went through the centre of the village, she took a moment to appreciate the picturesque scene.

It calmed her, centred her thoughts.

For the first time in her life, rather than moving towards safety, she was stepping outside her comfort zone and embarking on an adventure. There was no way to know how Theo would respond to her admission of love, but it was something she knew she had to do for herself. Instead of her habit of planning everything, and wanting all the answers right away, all the questions she had would have to wait.

One step at a time.

And all the pain she'd been through in the past, instead of being a negative, really was the reason she knew, no matter what happened, she'd be all right.

As long as she knew Hope and Theo were safe and happy, with or without her, she'd be happy too. Or as happy as possible while pining for something you knew you could never again have.

She was stronger that she'd ever given herself credit for, and she was ready to use that strength to her advantage.

Putting the car in gear, she made her way along the lane to Theo's house, feeling a sense of homecoming that had been missing when she'd arrived at her own cottage earlier.

Taking a deep breath, she exited the car, noticing Theo hadn't turned on his Christmas lights, and wondered if that was an indication of his state of mind. In a strange way it gave her a sense of optimism, so that when she got to the front door she didn't even hesitate, but knocked straight away.

When Theo opened the door, her breath caught in her throat, and as the expression on his face morphed from polite inquiry through surprise to delight, she knew it would all work out.

Theo held out his hand and, instinctively, Nya took it, feeling as though the world had suddenly righted itself, and she was exactly where she needed to be.

* * *

Theo couldn't seem to catch his breath, anticipation wrapping itself around his chest and making him light-headed.

Nya, a little smile tipping the edges of her lush mouth, stepped easily into the house, and into his arms as the door swung shut behind her.

How could he resist her upturned lips? Why would he resist, knowing that kissing her was tantamount to being thrown into paradise?

When their lips met, and she melted against him, Theo knew that if he had his way, he'd never let her go. They fitted together perfectly—physically, emotionally, intellectually—in all the important ways.

She was what he needed to move forward and live happily again.

But he needed to know exactly why she was here.

Was it just for sex? Or something more?

Dared he actually hope that she had feelings for him that went beyond friendship with benefits?

Yet, the magic of their kisses kept him enthralled, and when Nya nudged him further into the house, he didn't resist.

She pulled back, just far enough so her breath rushed, warm and sweet, across his lips when she said, 'Make love with me.'

Everything inside him strained towards her, wanting to do what she asked without question, except the one, small part of his heart that whispered, *I need to know*.

He couldn't stand the pain, if all she wanted was the physical connection, and not the emotional.

'Why, Nya? What do you need from me?'

Nya drew back a little more, her gaze searching his, shining and intent.

'I don't need anything from you, Theo.' His heart clenched, and a cold ball formed in his stomach. 'I want your love, but that's not something to be demanded. I want your love, because I love you.'

That was all he needed to know. To hear.

A wave of heat crashed through him, washing away the icy fear. Picking her up, he carried her through to his bedroom, telling her, in between kisses, that he loved her too.

When he laid her on the bed, she twined her arms tighter around his neck, and tugged him down with her.

'I never thought I'd love again,' she whispered against his skin, before tracing the tendon along his neck with her tongue. 'You've brought me back to life.'

Later, he thought, they could talk more. Tell each other all that needed to be said. But just then he wanted to show her exactly how much he loved her, with his body, and his actions.

And it seemed she felt the same way too.

They rolled and kissed, taking off each other's clothing, touching each bit of skin as it was exposed. The scent of her filled his head, an aphrodisiac more potent than any liquor, and everywhere her hands skimmed was brought to tingling, straining life.

Time seemed irrelevant, as though they'd fallen into a place of enchantment where only they existed. Although his need grew to almost desperate levels, Theo forced himself to love Nya slowly, thoroughly. The sounds she made as she climbed towards orgasm, the way she cried out his name on culmination, pushed his own arousal even higher.

When she rolled him onto his back, and began her own slow, exploratory journey of his body, he knew it wouldn't take much for him to lose control.

As though knowing this, she teased him gently, keeping him hovering on the edge of release, then easing him back. There was something so erotic about her total concentration, he found himself having an almost out-of-body experience. As she caressed him, his vision narrowed until she was all he could see, and even though his heartbeat echoed in his ears, he also was aware of every breath she took, every soft sound she made.

Then her gaze lifted to his, and Theo reached down to pull her up and over his chest so he could kiss her, long and hard.

'Now, please, Theo.'

Her words made him tremble as though they were a touch. Rolling her to one side, he reached for a condom, going up on his knees to put it on, her eyes, dark and heavy-lidded, watching his every move.

She opened for him, her arms reaching to hold him, pull him close, and then closer yet, her gaze not wavering, holding his captive.

And he knew that as long as he lived, he'd remember that moment as one of the most beloved of his life.

Her need for him, and his for her, were the culmination of rough roads and heartbreak, but the two of them together, just then, had created an instant of pure perfection.

'I love you,' they whispered at the same time, and Theo thought his heart would explode with sheer, unadulterated joy.

He'd planned to go slowly, give her as much pleasure as he could, for as long as he could, but Nya took control of the pace, undulating beneath him, rocking faster and faster.

Gasping, he gripped her hips, trying to return to a more leisurely pace, but she just laughed, and somehow the sound of those delicious giggles made him even wilder.

'Yes,' she cried. 'Yes, Theo. Just like that.'

Then she was coming, arms and legs locked around him, pulling him into the whirlwind of her orgasm, and he felt as though he were flying.

Still entwined, they rolled together onto their sides, lying face to face, and he gazed into Nya's eyes, savouring the present, unimpeded by the past.

Free, except for the chains of love binding him to her.

'You say I brought you back to life, Nya, but in reality you did the same for me. You and Hope filled my heart, chased away my loneliness. Made me believe in love again.'

She nodded, her smile so glorious he was almost blinded by it.

'I realised I had to put my fear aside, so as to be with you, Theo. Take the chance that you might not want me, but find out one way or another. Being with you showed me I'd rather risk everything, give up anything, if I could be with you. If you want to move from Carey Cove, and want me to, I'll go with you.'

That was when he knew, without a shadow of a doubt, that Nya loved him, fully, completely.

Carey Cove had been her refuge for years, but she was willing to give it up, to be with him.

He shook his head, then leaned in for a kiss.

'This is our home. If I have any say in it, we're not going anywhere.'

'Oh, Theo.' Throwing her arms around his neck, she hugged him hard. Then she giggled, and said, 'Maybe we should move, just so I don't have to hear my mother repeatedly saying she knew there was something between us, and telling me she told me so.'

He chuckled with her, hearing their mingled laughter like a miraculous symphony of love.

One he hoped to hear for the rest of his life.

EPILOGUE

EVER SINCE KIARA had taken decorating to a whole new level the year before, a percentage of Carey Cove residents had been plotting to unseat her as Queen of Christmas. The result was the village being positively awash with elaborate light installations and ornaments of every style, size, and type, from old-fashioned to new wave.

'I didn't know the old village could look this good,' TJ said, as they stood in the foyer, taking off their outer wear, having just come home from a leisurely stroll down to The Dolphin for dinner. 'Nothing like a little competition to make things go completely over the top, is there?'

Nya laughed, as Theo replied, 'We almost had a fist-fight the other night, at the tree-lighting ceremony, between Keith Platt and Tony Wednesday, both of whom insisted his light display was best.'

'Silly men,' Gillian interjected. 'Anyone with eyes can tell that Kiara has them beat, hands down. Right?'

The last part was addressed to Hope, who nodded,

gazing up at Gillian as though the sun rose and set in the young woman.

Everything was almost perfect, Nya thought, as she headed to the kitchen to put on the kettle, while Theo and the young people moved into the living room. Life was exceptionally good.

It had been nine months since Hope had come to live with them in Carey Cove. Her mother, Willow, had tried her best, but ultimately felt the now one-year-old would be better off in permanent foster care.

But only if Nya and Theo would agree to take her.

'I want to go back to school,' Willow had told them, when they'd met to discuss the matter. 'And, to be honest, I just don't feel like I can manage her, you know? Will you take her?'

She hadn't had to ask them twice. Making Hope a permanent part of their family had felt so right.

'We'll be her surrogate grandparents,' Nya had told her. 'You'll always be her mum.'

'And always be a part of our family, too,' Theo had added, the sentiment bringing Willow to tears.

Gillian and TJ had come to visit not long after Hope had come back to Theo and Nya's, and Hope had taken one look at Gillian and decided she'd met her idol. She'd gone crazy with excitement when she'd seen Gillian arrive to spend Christmas, and the young woman had been so sweet to Hope. It made Nya happy to see them together.

And when Mum was in the mix, it was even more adorable, since both Hope and Gillian loved being with Iona.

'There you are,' Theo said, coming into the kitchen to wrap his arms around her waist and dip in for a kiss. 'You're taking a long time.'

She laughed. 'I've been in here for two minutes. You're awfully impatient.'

'Well, it seemed longer to me.'

Turning fully into his arms, Nya raised her mouth for another kiss, then said, 'Good thing I bought you a watch for Christmas.'

'Ha-ha. You're so funny.' Theo's watch collection was already too big. Then he lowered his voice to ask, 'Have you heard from Willow?'

That was, in Nya's opinion, the one fly in the Christmas ointment—Willow's absence. True to her stated aim, the teen had gone back to school, as well as working at a store in Newquay. She called often to ask how Hope was faring, and had visited a couple of times. When Nya had suggested she come and spend whatever time off she could get over the holidays, she'd said she would let them know. She'd seemed to have enjoyed the previous Christmas spent with them, and had forged a sweet bond with Mum too, but neither Nya nor Theo had heard from her since.

'Not yet,' she replied, trying to sound upbeat. 'Just because it's already Christmas Eve doesn't mean she might not turn up.'

Dropping a kiss on the top of her head, Theo agreed.

'You're right. And your mum should be here any moment.' Giving her waist another squeeze and then relaxing his arms, he continued, 'This is turning into an amazing Christmas. The entire family here, my lovely lady on my arm. I don't know how it could get any better. Except, maybe, if you'd agree to marry me.'

Nya searched his gaze, trying to sense his mood. Last Christmas he'd told her that, as much as he loved her, he didn't feel ready to get married again, and Nya hadn't cared. She knew he loved her, and she'd promised herself that she'd never push him for anything he didn't want to give.

'Are you sure, Theo? It's completely fine for us to be going along the way we are.'

Nya had sold her cottage and moved into Theo's, and she'd never been happier. She didn't need a ring to tell her they were made for each other.

'I am sure,' he replied. 'You and Hope are my Christmas miracles, and you would make me the proudest, and happiest, man if you'd agree to be my wife.'

And what could she say to that, except a resounding, 'Yes!'?

As he pulled her close again and kissed her once more, there was the sound of a commotion in the hall. Their lips parted, but as Mum's voice and Willow's, Hope's shrieks of joy and multiple cries of welcome echoed, Nya knew, without a doubt, they'd found all they could ever desire.

Comfort.

Joy.

Home.

Love.

* * * * *

SINGLE MUM'S MISTLETOE KISS

RACHEL DOVE

MILLS & BOON

In memory of Jean Wrigglesworth,
who loved life, and reading Mills & Boon.

Dearly missed and for ever loved by all.

Also for Oliver, my darling dog and writing buddy.

Run free on the rainbow bridge, my little love.

Max will look after you.

CHAPTER ONE

LORD, THESE CHAIRS are *surprisingly uncomfortable. I'll have to mention it to Nya when I'm back at work. Get the cushions restuffed or something.*

Marnie adjusted herself in the seat, smiling at the other visitors in the waiting room as she waited for her turn. It was weird to see the other side of the curtain, so to speak. It was health visitor day, and she was here as a patient. A new experience for her. She felt a little weird, used to being the one helping new mums.

It was a cold December day, one that she'd been looking forward to since having her baby. The last time she was here, she was giving birth. Her baby being delivered by the colleagues she loved and cherished in her own place of work. She loved the symmetry of it all. It gave her a real sense of belonging, and her previously wanderlust-filled heart was not only healing, but it was also full. She'd gone from broken-hearted single midwife, to becoming a mother in the community that she loved and lived in.

She'd come so far from that beach in Bali. From the girl laughing in the photos with Oliver, as the world's sights and landmarks provided the backdrop to their trip snaps. Living with a lie she didn't discover till it was painfully late. She'd returned home with sand in her suitcase and devastation in her heart. Carey Cove had been somewhere to retreat to. Somewhere to start a new life, one she'd never thought would be on the cards.

Now she was the rather tired hormonal mother, sitting with the other new mums and babies in the beautifully festive decorated waiting room, waiting for her six-week check with the other patients. Her back was aching, and the seat of the thinly cushioned chair was too rigid for her still recovering body. Violet snuffled in her arms, and she adjusted her to stop the arm cradling her going dead. Her newborn daughter settled straight back to sleep again, and, looking at her, Marnie was overwhelmed by a rush of love once more.

She often felt it. It slapped her right in the face sometimes. When she looked at her child and wondered how on earth she'd got so lucky. PCOS had been part of her working and professional life for years. She'd held many women, crying over their condition. What it meant for their fertility. For the children they wanted but couldn't have. She was one woman who didn't take her fertility for granted, ever. She'd been lucky, she knew. So lucky, and whenever she looked at Violet, she was reminded of that.

Yesterday she'd cried tears of pure joy because Violet had sneezed in a cute way. The day before that, it was seeing her tiny little outfits all freshly washed and drying on the radiator. She was besotted with her, utterly in love with the wondrous bundle in her arms. She still couldn't quite believe she was a mother. She'd always thought that it was something that would never happen to her, so every sneeze, every little snuffle—it was all just so joyful.

She'd given birth here, of course, so she had gone through every experience she could here. In the best place too. Her place. Hers and that of the women who ran the place. The men too, of course, but everyone knew who the real bosses were. Even St Isolde's, the hospital in Falmouth they worked with, knew how instrumental Carey House was in the care of the patients in the community and beyond. Theo was one of the main doctors there, and she knew that Carey House held a special place for him too. Everyone felt it, the minute that they walked through the doors.

She wondered how her replacement was getting on. She hadn't spotted any new midwives there so far, and the girls had been very quiet on the work front. They kept telling her to forget the place, and her patients. That all was in hand, and she should just enjoy the time with her child. Which she was doing, but she couldn't quite quell the curiosity about her replacement. They were in their second week now, she knew they'd be feeling pretty settled already. Carey House didn't have the need for many agency staff; once people came, they tended to stay. It spoke a lot for the place, she thought. Whoever was taking over her role, she knew that they'd enjoy their time there. It was hard not to.

Even now, the waiting room felt more like a cosy sitting room rather than the usual colder, clinical waiting areas health buildings usually defaulted to. Here, it was more like coming to a boutique hotel to have a baby. It was a unique place, and the staff who ran it worked tirelessly to keep it that way. It wasn't uncomfortable sitting here waiting, aside from the slightly lumpy chairs. She found she was enjoying being an observer for once. Violet was great, but with her cottage being the only occupied house on her lane, it was quiet. Violet couldn't exactly talk back yet. It was nice to be amongst the chatter of life once again.

The other mums were chatting amongst themselves. She heard the odd snatch of conversation. The whole place was festooned in Christmas decorations, which reminded her that she was normally trimmed up at home by now. She'd made a start, but, with Violet to care for, she was finding it a little harder to get her bigger jobs done. She had enough to do sanitising every surface in the house when she got a little restless or bored. Not that Violet was an annoyance. She couldn't stop looking at her daughter, marvelling at every little noise and facial expression. Babies were far from boring, but she was missing the routine. The laughs with her colleagues.

The twinkly lights from the tree nearby were making her feel cosy, and tired. Hopefully she'd be able to get a nap in that afternoon, while Violet slept. She could leave the rest of the decorations to another day. She'd made a start with adorning her fence with cane decorations, but some of her other pieces took a bit of putting together. It wasn't as if she had neighbours to compete with. It was just her and Violet on their little lane. She had no one to impress but her babe, and that was just the way she liked it. One of the women laughed across the room, and she found herself listening into their conversations.

'A whole six hours! Wow, I wish mine would sleep that well. I swear, I slept in front of the dryer the other night. The sound was the only thing keeping this little monkey from screaming the place down!'

'Don't talk to me about cracked nipples. With my second, I was about ready to punch the next person who called me Dolly Parton. I was in so much pain. What's the point of huge jugs when they feel like two hard rocks? I swear, I don't know how we conceived our third after that. I was done!'

A giggle of laughter rang out now and again. Women swopping horror stories. Marnie sat there, cradling Violet to her, enjoying every minute. Now she wasn't just a bystander to these stories. She didn't have to just nod and empathise any more! Now she had her own stories to share. Although she was feeling pretty smug at the moment. Things were good. Hardly any hormone swings at all. If she could get some decent sleep, life would be pretty perfect. Just as she'd hoped it would be, after Oliver, her no-good lying ex, after everything she went through to become a mother. She felt as if Violet was the prize, her future dream realised by her and her alone.

'These chairs are a bit hard, aren't they?' Another mother sitting next to her shuffled in her own seat. Her baby was sitting at her feet in his infant carrier, wearing a little blue outfit of dungarees and a giraffe T-shirt. He was fast asleep.

'I'm glad you said that. I thought it was just my

creaking back,' Marnie replied with a smile. 'I love his outfit.'

'Aw, thanks, it's his second change of clothes this morning, to be honest. We had a bit of an explosive-number-two incident this morning. I filled a washing machine load with everything he marked. It was up to his ears!'

The two women laughed together. 'I'm Vicky, by the way, and the poop machine is Benjamin.'

Marnie shook her hand, feeling the warmth from her fingers wrap around her own.

'Marnie, and this is my little Violet. Is he your first?' Marnie didn't recognise her, but she was on maternity leave from Carey House, the cottage hospital she was currently sitting in. She didn't deal with every mother who came through the doors. She felt a pang at missing work, but it soon passed when she looked at Violet again. She was in no rush to get back quite yet. Delivering babies was addictive, and it was nice to be back in the butter-coloured stone building that she loved, but she wasn't in that much of a rush for her maternity leave to be over. She wanted to enjoy every moment with her baby daughter before things got hectic. 'Violet's mine.'

'No, I've got a three-year-old too. Jaxen. They say you forget how tiring it is, your first. Feels like my first-born sometimes, when he's screaming at three a.m. It's amazing what you forget. Or block out!' Vicky laughed again, and Marnie nodded.

'Ah, well, it's all new to me still.' She didn't let on that she worked there as a midwife, had delivered hundreds of babies inside these very walls. 'It might just be the hormones, but I'm loving every minute.' Marnie knew it wasn't just the hormones, but she wasn't about to wax lyrical in the waiting room. Even at three a.m., when she was feeding her daughter and feeling as though she hadn't slept in a month, she knew it was worth it. Every little bit of her journey had given her the perfect little bundle in her arms, and she didn't take a second of it for granted. Or forget how long she'd longed for her. How much effort it had taken to get there on her journey to motherhood.

'Nothing like it, is there?' Vicky agreed, looking down at her son Benjamin who was awake now and busy trying to eat his little fist. 'I swear, I never thought I'd have another. You know, you get busy, money gets tight. He's worth it though.'

'I totally agree,' Marnie said, thinking about the months of IVF she'd gone through. She'd go through it again tomorrow to get to be sitting in this chair today. 'It's the best. Tiredness and poo incidents aside, of course.'

The two women got to chatting, and Marnie found that she was really enjoying herself. It was like being admitted to a club that she'd been denied access to before. She felt as if she'd been looking through the windows of parenting as a bystander for so long. Wondering whether she would ever get her chance, like millions of other women out there who found it so easy. Sometimes she couldn't believe she'd done it. She had arrived, and her baby had been delivered by her colleagues in this very place. Well, had she taken a longer walk, Violet

might have been born on the beautiful front lawn! It
had felt so right, as if she'd come full circle.

She was a member now, a fully-fledged mum. No
longer would she have to listen to anecdotes of sleepless nights and other parenting nuggets that she wasn't
a party to. She finally had the status that she'd longed
for and feared she'd never have. Mother. Vicky was telling her about the local nursery in the area that her son
went to, but she suddenly fell silent.

'Vicky?' she asked, wondering why she was staring
across the room doing a pretty good impression of a
goldfish out of water. 'Are you okay?' Benjamin passed
wind and even that didn't rouse Marnie's waiting-room
companion. Her lips moved, but nothing came out. Marnie looked around the waiting room. The mothers were
all aflutter in the room, she noticed now. She felt as if
the wintry temperature had risen by a few notches, felt
the tension change in the air. At her side, Vicky's elbow
jutted out, knocking Marnie's.

'What?' Another nudge, and Marnie turned to see
what she was looking at agape. Another new mum patient had just come back into the waiting room, and a
man was standing talking to her, his back to them. Marnie noticed his clothing and frowned. He was dressed
in the staff uniform. 'Who is that?' she half mumbled.
She took in his rear profile without meaning to. It was
hard not to; the man was like a side of beef. He was
easily six feet tall. She could tell from her sitting and
gawking position. Trust her to be on maternity leave
when they had a hot locum in.

A locum… *Oh, no.* Was this muscled Adonis her temporary replacement?

'Have you seen him before?' she asked Vicky from the side of her mouth.

Her replacement was supposed to be in situ already. Perhaps he wasn't hers. Or rather, her replacement. Marnie shook her head. Maybe the hormones had resurfaced a little bit. She was a teeny bit hot and bothered by the vision in front of her. She kept wondering what he looked like. The back of his head was pretty enough. Short dark brown hair atop a strong neck and a thick set of shoulders, leading down to a well-packed torso.

'No, and I don't know where they got him from,' Vicky breathed at the side of her. 'But they should get more like him. He's easy on the eye, isn't he?' She didn't whisper the last bit, and Marnie was sure that she saw the man's back stiffen. She could see the set in his shoulders rise somewhere around his earlobes. She blushed despite herself.

Caught ogling a man on her six-week check. She could just imagine what her colleagues would make of that.

She fanned her face with her free hand, trying to circulate the air back into her lungs. That was not what she was here for.

The mystery Adonis kept talking to the mother, giving her a pamphlet while the patient thanked him. Marnie focused back on Violet, trying to distance herself from the conversation. She never earwigged in waiting rooms, not on private conversations. She wasn't about to start now. Or here. She was here as a new mum, just like the others. Here for her six-week check, something she'd been looking forward to. Another club she was now a member of after waiting and wanting Violet so long. She was still on leave. It wasn't her concern, not yet.

Who was he, though? Had he come from an agency?

'See, you can't even speak. How come he works here? It's a bit of a waste, if you ask me. He should work in the fertility clinic.' Vicky was obviously not afraid to speak her mind. Or one to lower her voice. 'Cart *before* the horse, that way.'

God love the Cornish candour, Marnie thought to herself as she saw the man turn slightly in their direction. His ears were obviously burning. Quite obviously in fact. The tips of them were bright pink. She cleared her throat to stop the laughter that threatened to burble up as she looked away quickly. The man returned to seeing the woman and the baby she was holding out.

'I think he heard you.' She smiled at her rather funny seat-mate. 'I don't know who he is, I've never seen him before either.' She didn't bother divulging her bemusement and slight irritation about it either. Or the fact that she'd watched the way his shoulders had bunched the material of his uniform as he'd turned towards them. She found herself wishing she'd had the energy to put some make-up on that morning. She knew she didn't look her best. Sleep deprivation did that, despite all her planning.

Wait, what? It's just a man, Marnie! What do you care anyway?

'Well, I think you might be about to find out.' Vicky broke through her flip-flopping thoughts as the man turned and set his eyes in their direction. And his rather long legs. She was wondering to herself what shoe size he was when his feet stopped right in the middle of the room.

'Heads up, ladies!' Vicky stage-whispered as he approached. The ladies in the waiting room all collectively sat up, smoothing down errant locks and reaching for compacts from their changing bags. Marnie remained frozen in place. She wasn't about to preen for a man. Even a huge hunk in midwife's clothing. She couldn't have moved if she'd wanted to. He was looking straight at her, and she couldn't seem to break her gaze away. Hazel eyes demanded it, and she found that she couldn't look away from them.

Was this her replacement? Oh, her workmates were in trouble now. A heads-up would have been nice, ladies!

'Ladies, if I could just grab a second of your time.' He nodded to the health visitor who was busy weighing babies in the corner of the room. 'Sorry for the intrusion.'

She heard Vicky mutter something along the lines of 'you can grab what you like' beside her as she nodded, almost mute. The back of his head was unfortunately not his best feature, as she had previously pondered. The front of his head, well. Wow. The man was gorgeous, for want of a better word. Fit, for another. He was like a huge tree trunk standing in front of her. Momentarily an image of her as a squirrel popped into her head, but she shook it back out when he continued talking. She tried not to focus on the shade of hazel in his eyes. It reminded her of the trees in spring, the ones that grew around the place. The green and the brown flecks in his eyes making a colour all of their own. One she couldn't quite place.

'I'm Ash Ellerington, the new temporary midwife. You might have to bear with me a moment, ladies.' He raised his deep voice to address the room. 'It's my first day here at Carey Cove, but I'm a very quick study. I know my predecessor is already really missed, but I hope that I can help while I'm here.'

His smile was charming, and Marnie watched the women all fall under his spell. Further than they already had from mooning over his physique.

Well, he certainly has a way with women.

He turned back to her, bringing his smile with it. She looked away.

I don't think so. You're not winning me over.

'Replacing who?' she asked, already knowing the answer but still not wanting it to be true. He was late, anyway! First day today? What the heck? He was supposed to have started two weeks ago! She thought of her patients, of her colleagues sharing her workload while she looked after her new baby and got to grips with being a single mum. The thought irked her. Why wasn't he here two weeks ago? Why had they waited for him, and not just booked someone else? The man looked around the room, noticing the obvious interest in their conversation.

'One of the midwives, maternity leave,' he replied vaguely. And rather dismissively, Marnie thought to herself. She'd already made the decision to dislike him, it seemed. Did he not even know who he was replacing? The girls must have told him her name. She felt the pang of work stress down her spine and hated him for making her feel like this on such a good day. 'If you'll excuse me, ladies, I had better get on.' He half bowed at them, which made Vicky swoon at the side of her. Marnie kept her body rigidly straight, watching him turn and walk away.

He had better be doing a good job. First day indeed!

She watched him talk easily with a couple of mothers at the other side of the room, and she busied herself with her turn, her name being called to go and have herself and her baby checked. Soon she was focused back on her appointment and Violet. The six-week check was important, and Violet was hitting all her milestones. She didn't see the man again, and her appointment was over before she thought about him when it was time to leave.

She'd bundled them both up against the cold, and she was not long out of the doors of Carey House when she heard her colleague's voice from behind her.

'Marnie, glad I caught you! Have you got a minute?'

She turned to look at her friend Nya and was shocked to see Ash standing beside her. She felt her eyes narrow in his direction instinctively. As if she were observing a cuckoo in her nest.

'Hi, Nya! I would have said hi, but I know you guys are busy.' She looked Ash in the eye. 'First days tend to be busy.' Her dig went unnoticed by Nya, but she was satisfied to see Ash wince.

Nya had since closed the gap between them both and enveloped her in a huge hug. Violet protested from the car seat in Marnie's hands. Nya bent down to look closer at the little girl. 'Sorry, my little beauty! We just really miss your mummy here!' She reached out and smoothed her blankets a little against the cold before turning her hundred-watt smile back to Marnie. She sure was happy these days. Marnie was so happy for her friend, and Theo was such a great guy. It was easy to love the two of them together. 'I didn't want to keep you out in this December weather, but I did want you to meet Ash.'

Ash stepped forward then and grew about a foot. He seemed to stand straighter as he locked his eyes on hers again. She thought of her irritation that this man was taking over her job. Go figure. She was trying to live her life *without* a man, and now she had one covering for her career. Seeing her patients. Still, it was hardly his fault. He was here now, that was the main thing. She'd be back before she knew it, and he'd be gone. The last man in her life that she would ever need. She rather liked the sound of that. Another piece of the man-free plan to tick off.

Nya was still chattering away animatedly about the comings and goings; about the Christmas babies they were expecting to arrive. Ash cut through her voice and held out his hand.

'Hi, Marnie. I'm Ash, as you know.' He blushed. 'Nice to meet you. I hear I have a lot of midwife skills to match up to.' He raised a brow, and she smiled politely right back.

'Nice to meet you, Ash. I hope—'

Then she made a mistake. A rather big mistake that took her completely by surprise.

She shook his hand. Now, it could have been the fact that she was blindsided, seeing this man and realising he was filling her shoes. It could have been the fact that while she was loving being a new and proud single mum, she was also a woman. A hormonal one at that. She could have put it down to many things, but she knew what she felt. It was as though a bolt of lightning had shot through her body. The very second he closed his fingers around hers, it was as if they had welded to each other. She'd gone from feeling electrocuted by his touch, expecting them to be blown apart, to being a hundred per cent certain that they were stuck together for ever.

When she managed to remember where she was, she focused on his face. He looked as confused as she must look. His lips parted, and his tongue peeked out, moistening his dry mouth. She understood. Hers felt like the Sahara. She swallowed, realising that she'd stopped talking mid-sentence. Instead of replying like a competent professional woman, she openly gawked at him instead. Their hands were still stuck in the handshake between them. Marnie seemed to slightly recover first.

'Sorry, I was going to say welcome, and thank you. I know everyone will make you feel at home here—it's our thing,' she said in a rush, and that was when she managed to get her fingers to move. She broke the contact, and saw Nya shooting her an odd look.

What was wrong with her?

Loved-up Nya was so happy. She hoped Nya didn't

get any ideas. She wasn't about to be subject to some maternity-leave cupid caper. He could cover her job, sure. That was as far as she was willing to go with another man ever again.

Ash didn't bear witness to the women's little exchange. He'd already tilted his head to look at Violet. Marnie watched him grin at her daughter, and then the little madam grinned right back.

She smiled! At him! Have I taught you nothing, Padawan?

She would have to be having words with her progeny. 'Smiling already, eh? Clever girl!'

He pulled a funny face at Violet, and Marnie watched as her daughter showed her cover man a gummy smile. A full, beaming grin of pure happiness to see him. It was as if ruddy Santa Claus himself had peeped his head in to say hello. It made Marnie's heart clench.

Yeah, post-partum hormones and Christmas don't mix. I'm one Hallmark movie away from being a total festive softie. I've been waiting for her to smile, and she gives it up to him? I hope it was just wind.

She knew better, but even the midwife in her was willing to go along with the self-told lie.

You're smiling away at our enemy, little one.

She had expected her daughter to have her back, but obviously she was a sucker for a handsome face. Not that he was handsome, per se. Well, he was, if you went for the whole tall, dark and handsome package. Which she didn't.

She wrapped her coat around her a little tighter as the wind picked up around them. The summers here in

Carey Cove were amazing, and the winters beautiful, but cold. Ash gave her a look of concern, but she ignored him. She didn't need his help.

'I'd better get her in the car.' She held the car seat a little closer to her body. 'Nice to meet you. Nya, call me.'

'You too.' He took a step back from Violet and her. 'It was lovely to meet you both.' He nodded to Violet. 'I'll let you get warmed up.' Still feeling frazzled from the excitement of her morning, and freezing rapidly, she looked at Violet. She was still looking at Ash, bundled up. It looked as if Marnie wasn't the only Richards girl to try to size him up. Violet was staring at him so hard her eyes were almost crossed.

'Thanks.' She smiled at him while avoiding those hazel eyes and nodded to Nya. 'I'll see you soon, Ash.'

The two of them said their goodbyes, and Marnie headed off. When she was out of sight, she stopped and looked at the palm that had touched Ash. She could still feel a tingle on her skin that she knew was nothing to do with the Cornish winter.

She was still thinking about him when she got home. The jolt she'd felt when she'd shaken his hand was still affecting her now.

What the heck was that?

She'd had quite a crush on a few people when she was pregnant. Idris Elba in…well, anything, for example. She'd watched *The Avengers* on repeat. She understood that behaviour. She was a midwife, she knew all the stories, all the tales of weird cravings and urges. Crushes on celebrities while they were growing a human. But now? She was done with men. Ash felt like a fence post blocking her new man-free life. One where she delivered the next generation of babies and raised her daughter. All on her own. Just the two Richards women. They were going to be the Gilmore Girls, sans the cute and rather surly café owner. That was what Ash was. He was a café owner in the plot of her life. An unnecessary character that she knew belonged on the cutting-room floor.

Lightning bolts? Pah.

She didn't need it. Or want it. Plus, he was leaving anyway. He was a temp, filling in for her. She reminded herself of her earlier resolve. She was never going to be at the whim of a man, ever again. She'd had her baby without a man at her side. IVF had enabled her to finally follow her heart and fulfil her dream of becoming a mother. If she could do all of that single, then she wasn't about to change it.

Not that he was even interested, of course. She'd seen the odd look he'd given her after her handshake. Violet liked him, but she was a fickle baby. Her mother had plenty of time to teach her beloved child that a woman could do anything she wanted. With or without a smiling man with lightning-bolt handshakes. Ash would be gone soon, and she'd be back at work. Job done.

CHAPTER TWO

'MARCH MADNESS,' I tell you. All these babies, it's the product of the March madness.'

Sophie fast-walked down the corridor, a delivery kit in her arms. 'Ash, you are in for a hell of a first day! Shout if you need anything!'

She rushed into one of the delivery rooms, the shouts of pain from the labouring woman inside escaping till the doors swished closed once more. Ash was left alone on the corridor. The six-week check clinic was done for the day, and he was now due to deliver his first Carey House baby.

'Good afternoon!' he said jovially as he entered the delivery suite. 'Mr and Mrs Evanshaw?'

The patient, a pretty young woman called Hayley, was sitting on the hospital bed, her legs flat in front of her. The monitor was strapped to her bump, monitoring the baby. Ash walked over to the printout, checking everything was fine with mum and baby. Mr Evanshaw was hovering by the far side of the bed, looking very worried. He was ashen-faced.

'Hi, Hayley, please. This is Tom.'

'Hi, Tom.' Ash held out his hand, and noticed how the expectant dad's hands shook. He'd already read her case notes. Mum was forty weeks plus five days, and more than ready to meet her first child with her new husband. Hayley was fine, relaxed even, but Ash could feel the tension coming off the father in waves. 'So, first baby today, eh, Dad?'

Tom grimaced rather than smiled back, and Ash patted him on the shoulder. 'Don't worry. I'm Ash Ellerington. I will be your midwife today. I'll be back to check on you both soon.'

He made the rest of his checks. Hayley was five centimetres dilated and progressing well. Baby was fine. A textbook pregnancy, it seemed. First babies were often late. He had a nice easy afternoon ahead of him.

He headed to the nurses' station. Nya was working on the computer. She stopped the second he approached and gave him a grin.

'Hi, Ash, how's it been? Your first patient going to plan?' She nodded her head towards the delivery suite he'd just exited.

'Smooth sailing so far. I just came to get my rota.'

Nya nodded in recognition. 'Oh, yes, I'll get one printed off for you.' She lowered her brows inquisitively. 'You didn't put down any days off you needed. Do you want to let me know?'

She was so nice, but wrong. She was assuming he had a life outside this place. He shook his head, plastering a jovial face over his features that belied how he felt.

'Er…no, I'm good. I don't have anywhere to be particularly.'

He didn't have a home either, really. The rental place he was staying at was nice, but one of a dozen places he'd stayed in over the last few months. He never stayed in one place for too long. It was how he liked it.

'At Christmas?' Nya sounded incredulous at the thought. 'Well, you won't be bored here.' She shot him a mischievous look. 'Things happen round here, especially in winter.'

Ash had no idea what she meant, but her smile brought out his own.

'Really?' Hayley's room buzzed, and his head instinctively turned towards the sound. 'Well, I'd better watch out for that.' He headed back to the room. Whatever magic this place held, he doubted any of it would rub off on his short stay. He was here to work and move on. Work, sleep, move, repeat. He had no time for magic. He knocked on the delivery-room door, and headed in. You would never tell by the smile on his face, his easy manner, that he was a man in pain. He liked it that way.

'Something's wrong,' Hayley moaned, her head slick with sweat. Tom was trying to mop her brow with a cold flannel. It just agitated her more in her discomfort.

'Tom, knock it off.' Ash was gowned and gloved,

checking the baby's position. The baby's head was crowning, but Hayley was getting tired. The baby's stats were starting to change, and not for the better.

'Ash, what's wrong? Ash?' Tom was getting anxious, on top of his already jangled nerves. Ash needed to keep the situation calm, not scare Hayley. On top of that he had to soothe Tom, who was a neurotic mess. Things could escalate quickly in these delivery rooms. He thought back to the one he'd been in. How that had ended. It made him all the more determined to keep the parents calm and deliver their baby safely.

'Okay, Hayley,' he started, getting her attention while motioning for Tom to take her hand. 'Tom, I need you to stay calm. You're getting tired, and we need to get this baby out safely. The monitor is displaying signs of distress.'

'Distress?' Tom echoed, his voice a high squeak of panic. 'What do you mean? We don't even know what we're having, and now we have distress? Hayley, are you okay?'

Hayley had started to cry. Her contraction wasn't far behind her tears. Ash took charge of the situation.

'Tom, Hayley, look at me.' Both parents turned towards him, their fearful eyes wide. 'Hayley, on the next contraction, when you get the urge to push, I want you to push. If I say stop, I need you to stop. Okay?'

Hayley nodded, lifting her head up a little as though she were preparing to go into battle. 'Okay.' She gripped Tom's hand tight. Tom was so pale he was transparent, his eyes bulging with terror.

'Tom,' Ash prompted, 'it's going to be fine. You're going to meet your baby any minute.'

That brought him back. He started to smile, nodding, and he reached for his wife's other hand. When the contraction took hold, Ash moved into action.

'Push, Hayley!' Tom said, his face streaked with tears now. 'Push, baby!'

Hayley's face went puce as she bore down, grunting with the pain. The head was coming. Ash helped her to deliver the rest of the little baby's face. 'Pant, Hayley!' he urged. 'Well done, I can see his head.' That wasn't all he could see. The reason for the slowing stats was wound around the baby's neck. Tom went to move closer to take a look. Ash saw his face as he took the umbilical cord in. He looked to Ash, and Ash shook his head at him. His expression telling him not to tell Hayley. 'Your baby is beautiful!' he said to Hayley, moving swiftly to pull the cord from around the baby.

'Is it—?' Tom began to ask.

'Perfect.' He cut him off with a smile. The cord was removed, and Ash could see on the monitor that the baby's stats were already climbing. 'On the next contraction, we're going to push some more. You tell me when you're ready, Hayley.'

Tom lost his squeamishness after that. He gripped Hayley's hand tight, one hand around her thigh as she pushed their baby into the world. Ash handed him to one of the nurses. He wanted the little one to be triple-checked. Put both his and the parents' minds at rest. It was a complication, it happened. He knew. But the baby was shouting, its annoyance clear at being removed from such a comfy home. It was fine. Healthy lungs. Glowing pink in colour. Shivering from the ordeal of being born, and opening eyes to see things for the first time.

Tiny fingers and ten toes. A little clump of hair on top of his head. He had a look of Tom, Ash thought. He held the little boy for a second, taking him in before putting him straight onto Hayley's chest. The little man let out a lusty cry, and when he locked eyes with his mother, he stopped. Decided to take to gazing at her instead. Tom had his arms around both of them, whispering barely coherent words of love and joy to the family he'd just helped create.

Ash administered the drugs to deliver her placenta. The nurses were cleaning up, Sophie brought in tea and toast for the mother. Ash worked methodically, completing the paperwork, and the checks. Making sure everything and everyone was taken care of.

He didn't try to listen to Tom, but he couldn't escape them. 'I love you both so much. Hayley, look at him. You did it.' The baby let out another cry, and the pair of them broke into sobs of teary laughter. 'We're a family. Finally.'

Tom was cradling both of them to him, he and Hayley openly crying and smiling as they looked at their baby.

'Congratulations,' Ash told them both, looking at the bundle of soft blanketed perfection in their arms and feeling a pang in his heart that almost knocked him off his feet. 'You have a lovely little boy.'

'A boy!' Hayley beamed. 'Tom, you got your son!'

Ash could tell from the look on Tom's face that he didn't even care. He could have become the father of a bright yellow alien, and he'd have still had the same ridiculous, goofy expression on his face. Tom was just grateful that they were both here, and okay. That was why he held them so tight. They were his world. Tom kissed Hayley, crying again. 'I was so scared, Hayley. I felt helpless then.' He looked across at Ash, pulling himself together a little. 'Thank you, Ash, really.'

Ash waved him off. 'Hayley did the hard work. Congratulations again, the nurses will be in soon to check on you but if you need anything, just press the call button.'

He was just outside the door, collecting his thoughts before getting back to work, when Tom came out to find him. He held his hand out to Ash. Ash went to shake it, but Tom pulled him in for a hug.

'Thank you. I panicked, seeing that cord around his neck. You never even told her.'

He pulled back, and Ash gave his back a pat.

'No point in worrying her when she was already busy,' he said, deflecting the seriousness of the situation. Cords got wrapped around babies quite often, it wasn't as though he'd not seen it before. It was just weird that his first delivery had sparked so many memories of his own. 'She did really well. You have yourself a beautiful family there, Tom.'

It almost broke him to say it, but he meant the words that wounded him on the way out of his mouth. He always meant them. He cherished life. That was part of the problem, he guessed.

'Thanks,' Tom gushed. 'He's amazing. We're calling him Noel, after the season.'

Ash laughed. 'Perfect name for a Christmas baby. I like it.'

Tom nodded. 'Hayley picked Ashley, for his middle name.' Ash didn't know what to say. It hadn't happened before, in any of the places he'd delivered babies. A little boy in Carey Cove was going to have his name. 'I told her, what you did. We both really want to give him your name, if you're okay with it.'

Ash nodded, swallowing his emotion down before trusting his voice not to let him down like a hormonal teenage boy.

'Tom, I'd be honoured. Thank you.'

Later on, when they were coming off shift, Sophie pushed a photo under his nose.

'Here you go. Your first baby for the wall.'

It was a photo of Noel, dressed in a Christmas outfit with Christmas-pudding-themed mittens on his little hands.

'Wow, thanks.'

Sophie beamed at him. 'He's a little cracker, isn't he?' She passed him a pen, putting her bag over her shoulder and fastening her coat. 'Don't forget to put the details on the back. Night, Ash.'

'Night, thanks again,' he said, watching the other staff leave while the cleaners hoovered around them. A radio was playing somewhere in the background, Christmas songs playing on a loop of modern and clas-

sics. The Pogues started up as he unlidded the pen. He
wrote the date, followed by the baby's name.

Noel Ashley Evanshaw
7lb 14oz
Delivered by Ash Ellerington.

He pushed back from the desk, getting up from the
chair and pinning the photo to the board. A sea of babies
looked back at him. He took in the faces of the families. All so different from each other. Siblings cradling
their newborn siblings. Women giving birth with their
mothers and partners supporting them, witnessing their
family expanding first-hand.

Ash's eyes stopped on a photograph. Marnie. Her
birth photo was up here too. He looked around, but no
one was watching him. Taking the pin out, he looked at
the photo closer. No man or mother in the room, by her
side. On the photo, Marnie was grinning from her hospital bed, her colleagues around her bedside. He turned
it over. Violet's date of birth was on there, just a few
short weeks ago. Her birth weight, and her name. Under
that, someone had written 'Marnie's miracle baby', surrounded by a love heart.

He didn't recognise the writing from any of the paperwork he'd seen before. He wondered whether Marnie had written it herself. He ran his finger along the
elegant scrawl, and then carefully put the photo back in
place on the board. It was near the photo of Noel and his
parents. Ash moved the photo till it was a little closer
to Marnie's. He didn't really know why. Maybe it was

just that he felt as if he were working for her. Marnie would have delivered Noel, after all, had she not been on leave. Noel belonged to her too, he figured. That was why they were better together amongst the sea of happy faces.

It was coming to the end of his shift, and he was moving photos on a board. It truly was the weirdest first day he'd had in a while. That was without thinking about the thunderbolts he'd felt when he'd shaken her hand. A truly weird first day. Ash had loved it.

CHAPTER THREE

Ash signed his name with a flourish, a stack of paper-work to get through. He did a double take as he noticed the pen hadn't inked the page. Tutting, he threw the pen into the wastepaper bin at the side of the neat, colour-ful desk. He glanced back up at the photo collage on the wall, interspersed with thank you cards and little messages of gratitude.

Reaching across the neat and organised desk, he took a pen out of the pen pot and got back to work. He'd al-ready started late, he didn't want to leave things unfin-ished on his first day. Carey Cove ran like a well-oiled machine, and he could tell the staff there were com-mitted. He didn't want to show them anything less. As he filed the papers away, his eyes fell on the photo of Marnie again. Ash loved that she'd added her own birth photo to her wall, but he found it hard to look at just the same.

Babies were always the best part of Ash's job. He loved it. Bringing new life into the world, seeing peo-ple creating new families. Observing them adding to that family over time. Distracting nervous dads with talk of the sports results. Seeing the love and adoration, helping them to quell their fear and enjoy the moment when another person joined the population. Every new baby he delivered had him thinking of what his might be like, one day. How it would feel to be an expectant father in the room himself. Giving control over to the team of professionals, supporting his wife as they joined the parent ranks. He'd imagined it so many times. He couldn't wait. To be a dad, to be at the other end of the delivery room bed for once, waiting for *his* child.

He'd imagined everything.

Almost. He'd been stupid, he knew now. Gullible even. Naïve. He knew more than most expectant fathers. He'd seen it before first-hand. He knew the risks, the cruel twists of medical fate that could and did occur. It was life, and with that came death. It was part of the job. He'd known that. Or he'd thought he did.

Till the day he ended up leaving hospital, much later. A lifetime later. Alone. Then he knew he didn't have to imagine any more. The worst had already happened. His family hadn't started in that room. It had died. Despite his training and experience there had been nothing he could do to help. He couldn't save them. There would be no car seat, no slow drive home with their precious cargo in the back seat. He'd left tear-stained and broken.

His sisters had picked him up off the floor of his living room. Literally and metaphorically. They'd fed him, bathed him, nagged him to drink less coffee and more water. To remember to eat, to sleep. They'd cleaned his house, they'd cleaned him. Ash had barely noticed. He hadn't wanted to do any of those things for a long time.

All he'd wanted was the family he'd created. The one that was gone for ever, before he'd even had a chance to enjoy it. He'd just wanted to be with them, in the early days. He'd missed them too much to function for himself.

When he finally had started to emerge from the cloud of grief, he'd known he'd had to leave. He'd had to change his scenery, to get away from the place that held so many memories of the life he'd loved but had lost for ever. His sisters had their own lives: families, friends, jobs. He loved them dearly, but he'd needed to move on. Somehow.

Babies always gave him joy, that never left him. He was grateful for that if nothing else. Grateful for the time they'd had together. He knew more than anyone how precious the moments were. So he'd gone back to his work, back into the delivery rooms filled with pain and joy and life. He'd put his own pain aside and gone back to fulfilling other families' dreams.

Ash pulled up to his new temporary home, turning off the engine with a deep sigh. He was bone tired, the quiet of the lane he now called home soothing. It was beautiful here in Carey Cove. From the moment he'd arrived he'd really liked the feel of the close-knit beauty spot. He'd felt the same when he'd walked through the doors of Carey House. It was a good place for him to be for now. A nice little place to retreat to for a while.

The staff seemed nice too, a welcoming, friendly bunch. Tight-knit without any cliques. Everyone who walked through the doors was treated with the same smile, respect and care. The midwives ran a tight ship, but his first day had been smooth. Given that he was two weeks late to the post, their reception had been both a relief and a revelation. He rather liked it there.

He'd gone through the day-to-day running of the house details with Nya, and he felt better about his second day. He had his shift rota, and now he was ready to settle into his new temporary home and looking forward to getting to know Carey Cove and its inhabitants.

Thinking about the people he'd encountered on his first day, he found Marnie popped back into his thoughts again. He looked down at his hand as he reached the front door, keys in his other hand. When they'd touched, he'd felt something intense. A zap in his fingertips running right up his arm. He'd just stood there in shock. Like a prize fish on a plaque. Glassy-eyed and open-mouthed. She'd looked at him in confusion.

Probably wondering why I'd lost the power to control my face the second she took my hand.

She was no doubt at home now, talking to her husband about the total idiot who'd come to cover her mat leave. A woman like that would have someone to come home to.

He rubbed his tired eyes as he let himself into the cottage. The house he was staying in was so beautiful, even in the moonlight it looked inviting. Even though the windows of the place were all without light. He certainly wasn't expecting anyone to be at home waiting for him. The thought slammed him deep in his gut. Sometimes, in some places he worked in, it made it worse. Here, he felt oddly comforted by his new digs.

His cottage was at the end of a lane, with only one other house next to his. Perfect. The night was full of the sounds of the Cornish weather around him, but nothing else. No people. Not even a dog barking. It felt oddly welcoming. Calming. Less eerie feeling than the place he'd just left. He pushed the thought away.

It felt as if a whole lifetime had passed since he'd turned up to his first shift that morning. As ever, he searched for the positives in his day, to push the dark, lonely thoughts away. Carey Cove was a definite plus point. The minute he'd arrived, he'd felt it. The magic of the place had soothed his tired bones. His first day at work had been great too.

Marnie's hand. Wow. Where did that come from?

The minute they'd touched, it had felt as if his soul had been lit up from the inside. For half a second, when he'd locked surprised eyes with hers, he'd thought he saw a flicker of something cross her features too. Her lips had parted, her mouth falling open before she'd pulled herself back tight together before him.

Did I really see that?

He felt sure that she must have felt it too. He remembered looking down at the floor to check for scorch marks. It felt as if lightning had struck right by their feet. Madness, he knew. She was a colleague, for a start, he was the person covering her duties while she was tending to her new baby daughter. Violet, he remembered. She looked just like her mother. He'd seen it as soon as he'd set eyes on them. There was no way she would be single. She had to have a man at home, keeping the lights burning.

He turned to look at his neighbours' cottage. It was a carbon copy of his, but a better, finished version. He found himself drawn to the warm light spilling from the windows, the interior looking neat and homely. Christmas lights hung from the roof, twinkling and lighting up the neat painted wooden window frames. The house was well kept, and that extended to the garden. Oversized candy canes on red ribbons adorned the bushes at the side of the neat lawn, and there was a dusting of snow on the inside of the windows. It looked like a festive picture postcard, and made his pad look unlived-in and pretty unloved. Like he felt. At least it was pretty. Misery loved comfort, and he shrugged as he entered the front door, closing it behind him with a deep, tired sigh.

He switched on the lights, his half-closed eyes taking in his surroundings. The living room looked comfortable. On one wall there was a swept fireplace, an armchair placed perfectly in front. He could already see himself after a long shift of delivering babies, warming his feet by the fire. He looked around the hearth and saw that there was a wicker log basket containing two logs.

Shopping trip tomorrow. Food supplies, wood. Get stocked up before the festive baby rush really gets going.

He ignored his slightly empty stomach as he worked to get the fire started with the last of the logs.

Once the fire started to lick around the logs, he sat down in the armchair, his socked feet hanging over the end as he reclined back. He needed to get showered, drag himself to bed, but he found he couldn't muster the effort to walk up the stairs. He'd warm his feet first.

As always when he was settling into a new posting his thoughts invariably turned again to his lost family. His late wife, Chloe, their infant son, Sam. It had been several years since their passing, but the pain of their loss was lodged firmly in his heart. Less intense now, more of a dull ache, but always there, serving as a reminder to keep his heart guarded and giving him a reason to carry on with his nomadic lifestyle. And while he moved on, from place to place, he took comfort in knowing that, wherever they were, Chloe and Sam were together.

The fire crackled around him, the cosy feeling of the room amplifying as the warmth from the flames thawed out his overtired and rather cold feet. The silence of the room filled his ears, the occasional pop from the wood on the fire like a lullaby. He could just rest his eyes for a second…

Bang! Bang! Bang! Bang!

'Wha—?'

Ash's head snapped up from the back of his armchair. His neck cricked in protest as he wrestled his way out of the chair. The fire had burned down, the embers still glowing red hot in the darkness of the room.

Bang! Bang!

There it went again. He managed to put his feet onto the floor, tripping over the rug in the middle of the room he hadn't even noticed when he'd walked in. He got to the door just in time to stop the next bout of hard knocks.

'Hello?'

Ash saw the hat before he took in the officer's face.

'Good evening. Could you step outside for a moment, please? We've had reports of a disturbance.'

'Disturbance?' Ash stepped out of the front door, past the police officer who had knocked him out of his slumber. 'Where? There are just the two houses, right?' When he looked across at the house he'd admired earlier, Ash was sure that he saw a twitch in one of the upstairs bedroom windows. A second later, he saw the light go off.

What was going on?

The officer was eyeing him, from his ruffled bed-head hair, his crumpled clothing, to his socked feet. 'We got a call that someone had entered the property here without permission. Are you staying here?'

Ash rubbed his hand through his hair, hopping from one foot to the other to ward off the bite of the cold weather.

'Er…yes, my first night—rental. I'm working at Carey House, as a locum midwife.'

The officer raised his brows. 'Carey House, you say?' Ash saw his gaze flick across to the other house, before looking beyond Ash to the open cottage door. 'Okay, do you have identification?'

Marnie hid behind the curtain when the man standing with the officer looked up at her window. Lunging for the switch for her bedside light, she flicked it off and hid.

So there was someone there. How scary.

She'd been up feeding Violet when she'd seen lights

on next door. The knowledge it was supposed to be empty had had her reaching for her phone. Violet had fallen asleep in her arms and was safely snuggled in her cot. She went to peep out of the window again and she saw the mystery man handing over some pieces of white paper to the officer, who shone a torch on the documents, nodding his head.

George! What are you doing?

Surely Carey Cove's favourite officer wasn't about to leave the man there. George said something to the man, shuffling one foot awkwardly, before handing the papers back and holding out his other hand. The man stepped forward, away from the cottage, and the torch shone onto his features.

Oh, Lord, no.

Marnie squeaked loudly, embarrassment and realisation making her body jolt. Violet let out a solitary cry of shock and then fell back to sleep. The two men shook hands, and George turned away to his police car. She'd have to apologise to him later for wasting his time and dragging him out in the night for nothing. She held her breath as she watched Ash shake his head in bewilderment, turn and walk back into the cottage, and close the door.

He'd looked ruffled in more ways than one. As if he'd just been woken up. She blushed at the thought of her mistaken actions. The midwife covering her job was now living next door, and she'd just called the police on him! She'd had no idea he'd be staying nearby. Seemingly alone too. No other lights had come on in the house, and no one else had come out of the door.

Was he here alone? Would he be alone at Christmas, or would someone come to join him?

She shook off the thought. It wasn't her business. People had their own ways to live their lives. She knew that more than most. She'd recovered from a break-up, and her dreams had disappeared in front of her eyes. She hadn't been able to see past Oliver and his betrayal for the longest time, but when she had decided her next move, she'd gone with it with her whole heart. She hadn't stopped to think what people might say. The closest people to her were who mattered, and they were all supportive. Just as they knew she'd not made the decision lightly. They believed in her, and now she was living that dream, and Ash *was* here to cover for her. She didn't want him to feel unwelcome. That was not her, or anyone at Carey House. She didn't want to leave a bad impression of herself. It was an honest mistake.

Violet stirred again, and Marnie knew she would be up again soon. She'd fallen back asleep before getting her fill. Marnie rolled her tired eyes and moved away from the window to throw some clothes on. Once she was dressed, she went to scoop up her daughter. One sleep-mitten-clad hand was covering her face, making her look so cute Marnie had to remind herself that this little bundle was here, and hers. She smiled and lifted her daughter into her arms.

Heading to the kitchen, she reached for the baby carrier from one of the cupboards and popped Violet into it, pulling her coat over her to wrap them both up against the cold. It was a good job she'd been to the village bakery that day. She reached for the box of handmade mince pies from the polished countertop, tucking them into the nook of her arm before heading out to make things right. Hopefully she could get some sleep then.

Since Violet was born, sleep had been in short supply. Even a nap felt like a spa weekend. The last thing she wanted was to have an upset neighbour. She remembered the way her hand had felt in his, marvelling at the feeling of familiarity and excitement it produced every time in her gut. She flicked a lock of blonde hair away from her eyes and knocked softly on the door. She didn't want to run the risk of waking him up again.

Ash's smile was the second thing she saw when he opened the door. The first was how good he looked. Unkempt, tired, but naturally handsome. It made her stomach flip, and her lips break out into a smile that matched his.

'Hi,' he said softly. He looked down at the baby carrier with a frown. 'Everything okay?'

'No, actually. I came to warn you about a crazy neighbour who calls the police on innocent people.'

His laugh was unfiltered, and amazing to hear. She laughed with him, her cheeks blushing with her embarrassment. And his friendly reaction.

'Ah, thanks. I'll keep an eye out for her.'

'I came to apologise properly; I had no idea that Mrs Quentin had rented the cottage out.' She looked down at the box in her hands. 'I thought you were a burglar.'

'Only on the weekends.' He smiled. 'You have no need to be sorry. It was an honest mix-up.' He frowned as he saw her shiver. 'You needn't have come out into the cold, especially with the little one.'

'I didn't want to leave…it. I wouldn't have slept.'

Ash surveyed her face, his brows knitted together pensively.

'Well, thank you. Please, come in?' She hesitated a second, the box still in one hand. He narrowed his eyes. 'It's really cold out.'

She stepped inside the door, Ash moving aside and closing it behind them.

'I'm sorry,' he said ruefully. 'I haven't had a chance to get any wood for the fire yet. Come through.'

Marnie followed him through to the sitting room. The fire was burning low in the grate, but the room was warm and neat. The recliner of the armchair was down.

Was he sleeping in the chair when George arrived?

She felt her cheeks redden.

'Sit down, please. Would you like a hot drink?' His face paled, but she was too focused on the offer of caffeine to notice.

'Oh, no, thanks. I can't stay. I just wanted to make amends. Here.'

She offered him the box of mince pies as he offered her a seat with a flick of his wrist. They both laughed. He took the box, his fingers touching hers for a split second. *Bang!* There it was again. The jolt. Ash licked his suddenly dry-looking lips and motioned behind her to the sofa.

He pushed the armchair back into its sitting position but didn't sit till she was installed on the sofa with Violet in her carrier. He opened the bakery box, and she saw his eyes light up.

'The best mince pies bar none.' She grinned. 'The bakery round here is amazing.'

He lifted one to his lips and made short work of it. 'Mmm… Wow.' He swallowed the rest of the tasty morsel, reaching for another after a pause. 'Thank you for these. You really didn't have to, though. I'm sorry if I scared you.'

'I was up feeding Violet anyway.' She rebuffed his apologies. He was being so nice about it all. He must have had a long day too, given his current look. 'I don't sleep much these days, thanks to little madam here.' She noticed he had lifted a third mince pie to his mouth, and she realised he was starving. 'Listen, the local bakery delivers.'

His eyes met hers, and she was once more looking at the hazel hue of his irises.

'It's really handy when you're on shift. The supermarket delivers up here too. I don't mind taking in any parcels you get. I'm around most days at the minute.'

'That's really kind of you.'

'I'm like that with every burglar I meet,' she quipped, making them both giggle. 'It's no trouble, honestly. It gets pretty busy at Carey House.'

'I got that idea. I like it there though; I get a good feeling about the place. Nya's lovely.'

Marnie's white teeth flashed. 'Yeah, she's the best. She's a good friend.' She patted Violet's back softly in the carrier. 'She supported me when Violet was born too, so we have a bit of a bond.'

'That must have been lovely to share.'

'Yes, it was all a bit of a rush. I'd imagined going

into labour a lot, what with our experience, but yeah. I was definitely taken by surprise.' She noticed Ash was looking at her intently. 'She was safe though. That's all I wanted.' She saw his shoulders relax visibly. He was a heart-on-a-sleeve guy, she realised. It was nice. He'd fit in well with the others. She felt proud that he was covering her role in that moment. He was definitely an improvement on the neighbour front. Not that the stakes were high, given that she'd thought he was some light-fingered shadow in the Cornish night.

'Must have been a worry for you all.'

'Well, yeah, but Nya and the team had my back.'

'Does your partner work in medicine?'

It was a lame question, but she kept saying I. No mention of a 'we'. He was curious about the answer.

'No.' She shook her head. 'It's just me and Vi.' Her green eyes flashed with something when she spoke. Ash lowered his eyes.

'I'm sorry to hear that.'

Marnie's smile widened. 'Don't be. I chose to have Violet on my own.' When Ash's brows furrowed in question, she waited for him to quiz her on where the father of her baby was. He didn't. What he said next shocked her.

'Well.' He was smiling now, the last mince pie sitting in the open box. He offered it to her, but she declined with a shake of her head. He looked as if he needed a good meal. She hoped he'd take her up on the offer of taking his deliveries in. It would be quite nice to have someone in the house next door. Tonight had rattled her a little. It felt different now she had Violet to care for too. She felt a little more vulnerable. 'I think that's amazing. How's it been going?'

He sat back in his seat, as if he was getting more comfortable to hear her story.

Wow, he really cares. He's such a nice guy. Oh, enough, Marnie. Surely it'll take more than a pair of eyes and a gorgeous smile to make you even contemplate going near another man.

She focused on the question, willing her cheeks not to burn. He was still looking at her, intent on her features. It made her oddly nervous. She wasn't used to the feeling. It wasn't entirely unwelcome, but what did it matter anyway? She might as well just enjoy the chat with an attractive man. Attractive with a capital A.

'Good.' He lowered his brow, and she caved immediately. 'She's amazing. I love being a mum. It's mostly great, but it is tiring.'

His face dropped. 'I'm keeping you up too.'

Marnie waved him away, getting to her feet. 'No, it's fine. I spoiled your evening. Don't forget about the deliveries, okay?'

'Yeah, thanks. If you're sure.'

Marnie walked towards the front door, Ash close behind.

'Of course, that's what neighbours are for.' She turned towards him as he leaned in to open the door for her, and she felt it again. That jolt. There was no mistaking it this time, or his sharp intake of breath. The one that matched hers. Her head had snapped around to face his, and his hazel eyes, so entrancing. As soon as she looked at him, she knew he'd felt it too. She'd

known it the first time but had talked herself out of that
way of thinking pretty quickly.

'Sorry,' he breathed.

'It's okay.' She was flustered. 'These hallways are
pretty snug.' They both laughed, and the moment of tension fizzled away. 'Night, Ash.' She slipped out into the
night, and he walked out to watch her get back home
safely.

'Hey, I like your decorations.'

Marnie rolled her eyes. 'I made a start, but I normally
do a lot more. I love Christmas, and it's Violet's first
one. I still need to make the Cornish tree.'

'Oh, yeah? That sounds nice.'

She smiled at him. It was there again. That full,
toothy smile of happiness she had.

She waggled her fingers at him when her key was in
the lock, and she was gone. He found himself still staring till the upstairs bedroom light came on.

Sitting back on the couch, he looked at the empty box
and thought about the night's events. He'd gone from
being a suspected burglar to a neighbour she wanted
to help. She'd fed him. He hadn't even thought about
how hungry he was. And sitting with Marnie had been
nice. She'd looked tired—maybe he could be a bit of a
neighbour to her too. Being a new mum wasn't easy,
he knew that much. Her being a mother on her own, in
this isolated lane, he felt an odd surge of protectiveness
towards the pair. There was no mention of a father, and
she'd actively told him there wasn't one. People went it
alone all the time. Working in medicine over the years,

in his various roles, he knew how complex and unique family set-ups could be, and how they worked. Marnie seemed so happy; it was nice to see.

Ash couldn't quite believe that a man would walk away from her—was there even a man *on* the scene at all? Had there ever been? Oh, Lord, he was driving himself mad with his theories and wonderings. What was the point? He wasn't up for a relationship. Heck, he wouldn't even be here. He was here to cover her maternity leave, and then he'd be packing up and off to his next job placement. It was how he liked it, wasn't it? It made sense to keep moving. Keep things fresh, turn things around and move on to the next place.

He loved delivering babies, it gave him joy. A sense of satisfaction. Maybe even chasing a few little demons away along the way. Marnie wasn't the one for him, it was just a passing attraction. Sure, it had happened more than once. The jolt he'd felt both times was hard to ignore, but his heart wasn't in danger. He kept that firmly locked away. He couldn't even think about getting into a relationship.

Besides, Marnie was independent. He could see the strength and warmth emanating from her whenever he was around her. Felt it whenever his new colleagues mentioned her at Carey House. He'd been there one day, and he knew that she was dearly loved and missed. It made him all the more curious about what it was that drew him to her, and all the more determined to ignore it. It was just another job.

Picking up the empty box, he tidied up. Hopefully

he'd get some sleep in his strange new bed. He had a busy day at work tomorrow.

As he got into bed later that night, turning off the bedside lamp, he lay in the darkness. Marnie's light was still on. He thought of her, looking after Violet, her blonde hair half over her face as she bent to kiss her daughter. He fell asleep, the light from the house next door the only light in the darkness around him.

CHAPTER FOUR

'RIGHT,' MARNIE SAID, pulling off her rubber gloves and laying them over the sink tap. 'I think we're done, little madam.'

She looked down at Violet, who was half asleep in her snug baby carrier on Marnie's chest. They'd had a busy morning and Marnie was excited to get into the festive spirit. She'd slept like a log after going round to see Ash, and Violet had even slept in a little. The wintry weather was the perfect backdrop to her mood. This was the first Christmas she was going to have as a mother, and Violet's first Christmas ever. She was really excited to get organised and embrace the season. She loved her cottage, especially at Christmas when the whole place looked magical. Oliver had never embraced the season as she always had, so this Christmas was going to be different in many ways. All of them good, in her eyes.

As she passed the dining-room table, her fingers reached out to touch the silk of her mask. This weekend was Carey Cove's Guise Festival, and her mother had already offered to babysit Violet so that she could have a night off. She couldn't wait to have a night off.

Feel like a woman first for the first time since she'd got pregnant with Violet. She was really looking forward to it and it was a great practice run for Christmas Eve. Sophie and Roman's engagement party was going to be huge; the whole village was invited, and everyone was full of support for the loved-up pair. Eager to celebrate it together.

She'd been on a cleaning and organising frenzy all morning. The 'lie-in' had made her feel like a new woman, and she was taking advantage of the adrenalin burst. Once Violet was down for an afternoon nap, she adjusted the hairclip holding her short blonde hair back off her face and headed downstairs. The sun was fading, the approaching dusk painting the sky with stars that twinkled above her home. She loved the summer and the late sunsets, but in Carey Cove the season never impacted on her mood. Christmas was Christmas. It was always a good place to celebrate it. The people here made it so special.

She headed outside to the workbench she kept at the front of her house. She loved gardening and tending her home. It gave her peace. She gathered together the materials for her Cornish bush decorations. Violet would be happy for a while. Marnie smiled as she looked at her sleeping daughter on the baby monitor she'd brought out. She was such a good baby; she'd slotted right into Marnie's life.

She felt very blessed as she put the withy in the centre of the bench and got right to work. This was the life she'd envisaged. Last Christmas, when she was making these very decorations, she had been hopped up on hormones and scared to death at the prospect of the IVF not taking. She only earned a nurse's wage, and IVF on the NHS was not routinely given in her circumstances. For a single woman like her, it had made it a little harder too, given that there was no father involved. It involved more ingredients to bake the pudding, so to speak. It meant a lot to her; she could still remember how she had longed to know the future. She did that sometimes, at a fixed point in her memory. Making the Cornish trees outside her home, wondering what the woman who would stand there a year on would tell her if they could meet. If last year's her were here now, she'd tell her everything would work out.

'Everything worked out,' she repeated aloud.

'Yeah, looks good from where I'm standing. Very festive.'

Ash was standing at his gate, looking tired but bright-eyed.

'Thanks. Good day?' Her work curiosity was piqued.

'Yeah, great. We had a Noel come into the world, and a Holly-Mae. Sophie thought it was hilarious.'

'Aww, that's cute.'

'Yeah, I think so. You had a good day? Had anybody arrested yet? The postman, perhaps?'

'No.' She levelled a steely gaze his way. 'I like our postman.'

'Ouch.' He laughed. She laughed along with him. 'Well, I need to get in. I'm starving.'

He touched his hand to the gate but looked back. 'You eaten?'

She was just adjusting a twig when her stomach rumbled. 'Well, I…no.' She looked around her at the piles of decorations. 'I guess I got a bit involved in my project. I don't do well watching TV. Or relaxing, really.'

'You like to be busy. I'm the same.'

Marnie watched him wrestle with something. She could feel the tension emanating from him.

Is he nervous?

'Fancy a takeaway?'

Whatever it was, it's gone now. Why are you here, Ash?

She wanted to hope for the best for him, that he would just leave, and she would move on. The annoying part was how much he intrigued her. She wanted to reach out and touch him almost, as if touching him again might crack the puzzle.

'I bet you know of some good places that deliver, neighbour.'

Was that a little flirtation, Ash? I mean what are you doing? This woman almost had you arrested straight out of your sleep. You were late to cover her job too.

But she didn't seem too mad about that now. He'd had a good reason, but he had felt bad about it. Reliable was something that he disliked being called these days, but it was true. He was usually the best at whatever he turned his passion to.

It had kept him going these past few months. Helped him get up every morning and put one foot in front of the other. He was alone, but he didn't have just himself to think about. He wasn't here to romance the woman he was covering for. He was here to do the job and move on to the next one. Check in on those who loved him, visit them when he could. Chase the bad feelings away with a move to the next town. The next set of faces he would forget the instant he got to the next shift. The next place had a new sea of faces to get to know professionally, new ways of working, and quirks, to learn.

As he quickly showered and changed, he thought about his neighbour. She was bristly. Good at her job, he knew that. Her colleagues were singing her praises, but he knew that they spoke so well of her earnestly. They all loved Violet, but Ash got the sense that Marnie was keenly missed. As much as they welcomed him in with open arms. She was quite a person to work out.

'Idiot,' he said to himself. He half threw the shampoo bottle onto the rack. He'd washed his stupid hair three times while thinking about Marnie in the shower. He was losing his mind. Maybe that was why he got dressed so fast. He even squirted himself with a little cologne, still in his suitcase from his last place. Where it had stayed in the case. He frowned, realising he was overthinking yet again. Running a comb through his short brown locks, he checked himself over. He looked a little brighter than he'd thought he would. It was the prospect of food. The company wasn't bad either, of course, but he knew how to lie to himself well enough by now. He was nearly as good at it as he was at lying to everyone he met. It came naturally to him now, which was the thing that worried him the most.

Grabbing his wallet from the dresser, he slammed his front door a little too hard, and composed himself when he realised Marnie was still outside. She was standing there looking at him, a box of decorative bits in her hands.

'Everything okay?' she asked him easily.

'Yep.' He nodded, as easily as drawing the breath that filled his lungs whenever he looked at her. 'Everything's great.'

'So, like this?'

Ash held up his first attempt at decorating the withy bush, ribbon and decorative pieces all spaced out perfectly on his design. It was actually pretty good.

'You sure you've not done this before?' she asked as he jumped in the air.

'Holy— Argh!'

He'd received another scratch on his arm from the sharp leaves they were working with. He'd drawn blood already but brushed it off when he saw her looking. She knew it hurt. The first time she'd made one she'd been cut to ribbons. He flinched again, and she saw his hand pull back. A giggle erupted from her, her breath misting the air around them. It was getting on for time, the sun long gone. She snipped another piece of holly into the shape she wanted, trying to keep a straight face when his head snapped in her direction.

'Oh, find it funny, do you? This holly is lethal. I stink of apple. I'll probably get some kind of plant-mutation disease, end up with branches for legs.'

Another titter erupted from her chest before she could stop herself, and he glared at her.

'I'm serious! This is a decoration? I could use this thing as a weapon.'

'Oh, really?' she asked, trying not to let the laughter take over her voice. 'How?'

'How what?'

'How would you use a Cornish bush as a weapon? It's a cute decoration, a tradition!'

'So is bullfighting, and you don't see me doing that either.' He assessed his creation again, as a blacksmith assessed the steel blade of the sword he had just finished forging. 'I'm pretty sure if you threw it at someone, or them into it, it would hurt. The holly sprigs alone are lethal.'

Violet was still to get restless. She was lying in her Moses basket, wrapped from the cold and positioned so Marnie could see what was happening on the baby monitor screen. Marnie peeped over at her, taking the opportunity to try to stop laughing at Ash.

'True,' she finally said when she could trust herself to hold a steady tone. She clipped the last piece of holly into her efforts. 'Well, I think I'm done too. Food will be here soon. I'd better feed and change madam here.'

'Want me to clean up here?'

Marnie's heart swelled. It was kind of nice to have a bit of help.

'You sure?'

'Yeah, but if you hear a woman screaming now and again—' he pointed to the offcuts of holly waiting to be picked up '—just ignore it.'

She was still laughing when she was in the house, changing Violet. She liked this side of Ash. He was caring, intelligent. Kind. Understanding. Given that she had tried to have him arrested and removed from his own home, that was something. Even in the friendly little haven that was Carey Cove. He'd just fitted in, she mused. As if he'd been one of them the whole time.

The fact that she couldn't forget hit her in the face again. All of this, this ridiculous inner turmoil over him while he was here solely to cover her job while she was on maternity. Thinking about it that way, she actually felt a little judgmental towards him for how nice he was to her. More confusion. She had been pretty prickly. Him being late for her job had added to her guilt about not being there at work, even though she knew her colleagues were not the ones stressing over it. They were all really happy for her, and they'd obviously held the fort down in her absence.

She had to admit, though, she'd thought she'd meet her mat-leave cover in different circumstances. She'd assumed it would be a woman, which had been presumptuous of her, looking back. Was she so sworn off men that she didn't see them any more? Unless they were a barcode number on a vial of sperm, she hadn't really cared a jot about men. She reminded herself that, whatever this was or wasn't with Ash, life wasn't due another change. She looked herself in the mirror again, Violet in her arms looking cute in her 'I love Santa' sleepsuit. One of the women at work had bought it for her.

'You are adorable, do you know that?' She dropped a kiss onto her daughter's smiling face. 'Come on, time for us to eat.'

Once Violet was changed and dressed ready for bed, Marnie wasted no time in heading back downstairs.

'It's nice to have company, isn't it?' she murmured into her daughter's ear. She got the bottle she'd been warming and took it through to the lounge. From the window she could see Ash tidying everything away. As though she'd called him, he turned and looked straight at her. She gasped a little. The jolt definitely didn't need a touch that time. He looked back, his face blank on first look, but then his expression warmed into a smile. His cheeks were bright pink from the cold December night. It had started to snow a little more, and soft flakes now broke up the black glossy surface of his hair in the darkness surrounding him. Even through the glass, he looked clear to her. Crystal-clear and absolutely gorgeous.

She smiled back, before turning her attention to Violet. Once she was drinking heartily from the bottle, her little hand stroking Marnie's arm, Marnie relaxed a little. Violet always did that, up and down. As if she loved to be in her arms. Looking at her, she grimaced.

'Well, that was those hormones I was telling you about.' She puffed an errant hair back into place, her face a picture of embarrassment. Violet kept drinking, staring back at her with those beautiful blue eyes. Listening, Marnie knew. To her mother, who was still swirling emotionally because of the birth and was now lusting through the window at her neighbour, who was tidying up their—her Christmas decorations, not laying pipe. She blushed again at the thought of that, and then he walked back inside.

She heard him shake his coat off, tap and remove

his boots. He came through to the lounge and seemed to pause in the doorway.

'Please, make yourself at home.'

That was a bit much. You might as well ask him about the pipe laying.

'I'm just feeding Violet.'

He came in and took a seat next to her on the sofa.

Interesting.

She looked at the armchair, and he followed her gaze.

'Sorry.' He went to get up. 'I'll sit over there.'

He stopped halfway in his ascent because she'd put her hand on his leg. She yanked it back, wrapping it under Violet as if to keep it safe.

'No, sorry. Please, sit down. I'm just not used to company.'

He looked conflicted for a second, as if he'd sat there without thinking about it beforehand. She hated that she'd taken that easiness away. Even if she'd had to brace herself to ignore the feel of his leg against hers.

He sat back down but kept a little distance between their bodies. She reached for the takeout menus she'd taken down from the fridge.

'Thanks.' He looked at Violet, smiled at them both, and turned his attention swiftly to the menus.

'So are we sharing, or doing our own thing?' she asked. She was willing her own empty belly not to give her away. Especially in this proximity. Her stomach, however, had other ideas. She'd had a busy, exhausting day, and she needed nothing more than to stuff her face. She was even willing to risk it in front of Ash. She recognised the fact he was hot, but she was off men, so food won. He might as well be a unicorn really. A nice unicorn, but something she would never have just the same. So food it was. She just wasn't sure that he was ready to see her rip into her food like a rabid hyena.

'Well, I don't know about you—' A gurgle broke the conversation. Both sets of eyes, well, even Violet's eyes, widened. 'Listen, that was my stomach. I didn't get to finish my lunch today—we had a bit of a rush on.' His cheeks reddened even more than when they were warmed by the fire close by. 'I apologise for that in advance, ladies, but I am going to order a lot.'

He waggled his eyebrows at her, making her laugh again. She noticed he seemed happier when she laughed. She was noticing far too many things about Ash Ellerington. Full-naming him again. As if he were some earl from those regency romances she loved to read. Well, she wasn't an eligible miss. This wasn't a book either. She pointed to the menus in his hands and jabbed a finger at The Imperial Palace. It was actually a restaurant, but they delivered too. The food was to die for. She never usually indulged. Tonight, though, she had company.

'Chicken and cashew nuts, prawn crackers, spring rolls, plum sauce, please.' She started to burp Violet, jerking her when she remembered something else. 'Prawn toast too!' She scrunched her nose up as Violet let out a resounding burp the second her hand patted the little one's tiny back. 'There you go.' Noticing that Ash was standing looking at her, open-mouthed, she shrugged. 'I'm hungry too.'

* * *

Wow.

Ash had seen some things when he was dating, before he'd met the woman he'd married. He'd dated nurses mostly, when he was training. Working in close proximity, the unsociable hours. It happened from time to time. He'd been on some horrible, awkward dates. Especially around food. Which made it all the more surprising that he was really enjoying himself. Marnie had relaxed the second Violet had settled, milk drunk, and she could eat. She'd eaten a full plate full of chicken and cashew nuts, and she had a prawn-cracker shard stuck to her trouser leg. Ash kept looking at it, eating his own food as he watched Marnie eat her fill. Now, this wasn't awkward. He felt comfortable here, with her. Violet got cuter every time he saw her. Which was from afar, of course. He wasn't one to get attached to babies.

Not any more, a weak little voice inside him said.

He silenced it with a spring roll.

'Good, eh?'

Marnie was sitting back against the couch cushions now, Violet still in the crook of one of her arms. Lazing, Ash would describe it as. Drunk on milk. His heart squeezed, and he focused back on his plate, and the conversation.

'It's the best I've had in a while.'

'Ah, well,' Marnie breathed. 'I bet you get to taste a lot of different stuff though, travelling.'

'I'm hardly backpacking around India. It's all in the UK.'

'Still, you get to come to places like this.'

'True.'

'You like it here, don't you? For you temporarily, I mean.'

Ash looked around the cottage, and then stopped himself. It made it look as if he were thinking about her home. Not that he wasn't. God, he was just stuffed from all the food. Tired too. It had been a busy day. It was late. He kept lying to himself over and over.

'That bad, eh?' She jostled his elbow with her free arm, putting the plate down and stretching her arm out.

'No!' he said, a little too loudly. 'No. Of course not. It's…great here.'

'Better in summer.' She smiled, getting a faraway look on her face. 'I can't wait to introduce Violet to the ocean.' She caught his eye. 'Still, Christmas isn't bad either.'

The air changed in the room, but Violet didn't feel it as they did. She started to cry, breaking the eye contact that felt charged between them.

'She's tired. I'll have to try to get her down.'

Ash smiled, not knowing whether to be disappointed or relieved by the intervention. Judging it by the thick slab suddenly lying across his chest seemed unreliable at the moment.

'She's got an excellent set of lungs on her.' He leaned in closer. 'She looks just like you.'

'You think?' Marnie turned to look at him, and her hair brushed his cheek. He half closed his eyes at the contact. 'I think she does, but I didn't like to just say it.'

'She's just like you.' He looked back at Violet, who

was looking right back at him. It was as if she were sizing him up.

I can't be your daddy, little one. I'm just passing through.

'Beautiful.'

She was so close. So very close. His arm tingled with the effort of not bridging the gap between them. Could she feel this, really? She acted as if she wanted to push him away from her for ever and drag her to him and beg him to throw her up against the wall. All at the same time. To push against her with his body, while she claimed his.

Could that really be in her eyes? Was that what this was? Why did this have to happen? How could he attempt to walk away from this intact? Without action, too? God, the world was so cruel it twisted his guts. She felt to him like a light, pulling him to its warmth. Violet snuffled, and her head turned back to her daughter. She moved Violet to the other arm, giving the other one a little shake before turning back to him.

'Would you like to hold her, before I take her up? I won't be long. She's already asleep.'

Ash's mouth went dry. The room shrank to half its size before his eyes. He felt trapped for a moment.

Too much. I thought these things had stopped.

'Er... I don't think I should. You know, I've just come from shift.'

He thumbed at his top, belatedly remembering that he'd been home and showered. Marnie knew that too, but she didn't comment.

'What am I saying?' He slapped his palm against

his forehead, before gathering some empty dishes with shaky hands. 'I got changed. Listen, I think I should get some sleep before I forget something else.'

She called after him, telling him it was okay, she would clean up, but her voice on the stairs went unanswered. When she came back down from putting Violet to bed, the living room was clean, and empty. He'd left a note on the counter.

Thanks for a great night, neighbour.
Ash

He closed Marnie's front door with a slow click. He waited till he was at the bottom of her garden before he paused to take in a big shuddery breath. He'd had to get out of there. He could never have explained himself. Especially not to Marnie. Just before that, he'd been wondering if he should kiss her. Wanting to kiss her. Needing to.

Sam. That was what had sent him running from there as if the whole place were on fire. Sam's cold little face. Not pink, and full of life like Violet's. She'd been snug in her mother's arms. The happiest little baby. Sleeping after a busy day. Not like Sam. He'd never even opened his eyes. Never looked on the world, on a single human face.

When Ash had looked at Violet, he'd seen Sam's face instead and he'd frozen. The thought of holding Violet, a wriggling baby, in his hands when they'd held tiny Sam for so little time. He'd frozen to the spot, and then run for the damn hills. Left Marnie a vague note that anyone could leave. It didn't serve as a good ending to such a good night.

He'd been fine around babies before. It was his job, for goodness' sake. Why this one rattled him was a mystery he didn't want to poke at too much. He knew Marnie was a mother. One all on her own and happy with the outcome. Violet was perfect, and Marnie was a great mother. All of that was attractive to him, but not exactly what he was looking for. He wasn't looking for anything. Peace perhaps.

Tonight was a reminder of why he kept moving on. Why he didn't form attachments any more. Because they caused pain. To others. Marnie's face when he'd dashed away like some thief in the night. She'd been so close, right there. Lips inches apart. God knew when he'd be that close again, and what he would be able to do and not to do if they ever were in that situation again. Would she slap him for setting his lips on hers, as he wanted to?

He took another shower, for no other reason than he felt dirty for his cowardly exit. By the time he slipped under the sheets, his mood was even worse. He loved Sam, so much. He'd held him for the shortest time, but he would love him for the longest. Till he stopped drawing breath himself. After that too, if he had anything to do with it. He loved his wife too. They were gone, though, and being here alone in a strange new place reminded him that he was still here.

He turned over for the ninth time, his naked form now only half under the covers. He felt strangled in them, confined. He wondered if the woman next door was sound asleep or thinking about his abrupt exit. Or him. As he was her. Squinting at the clock, he rubbed at his eyes, and went to get a tumbler of whiskey to help him on his way to slumberland.

CHAPTER FIVE

'Hi!'

'Hey, you! Aw, come here and give me a hug!'

The two women embraced on Marnie's front doorstep, with Marnie ushering the two visitors inside. She'd been cleaning up all morning, waiting for their visit and using her nervous energy up on chores and little jobs around her cottage. A tray of freshly decorated Christmas cookies sat on a plate in the sitting room. They were iced with different designs—she'd had a bit of a creative morning to channel her thoughts away from her neighbour.

'Come in, come in! It's so nice to see you both! I need all the gossip from work.' Violet was in her Moses basket, kicking her little feet out from time to time as she lay watching the three women enter the sitting room. 'How are you getting on, Lorna?'

Lorna stepped forward, giving her a broad smile and an outstretched hand. 'Ok I think, Marnie.' Marnie settled the pair of them in the lounge, bringing a tea tray through to go with the cookies. Nya picked up one decorated to look like Rudolph, taking a bite and closing her mouth in pleasure.

'Wow, you've been busy, Marnie. I thought you sounded chipper on the phone.' Marnie blushed, looking away to pour the tea. Perfect action to hide from her friend's scrutiny. 'Lorna's doing great as our trainee midwife!'

Marnie took her friend in for the first time. She was searching now for clues, while she hid her own about Ash. Something was weighing on her mind; Marnie could tell the second she'd looked her mate in the eye.

'Glad it's going well, Lorna. I know it can be a bit full on,' Marnie said smoothly, taking in Nya's companion fully now too. She'd already heard good things on the grapevine. Their vetting procedures were pretty thorough—anyone given a job was always a good fit. They weren't cliquey, or a cult, as it sounded. They were just a group of passionate, caring people who sought out the same. She thought back to her travels with Oliver, half a world and a lifetime ago. Even now, when she was still recovering her body fully from childbirth, and surrounded by the winter weather, she wouldn't trade it. Not for now. One day, she'd take Violet with her to explore.

Nya nudged Lorna from her seat on the sofa, pointing to the plate of cookies. 'Lorna, I'm sorry we're so informal, but you know Marnie's one of us.' She finished the cookie and headed to the Moses basket. Violet looked up at her with her gorgeous bright eyes, and Marnie felt a swell of maternal pride.

'Well, little miss Violet, you have grown!' She turned

to Marnie, beaming. 'She's got a little bit more gorgeous too.' Marnie laughed.

'Well, I'm biased, but of course I'm going to say yes, she did.'

'Are you okay for Lorna to do the checks on Violet here?'

'Of course.' Marnie grinned at Lorna, to put her at ease. Everyone had to train. No one was born knowing how to be a midwife, not with modern medicine ever evolving too. She remembered how nervous she'd felt inside on her first few months of training. It was daunting, the job they did. Definitely not a walk in the park. The highs of delivering a baby though—the only thing that had surpassed that was giving birth to Violet. 'We're a team, right?'

Lorna visibly relaxed. Once she was getting on with attending to Violet, Marnie took the opportunity to quiz Nya further.

'So, how's work been?'

Nya, sitting next to her on the sofa, gave her the side-eye.

'What?'

Nya laughed. 'Come on, Marnie, how's work? We're here to check on you two! Don't be worrying, we're coping.' Marnie felt a pat on her arm. 'We miss you, of course, but Ash is doing a good job.'

Marnie willed her cheeks not to explode into colour. 'Oh, really? Not too good, I hope.' Her too shrill laugh rang out into the room. 'So, what's he like, then?'

'Ash? He's nice. Really good with the patients, he's

quite intense about procedures and equipment set-ups, but that's not a bad thing. Methodical, but fun with it.'

'Sounds perfect,' she replied without filtering her thoughts. Nya's eyes were on her again.

'You must know him better than us by now, though!' Nya threw back at her like a casual bomb. Marnie turned, making sure Lorna wasn't looking. She was busy with Violet, noting something down on the tablet they'd brought with them.

'Why would I?' There it was again, the high pitch of her voice coming to the fore with her nervous energy.

'Er, he lives next door? You must have seen him around.'

'Oh, yes, of course. I don't know him that well.' She got the urge to ask more, but she knew it would be obvious. They didn't gossip about people, especially not temporary workers. 'He seems nice. How's baby Hope coming along?'

She was changing the subject, but she did want to know. The little one had been left on the steps of Carey House. She couldn't imagine leaving Violet on the butter-coloured stone steps, in any circumstances, but she knew she could never judge. She was ready for Violet, in a good financial position. She had a steady job in a career she loved and friends and family around her if she ever felt alone or needed help. Hope's mother had taken her there to give her the best chance at life. Marnie knew that was all a mother ever wanted because she wanted that for Violet too.

Hope was being cared for by Nya and Theo, who had recently discovered that they were interested in more from their relationship than friendship and co-parenting. Marnie was thrilled for her friend and boss.

'She's doing well, hitting all her milestones so far.' It sounded a little technical, but Marnie understood. Perhaps she was trying to keep a professional distance. She got that. She'd done it herself for long enough. It was hard, seeing everyone else have babies. 'She's settled down really well. Theo and I love taking care of her.'

The three women chatted easily for a few more minutes while Nya and Lorna finished their cups of tea and ate a couple of Marnie's Christmas cookies. Finally it was time for them to leave for their next appointment. 'Are you looking forward to the ball?' Lorna asked her as they were leaving. 'I've been told it's quite the event around here.'

'I am actually. Looking forward to seeing you there, Lorna. Bye, Nya.'

'Bye, my lovely,' she said, enveloping her in a huge hug.

'Call me if you need anything, a sitter, anything.' Two babies wouldn't be a bother to Marnie. It would be nice to have company for Violet too. Socialisation could never start too early, especially when you had a whole cove of people around. It might just keep her busy too. She seemed to get into trouble when she was at a loose end. It wasn't itchy feet, but something like it.

She thought about it later that night, once Violet was asleep, and she'd run out of cleaning to do. She pulled an old photo album out from the bottom of her wardrobe. Paris. They'd taken the usual tourist photo in front of the Eiffel Tower, Oliver pulling a funny face at the last second before the photo took. She looked at the snap, at her laughing into the camera at his antics. She couldn't say it had all been bad. It hadn't been, till the end. They'd seen the world together. She kept flicking through the album till she found what she realised she'd been wanting to see. The engagement photo.

Oliver had handed his camera to another traveller, asking them to take a shot of them on the beach. It was a beautiful, hot day. Her face was sun-kissed, her hair blonder than when they'd started out. She wore her hair in surfer chick waves then, which she'd kept pinned up for work. Recently she'd opted for a sleek blonde bob. She now had a different life, and it was a different woman who was looking back on that photograph.

Oliver had dropped to one knee, and that was that. Their magical moment, now a snapshot in an album and a fading memory in her head. Two weeks before they'd been due to fly home, the bubble that was Oliver and Marnie had well and truly popped. Instead of flying home to a wedding, and their life together, she'd returned alone and changed.

Had she been naïve, back then? She thought so afterwards. Scrutinising every moment of their last few days together, to see if she could pinpoint the issue. At the time, she'd thought she'd never recover. She knew differently now, but did that mean that girl on the beach was gone?

Marnie put the album away and looked out of her side window at the house next door. There were no lights on save for one in the lounge. She wondered what Ash was doing. It was quite lonely on the lane. She pondered half a dozen reasons to send him a text, but then gave up and decided to go to bed instead. She didn't know what to say anyway. *I'm thinking about you? What are you up to?*

She snorted and turned to her side in bed.

'Don't be daft, Marnie. For God's sake, just stick to the plan.'

She pushed her phone into her top dresser drawer an hour later, a dozen more unsent texts to Ash on her screen.

CHAPTER SIX

WHAT A WEIRD week this was shaping up to be. Even for Christmas. Even for this Christmas.

'Overthinking Annie' was here again. Was this what happened to all new mothers, or just ones who had got a little bit smitten with their neighbour? Well, annoyed at first. Then intrigued. Smitten was right after that, even though the lightning thing had been there the whole time. She had no point of reference for that aspect. She'd never encountered it before.

So here she was, her first big night out, and she was wondering where Ash was. What he was doing. Thinking even. Ugh. It was annoying. So she'd come full circle. Annoyed, intrigued, smitten, confused, and back to annoyed. The sheer rainbow of emotions that she felt when she thought of him gave her post-partum hormones a run for their money. In fact, they utterly surpassed them in every single intricate way. Thinking of a man again. Great.

She huffed out a frustrated sigh. She would be back at work soon, back in something like her old routine. A working single mother, and a happy one to boot. That

was the plan. She felt as if she needed to keep reminding herself of that these days. Given her current swirling head, she wished she'd done what she'd almost done.
Called to cancel her mother, put Violet to bed and eaten
ice cream and chocolate in front of the TV. A thriller,
with no romance involved. She could almost taste the
chocolate, but she pushed herself to get back to the confident woman she'd once been. She was perfect, just as
she was. She was just having a bit of a wobble. That was
it. A bit of a flirtation with a passing stranger.

She thought of her movie last night but dismissed the
idea. No, Ash wasn't a spy. This was why she needed
to get out more, and why she was pushing herself to
go. She had been so looking forward to attending the
Guise Ball before this. She had a feeling tonight would
be different from the usual events though. She felt excited, and she didn't trust it. She needed the plan to
keep her sane.

'You are fine as you are,' she said aloud to herself,
and felt her shoulders straighten in response. She said
it to herself the whole way there, till the venue came
into sight. Then, her mouth felt too dry to utter a word.
'You...' She swallowed hard. 'You are sticking to the
plan.' She took another step, a more confident one this
time than she felt. 'You are fine as you are.' She bit at
her lip. 'Now stop talking to yourself and go and have
some fun.'

The nerves kicked in the second Marnie's heels hit
the grass of the village green. She felt odd. Naked without Violet and her changing bag. Alien in her own body
without her child with her. They'd been together for so

long, she felt lost. Careful not to ruin her sleek bob, she secured her mask and felt instantly better. Shielded. It was a little more glamorous than a bag full of baby wipes and rattles too.

She walked slowly across the grass, surveying the scene and taking everything in. She'd been so rushed lately, busy with work and Ash. His sudden departure the other night had really bothered her. But then, the mere fact that it had bothered her so much was so irksome that she'd been rattled by the whole thing. Why did she care anyway? He made her nervous. Wooden at times. It was embarrassing. She just couldn't resist being near him, but she wasn't going to tell anyone that. She wouldn't need to anyway. This secret had an expiration date attached to it.

He was covering for her for a finite time, not for ever. He rented next door, as temporary nurses often did when the occasion arose. He'd be leaving, to go to the next job.

Then she'd be back to normal life, and he'd be off to help at the next place. It would be a shame though. It was quite nice having a neighbour. Especially one like this particular neighbour. She chose to focus on the night ahead. She wasn't on show like she felt in her head. She was incognito tonight, and here to have some fun.

She nodded to a few people as she passed, enjoying the curious glances from them. They didn't recognise her! The mask and her now no-longer-pregnant body were enough to make people take a second look. She quite liked it as she walked under the hundreds of twinkly lights, all adorned around the place. The Christmas tree was all lit up too, the perfect Cornish Christmas postcard scene. It was an amazing backdrop to the ball going on around her. Carey Cove was transformed for the evening, and the people with it.

She herself felt like a different person. Free, confident. Sexy. It wasn't all breast pads and bath books, she knew. She told her patients often enough. To remember the woman inside the mother. She was actually stupidly glad she'd made the effort tonight. Violet was safe and being adored by her smitten grandmother, Marnie was wearing a nice dress, and she was going to jolly well enjoy it.

Enjoy it she did too. People-watching at parties was one of her favourite things to do. When the room was a happy one, anyway. She gazed at the masked people for a while, trying to work out who was who. In the end her efforts were futile, so she started to watch their actions instead. People were bolder wearing a disguise, she decided. It was quite daring. Nothing risqué of course, but there were more than a few longing looks, she thought. Maybe she was just feeling the post-partum effects again. She decided that she might have to keep using that line for a while. Especially given her recent daydreams. She needed to shake off everything for a few hours. Stop watching life and get back into living it.

As if fate was conspiring with her for the evening, the next song to come on was one of her favourites. She didn't even try to stop her feet from heading to the dance floor. Normally she'd need a couple more drinks before she started making shapes, but the mask was a little protective shield. She felt great!

Marnie swayed along, lost in the music the minute her eyelids closed. God, she missed dancing. She used to love going out with the girls, letting their hair down and dancing the night away. It felt like so long ago now. Oliver had changed things. She'd lost pieces of herself, for nothing. She smiled as she moved to the beat, feeling oddly smug at the thought. She'd come through it, and now she was dancing again while her child slept. Safe and sound. What more did a woman need?

She opened her eyes as someone brushed their arm against hers, and her smile dimmed. She was dancing in a sea of couples. She hadn't noticed it before. She felt as though her joy had been cut off. A little fish, swimming alone. She tried to shrug the feeling off. She shouldn't have had that glass of champagne when she'd first arrived. She'd glugged it for her nerves, but now she'd had one thought of Oliver. Not even Oliver, she reminded herself. Hell, if he were on this dance floor she'd be sinking her heel into his stupid foot and walking away as fast as her legs could carry her. She didn't long for him. Not any more. She did get the sense that she was missing something though, and she was back to feeling…

Well, she didn't know what she was feeling, but she didn't get a chance to prod at it. As she turned to head off the dance floor, and was striding towards another drink, something stopped her. Well, someone. Masked, tall, dark. Male.

Who was this guy?

She thought she felt a spark of recognition, but the man kept coming before she could get a good enough look.

She didn't need another look. She knew half a second later exactly who the man behind the mask was. She would never admit it, but she knew that, right now, she could pick Ash Ellington out of a crowd of any other men in the world. The truth of that fact rattling around her brain scared her to her core. It was the one thing she didn't want. His hand closed around hers, pulling her gently towards him. She knew the second his skin touched hers. The man was Ash. It was as if he'd charged her up from the inside. She felt as if she were glowing brighter than any light on Earth or above. Zap. The power of Ash's hand in hers. It was unmistakable. Even when she didn't recognise him, she knew him above anyone else. This was so far off her plan she might as well tear the thing up.

'Dance with me?'

That was all he said. She didn't even answer. The moment her feet moved in his direction, his hand was taking her free hand in his and twirling her. His hands were soft, but she felt the power in his easy grip. The warmth of his hand on her hip as he steadied her on a spin, her laughing as he waggled his eyebrows at her above the mask.

The song changed, but their steps didn't falter. She tried to focus on the eyes behind the mask, the cut of his suit, as if that would give her a hint. A reason why this man made her feel so alive, what his deal was. Every time they saw each other, she needed more. To know more. To work him out, and how to stop his hand-shake from turning her into a bumbling idiot too. Not much to ask from a very confused and slightly over-tired mother, surely?

She felt the thoughts float like feathers before she could catch them. His hands kept reaching for hers, twirling, dancing, and moving around each other. The other ball-goers were there, Marnie knew. She knew she was still on the village green; she could see the green brilliance of the Christmas tree reflected in the lights adorned around every tree and post. Reflected in every bauble and bright outfit of the guests. She knew where she was, that they weren't alone. They were not the only people there.

It felt that way though. Slowly, song after song, beat after beat. Every touch they shared; their bodies never not connected to the other. The mask helped her dar-ing side come out to play, and Ash matched her step for step. They danced as though they had done it for ever. The night went from slower songs to bigger beats, their dancing getting more fun and playful as the night wore on.

Marnie was hot, parched and she had laughed till her sides hurt. Her masked companion had come in like a bolt from the blue, and it had made her night. Most of the night, she thought as she caught sight of her watch under the lights. The rest of the dance floor were still going, the energy of the whole place in full frivolity. Ash nodded his head to the side, pretending to mop his brow theatrically. His eyes were bright beneath the mask, and she could see his heaving chest matched hers. He'd enjoyed it just as much as she had.

'I might need a minute,' she admitted over the noise of the music. He laughed, a deep rich sound she wanted to replay the instant it was over. When he reached for her hand, she took it, laughing as he led her off the dance floor. He led them away from the noise of the party and into a quiet, moonlit corner. Shielded from the noise, they caught their breath, still laughing.

'I'm really glad I saw you,' he said, pulling her a little closer behind a tree as a loud trio of people heading home weaved across the grass nearby. 'I wanted to apologise for the other night. I didn't mean to rush off the way I did. I enjoyed myself, I wanted you to know that. I feel bad for how it ended. I guess I was afraid I might pass out and drool into the spring rolls.'

He looked away, even when she attempted to smile at him. She got the distinct impression there was a lot more to the story of Ash. She ignored the questions within her. When it came to him anyway. She had told herself that it was just because he was helping her out, with work, even at the house. Ash was a neighbour, a friend. The tags she'd assigned to him on the way to the *Don't go there* bin she kept for men and romantic entanglements these days. Her last interaction with a man had involved a test tube and she had sworn to herself she would not break that rule. Even though they had just danced like lightning bolts, fast and full of electricity.

'Oh, that's okay.' Marnie was having trouble concentrating on his words. The proximity of him was overpowering her senses, and her strict 'no man' rules. She was drinking him in, the closeness of him. How good it had felt to be in his arms, twirling on the dance floor together. It wasn't just his body though, or the way he made her feel.

How did he make her feel? As if she were plugged into a damn light socket, the electricity coursing through her skin wherever he touched her. It wasn't just that, or the feeling that he was feeling the same jolt, the same sparks. It was his eyes that held her attention too. Intense, lustful flashes even, and something else. He looked upset, pained. Was he feeling the same doubts? Did he have the same rule about not getting involved with a woman? He didn't stay in one place, after all. What would be the point?

She wanted to ask him everything, but she didn't want to hear the answers either. Nothing good could come of it. Still, the sensation that he was going through something was unmistakable in his expression. She didn't want to care, but she did. So much. She felt alive when she was with this man. She felt things she'd never felt with Oliver, and that knowledge was something even her stoically single brain couldn't deny. She wanted to comfort him, be the one who chased his cares away. Even if it was just for the night. It couldn't be more: they were worlds apart, and soon he would be miles away too. Possibly making some other woman's heart fill with longing.

Ugh. Her heart clenched at the thought. She had no claim on him, but the thought of him with another woman made her heart hurt.

Would they feel the jolt from his touch too? She

doubted it. She doubted that there were two other people on the face of the earth who felt like this in the other's presence. 'It's okay,' she repeated, her voice barely a whisper. He looked from her eyes to her lips, and back again. His tongue darted out to lick the dryness of his own full mouth, and she followed the movement as if she were starved. Her tongue tingled with jealousy. 'Ash...'

She wanted to smooth the crease from his brow, but her hands didn't move. 'Did something happen? Is that why you left?'

She thought of their lips, so close on that sofa. *So close.*

'Was it something I did?'

'No, of course it wasn't you,' he cut her off softly. Once more his beautiful hazel eyes focused on her mouth.

Could he see the words hidden behind her lips, begging for release?

'It was me.' The pain in his eyes as he looked down at her stopped her from asking any more. 'I'm sorry.' She took off her mask, not wanting to shield her face from him in that moment. 'It's...complicated. All of this is complicated.'

'Ash, it's fine, honestly...'

All of what?

He was still staring at her. His eyes, those beautiful eyes, so unique. She couldn't stop trying to fathom their depths. The pain behind them was something she recognised; she knew it. She recognised something in

him. Was that what this was? This…this…thing between them?

He's right. This is complicated.

The rest of her words evaporated from her brain, the
heat from the dancing and the proximity of Ash turning
every solid thought into mush the second it was formed.
His eyes were locked onto hers, and they were closer.
Almost touching. Marnie didn't even know whose feet
had moved. Everything but his gaze felt irrelevant as she
looked right back. Seeing more than pain etched on his
pupils the longer she looked. He took a deep shuddering
breath in, and she couldn't stop her fingers from moving
any longer. She reached up to Ash's face, slowly pulling the mask away from his features. He didn't move
an inch, but she felt his hot sweet breath on her cheek
as she touched the skin on his temple. She wanted to
see his whole face.

'That's better,' she whispered. His lips twitched, and
her eyes feasted on the movement. He dipped his head
low, and she lifted herself towards him. The second
their lips met, the crack of thunder they both felt pushed
the two of them closer together. He wrapped his arms
around her waist, pulling her up and against his strong
body. She could feel his hands shaking as he held her
close. His lips were sealed to hers, the pain she'd seen
in his eyes moments earlier gone. There was no pain
in Ash now, he was right there with her. She felt sexy
when he looked at her.

Like a man starved. He twined his tongue with hers,
deepening the kiss just as much as she wanted him to.

She had her hands on his face, pulling him to her while their masks hung from her fingers from their straps.

'Marnie,' he breathed, in between long, deep caresses of her lips. Marnie whimpered at that, liking the sound of her name on his lust-filled tongue. This was the hottest thing she'd ever done. It wasn't just the masks either, the setting. It was as if she wanted to jump him, right here, right now. She'd laughed at that part in movies before, but, man, she got it now. *Ding-ding-ding.* She was on fire for the man. Wishing she were back in her cottage, and not with ice cream.

The twinkling of the lights behind Ash's head lit him up like a halo from behind. She opened her eyes just to check he was there and found herself drawn to his closed lids. She was at a ball, dressed to the nines, kissing the hot midwife who was covering her maternity leave. He was leaving, and she was sworn off men. He was hiding something, something dark, she knew it. She had dark corners of her own heart, and her pain thrummed with his. She felt it, just as deep as the kisses he was giving her with everything he had. She was drunk on kissing his lips, feeling his tongue dip into her mouth, exploring her and gripping her ever tighter. His soft, large hands were wrapped around her. She felt no cold, no breeze from the sea. She just felt warm, and safe. Sexy and daring. Like her. Marnie had got her groove back…

'Woo-hoo!' a rather drunken voice sang out behind them, and Ash's eyes sprang open. For a second, they grew lazy again when they locked with hers. He tightened his fingers around her, securing her to him. As if he was excited to find her there when his lashes lifted.

She felt the stirring of lust again even in her panic, and then the voice turned into voices. They sprang apart, Marnie grabbing her mask and throwing his into his waiting hands. As they put on their disguises, breathing heavy and hard, she heard Ash call her name just as the crowd drowned out his words. A few masked and rather sozzled party-leavers looked their way, Ash nodding awkwardly in their direction. Marnie took the turn of his head as her cue, and she ran off, towards the crowd. The spell had well and truly been broken. The coach was a pumpkin, and she was off like a shot. Not trusting herself to stay with him any longer. Embarrassed about being caught snogging in the bushes too. She had to stay living here after all. People talked to each other. Everyone loved a party story. She didn't want to be the subject of gossip. Not again. Heck, no.

'What have you done?' she chided herself under her breath. 'Dear Lord, Marnie! Get it together!' Her lips still felt white hot, swollen from Ash's attentions. Brushing at them, she still felt the tingle from his lips. She was surprised they weren't on fire, scorched from the crackle that flowed between them.

Imagine if you'd had sex, her horny brain spat out.

'Imagine? I nearly did…' she whispered back to the voice.

She was breathing hard, and she knew it was more than the running she was doing. She'd stopped only to throw off her heels and grab them, but she'd heard Ash call her name. More than once. She didn't turn around, she didn't stop till she was standing outside her parents' house, her hand on the doorbell. The whole journey there was a blur. There she was though, intact, deranged with the thought of what she'd just fled from, and still masked. She pulled it off her face as her mother opened the door. She twanged the elastic against the shell of her ear in her haste. Ignoring the sting, she painted on a smile.

'Hi, Mum, everything okay with Violet?'

Her mother was never one for missing a trick. Marnie knew she was rumbled the second her mother's brows knitted together. She never scowled, but the lowering of the brows was a sure-fire sign that she'd clocked something. Marnie continued her tactic of acting breezy and grinning like an idiot.

'Oh, fine—she went right off after her bottle. She's been good for her grandma as always. How was the ball?'

Marnie followed her into the house, eager to see her daughter again. She realised she'd forgotten about her that night, caught in the moment with Ash. She'd thought she'd feel guilty, but, surprisingly, she just felt like a woman who'd had a good night. Despite its complications. She didn't know how she would sleep though. Hot and sweaty probably, as her dreams no doubt would be.

'It was good. Fun. How's Violet been?'

'My granddaughter has been as good as gold as always. You've asked that twice since you walked in. I raised you, you know. I didn't do half bad either, I think.' Her eyes crinkled in the corners as she smiled.

Her eyes were still searching though, like bloodhounds after a scent. Marnie hoped she didn't look too dishevelled.

'How was the ball?' Her mother reached forward to pluck a blade of grass from Marnie's hair. 'Looks like you might have had some fun.'

Marnie didn't look her in the eye. 'It was good, I said. Lots of fun.'

Mostly in cosy darkened corners.

She felt her body get hot under her dress all over again.

'Hmm, I can see that.' Her mother started putting everything back into the changing bag, a knowing smile on her face. 'Your cheeks are flushed.' She smiled, her eyes dancing with mirth as Marnie looked at her agog. And very red-faced. She was flushed right through to the neckline. She felt as if she might combust. 'And your hair looks like you were dragged through a bush.'

Marnie's open mouth was her mother's only answer. Not that she needed one. She was too busy laughing while she packed up Violet's things.

The clock was a rather annoying concept. Time too. The clocks all ticked on, heralding the seconds of your life ticking by. Hours that you could be sleeping in. Much-needed sleep. She was lying in a comfy bed, warm and cosy. Violet was asleep, and she had time to get some much-needed shut-eye.

Which sounded perfect. Easy. Rare, given her new status as a single mother. She punched the pillow, looking once more at the clock. Three minutes had elapsed.

Marnie sighed and flumped face down on the duvet. It was no use. She couldn't sleep. She'd half dozed off an hour ago, but the instant her lashes met she was back on that green. Back in Ash's arms. In the shadows, kissing him. Tasting him. Exploring more. Fearful that she wouldn't find it, and wary that she would. Pulling him closer to her as he reached for her just as desperately.

How the heck was a woman supposed to sleep when she'd got that on her mind? Especially after a very long dry spell, and a 'no man' rule that was cast iron. She could plead temporary insanity or blame it on the mask, but when she'd realised he'd reached for her, she'd forgotten his abrupt exit. That was the problem. As her regency romances would say, she quite forgot herself when in the presence of that certain gentleman. This wasn't a book though. It was barely a chapter.

He was living next door, doing her job, working with her friends. He was getting entwined into Carey Cove. Into her life. Kisses in the dark were not part of any plan she had. She needed to stop thinking about her hunky neighbour and keep it as normal as possible till he left. Then she'd be back at work, tired, busy, and raising her daughter. Just as she'd planned.

She looked at the clock once more. Another four minutes lost to thoughts of Ash and the million reasons why kissing him again was a good idea. She'd felt more than his touch that night, and she wondered what his pain was. Why was a man like that single and travelling? Commitment phobic? She didn't get that kind of read from him. After Oliver, her instincts were sharp on that score. Maybe her resolve wasn't quite as steadfast as she'd thought, given her dalliance, but her instincts were always at play. But then, there hadn't been anyone *since* Oliver. Her friends had tried and failed to get her to go on dates. She'd rather die than be on some dating site. She had no intention of running that gauntlet. She didn't want a man, and she didn't need one either. Violet was proof that her plan was worth it.

She'd gone through the IVF alone. The injections, the appointments, the surging hormones. She'd cried buckets inside rooms at work, overwrought with the surges going on in her body while she was trying to work and not think about babies. Which, of course, had been impossible. They had been in her face all day long. She loved it, but her own longing had made it much harder.

As if on cue, Violet woke up, letting her mother know she was hungry with a good healthy squawk. Her unmistakable feeding cries. Balm to her ears after reflecting on the days before she came to be.

'It's okay.' Marnie smiled, rubbing her tired but wide eyes as she went to feed her daughter. 'Mummy's here.'

Once Violet was happily in her arms feeding, Marnie's attentions turned back to Ash. She could see a light on upstairs at his place, and she wondered whether he was restless too.

Are you thinking about me? I can't get you out of my head.

She'd felt it when they'd worked on the decorations together. Brushing her hands against his, seeing his reaction. She knew he felt it. How could he not? It was all she could do sometimes to stay on her feet when he was close. Her whole body reacted to him instinctively.

She'd never felt that with Oliver. Which made her wonder what she was in for.

She wasn't the type to go lusting after anyone. She didn't have the time or the patience for games. Or lies. Oliver had tested every limit on that score, and his betrayal was not something she was ever going to go running towards. She felt as if she'd been blindsided by him, and she was furious at the lies, the time wasted.

She felt the old anger and hurt rise within her, Violet picking up on it and wriggling. Marnie shushed her and pushed Oliver back where he belonged in her brain. Firmly in the waste basket labelled 'trash'. Which was where she'd placed all *other* men, if she was honest. The only male she had wanted to have any truck with was Violet's sperm donor, and that wasn't a man per se. More of a strong sample in a jar. That was enough for her. No pain, no games, or lies.

And now she was lusting after her neighbour. He was passionate about the job, just like her. Her friends had kept her up to speed on his work, and they were impressed. Not an easy feat with the ladies of Carey House. He'd got the seal of approval. The thought made her smile through her fatigue. As she looked out of the window at Ash's lit window, she thought of something else.

His masked eyes at the ball, so full of something dark, hidden. She recognised it as pain. She'd seen it in the mirror enough times after her own difficult time. Pre Violet. He looked as if he was in need of sleep, pretty much all the time. Even at the ball she'd noticed how drawn he looked. It made her want to look after him. She was like that with everyone. It was her nature. Ash was different though. She recognised that. She wanted to know more, to help him even. It could be anything.

As she burped Violet and settled her back into her cot, she turned off the light and hoped that sleep would take her. She wanted to stop thinking about it. Ash could have any number of reasons for who and how he was. She didn't need to drive herself mad with all the best- and worst-case scenarios. It was dangerous on two counts. Once she knew, she would have to deal with it. The easy way out was just not to know. Not to get involved. Because, as Marnie tried to close her eyes and not think of the man whose lips she craved, she knew. The second count was him, and how he made her feel. There would be no coming back from that loss. It was far better to keep her head down and just keep her feelings to herself. He would be gone soon, and the feelings would pass. She hoped for that as much as she did for sleep.

Turning over, she looked out of the window into the night. The curtains were half closed, leaving a nice gap for her to focus on. It was Christmas, she had the engagement party to look forward to. It was also Violet's first Christmas, and the time when all their family traditions could be formed. She did think that it would have been nice to have Ash around, but she knew it would just get her in deeper. She had the life she had wanted for so long. Sure, it would have been nice to have someone to share it with, but life wasn't perfect. What she had was enough before Ash arrived. She lied herself to sleep. It would have to be enough. It was the plan, and she always stuck to the plan. Whatever Ash's deal was, it was for the next woman he kissed to worry about. In the next place.

It was another two hours before Marnie eventually slept, but she still dreamed of Ash. Driving away from Carey House, as Marnie watched from the doorway.

CHAPTER SEVEN

'Wow, YOU LOOK how I feel.'

Marnie paused mid yawn. She had one hand on the doorframe, and the other scratching the mass of bed-head blonde hair on her head.

'Oh, cheers. Good morning to you too. Come on in.' She rolled her eyes theatrically at her friend, and moved aside to let Daisy in. She was rather weighed down with the big quilted black coat she was wearing, and she waddled like a duck through to the kitchen. Her fur-lined winter boots had a frosting of snow on their tops, and she smiled sheepishly.

'Sorry. For the snow and the snark.'

Marnie laughed, pulling out one of the chairs and helping her friend settle into it. Flicking the kettle on, she grabbed two mugs from the cupboard and checked the baby monitor. Violet was still flat out on the play-mat, looking up at the jungle gym above her. Marnie smiled at the sight, and, making the tea, let her friend vent. 'It's fine. Come on, tell me.'

'I'm just so fed up,' Daisy moaned. 'I've drunk all the raspberry-leaf tea I can stomach; we had a vindaloo the other night. I've been on a million walks, till the snow stopped me. And I'm a nightmare to everyone. I just want to snap everyone's head off. Braxton Hicks are the worst.'

Marnie put a mug of tea in front of her and took a seat. After one look at Daisy's glum face, she got the biscuits out too. Daisy threw her a look of pure guilt.

'I'm sorry. You're the last person I should be moaning to.'

'Give over, and moan away. I get it.'

'I know, but with everything you went through…'

Marnie's hand was on hers before the sentence was finished.

'Listen, we all have our own journeys to motherhood. Every journey is hard, no matter what road's taken. You're three days overdue in your pregnancy! You're tired, excited, nervous. You want to meet your baby. There isn't a woman in the world who wouldn't feel a bit down.'

Daisy smiled, through watery eyes. 'I knew you'd get it. It's worth it though, right?' Daisy looked across at Violet. Marnie followed her gaze, her whole face lighting up.

'It's the best.' She smiled back at her friend and squeezed her fingers tight. 'You moan away, have a biscuit. I'll go find a film.'

Daisy grinned, happy to be distracted. 'Popcorn?'

Marnie winked. 'You know it!' She looked through the movies with the remote, settling on a funny rom-com they'd both watched before and loved.

* * *

Marnie was putting a load of washing on when she heard Daisy from the lounge.

'Ooh!'

'Daisy? You okay?'

She half ran to the lounge, but Daisy was still on the couch, Marnie's ball mask hanging from her fingertips.

'Yeah, I forgot about the ball! How did it go?'

Marnie tutted. 'Daisy, I thought the baby was coming then! It was good. Great.'

Daisy shook her head. 'Listen, your daughter can listen to this conversation and not even know it, so spill.' Daisy was smirking now. Teasing.

Oh, crumbs.

Marnie's jaw dropped.

Gosh, did everyone know what was going on? Was it her face, giving her away? Were people talking? Oh, no.

'What do you mean?' She feigned ignorance but gave up when she realised Daisy wasn't buying it. It had been a pretty poor attempt. She couldn't help it but whenever she thought of Ash, even though she couldn't do anything about her attraction to him long term, she knew she lit up. It was driving her crazy, but she smiled at her friend and hoped she'd at least buy that. 'You're being weird.'

Daisy laughed. 'Yeah, I'm being weird.' She air-quoted her sentence, the epitome of sarcasm between the two of them. 'I saw you, dancing with that guy! You know, tall, dark? Wearing a mask? Who was he?'

'Oh, him.' She waved her away. 'Just a father of one

of the babies I delivered.' She groaned. Wow, that was pathetic. Thinking on the spot was normally her forte, but Ash made her mumble, blurt things out awkwardly.

I think I'm in trouble. Hormones! It's the hormones, calm yourself.

Thinking of being twirled in Ash's arms under the Christmas lights. The heat of his body against hers…

'Marnie! Hello?'

Marnie snapped her eyes to the impatient bloodhound before her. 'What?'

'I have never seen you act like that around one of the new dads before.' Daisy's smile was near smug, and Marnie blushed. 'Well, I'm sure I'll get it out of you.' She looked sincere. 'I'm glad for you, either way. You looked like you were having fun.'

Marnie didn't say anything, just busied herself with setting them both up for the film. It was a distraction tactic, of course, but it worked. Daisy was in need of a sit and a bit of girl time, and she happily let the subject drop in favour of sweet popcorn and a bit of Christmas cake. Marnie had done nothing but bake Christmas cake and cookies when she couldn't sleep waiting for Violet to come. Daisy could enjoy the fruits of her labour, so to speak. The thought made her smile.

She sliced some cheese to add to the slices of rich fruitcake, marzipan and royal icing before heading back to her friend. She was glad Daisy had come to visit. It was better than the two women spending the morning alone in their homes. They both needed something to keep them busy, albeit for very different reasons. Marnie found she really needed this too. As distraction techniques went, this one wasn't half bad for her either. It stopped her from thinking about that kiss, the jolt she felt when she was around Ash. She'd never felt like that with Oliver. She wondered now whether she would feel it with anyone else.

No, stop it, Marnie! There is no man in your plan. Read the fine print. Career, home, baby. That's it.

He was leaving anyway, and those eyes...

There was more to Ash than met the eye, and she knew it. That was half the problem, she guessed. Maybe she should just ask him outright. Maybe he was married, a total cad! Then all of this angst would be a moot point.

Oh, dear Lord, she thought to herself as she walked back to her friend. *You really need to get it together.*

One film turned into two, and the two women were having such fun. Daisy was more relaxed, and all baby and sexy colleague/neighbour frustrations were forgotten for the moment. Marnie was putting their plates in the dishwasher when she heard a sharp gasp behind her, followed by an unmistakably loud splash of liquid onto her kitchen tile.

'Marnie, I think the baby might be coming.'

'Really?' Marnie was shocked and excited at the same time. The excited friend had taken over from the seasoned midwife in her, and she'd not even moved.

'Er...yeah, my waters just broke on your floor.'

The two women looked down at the pool of liquid and back up to each other. After a long second, Marnie sprang into action.

'Oh, okay. Baby coming! Right!'

Violet chose that moment to let out a lustful cry,

and Marnie's training kicked in. She was going to need some help, and fast. She realised that she had it, right next door. She needed Ash. He picked up on the second ring.

'Marnie?'

'Yes, it's me, I—'

'Hi, listen, I'm glad you called—'

His voice was soft, and she wondered what he was going to say for half a second before Daisy let out another puff of air and a groan.

'I need you, Ash. Are you home? My friend's in labour!'

'What? Where are you?'

'At home—can you come?'

The line was silent for a half-second, and then his strong voice came through the line, as clear as a bell, even over the wails of Daisy and Violet.

'I'll be right there.'

He bounded through the front door, his kit bag in hand. Marnie, having quickly wiped up the spill on the kitchen floor, was just settling Daisy onto her sofa. She'd just put a new Christmas-themed throw on there. It wouldn't make it, but maybe her sofa would. She laid some towels down quickly and Ash headed to the kitchen. Marnie could hear him washing his hands in the sink as she settled Daisy as comfortably as possible.

'Have you rung work, let them know we have incoming?' Ash asked as he entered the room.

'I'll call now.' Marnie found the contact and fired off a quick call to Carey House. As ever, the staff were ready and willing to help, and by the time Marnie had hung up she knew they were organising transportation to get Daisy and her baby delivered there safely. She saw Ash watching her and turn to their patient the second he'd seen her looking. Marnie knelt down by Daisy at the foot of the couch.

'Hi, I'm Ash Ellerington.' He smiled easily at her friend, and Marnie was once again distracted by the smile on the man. When he flashed his pearly whites, she found herself utterly lost and incapable of speech.

Trouble, she reminded herself. Trouble was what this man meant. Chaos in the relative order of her life.

Daisy let out a low growl, which snapped Marnie back into the room.

'Hi,' Daisy said through gritted teeth. 'I would shake your hand, but...' Another contraction took hold, and they were coming faster. This baby wasn't going to wait for an ambulance. 'Argh!' She breathed through the latest contraction, Marnie timing it with her wristwatch. Once it passed, Daisy puffed out and relaxed against the cushions.

Ash laughed softly. He knelt down by Marnie's side, his leg jamming up against hers. A half-second later, she saw him jolt from the contact just as she felt it reverberate through her own body. She could feel the heat from his thigh warm her own. She resisted the urge to dry-hump his leg, given the situation, but only just. If there hadn't been a woman in imminent labour in the room, she had a feeling it would be a different matter. Ash was looking at her, his expression just as shocked as hers.

Is he really feeling this like I am?

Marnie felt as if the pair of them could burst into

flames. Just as she was trying to focus back on her patient, he broke her gaze, and it was back to business.

'Don't worry, Daisy, is it?' Marnie nodded at him as she helped Daisy to remove her underclothes. Once Daisy was relatively comfortable, the frown on her face softened a little. She smiled at Marnie, before turning her gaze back to Ash. Marnie recognised her mischievous grin a mile off. Her friend might be in labour, but she still hadn't missed a trick. She wondered momentarily whether Daisy had seen the sparks between them.

'Yeah, that's right. Nice to meet you, Ash.' She waved her arms around her. 'Not in these circumstances, obviously.' She turned to look him up and down fully, and Marnie felt her whole body tense. He passed her a pair of gloves and she avoided looking at him as they both put theirs on. 'Settling into Carey Cove, okay?'

Daisy's face changed from curious to uncomfortable again, and Marnie thanked her contraction for being a distraction. She was still timing it when Daisy spoke again. 'Weird—' pant of breath '—without your—' pant of breath '—mask on? *Eee-yah-ah!*'

The question turned into more of a steam-kettle noise towards the end, but she knew Ash had understood every word by the blush on his cheeks. Marnie focused on the business end of her friend and chose to ignore the other situation altogether.

'Daisy, you're fully dilated already, okay. When you feel the urge to push, push!'

She took her friend's hand, ignoring the vice-like grip and breathing right along with her, Ash by her side. The two women panted together and in a few short con-

tractions, Ash delivered the baby and placed him right
on Daisy's chest. The little boy let out a lusty cry, and
as Ash checked him over Marnie checked Daisy and
marvelled at the moment she'd watched her friend become a mother.

'Oh, Daisy, he's perfect! Well done. He was fast for
a first baby!' Ash's smile was so happy.

Daisy, her hair matted with sweat, pushed a lock
away from her forehead and, tearful, she kissed the top
of her new son's head.

'I'm so sorry about your living room!' She laughed,
and Marnie brushed her off. A tear fell down her own
cheek as she laughed with her friend.

'Don't worry, he's worth it,' she retorted. 'You did
good, Daisy. He's perfect. Ten digits, and ten toes.'

'Thanks, I'm even more glad I got bored at home
this morning now.'

The two women laughed together as Ash dealt with
the placenta, giving Daisy an injection to bring it along
a little faster and clearing away the debris of the very
fast home delivery. He watched the two women laugh
together, Marnie's ruined sofa not even a thought in
their heads. He'd witnessed something special today.
Something different. It felt more personal. Being here,
in Marnie's home, with her assisting the delivery right
next to him.

Birthing babies was always special, but watching
Marnie do it, with her friend as the patient, that was
something else. His heart was breaking wide open, and
that wasn't a good thing. Even just then, back there,
touching her body with his had reminded him of how

she made him feel. How he felt when he was around her. He'd never expected to feel anything like that again, but this woman, the feelings he experienced with her…and it was with her, he knew that.

As he left the two women to clean up, and enjoy the moment, he washed up in the kitchen and put the rest of his kit back into the bag he'd brought. All the while thinking of how Marnie's lips parted whenever she first saw him. As though a breath had caught in her throat, and she needed air back in her lungs. How he felt when he was near—

The horn sounded outside. The transport to Carey House had arrived. Zipping his bag up, he pushed the thoughts away and headed out of the cottage to meet the team outside. Relay the happy news of the birth and all that it entailed. Well, almost all.

CHAPTER EIGHT

MARNIE CLOSED HER front door, giving herself a minute before she turned back to the hallway. When she did, Ash was standing there, kit bag on his shoulder.

'Well, that was quite a morning. I can't believe Violet slept through the whole thing.'

Ash's gaze turned towards the sitting room, where Violet was snoring in her baby chair. She'd kicked up a fuss in the beginning but had nodded off just as things had got going.

'Well, I think she takes after her mother.' Ash's voice was husky. Like a dark whisper. It reached more than her ears and made a reaction. 'Nothing much seems to faze you, does it?'

Marnie laughed, mentally brushing off his words as much as her heart clung to them. 'Well, it's part of the job, isn't it?'

Ash put his kit bag down. It made a thud by his feet. 'I wasn't talking about the job. You're someone to watch, Marnie Richards.' He looked down at the hallway floor, as if deciding something. He bit at his lip, and Marnie felt that jolt once more.

He's not even touching me. Yet.

'I can't stop watching you. It's driving me mad.'

Somewhere between the biting of his lip and the words he spoke after, Marnie had found herself an inch from him, and his arms reached for her as if he couldn't bear to not touch her for a second longer.

'Me too.' That was all she could get out before they smashed against each other, groin to groin, her leg flying around his. He grabbed it with a steady hand and lifted her up, tighter against him. Holding her legs around him, he kissed at her neck hungrily before moaning in impatience. Marnie clawed at his back, pulling him tighter towards her as her back hit the wall. His arms were wrapped round her, his hand now grabbing her bottom. He dipped his head and kissed her again. Kissed her as if he'd been waiting years to do it. She ran her fingers up through his hair, ruffling it and feeling it flow over her fingertips.

God, he was sexy. She was desperate for more, for him. She'd never get enough.

'Marnie,' he breathed. 'Do you feel that?' He looked half mad with curiosity; his eyes boring into her up close. Now given that Marnie could feel how aroused he was against her, she could have answered with something cheeky, but she didn't. She knew what he was talking about. The attraction, the jolt.

'The thunderbolt?' She asked him out loud, and his face sparked with recognition as he took her lips with his again. He kissed her as though he wished to do nothing else for the foreseeable. As if he couldn't believe it was happening, and he wasn't going to waste a second of it. It was all very intoxicating. She couldn't get close enough to him, get enough of his huge, splayed palms spread across her backside. She rubbed mercilessly against him before realising what she was doing. She stopped, and his hands pulled her closer, him moving her body closer himself as he growled into her neck.

'Tell me about the thunderbolt,' he demanded rather than asked. What was it about Ash when they got closer? He turned into some kind of grizzled, husky mountain man. She absolutely couldn't get enough of it. She was still in his arms, tight in her hallway, pushed against the wall. Against him. When he pulled his head back to look at her, she was struck once more by the sheer beauty of his hazel eyes. She'd never look at another pair of eyes the same, not after his.

'It makes me crazy,' she admitted, and his lazy, satisfied smile made her insides turn to goo.

'Me too,' he said, dipping his head to kiss the tip of her chin. He didn't release his hands but hers were all over him. In his hair, touching the lines of his chest through his thin cotton T-shirt. 'What else?'

She reached to kiss him, but he pulled away, just a touch. She hummed at his denial, and he laughed. 'Tell me what you feel, and I'll kiss you more.' His eyes were half closed, hazy. He was as turned on as she was. She raised a brow at him and lifted the corners of his T-shirt up. Showing off a glimpse of his bare, chiselled chest in the warm light of the cottage.

'I feel abs,' she breathed as she ran her fingertips down the patch of skin she'd uncovered. Discovered more like. She felt like an adventurer, up here in his arms. She might as well be sitting on a table. She would be just as safe. Well, not quite. As turned on as she was, she couldn't deny how protected he made her feel, too. As if she were the only woman in the world that mattered to him. It was a rather heady emotion. No wonder the sparks had come. It was as if their energy had nowhere else to go but just zapped between them in frustration. She'd thought…well…

'Marnie,' he said, his face dipping into a frown. He looked concerned, and he was still breathing hard. She realised her hands were still in his hair, but she'd been miles away. In her own head.

'Marnie.'

This time, her eyes snapped back fully to his. His voice was stronger, more passionate, more…commanding. 'Are you still with me?'

His face had moved closer with each word, and she could feel the brush of his bottom lip against hers, then it was gone. Just half an inch away. Half a zap of lightning flashed between them, the prospect of what came next scary, but, oh…my…gosh. It would be…amazing.

CHAPTER NINE

HAVE I LOST this moment?

That was running on replay in Ash's mind as his arms still clung to her gorgeous body.

I'm so turned on, please don't stop this.

He knew he should be remembering something, that he should be staying away. He was so drunk on this woman, this amazing woman who didn't need anyone but made him want to protect her like some bear of a man from the Dark Ages—it was something he just couldn't shake. He was starting to dread the day he'd leave this place. The thing was, he'd kind of figured that out before now. His mind didn't drift, hadn't drifted. He was right here, in this moment and loving every minute of it.

'Marnie,' he said again, his voice sounding deep and broken, even for him. 'You with me?' He tried not to, but he touched his lips to hers. Just for a second, or five. He had to, he thought he might explode otherwise. It didn't help when she moaned in response.

Wow. I want to make her do that again. A lot.

The thing she did next was nearly the ending of him. He nearly dropped her on the stop. She answered him.

'Yes, Ash.' She brushed her lips against his, licking at them playfully when she pulled away. 'I'm with you.'

He smiled, and he wanted to say something else. A lot of things, some things that would definitely kill the moment and how he was feeling holding his own little spark of light in his arms. That was what she was, he thought as their lips came together again, their bodies pushing against each other to get closer.

She's a spark of light. A bolt I didn't expect, clear out of the Cornish blue sky. A star lit up on the Christmas tree.

So he was glad he didn't say anything. He didn't want to do anything, say anything to break their bubble. He wanted more of her. So he didn't make a sound. Someone did though. Violet.

His hand was on the outside of Marnie's underwear when Violet woke up. And, boy, did she wake up. Marnie's face dropped, and she wiggled out of his arms. He stayed her movements and placed her back down on the floor. She looked at him for a long moment, but he couldn't make out whether her expression was one of disappointment, or guilt. Or panic. She seemed to put a mask on the second her daughter alerted her. He felt foolish maybe, reckless, sure, but not guilty. That would imply that he regretted it. He felt more as if her dad had just walked in on them kissing in her bedroom.

'I, er…sorry.'

She was back, Violet in her arms now. The little one was teary-eyed and clearly still tired. It was only then that he noticed the tiredness was etched on her mother's face too.

'Let me guess.' He walked across to them. Violet observed him with features just like the woman holding her. He smiled at them both before answering. He felt as though he needed a moment to get over the sight of the two of them.

Was that it? Was that why he was attracted to her? A single woman with a newborn baby? No, he already knew he'd questioned that before. Without even quite knowing why. Well, he did know why. The first time they'd met, in the waiting room at Carey House. Wow, he'd thought he was going to pass out right in front of her that day. He knew he'd not even noticed her baby, or even thought about why a woman like that might be in the room. He'd just clocked her. Her questioning, curious eyes. Her sleek blonde bob, severe-looking on most people, but on her it just made her look fiercely beautiful. Especially now, he thought with a curl of his lip. 'She didn't sleep last night.'

Marnie shook her head. 'Nope. She just needs her nappy changing. I'll just take her up...'

'Oh, okay.' He took a step back in the hallway. 'Do you want me to go, let you...?'

He stopped talking when she met his eye. 'Can you stay?'

His nod was all he could get out without saying something sappy. Her returning smile nearly took him to his knees. He watched her carry her child up the stairs of the house that mirrored his in everything from size to layout but not in heart. This place was a real home. It reeked of Marnie, and Violet was everywhere now. Not in a hoarder kind of way, but just in the way a proud mother would want. Photos in frames, toy box ready in the lounge. Play mat out, bottles in the steriliser. Everything neatly stacked, in order, in the kitchen, he noticed as he looked around a little, walking slowly and taking in every detail.

He could make out Marnie's voice from upstairs. She was humming something about being over a rainbow, and it made him smile, but his heart clench. It wasn't because she was a mother. It was because of her.

He looked around the rest of the kitchen. It was neat, everywhere really. You could tell she was a new mother, of course, but he could tell she cleaned a lot. He did the same. He wondered whether she did it out of boredom too. Something to chase the feelings away.

He focused on the fridge, which was adorned with orderly photos weighed down by fridge magnets from places all around. She must have travelled at some point. Before settling down in her home town and raising a family. He was still travelling, and still carrying baggage. He felt his shoulders sag. This was messy, and he didn't want to hurt her. That was the last thing he wanted. The first thing was more of what they'd just done in the hallway.

He wanted to do more hallway stuff. Boy, did he, but it came with conversations, and talking. Longing and counting down days on his rota. Till the last day. When he would do what? Just leave and go to the next job, as if nothing had happened? He didn't relish any part of that in his future. He didn't have a plan, as such. He knew if he had, though, it wouldn't have included this. He'd met a woman like Marnie at a time that he wasn't looking or expecting to. Or wanting to, for that matter. He realised that his heart wasn't quite the swinging brick he'd thought it was now. The fast beating of his heart was testament to how strong that organ was at the moment. Half thudding out of his chest.

He heard the humming stop, and her footsteps on the stairs. This was it. This was the perfect time to escape again. He should just leave and avoid her for the rest of his time. He could do that at work, even though everything about Carey House seemed to remind him of her. She was part of the place, as noticeable as the paint covering the walls. He could take extra shifts if they came up. Bury himself in work for a different reason than normal. A less sad one, but still, a situation still best avoided.

He should contact the agency, ask them to replace him. He would be sent elsewhere. Something had stopped him though. He told himself it was because he'd already been two weeks late to start. He didn't like to let people down, and the staff at Carey House didn't deserve to be left in the lurch. He didn't want to upset Marnie either. She would probably blame herself, for not being there. Nya said that she would probably come back before the end of her proposed maternity leave. Maybe after the festivities were over, she would want to come back. Then all of this angst would be for nothing. He could stick it out another couple of weeks.

He'd been planning to ask to work over Christmas anyway. It wouldn't be any different to do that here. It would be easy. He could keep his head down, hide out in his cottage. Wait his time out. It sounded like a plan. A plan that had one question attached to it that he couldn't work out the answer to for the life of him. The question was why wasn't he heading right out of the front door? He had his keys in his hand, but his feet didn't move.

CHAPTER TEN

ALL THE TIME she was upstairs, soothing her very cranky and very tired baby back off to sleep, she was thinking of what came next. When Violet's soothed mood and now dry nappy lulled her back to sleep, and Marnie faced Ash again.

Thankfully, her baby daughter seemed to get the gravity of the situation and dropped right back off to sleep. Perhaps the totally sleepless night she'd endured had a good reason after all.

She half ran to the mirror to check her appearance, but she was oddly thrilled by what she saw. She looked drawn, sure, but she also looked like a woman she'd not seen in a while. A rather happy one with a blushing complexion. It was heady, spending time around Ash. Addictive perhaps.

She'd already spent some time daydreaming about what it would be like working with him at Carey House. How he'd looked in the waiting room haunted her. It would feel weird now for her to be there and not see him somehow. Her friends had spent the energy of many texts and calls telling her how well he was already doing filling in for her. How attentive he was, how good he was with the patients, and the team. He'd already won the girls over, Marnie could tell. They didn't say anything about a personal life though.

She quickly slipped on some strawberry-flavoured lip gloss, something she did when she felt a little on edge. It gave her confidence without looking too flirty. She straightened up her sleek bob, untangling the curls Ash had woven in with his touch. His lip on her ear, driving her mad enough that she'd lost the power of speech. It was as if time had stopped, but then Violet had stepped in. She knew she should feel guilty, but she was a single mum in every sense of the word. There was no father to hurt in this scenario. She was the sole parent to her daughter, and she was entitled to a life too. She didn't want to just be a midwife and mother, by any means.

Once she was looking more like herself, if a little tired and sparkly eyed, she checked on a sleeping Violet and headed back down the stairs. Ash wasn't in the kitchen, and her heart near stopped when she considered the fact that he might be sitting next door. Wondering how the hell he was going to get out of the situation he'd just walked and nuzzled and kissed himself into.

She turned towards the lounge and stopped in the doorway. He was sitting on the couch, legs spread apart, looking comfortable and huge on her sofa. He looked up when she walked in, his face changing from a pensive look to a wide smile.

'She went back down okay?' He stood and crossed

the room. His hand was in hers and she was sitting next to him on the sofa before she could utter a word.

'Yeah, fine. She needs the sleep, although it might cost me later.'

He chuckled softly, but then it died in his throat. 'Marnie, I don't want to complicate your life in any way.'

Marnie turned to look at him before she answered. She wanted to gauge the tone of his words by the expression on his face, but he gave nothing away. She played it safe.

'Well, I think that you saved me today. With Daisy. I needed the help.' Her face dropped when she realised she was sitting on said couch, but she had taken the covers off the cushions and covered them over with a new throw. He followed her gaze and laughed again. Once more, it didn't last long.

'I don't want to hurt you, Marn.'

Marn? No one had ever called her that. It sounded amazing coming from his mouth, but she concentrated on keeping her own face expressionless. Like his. He was giving something away though. His pain. It was there in his eyes. She knew it as she knew her own. She let him keep talking.

'I was married once.' She wasn't expecting him to say that, but at least she knew now. She could process it. He must have seen her facial expression. He held up his hands as if in surrender, his hazel eyes focused solely on her.

'I'm single now, but I don't stay in one place. My job

is covering for you. When you go back to work, that will be the end of…it.'

'I know. I've always known that, of course. I wasn't expecting this, but it doesn't change my plans.'

He took her hand in his, and that stopped her train of thought.

'Plans?' he asked, his thumb rubbing soft, slow circles across the back of her hand. It was very…distracting. Not annoying distracting, but harder to get her words out. And mean them.

'Yes…er…plans. As you already know, I had Violet through IVF using a donor, so I don't need a father for my child. I knew what the deal was, and I was more than happy with that.' She frowned at her use of the past tense. He tongue-tied her when he was this close. 'I am happy with that. I don't plan on being in a relationship.' Ash was looking at her intently, and it was the first crack in his mask. He looked disappointed. She was sure she'd seen it on his face before he looked away. When he looked back and locked her eyes down with his hazel orbs, his face was all business once more.

'That's that, then, we know where we stand.' They both nodded numbly at each other. He cocked his head. 'Why were you single, can I ask? Before your plan started.'

She sighed, remembering the details and feeling bored of the whole thing. And stung with shame too. Not as bad as before, but it still pained her to speak of it. She knew it had worked out for the best, but rising like a phoenix didn't mean that the ashes didn't still throw an ember of memory out from time to time. It still stung, that feeling of being so utterly betrayed by the one person she trusted the most. Now, she was free of it, she reminded herself.

'I wasn't, at least, not for that long anyway. I was engaged.'

His hand stuttered for just a second, but the circles continued. She half expected to see little blue sparks when she looked down at their hands, but it was just his huge hand covering hers. 'He broke it off just as we were about to get married. It was very public, and messy, and hurtful. I was humiliated and I didn't even see it coming.' She smiled when she made another comparison she probably shouldn't. 'A bit like you coming along.' His eyes focused on hers then. 'In a good way.'

'In a good way?' he checked; his brow raised. His hand started to move a little faster.

'Yeah, I think so. I know you said you used to be married, but…'

His hand stopped then. 'That has nothing to do with you though, it just means that I like to move around. I need it, I guess.' She nodded in understanding. She'd taken a good look at her life after Oliver and decided to take the plunge with what she wanted in life. Hers had just meant staying close to home. He wanted to be out in the world. Maybe that was what the sparks were about. Maybe he was just an interlude in her life. One that she needed to finally free her of Oliver and the stain he seemed to have left on her ability to care about men. At all.

'We're on the same page, as clichéd as it is. I don't want a relationship or a daddy for my baby, you don't want anything serious, and you're leaving anyway.' The look on his face told her that she'd laid it all out there rather bluntly. 'Sorry.'

'No,' he said a little bit too slowly. 'I get it. You have your life, and I have mine.'

'And a shelf life,' she agreed. She felt a little sad about that, but she didn't pick it apart in that moment. She could think about it later, digest it when Ash had left Carey Cove, and she was back fully into her new life. A working mum, just as she'd planned. That would be enough to juggle for anyone. She had no time for a man. Even one who looked like Ash. Who pulled her close as she was thinking of reasons to pull apart from him. From the touch she relished every time. The touch that made her body flicker into life. She went willingly, and they lay on the sofa together for the longest time. Holding each other in the quiet of the room and enjoying every moment. It was only minutes, but she thought of everything they could and couldn't be to each other. When she looked up at him, she knew he was contemplating it himself.

'It is a shame though,' she said out into the room. 'Another life, eh?'

'I just don't want to hurt you.' His chest rumbled his words through her, and she relished every single one, even if they contained twinges of something akin to pain too. 'I'm not here for ever—'

'I know.' She cut him off. He looked so stricken, and she needed him to know that it wasn't one-sided. She wasn't some lovesick teenager, hanging on his every word. She was a grown woman. He was the distraction

in her plan, not part of it. She'd be just fine after Ash.
She was before, right?

'Listen, we don't have to keep torturing each other
like this. You were married, I was almost married. It's
not like either one of us wants to run back down the
aisle. You're leaving, and I have my job to go back to,
and Violet to raise. After Oliver, I promised myself I
would never be in that position again.'

Just thinking about it now angered her. The humiliation, the betrayal was bad enough. It wasn't that that
gave her pause though. It was the fact that it meant that
she'd never really known Oliver at all. That was what
irked her the most. The fact that the man she'd chosen
to spend her life with was an illusion. The Oliver in her
head was not the Oliver she'd been due to walk down
the aisle with and she wasn't in a hurry to make a mistake like that ever again. 'Listen, I have my own plan
for my life, with Violet. I never had a man figure in it.
I wasn't expecting you.'

'I wasn't expecting you either.' He didn't look completely unhappy at the thought.

Good, I don't regret it either.

'We're both on the same page, as rubbish as the book
might be.'

'Exactly. Hey, if our exes could see us now. I wonder
what they would think about how much they messed
us up.'

'Yeah, well.' Ash let go of her to run a hand through
his already ruffled hair. 'If you ask me, Oliver is an
idiot. You had a lucky escape. He didn't deserve you.'

'I have to agree with you there.' Marnie laughed

softly. His jaw was tensed when she finally looked across at him. He was mad, brooding.

'I mean it. He's a jerk, hurting you like that.' He filled her eyesight, her senses, with those hazel eyes she'd come to love seeing day after day. 'I don't want to ever hurt you like that. I could never…'

She silenced him by doing what she felt. She kissed him. He wasn't a jot like Oliver. She didn't know much about Ash, or his story before Carey Cove, but she knew that much. He didn't have Oliver's arrogance, for a start. She felt as though she could trust him. He'd always been so different from Oliver, even if she'd been blind or too reluctant to see it when she'd first met him. As she kissed him, telling him everything with her tongue, she decided to just enjoy the moment. She'd have Christmas with him, surely that would be enough?

'Marnie.' Ash pulled away. Just enough to break their lips apart, but his arms came up around her. Encircling her in his grasp. She could smell the fabric softener on his clothing, the aftershave emanating from his delicious neck. His eyes were half closed when he focused on her once more. 'What are we doing? I thought we agreed to…' His words trailed off, his grip tightening. 'I don't think I can stay away from you. While I'm here, I—'

'Want to spend every minute with me?' she finished for him. He nodded, his expression hopeful, unguarded. She reached for him, tighter. One hand came up around his side, slowly brushing each finger along the confines of his clothing. He drew a ragged breath when her finger came up to brush his lips. 'I don't want to be away from you either. We have Christmas, right? I'm good with that.'

And she was. Whatever came after, she would remember her time with this heavenly man. Fondly, she hoped. And not wistfully. She didn't want Ash Ellerington to be something else she would have to survive through. Even if she knew every moment together would be worth it, his departure was ever looming between them. Of course, right now, in his arms, she was finding it hard to remember that fact. The thought of him being anywhere but here, right now, was more than she was willing to think about. For tonight, the plan was in the kitchen drawer of her mind. Something to be picked up and dealt with later. For now, on this snowy December afternoon, Marnie was choosing to live in the moment.

CHAPTER ELEVEN

SHE WAS OFFERING him herself, and Christmas together. Violet was still sleeping, but he knew she would be a part of the picture too. They came as a package deal. If he spent more time with Marnie, then Violet would be there too, of course. He knew that. He was well aware of her plan, and how important her daughter was to her. That little girl was the centre of her universe, and he'd known that from their first meeting.

He'd seen a lot of mothers over the years. Growing up with sisters, he was pretty in tune with the female brain, and how it worked. Add motherhood to that, and the woman changed. Whether she expected to or not. Some mothers were overwhelmed, which he understood. When he'd thought of being a father, he'd felt the weight of responsibility as well as the joy. Marnie was here doing everything on her own. He was in awe of her, and the thought of tainting it should have rung like an alarm bell in his head, but all he felt was happiness at the thought of spending time with Marnie, with both of them.

He shuddered as her finger continued its travels

along his lips, and he felt it deep in his…well, trousers. This woman, even just having given birth and cared for a child single-handedly mere weeks ago, was gorgeous. Her curves were in all the right places, she had the best shock of blonde hair in a haircut that drew him to his knees. That time they'd kissed, and he'd run his hands through her hair, wow. That night all he could think about in bed was how sexy she'd looked with her hair all messed up. *By me.* He told her that, minus the territorial comment. He did feel protective of her though. He wanted this to be a good experience for both of them. In all ways. If it was going his way.

'I think we should go upstairs,' she said, as if she'd plucked the thoughts right out of his head.

'Okay,' was all he could croak in response. Marnie picked up the baby monitor and took his hand. He was out of the arms of that couch and into hers in half a second, and he drew her to him. Lifting her. She wrapped her legs around him, giggling into his neck.

'Sorry,' she started, but he shook his head. The smile he threw her probably gave too much of himself away, but he was out of breath. Not from carrying her, he was meant to do that. He could feel the jolt between them, pulsating the more they touched. Out of breath from looking at her. He dropped a kiss on her lips and headed for the stairs. She pushed open her bedroom door with her dangling foot, and Ash walked right over to the bed and sat down. Her knees brushed the surface of the duvet, and she clenched her legs around him.

'Don't panic,' he said softly, aware that her eyes

had widened when they hit the bed. 'We don't have to do anything.'

She blushed, her eyes falling to his lips before she met his gaze again.

'I want to, it's just…been a while.' She rolled her eyes, a comical grimace crossing her features that he'd never seen before. 'Oliver.'

He felt his throat constrict and swallowed hard. 'I understand. It's been a while for me too.'

She waited for him to elaborate; he could see it. It took him a moment to get the voice to answer.

'My wife.'

Oh, God, don't ask me to tell you any more. I can't bear it. Not now.

She nodded slowly. 'We're in the same boat, then.'

He relaxed when she smiled at him, her eyes on his lips again. The mood was far from broken, but it took him a moment to focus again. He was close on that one. It was getting harder now not to have the conversation, but after her comments on the single-mother thing, it wasn't the time. He couldn't break this moment if he tried. He would probably be struck by lightning the second he walked out of the front door.

'I have something else to tell you.' She was biting her lip now. He braced himself for what she had to say. It would take a lot for him to leave. Probably the house caving in wouldn't stop him. He was enjoying being with her too much, even with the secrets and the inner torture of opening up his heart, his life, even to another person. Even temporarily. He was never the love-and-leave-them kind of man, and he didn't relish starting now. Especially not with the woman currently sitting astride him. 'I just had a baby.'

He laughed, part relief, part loving her sense of humour. 'Marn, I am aware of that fact. A Carey-House-delivered baby.'

Marnie smiled. He knew about her birth story. Her girls at work had been meddling, he could feel it. Oh, they hadn't revealed any patient details, but he knew them well enough to know them to be a very romantic bunch. No matter what they might have protested. Nya was the worst meddler, but she had a heart of gold that even outshone the rest of the team of angels he worked with. They adored Marnie, and he could see why. In about fifty different ways. Just off the top of his head.

'That's right, I'm just saying. I have a new mum body.' He laughed again, but her look stopped it.

'Oh, come on.' He shook his head, and caught her chin in his grasp. He kissed her once, twice. The third time because he couldn't resist, even though he wanted to get his words out. 'You are breathtaking, Marnie. I really fancy you.'

She smirked then, and he rolled his eyes. 'I sound about twelve.'

'No.' Marnie shook her head softly. 'I really fancy you too.'

There was no more talking for a while. Marnie slowly undressed Ash, as he undressed her. They stood together, taking each other in for a long moment before coming back together on top of the covers. They wanted to take their time, but, with Violet to think about, Ash knew that this time would never be enough. He would want more, even before he'd had it.

They kissed and explored each other, running fingers along each other's skin and learning the maps of each other. He wondered for a moment how it would feel when it came time to leave, but she reached for him then, and the thought floated right out of his head. Reaching for his wallet from his trouser pocket, he pulled out a condom. She lay beneath him, her hair messed up and wild across the sheets around her head. She was stunning, and it took him a second to gather himself before he lowered his lips back to hers. He lined himself up, her gasp as he pushed against her opening driving him wild. He didn't push any further, choosing instead to kiss her some more. He couldn't get enough of kissing this woman.

She wiggled her hips beneath him, and his resolve was broken. He slid in slowly, giving her a chance to adjust to him. The second he pushed in, they gasped together, his groan a low rumble that skipped across her chest. Her hands were in his hair as he rocked against her, slowly, languidly at first, but then harder, faster. She moved with him. He was enjoying every second and wanting to kiss her lips clean off her face. He grunted when she moved slightly beneath him, taking him in further.

'Slow down,' he urged. 'I don't want this feeling to stop.' He never wanted this feeling to stop. Who would? Marnie Richards had blown his nomad world apart.

That only seemed to spur her on, and he reached between them. Rubbing her with his thumb, enjoying every little grip of her hands on his body and little moan in his ear or against his mouth. She pulled him closer, kissing his neck as she reached release. Clinging to him, she enjoyed the aftershocks of her orgasm.

'Babe,' Ash breathed. 'You're killing me here.'

She realised she'd been clenching down on him, and she smiled devilishly at him, moving her hips again. He knew his goofy expression had turned back to lust. He moaned as he thrust harder, deeper. Kissing her all over, telling her how good she felt. She did feel good. She felt like the only woman on earth. It was quite a heady feeling and not one he'd been expecting to feel when he'd woken up that morning. Or any morning.

His movements grew jerky, his voice less coherent. He kissed her fiercely, his thrusts quicker as he came. His kisses didn't stop, they just tapered off as he came back down to earth. When he did look at her again, he marvelled at just how happy and satisfied she looked. She lifted her head, slowly kissing him. A different kiss this time, he felt. The jolt was still there, but something else was there with it. When she pulled away, he checked her expression for clues as to how she was feeling, but she turned to the side. Her mind was on the monitor. He couldn't blame her for doing that. She stiffened when she saw him watching her.

'Sorry.' The rueful smile on her face was another thing he wanted to store up in his brain and remember. 'Habit.'

'Don't apologise for being a mum. It's kind of cool to see you two together.' He didn't imagine his wife and child when he observed Marnie either. Was that a good sign, or a bad one? Another thing to wrack his brain over later. When he was alone again. 'Give me a second.'

Getting rid of the condom in the bathroom, he walked into the bedroom just as she sat up in bed. He hadn't put anything on, but he didn't show any signs of being shy around her. He didn't feel shy, it felt...normal. Their time together was short, he was going to live it to the full. Squeeze every last drop of juice out of the moments they shared.

He got back under the covers, pulling her to him so she was snuggled in the crook of his arm. Her head on his shoulder, he could smell her shampoo. And him. There he went again, feeling all alpha wolf. Given that he wasn't about to start peeing on the Christmas trees surrounding her property, he squashed the thought. Next Christmas he wouldn't be here. He'd probably be a distant memory to Marnie. Someone would snap her up when she least expected it. He wasn't daft. If things had been...

'Violet will be up soon, but if she wakes up, don't feel like you have to go.'

'Okay.' He couldn't see her expression. Was she hinting for him to go, or reassuring him that he didn't have to? Nah, she didn't play games like that. Neither of them did. She meant what she said. Her stomach grumbled, and he realised with the events of the day, she'd probably not even eaten. 'Do you fancy some food? I cook a mean omelette. We can have a break from all the Christmas food. I'm maxed out on marzipan this week anyway.'

He patted his non-existent belly and Marnie pushed him till he theatrically pretended to flail at the edge. She pretended to save him, and, somewhere in the tugging and the laughter, he'd flipped her on top of him and they were kissing again. And doing other things that they probably didn't have time for. Violet truly was a good baby. She didn't stir till they were laid happily in each other's arms again. It felt so domestic, he should have been running. He didn't move anywhere but closer to Marnie.

By the time they were downstairs later, Violet having a feed while Ash cooked for them both in her kitchen, Marnie realised that having a new neighbour might just have been the lift she'd needed to finally move on fully. She'd realised something else too, as he brought her a steaming hot cup of cocoa, with whipped cream and marshmallows. She couldn't give a stuff about Oliver any more. The man could go off and rot in her back story. She was onto her new life. Sure, it might not involve this picture, but she'd have this memory, right? Of something that was easy. And hot to boot. After the day's events, she was definitely feeling the festive spirit.

Thinking about Christmas, her mind wandered to thoughts about Ash and his circumstances. He always just seemed to work or be around here. While she knew he'd once been married, he'd not mentioned any friends, or any family. Maybe he really was alone? Did that make him lonely?

She thought back to her time after Oliver but before

Violet. That had been a lonely time. Even with all her friends and family around her. So maybe Ash needed just as much fun as she did? She was wanting to get out more too. It was great going out with the girls but talk often did drift to men. Which left her nothing to speak about. She wasn't going to tell him about this, either, mind you. Not when it was only a fling.

She'd always hated that word. Holiday romance sounded better. A Christmas holiday romance. Why not? She sipped at her cocoa, watching Ash as he moved around her space. He filled every space he was in. He made his presence known without even meaning to. It was a shame that he spent so much time alone. She had a feeling she wasn't the only one in need of fun.

'Do you fancy coming with me to an engagement ball? I mean, Sophie and Roman's engagement ball. You've probably been told everything about it already. They've probably already invited you, but—'

'They did, and I'd love to go with you, Marnie. I'm already looking forward to it.'

Wow. She *was* going to have a good Christmas. She didn't need Santa this year. Just the neighbour she couldn't stop thinking about. As he brought over a pasta dish that made her mouth water, she thanked her lucky stars.

Ash nudged her arm, and her eyes fell onto his effortlessly. She always seemed to lock on. He did the same thing.

'Eat up.' He winked seductively. 'You'll need all your

strength.' He licked a bit of sauce off his thumb. 'For all that dancing.'

'Yeah,' she agreed, tapping her fork against his. 'We have to dance. It's Christmas.'

CHAPTER TWELVE

MARNIE HAD HAD a busy day. Ash had been working, so she'd decided to finish the house completely for Christmas. She'd changed her sheets, cleaned everything. Taken Violet out in her carrier for a bracing walk. The stuff she normally did, but that day she'd had an extra spring in her step.

She was happy—really happy. She felt sexy and seen, she was killing it at being a mother, and she was involved with her neighbour. In lots of delicious ways that made her skin blush pink even in the cold Cornish weather. She tried to plaster on a normal expression, dulling her smile to an acceptable level. Her cheeks were hurting anyway from doing it all day.

She'd received the odd text from Ash when he was on a break. Telling her he was excited for the night ahead. To see her again. Asking what they were both up to. He was good with Violet too, not hands-on, but he always asked about her. She'd noticed the other night, when he'd cleaned up. He'd put all Violet's bottles in the steriliser. Folded her laundered pink baby blanket and left it on the side. It showed he thought something of her.

Oh, God, she was thinking again. There was no time for this. Her mother was coming through the front door. No time for wistful thinking that was neither part of the plan, or possible. It was a holiday romance. Holiday. Romance. She drummed the thought into her brain even as her heart tried to pump it out.

Oh, hell, no. Suck it up, Marnie!

'Hello!' her mother trilled the second she was through the door.

Marnie steeled herself for some subterfuge. Aka hiding the fact she was sleeping with her neighbour every chance she got. Or was planning to anyway. While she could. While the feelings creeping in were still manageable.

'Hi, Mum!'

'Don't worry, the cavalry's here,' she called from the hallway. 'I'm so glad you're going out again, love. Where's my granddaughter?'

'Up here,' Marnie called down the stairs. 'Bring up that glass of wine from the side, would you?'

Minutes later, Violet was in the arms of her cooing grandmother, and Marnie was sipping at the cold wine and looking at her reflection in the long mirror.

'You look beautiful, Marnie. That dress is perfect.' It was a good find. It was a normal dress, just a size bigger than she'd usually wear, but she'd altered it. It had ruched, sweeping material across the tummy area, giving her confidence with her post-partum tummy. She loved her body for what it had achieved, but she wanted to feel good tonight. Confident and not giving a moment to adjust her outfit or worry about this tiny fold or that.

Her body was beautiful, and she felt like that now. She knew the confidence had come in part from Ash, but it was down to her too. She felt as if she was finally living the plan. With a sexy six-foot-odd midwife bonus.

This dress was perfect for that. In a liquid, molten gold silk material, it made her feel as if she could hold her head up. She'd stuck with her usual sleek bob, knowing with a thrill that Ash loved it. It would no doubt be messed up by his hands by the end of the night. The thought of that gave her a frisson of butterflies in her stomach. Tonight felt really special. Oh, she knew that at Christmas most things felt special, everything was heightened. Good and bad, but it was more than that. She was thrilled to be going out with Ash. Even if her mother was there to witness them together before they left, with all her feelings on her face. Like mother, like daughter. She shrugged.

When Ash arrived at her door, he agreed with her mother about her dress. He looked at her in a very different way though. One that made her whole body quiver under the material.

'Marnie, that dress is beautiful. You look amazing.'

She smiled. Normally she would have rebuffed the compliment from men but, from him, she didn't feel the need to.

'Thanks, you look handsome too.'

He was dressed in a smart black suit, the hazel of his eyes sharper against the dark blocks of colour. His tie matched her dress, she noticed. A matching gold that shimmered when he turned. They would look like a couple. She wondered whether he'd thought of that.

As if he had put thought into the tie. He'd obviously taken note when she'd told him what colour dress she was wearing.

'Nice tie—is it new?' she added, and was rewarded with a smirk. A woman couldn't analyse a smirk, so she decided to stop trying. They weren't about games; they spoke about what they thought. If not fully what they felt. What she felt.

'Thanks. I thought it would complement your outfit, but nothing could beat that.' Her mother was busy fussing over Violet when she saw his gaze check on them. He leaned closer. 'You really are trying to kill me.' He half chuckled. 'You look amazing. I can't wait for tonight to be over.'

'Aww.' She was enjoying this. Teasing him. Driving him wild. 'No dancing?'

He gave her a look that almost had her reaching for the zip of her dress prematurely.

'Plenty of dancing. Nice and close.' He practically whispered into her ear. 'Hot and sweaty too, I should think.' He pulled back just as her mother turned back to face them. He gave her a smug little smirk, a secretive little move that made her whole body react and held out his arm like a perfect gentleman who never made a woman blush with his wicked ways. When he looked back at her mother, the simpering smile she gave him told Marnie that her mother was already sold. This was getting messier the more time went on.

'Shall we?'

She tucked her arm into the crook of his. Messy, but thrilling.

'Let's go. I'm itching to get on that dance floor.'
She gave him an innocent enough look for the benefit
of her mother, but her sultry eyes were all for him. The
squeeze she felt on her arm as he tucked her in closer
to him was all the answer she needed.

The evening was chilly, but thankfully mild for December. Their breath still condensed in the air around
them as they walked away from her cottage. It wasn't
too cold though, even though the snow was sparkling
with the ice contained within the white surface. With
her silk shawl, she felt quite comfortable. Unless this
was just down to the heat of the man she was walking
with. Her arm was still in his, and he'd slid it down for
her hand and held it in his the minute their houses were
out of sight. It was romantic, walking up to the hall.
Everything was lit up. Fairy lights hanging high in the
branches of all the trees they approached. It was like
a fairy walkway, and the closer they got to the party
venue, the bigger and brighter the lights and Christmas
decorations grew.

'It looks like your front lawn,' Ash quipped, and
she poked her tongue out at him. He'd helped her drag
the rest of her lawn decorations out when he'd seen
her struggling one day. It was yet another Christmas
memory of him that had woven into her memory. When
she was dragging them out solo next year, she already
knew she'd be thinking of him. The thought of it was
enough to make her miss him. Even while she was by
his side right now. She pushed the thought out of her
head and watched it freeze in the snow. Tonight was

not for thinking ahead. It was Christmas Eve. She was going to enjoy herself as much as she could.

'You should see some of the other houses around here,' she countered, thinking of one friend in particular. One who loved penguins and decorating even more than she did. 'Some of them make mine look like the Grinch's place.'

'I don't doubt it.' Ash nodded. 'Are you excited for tomorrow?'

'Very.' She beamed at Ash. 'Violet's first Christmas.' They could see the engagement party venue now, their feet picking across the grass. Ash was holding her tight, as though he was scared her heels would spike the ground and pitch them both forward. 'Oh, doesn't it look festive?'

Ash took a beat longer than normal to respond. Actually, he had been a bit quiet since they'd left the house. Maybe he wasn't looking forward to tomorrow as much as she was? He'd already told her he'd put himself on the rota at Carey House for the day, explaining he'd happily take the hit, being the new guy at work, and a temporary one at that.

'Ash, are you okay?'

His gaze fell to hers, and his face changed again. He looked almost peaceful. The frown gone from his features as if it were never there in the first place.

'I'm great,' he said, nodding to the revellers. 'It looks like the whole village is here.'

'Oh, they are.' She had no doubt that most of the villagers would be here. Everyone loved Sophie and Roman. They were really happy as a couple. They didn't much take their eyes off each other. Even when they were talking to other people. Marnie could see them, looking for the other over shoulders and sides of heads. It was cute to see. It made her heart ache a little too. They had their whole lives together. She had the rest of her maternity leave. If that. 'What do you think?'

She'd asked him an innocent enough question, but he couldn't tell her what he was thinking. The enormity of it was still hitting him. Leaving his cottage tonight and making the short walk to Marnie's house, he'd had a feeling brewing inside him. He'd felt it at work too, the more he recognised people who came to see him, saw babies come back in for development checks. Babies he'd delivered were out there now in Carey Cove. Some of them might even be Violet's classmates down the line. He had felt the odd pang of not seeing them grow up around him. How Violet would grow up without him. Hell, she wouldn't even remember him, not that he would expect her to. It would be better if she didn't remember a man who came and made her mother happy, then disappeared.

Would Marnie miss him? How long would it be until some other man saw what she was and set his sights on making Marnie his? Ugh. He'd been down this way of thinking before. Another man in her house? The thought made him feel sick to the pit of his stomach. He felt at home on their little street, in Marnie's house. He felt at home everywhere in Carey Cove. It was an odd feeling, but he was fast growing to like it.

He watched his colleagues around him. Nya and

Theo were dancing, smiles on both their faces, as they watched Sophie and Roman pass by. He was twirling her on the dance floor, her laughing her head off. Her ring twinkled like a bauble under the festive tinted lights above them. He needed to shake this melancholy off. He wanted Marnie to have fun tonight—she deserved it. He wanted to make the night amazing. Just for her.

'Do you fancy a drink?' he asked her. He could do with one too. To take the edge off. Push the dark thoughts away from the corners of the dance floor.

'In a minute.' She grinned back. 'I'm enjoying the people-watching.' She pointed out one of the darker corner tables. Ash looked across, scanning till he saw Lucas. He didn't have Harry tonight, and he was obviously enjoying his night off. Kiara was giving him little kisses, the pair of them whispering to each other. Wrapped up in their own little world.

'Those two are so cute,' she breathed. 'I love the two of them together.'

He raised a brow, and she brushed him off. 'Hey, just because we've sworn off love, doesn't mean I can't appreciate romance.'

He looked back at Kiara and Lucas. He'd thought he was sworn off love too, once upon a time. He hoped Marnie didn't really think that. He already knew that they were lying to themselves about this just being a passing attraction between them. They both knew it was more than that. They felt it. He was sure of that.

This place, he was sure of that too. He didn't want to leave. He could really see himself living here, putting down roots again. It was such a surprise to him, but it was there, just the same. He'd felt so lost when his family had been taken from him. He'd given up the home he'd shared with Chloe. His parents had sold their farm, his childhood home, and moved away years ago. They wanted to enjoy as much of their retirement together as they could. It was always their plan, and he was thrilled for them. They were enjoying their life, happy together in their twilight years. Chloe's own parents had recently sold up their own neighbouring farm, starting a new chapter of their lives too. It seemed that everyone was moving on, while he just observed and moved from place to place.

Marnie had drifted away with a kiss on his cheek, done on the sly. They weren't exactly hiding their status, but they didn't even know how to classify it themselves. A festive fling sounded tacky, and far off the mark from what he felt. He watched her chatting with her friends. She came alive around her friends. Animated hand movements, head thrown back in laughter. Marnie might have sworn off love, but it hadn't left her.

She had it in abundance for her daughter. He saw how loved and cherished Violet was. Marnie as a mother was a joy to see. She found it easy, and every little task was an honour to her. Not a chore. Even when she was tired, and half asleep, she still showed how lovely she was. How kind, how thoughtful. A man would have to be a lunatic to walk away from a woman like that. God knew, he would never have walked willingly away from Chloe. Oliver was a man he hated despite having never met him. Any man who would allow a bride like Marnie to escape was a fool, in his book. If he were Oliver, he would have married Marnie and never looked back. That would have been the best way to spend his twilight years. Being loved by a woman like that.

Marnie's eyes searched for his across the room, and she found he was already watching her. He could see her cheek flame, and as she looked at him with that knowing grin he felt his body stir. His heart too. He wanted this, but it was too messy. Too hard. Hell, he'd arrived late to this job. Perhaps he should never have come at all. The agency would have hired someone else. Marnie would never have known him. He would never have met someone he knew was a game-changer. He wasn't even playing the game, was he? He hadn't planned to. He hadn't planned anything. What was the point in planning when everything was lost? When he'd been on that floor, being fussed over by his sisters, that was all he would say to them.

Wash your hair, Ash. You look like a scruff.

What's the point? She isn't here to see my hair. Run her fingers through it.

He remembered how final things had felt. How ended his life had felt. Yet he was still here, expected to keep living it anyway. All he'd had left was his job, and a house he hadn't wanted to live in any more.

Marnie was still deep in chat with a small crowd, no doubt asking the work gossip and catching up on what she'd missed. When he'd arrived in Carey Cove, late and still a little broken, he'd felt as if he'd simply closed yet another chapter. He hadn' realised Carey Cove would make him yearn to open up another one.

The time he'd spent here at Carey Cove, developing relationships at work, spending time with Marnie and Violet, hanging out at their houses, it was all so happy. Hopeful. He'd felt a sense of belonging, and he felt it even more strongly now as he watched the people around him at the ball. He was sitting alone, Marnie occasionally looking over and meeting his eye with a sly smirk. A smile she only gave to him, he noticed. He felt territorial about that smile. It was just his. If he weren't here, would it disappear from her face for ever?

He winked at her and enjoyed seeing her flush before she turned her attention back to what Sophie was saying to the group of excited friends at the bar. Marnie was next to be served. He didn't have long before she was back. He thought of Chloe and Sam then, and recalled the last time he'd visited their graves. He'd sat on the grass by their headstones for the longest time, telling them that he loved them. That wherever they were, they were always with him. He wondered, now, what they would think if they knew about Marnie. How he'd met a woman who made him happy. A place that made him want to stay, instead of run. He was healing. He had healed a lot. Especially in this place, with these people.

Marnie was being served at the bar now, and he watched her smile at the barman. Her gaze flicked over to his, and he smiled over at her. Her whole face lit up when she smiled back, and it made his heart swell. He didn't want to leave this place. Marnie really was an amazing woman, and he couldn't imagine not staying put to see where this could go. It wasn't just the newness of it all, the twinkly lights and festive spirit overpowering his nomadic brain. When Marnie got back from the bar, he fully intended to ask her to be his girlfriend, to date properly. He'd tell her about his past, about Chloe and Sam, about the love and the loss he'd experienced, about how it had set him off on the path that had eventually led him to Marnie, and Violet, and a fresh start for them all.

He could find another job when it was time for Marnie to go back to work, and he'd keep living next door. He could picture it, them spending their nights together, sweaty and laughing wrapped in bed. Walking on the beach, making sandcastles with Violet as she grew up in front of their eyes. He wanted that, he wanted all of it. He wanted Marnie. He couldn't wait to ask her to be his. To see this through. Together.

His phone buzzed in his pocket, and when he saw the name on the screen his heart lurched in shock. It was Chloe's mum calling him. The timing couldn't have been worse. He felt a wave of emotions. Guilt at what he was just thinking seconds earlier, how happy he'd felt before the call had interrupted his daydream. He was about to change his life, but it would change Chloe's parents' lives too. He was thinking about moving on, starting again, but although they'd physically moved, he knew that they would never be able to move on in the same way.

He loved them dearly, but their relationship caused him sadness sometimes. Like now. When he felt as if he was finally ready to move on, but he didn't know how to do it without causing more pain to others. He answered the call, trying to sound jovial and hoping she wouldn't hear the background music of the ball.

He didn't want her to think he was out having fun all the time. Another pang of ridiculous, crippling guilt. He listened hard, but he couldn't make out his mother-in-law's voice above the noise. He headed away from where they were sitting, taking the nearest exit into the cold December air.

The ball was in full swing. Sophie and Roman were enjoying every minute of their engagement party. It was a beautiful event, all twinkling lights, tasteful Christmas decorations and Cornish ones too, making the party look magical. Everyone was dressed in their finery, and Marnie had had so many compliments on her dress, how glowing she looked. Little did they know the reason why. Her stomach still flipped at the thought of her and Ash together. The shocks he brought to her skin every time he touched her.

She walked over to the table she'd left him sitting at, champagne glass in each hand. She was going to ask him to stay over, she'd decided. Sure, her mother would raise her eyebrows and she'd be straight on the phone tomorrow to find out the gossip before she went to Christmas dinner. It would be worth it though. She didn't like the thought of him waking up in his house next door, alone. What was the point, when he could wake up next to her and have Christmas with them? She could easily share her first Christmas morning with Violet with him, then he could go in to work at Carey House as he'd planned, but be back to spend the evening with her.

The table was empty. Strange. She'd just seen him

there. The napkin he'd been fiddling with was sitting on the table, right where he'd been sitting. He'd looked fine the last time she'd set eyes on him. She hadn't seen anyone speaking with him. She stood there, glasses in hand, scoping the room for his hazel eyes. The back of his head. No matter how she looked for him in the crowd, she knew he wasn't there. Had he left? Maybe it had all been a bit too much. Did he regret them? He didn't seem to show any signs of regret. He'd nuzzled her neck before she'd left his side to go to the bar.

She remembered where she was. Staring at an empty chair with two glasses in her hands. She took a seat on the chair he'd just vacated. Putting the drinks on the table without spilling them was no mean feat either. Humiliation was running through her whole body, making her hands shake. He could just be in the toilet, she reasoned. He'd pop back up any minute, and then she'd feel like an idiot.

She calmed herself down, checking around to see if anyone had clocked her mini meltdown. If they did, they showed no signs of knowing. The party was in full swing, people in love all around her, having fun. She reached for her glass, drinking till the glass was empty. Having fun. As they should be. It was Christmas Eve, what had—?

Her phone was ringing in her bag. Grabbing for the clasp and dumping her glass on the table, she reached for her mobile phone. It was Ash.

She went to say hello but was stopped by a large crackle on the line. She listened. The line was awful. It sounded like the daleks were invading. She could hear a voice, faint. *Ash!*

'I know I need to go.'

What was he talking about? She listened again. The line kept dipping in and out of sound, the crackles cutting everything off. She had to force herself to keep the phone to her ear. As she did, she could hear Ash again. Mostly it was just his gravelly voice she heard, the words not quite making sense to her ear. Till three did that made her blood cool.

'Wife and son,' was what he said. It was clear to her ear, even as her mind took a while longer to process the news. So, he was married? And they had a child? He did regret their night together. Because he'd crossed the line. What the hell was he doing with her here, on Christmas Eve, if he had a wife and child at home somewhere?

She never went out, and she'd thought that he was worth it. For this short while. She'd even hoped he'd stick around after, not that she'd discussed it with him. Now all of that, all of this, was laughable. The line went dead, and she pushed the phone back into her bag. He didn't ring back. She had a feeling that she wasn't meant to hear his words. She wished she hadn't either.

She wanted to run home, tell her mother everything, get drunk and cry in bed. The old Marnie would have done just that. She was a mother now though, and she had heard only a snippet of a conversation. She owed Ash the chance to explain. She wanted to hear it, actually. She felt as if she needed to look him in the eye, if only for one last time. She was done hiding from men, and she couldn't write Ash off yet. She drank his glass, pulled herself together and headed back to her friends. Whenever anyone asked her where her date was, she smiled and told them that he had a personal situation.

Did he? she thought to herself. That was the million-dollar question.

She cared too much about the answer. He wouldn't be there tonight, in her bed, talking about their evening together. Or in the morning, when Violet woke up to discover that Santa had been. Not that she really knew, being that young, but Marnie didn't care.

She still knew.

She could do it alone. That was the plan anyway. She pushed aside all thoughts of Ash, and partied with her friends, trying to dance and laugh her cares away. It was Christmas after all.

She had the best night ever, or she would have had. If not for Ash. Him not being there just felt wrong, even though she was used to seeing the faces that she'd spent her nights with pre-Violet. It felt weird Ash not being there. She came home alone, which also felt weird. Ash's house was in darkness when she headed to her own front door. She resisted the urge to sob. Pulling it together once again to greet her mother, regale her with enough happy stories of the night to send her on her happy way home with thanks from her daughter. She went to kiss Violet goodnight, smiling as she watched her snuffle softly.

'Happy Christmas, Vi,' Marnie said, before pulling the nursery door half to. The night light lit up enough of the room to make it cosy.

The little LED Christmas tree on her dresser was twinkling. Marnie looked at it for a long time, before heading back downstairs. She had a few more gifts to wrap, and a bit more wine to drink. Not too much. She wanted her daughter to have the perfect day tomorrow. But tonight, tonight she allowed herself to be just a little sad. And eat the rest of the mince pies, she realised as she headed to bed a couple of hours later. She needed to get some sleep or Santa wouldn't come, she told herself.

What little lies we tell our children.

That was her last thought before she fell to sleep, mince-pie crumbs still round her mouth.

CHAPTER THIRTEEN

Christmas morning

VIOLET STARTED STIRRING in her cot around half-six, but Marnie had been awake watching the world through her open curtains. She'd watched the inky black night, and the stupid twinkling stars, and she'd got into a mood with herself. About being so bothered by another man who was a feckless idiot. A temporary relationship to boot. What was all that about? Was his child unborn? Was that the reason for the time limit, other than his leaving when the job ended? Obviously, there were other midwife jobs available in Cornwall.

Oh, for the love of safe deliveries, now she was mad at him for leaving, when she knew that was the deal anyway. She'd *wanted* that deal, she couldn't rewrite history now she was mad at him. She *was* mad at him, but she had known the score. She wasn't some lovesick teen, still hopeful of finding the perfect 'one'. She'd lived life a bit more to realise that was for the movies.

Violet's cry stopped her ridiculous hop-skip-and-jump thinking, and she decided to do what she did when she was at work. Switch off the personal-life button in her brain, and focus on the fact that Santa had been, and her baby was having her first Christmas. The best present for Marnie was undoubtedly spending the day as Violet's mum. She couldn't wait to watch her daughter, year after year, growing up and becoming her own person.

She leaned over the cot, her elated expression matched by her daughter's. It was the same all the time—they were just smitten with each other. Their eyes lit up at the sight of each other. Just like the mums and babies she'd seen over the years, when they all took their first look at each other.

'Good morning, my little gift. Happy Christmas.'

Marnie gummily grinned up at her. Her baby was growing up fast and meeting all of her milestones and Marnie was getting better at listening to the midwife training in her brain as well as the mushy goo that was her mum brain. Her mushy, sexy, messy brain goo. She'd lost a man, had a baby, met a man she could never have, been crushed by the man she couldn't have, and what else? Oh, yeah, she'd still wished for him. That moment, in the split second before she'd had her first coherent thought, her hand had reached across the bed. Not for Oliver, like some remnant of their relationship, but Ash. A man she'd spent far less time with. It was enough to distract a girl, but she was determined to have the best day.

Later on, the doorbell rang. That was the moment that Marnie should have steeled herself. A pre-baby Marnie would have, but doting mum Marnie was so happy to see her daughter enjoying her first Christmas and enjoying babbling away to the music she had on low. They were both sitting in her rocking easy chair, her favourite place in the house when she was wanting to feel normal. Grounded. That was why she didn't think it would be Ash at her door, on Christmas morning. She didn't prepare herself, she just got up and went to the door, Violet in her arms.

She opened the door. It was Ash. Standing there looking gorgeous amongst the Christmas decorations in her front garden. Her heart beat faster even as her hand tightened on the door. She might have been thinking about him, but she didn't want to see him right now. She was so angry, and she didn't want her first Christmas with Vi ruined either.

She was all set to give him a tongue-lashing and boot him off her front step when she clocked his clothes. He looked dishevelled, crumpled up like a paper ball and half-heartedly smoothed back out. He didn't look as though he'd seen a wink of sleep. She hated that they were at odds then. She wanted to know what was wrong, even if it was to do with her discovery. They'd slept together once, and he was leaving. Perhaps they could just forget this had ever happened, fly under the scandal radar till he left Carey House? She could see the pain in his eyes, and she remembered all those other times the pain had been there. Giving her a clue to an answer that she felt sure she still didn't have. Was Ash really as devious as Oliver?

She didn't think so, and she wasn't stupid. Or easy to sway. Ash was the only man she'd been interested in since Oliver. But she'd already consigned him to history. He was still going to leave.

'Listen, I—'

'I'm really sorry for leaving you last night, but it was important. I need to talk to you, Marn. Please, can I come in?'

His face was determined, and she felt her feet step to the side to admit him. Here they were, back in the hallway, a very different mood in the room.

'Happy Christmas, Violet. Is that smile for me?'

Marnie looked at Violet, and she was. She was smiling. Right at Ash, her angelic face lit up as if he were Santa himself. Marnie's heart clenched.

He's not ours, Vi. We can't keep him, baby girl. He's not ours to keep. He never was.

'She smiled at you again!' She tried to pass off her feelings with a laugh, but it sounded dull even to her own ears. She got mad instead. The feelings had to come out somewhere.

'She only does it for me usually. You're privileged, clearly!'

'Sorry,' he mumbled. 'Not a great start. You seem angry.'

'I'm not angry,' she lied through her clenched, smiling teeth.

'I just came to say—'

'Happy Christmas?' she blurted out. She couldn't listen to his explanations about his family. She couldn't bear it. She just wanted him to go. In fact, no. She didn't want that. She found herself wishing she'd never set eyes on Ash Ellerington. She wouldn't be feeling like this now.

Why does this hurt more than Oliver? How is this man so linked to my happiness?

'Listen, I really can't do this today. I'm sorry. It's Violet's first Christmas and I—'

'I know.' He went to stand closer to her, but she backed away. 'Marnie, the last thing I want is to ruin your day. Hell, I never wanted to ruin any day, any hour of yours. I just need you to listen.'

'Ash, I—'

'Marnie, please. Hear me out.' He stood before her, his hands up in surrender now. As if she were the one holding a weapon that would wound him. She couldn't hurt him now, not even if she tried. No matter what lies he had told, it was too late. Ash already had her heart. He'd wound himself around her heart tighter than Oliver ever had. She wasn't sure that she could get over this. 'I don't want to spoil your Christmas. That's the opposite of what I want for you.'

She wanted to slam the door in his face. She wanted to shut the curtains and hide away till his job ended and he left Cornwall in his rear-view mirror. She wanted that, right?

'Okay,' she half whispered. 'I'll listen.'

Ash's shoulders dropped half a foot with relief. She resisted the urge to tuck herself into the nook of his arm, pull him into her arms as she'd done before. How she was going to get through the rest of Christmas without his touch, she didn't know. The rest of her life? Impossible.

'Thank you. I'm sorry I disappeared. Last night. I didn't intend to do that.'

'Kidnapped by elves, were you?' Marnie's snarky tongue had woken up. 'You live next door. You have my number.'

'I know.' He ran his hand through his hair, sticking tufts up at odd angles. 'Marnie, I never meant to hurt you. I told you that, and I meant it. I got a call, last night. When you went to the bar. I never would have left otherwise, but it was important. It was Chloe's parents.'

'Chloe?' Marnie didn't want the answer to come from his lips, but she couldn't stop herself from asking anyway.

'My wife.' She flinched. 'Don't look at me like that, Marn. I can't take it.' She tried to move her gaze from his, but she just couldn't do it. 'I'm not married any more, you know that. I didn't lie when I said I used to be married.'

'Okay,' she plumped for. 'But you obviously didn't tell me the truth either. Not everything, and that's the same as a lie.' She walked through to the lounge, taking a seat on the couch with Violet in her arms. He'd paused in the doorway, looking at the domestic scene before him. He pressed on, striding across the room and sitting next to her on the sofa without being asked.

'I was married, but that's not the full story. The truth is that Chloe, my wife, she died. I'm a widower, Marnie. I have been for a few years. Chloe died giving birth to our son. Sam didn't make it either. There were complications. It happens.' He shrugged bleakly, as if going over a memory. 'I went over and over the case. I was there in the room. It was just, too much.'

'I'm so sorry,' Marnie murmured. She held Violet that bit tighter. She'd seen him deliver babies, be around them. Around her daughter. She'd never had an inkling that his pain was from the loss of his wife and child. She could relate to that more than most. Longing for a child. The difference was, Marnie's was safe in her arms. Ash's baby had never had a chance at life.

'I thought you were in pain, but I thought it was just from the divorce. That you didn't want to get involved because of that. I understood that.' She brushed some water from her cheek. She was crying. 'When I heard you say about your wife and child on the phone, even though the line was terrible, I thought...'

'You thought I was a cheat, and no good. Like your ex. I would never hurt you intentionally, Marnie. That's not me. Oliver was a fool. I owe you an explanation. Will you hear me out?' Ash looked so devastated that Marnie could never refuse to hear what he had to say. Silently she nodded.

'Chloe and I truly were childhood sweethearts. We married quite young, and we were each other's world. When we discovered that we were pregnant we were so excited. Our families were too. Our parents were neighbours, and we were all so close. I loved Chloe, and my son. And after they died I truly believed that I was better off alone. I guess I stopped living too.'

He paused then, and Marnie gave him the space to continue with his story.

'But I did keep living, Marnie. Only I had to find a

new way to live, a way without Chloe and Sam and the life we could have had and away from the memories that were suffocating me at times. And so I opted to move around the country, only taking short-term contracts. And those moves eventually led me here. To you, and to Violet. And honestly, for the first time in years, what I've found here, with you, and with Carey House, feels like it could be home.'

He swallowed.

'And last night, seeing you at that party, looking so relaxed and happy, and knowing what we'd already shared, I wanted to tell you everything. About Chloe and Sam, but also about how I hoped that you might be starting to feel the way about me that I feel about you.'

He paused again, before taking a deep breath and continuing.

'Only before I could talk to you, I got a phone call. It was from Chloe's mum. It totally threw me. I realised how selfish I was being, I hadn't even given them a second thought. Hadn't considered how me falling for you would impact on them. I am the only other link left they have to their daughter; how would they feel knowing that I might be moving on with my life? The last thing I want to do is hurt them.'

'You love them,' she said simply. 'That doesn't change just because their daughter died.'

Ash nodded.

'Exactly. I can't break their hearts to gain my own happiness. I needed them to be okay with it. I don't want to live out of a bag any more. I don't want to be the new guy no one remembers. Not now. I want you to remember the hell out of me, but I don't want to leave you either. Ever.' He took the pair of them in, smiling. 'I'm not trying to get some ready-made family. When we met, I just felt such a jolt. I've never stopped feeling that. It's you and me now, and Violet. If you'll have me.'

'Ash, I—'

He locked the eyes she loved so much onto hers and strode over to her.

'Please, Marnie. Forgive me for not telling you the whole truth. I swear on everything I am, I will never hide a thing from you again.' He was in front of her now, and she looked up at his face, believing the words coming out of the mouth of the man before her. Everything clicked into place now. Why he was alone and not dating. The pain she'd seen in his features from time to time. They'd met each other in this Cornish corner of the world and healed each other without even realising it.

'I believe you,' she said, reaching up and touching his cheek. 'I trust you.'

His face lit up, and he bent to kiss her. Violet was taking in the whole scene around her from her vantage point of her mother's arms. Marnie thought she saw her grinning at Ash. The little madam knew the score from the minute she met him, Marnie thought to herself with a swell of pride. Her daughter was going to be a little genius.

'You do?'

She kissed him again, her pulling him in this time.

'Yes, Ash, I trust you. I'm so sorry you went through that.' She bit her lip, but the plan was screwed anyway. If it was in paper form, it would be crunched up firmly in the bottom of the wastepaper basket. 'I love you. I do.'

'Despite your best efforts?' he quipped, his arm around both the Richards women now as if he didn't want to let go. 'I love you too, Marnie. You blew my world apart.'

He got down on one knee in front of the sofa and pulled a small box from his pocket.

'Which is why I want to marry you. For us to be together, now. No games, no plans. Just us.' He took her hands into his. 'Will you be my partner in the next adventure, Marnie? I only want to travel by your side from now on. Make a home here in Carey Cove. Help raise Violet. Love you for ever.'

Marnie cocked her head to the side. This man. He was so off the plan he was the antithesis of it. Perfect for a lover. No strings. No drama, just the fun stuff. And yet there was more, the spine-tingling feeling when you were close to a lover, one who seemed to understand you as well as you did yourself. Even after a bumpy start when they'd clashed. She'd wanted to hog-tie him and chuck him into the salty cove when she'd first met him. All the way through, the jolts of electricity between them had been undeniable. She felt them now.

'Ash, I would love to marry you. Where the hell did you come from?' She laughed, and he took a beautiful ring out of the box. He laughed with her, bending to kiss her.

'Hell, Marnie.' He kissed her. 'I came straight from hell, angel. Right to you.'

'Don't joke.' Her tone was cautious. 'Are you sure you want this? Is it not too soon? Do you need a—?'

He kissed her again, harder and more fervently this time, and she got the point. 'I'm not kidding, Marn. I came from hell. I hid all around the country, and then I came here. I was happy to blend into the background, helping other people start their families, see their joy and just move on. Save the mothers who got into trouble. It drove me, I guess. Till coming here. Till that day in the waiting room. When we touched, I just felt it. Even before then. Your hair, your eyes. They made me look right at you. That was it. That was the moment. I just realised it. I didn't realise it at the time, but I came here for you.'

'I felt it too, but I resisted the whole thing straight away. I put it down to hormones, being tired. I don't know. It scared me, I guess. I've realised now though that my past was getting in the way. I had Violet on my own, but that didn't mean I had to stay alone for ever.'

'I get it,' he comforted her. 'After I was widowed, I just thought that I'd had my chance. I wasn't looking. Are you sure you're ready to trust someone like that again, Marn? I trust you completely, but if we do this…' He seemed to struggle for the right words, and she saved a breath. 'If we do this, we're all in. I know it's fast, but I know it's right.'

'I trust you completely.' She beamed at him. 'That's my point. I felt safe the minute we met; it was like…'

'Instinct.' They said it together.

'I just didn't trust the feeling as that, is all. I want to marry you, Ash. I think we'd be so happy.'

It was his turn to beam then. He moved closer, taking her hand in his. 'I want this more than anything, Marnie Richards.' He dipped his head to a smiling Violet. She already had him wound around her little finger. Like a daddy's girl. Marnie wasn't even shocked at the thought. It felt right. 'I love you.' He said it to them both, but his hazel eyes were looking into hers, and they sparkled when she said it back. Wow, she was becoming such a sap. She filled up with tears, and they kissed again.

'I love you too,' she told him again the second their lips parted. 'I'm glad you came here. Came home to me. Happy Christmas, Ash.'

'Happy Christmas, darling. The first of many.'

'That's the plan,' Marnie agreed, and they kissed over the top of Violet's head. That night, they would do a lot of kissing, and a lot more besides. She wouldn't need the thermal reindeer pyjamas she'd bought herself as a Christmas treat, that was for sure. She reached under the tree and produced a present she'd bought for him earlier. A new sweater that would bring out the hazel in the eyes she adored.

'First Christmas as a family.' She smiled. Ash's kiss told her how thrilled he was with the idea. She felt the same way. The lightning bolt told her all she needed to know. She was going to live this adventure with Ash, and Violet, and enjoy every minute of their lives together. They had both been on very long journeys to find each other. It was time to enjoy it.

'Oh, no!' Marnie suddenly pulled away, her hand up to her mouth in horror. 'We can't do this.'

'Why? Yes, we can!' Ash was on his feet, startled, and Marnie giggled when she saw his reaction.

'Not us.' She reached out to him and he pulled her up, steadying her and the child in her arms. 'I love you, but we have other plans.' She pulled a face. 'You have to work and we have to be at my parents' house, for Christmas dinner.'

Ash smiled as she added, 'Want to come after your shift? I figure you can help me tell them our news.' She pulled him in one last time to kiss him before they went and saw the world together. As they would stay, by each other's sides, for the rest of their lives.

EPILOGUE

A LOT HAD happened in the last twelve months. Well, if Marnie looked back over the last few years, she wouldn't recognise her life now. She didn't have the wanderlust any more, even though Ash was keen to book a holiday soon. He wanted to start showing Violet the wider world, and she adored him for it. She could just see the three of them, jetting off to see the corners of the world.

She couldn't wait for her daughter to learn more, really experience life as she once had. Home was where the heart was though. She wouldn't trade any sunset beach in the world for this cold Christmas at Carey Cove. The world would still be there in January. The beaches and sunsets would wait for her family to discover them. For now, she had the magic of the season. Something the Cove had in spades. The girls had always thought so, but after the events recently in their own love lives, they were in no doubt of its existence. Any more than Marnie doubted the way she felt when Ash touched her.

The sparks still flew between them, a year on. She

doubted she would ever get enough of Ash. She would often joke, call him her little 'plan derailer'. The anticipation of becoming Mrs Ellerington only brought her joy. Her fear of weddings and everything relating to love felt like a lifetime ago. Here she was, at their engagement party and she hadn't even brought any crucifixes or garlic around her neck. Ash had laughed when she told him.

'*Marnie,*' he'd murmured, pulling her close and making her forget what they were even talking about with kisses to her neck. 'You might as well face it. We are incurable romantics now. Thunderbolts and all.'

She'd agreed, with a little more persuading from the love of her life, and his kisses.

Last Christmas, Ash Ellerington had asked her to be his wife, and she'd agreed. They'd become a family that day, with Ash moving in pretty much the minute his lease was up. He'd barely slept there anyway. He always seemed to gravitate to her place, and soon she couldn't remember a time he wasn't there. She wasn't in a hurry to remind herself either.

They'd decorated the house together this year, Ash even getting a little competitive with Nya and Theo. Marnie thought it was going to be a duel at one point, Ash and Theo lining up on the beach, each armed with a Christmas novelty light-up penguin. It was hilarious, even Nya and Marnie had wound them up in the end. The kids thought it was amazing that their dads were so excited about trimming up. Ash had made good buddies with Theo. The two men were the perfect complement to each other, and they both adored their family time.

Ash was working and living in Carey Cove, choosing not to work away and miss a minute of their lives together. He was there, full-time. A great father to Violet. The pair of them were like a comedy duo.

Ah, Violet. Her daughter wasn't quite a baby any more. She was her own little person now. She was still adored by everyone she met, of course, and she was a sociable little girl. Always babbling, waving and smiling at friends, family. She was a joy to have. Ash's face lit up whenever she was around, and the pair of them were inseparable. He'd crashed into Marnie's life, to cover for her while she became a mother, and then he'd shown her a world she hadn't thought possible.

The engagement party was perfect. Everyone had been so excited for the day to come, and now Marnie and Ash wanted to take in every little detail.

Together, they watched their friends and family have fun as they took a moment to enjoy the Christmas Eve festivities. There weren't many Christmas babies happening for once, so they were enjoying the peace. Nya and Theo had walked in earlier and blown that apart though, with news of their engagement! The whole place went wild. The pair of them had said that marriage wasn't on the cards, but obviously love had changed their minds and Marnie and Ash couldn't be happier for them. Nya was a woman Marnie loved dearly, and she couldn't be happier for her. After everything they'd been through together, the fact that their happy endings were here was amazing. Marnie couldn't wait to watch her walk down the aisle to Theo, their family and friends all there to share in the pure joy of the day.

What it meant for them, starting their new lives together after finding each other. She squeezed Ash's thigh, as if to remind herself that he was still there.

'Reminds me of our festive proposal,' his deep voice rumbled against the shell of her ear, and she felt the familiar, still-take-your-breath-away jolt that she always felt from him. 'Another wedding, eh? You lot are all going to be married off, you romantic bunch.'

She laughed. After Sophie and Roman had got married, Lucas and Kiara weren't too long after. Now Nya had fallen too. No more single girls, Marnie mused. They all looked so happy. Hope, Theo and Nya's adorable foster daughter, so beautiful with those Cornish blue eyes. Her brown hair was held back with pretty clips, sparkling sequins depicting little penguins. Nya always did dress her well.

They often went shopping together on their days off, the kids ending up in soft play while the two of them talked shop. Marnie had never imagined getting to do that with her friend. It made the trips all the sweeter to have. Hope was a lovely little girl. Marnie hoped the two of them would be as close as their mothers when they grew up. Perhaps they would even train as midwives. The next generation running Carey Cove. Hope and Violet, delivering babies. It would be just too perfect.

Hope was laughing at something, Violet giggling right along with her. Those two loved to play. They were always giggling. Just like their mothers, she thought to herself. Nya caught her eye, and the pair of them laughed. They knew they were thinking the same thing. It warmed her heart.

'I love how close Hope and Violet are.' She reached for Ash's hand, and it enveloped hers as always. He brought it up to his mouth and kissed the back of her hand. She forgot her train of thought for a moment, but Ash picked up the conversation.

'Sophie's pregnant too,' he said softly. 'They're just waiting to tell Roman's parents before they announce it.'

'I know.' She smiled. 'I'm so happy for them. I love how you care about our friends.'

'Of course I do.' He put his other hand over hers, sandwiching it between his mighty hands. 'It got me thinking too.' He nodded back to the two playing girls. 'It might be nice for Violet to have another kid to play with.'

She heard that. Loud and clear. 'Mr Ellerington, are you suggesting we have another baby?'

He pretended to consider it for a moment, and then waggled his brows devilishly. 'At least one.'

'At least one!' Marnie exclaimed. He shrugged.

'At least. I figure a boy might be nice.' He looked over at Violet, a grin of adoration crossing his features. Violet and Ash were two peas in a pod. She adored him. Had from the start, Marnie remembered. She gave her first proper smile to her new daddy. Even before Marnie knew, Violet did. She knew the man she'd met at Carey House was supposed to be in their lives.

Marnie followed his gaze, looking at her daughter, who was dancing comically with some of the other little ones. She was off now, making her own first little steps into the world. Ash followed her like a papa bear when they were out in Carey Cove. A big, tall protective warrior dad, his two fingers always wrapped in a pudgy little hand as Violet clung to various surfaces. She was always babbling away to him. Ash hung off every little word and declared her a genius daily. 'What do you think?' He took her chin between his fingers, kissing her. 'For once I can't tell what you're thinking.'

She snorted. 'You could never tell what I was thinking!'

Ash looked shocked. 'In what way?'

'In every way I wanted to do things to you.' She smiled cheekily at him. 'We didn't play games, but we both hid a little something. That afternoon, after we'd first made love, I looked at the three of us in the kitchen, and I just knew that I would find it near impossible to let you go.'

He was looking at her in wonder, the same way he'd locked those hazel eyes onto hers when she first told him that she loved him.

'You never told me that,' he half whispered. 'I felt exactly the same. You know that, right?'

She kissed him to say yes, she did. When she pulled back, another daydream popped back into her head. She'd had it the other night. They'd taken Violet to her mother's and gone for a meal with their friends. A real Carey House couples' night that had been such a good time. When they'd gone home that night, the house had been quiet without Violet, and as she'd drifted off, hours after they'd gone to bed together, she'd thought of something. How nice it would be to have a sibling for Violet. For Ash to have a child of his own. Oh, they didn't do the labels. He wasn't a stepdad. He was a father to

Violet—he'd been there from the start. It wasn't that, but she wanted more children. With Ash. She wanted to give him a child. They'd never talked about it before, but she had considered since last Christmas.

'You sure? The girls always said that I was a little bit of a tyrant when I was expecting Violet.' His belly laugh told her he didn't much care about that. Her heart swelled, as it did every day around him. With Ash coming to Carey Cove, it was as if her life had been completed. He was the missing piece. The thought of bringing another child into that, having a baby with her husband by her side. It was not part of the plan, that was for sure. She thought back to how steadfast she'd been on her actions. When she'd been expecting Violet, she'd decorated the nursery alone. It would be nice to do those things again, with Ash. She narrowed her eyes at him. 'Are you being serious?'

He looked at Violet, who was playing with Hope, Nya watching them both with a huge grin on her face. Looking back at his beautiful fiancée, he couldn't imagine anything better.

'I don't think we should put any pressure on it, but yeah.' He leaned in, kissing her slow. Just how he liked to kiss the second love of his life. The one he'd never looked for, but now he couldn't stop. God, whenever she was out of his arms, he looked for her. He was ridiculously in love. The way she felt in his arms, it still took his breath away. Waking up to her every morning was bliss. Her friends were now his friends too, and he was already seeing the babies he'd delivered grow around him when he was out and about. A couple of mothers were already seeing him for their next pregnancy. He could already imagine walking Violet to school, seeing those babies at the gates in their little uniforms. He wanted that, and more. He wasn't scared any more. He knew that even if lightning struck, the jolt of love between them would be enough to be worth every moment. 'Have you not thought about it?'

'I've thought about it.' She took a sip of her champagne. 'I wanted it to come from you, I think. If and when it was time.' She gave him a small little smile, her sexy bob making her look fierce but adorable.

'I know what you went through to get to Violet, and with Sam… I just knew that it wouldn't be straightforward for us.'

He talked about Sam, and Chloe now. Marnie had told him not to hide the precious photos he had. The life he had with Chloe before was part of him. Sam was related to Violet, through them. One day, they'd tell Violet about Sam, too, and his mother. How they were dearly loved but didn't get to stay on Earth. It was important to Marnie that Ash not forget them, and Ash loved her all the more for it. They'd even travelled to see their graves together. Marnie had even spoken to them both. Ash never knew what she had said. He'd taken Violet to see the flowers instead. He figured what they were talking about wasn't for him to hear. It was between them.

The more he'd thought about it lately, the more it made sense. He was ready to be a father again. Sam and Violet were perfect, and he knew that a baby would be the icing on the cake.

'I love you, Marnie. I've thought about it for a while.

You already made me a daddy. I love being Violet's father, and I want to do it again. Soon, hopefully.' He grinned, giving away a little of his eagerness. 'I would love to have another child with you, Marnie. It would be just...'

His smile took over his speech, not letting him get his words out. Seeing Violet play with Hope in front of them really cemented what he'd been feeling lately. They'd been together a year now, but it felt so much longer. They loved life on their little lane. They had talked about moving somewhere a little bigger, to buy a house together. They'd never got very far. The truth was, her cottage was home for them. Their little lane was home. Besides, they had an extra bedroom to fill. Why bother leaving paradise?

'Perfect?' she finished for him. They grinned at each other. Ash pulled her closer, his heart swelling with the jolt of electricity she gave him with her touch.

'I think so.' He dropped a kiss onto the bridge of her nose. The one she scrunched up when she was concentrating, or laughing heartily at work, or with Violet. 'Well, let's practise, eh? See what happens. No pressure. PCOS didn't stop you before, and we have contacts in the right field.' He thumbed over to the other people who lived and worked in Carey House. It was true, the gang would be thrilled. They would be ecstatic for all three of them. 'Besides, we haven't spent any time in the hallway lately.' His hazel eyes grew darker, lustful. 'Be a good place to start.'

She shook her head at him, but she was grinning. 'You're naughty.'

'I know,' he retorted. 'You love it.' Another sneaky kiss attack from him. He always did that when they were close by, talking. She'd be doing the dishes one minute, kissed senseless the next.

Marnie guffawed with laughter.

'Oh, really?' She looked back at the girls, who were being twirled around the dance floor in the arms of Kiara and Nya. 'You really want a baby?'

'I really want a baby, Marnie.' He leaned in. 'Our baby. What do you say?'

One look into those hazel eyes, and she knew the answer. It had been hard to get Violet. Frustrating, expensive, maddening. Then she thought of what Ash had been through. Losing Sam before he got a chance to know him.

With the job that they did, they were better placed than most to know how things could go wrong. Not work even. Fail. Complications happened. Emergencies happened. Not every baby delivered got the privilege of drawing their first breath. They knew all of the lows, but, looking at the girls, she remembered the highs too. All the lives that had come into the world. Some of the babies they delivered would be in the same classes as Violet, and their baby. Marnie knew that even knowing everything that could go wrong, it didn't stop people. That was life. You rolled the dice, strived for happy. That was what they would do. Strive for happy, and if the worst happened, they had the other to lean on.

'Okay, deal.'

He waggled his eyebrows again, taking her answer in. 'Really?'

'Really. I love you, Ash. Let's make a baby.'

'Woman,' he said, sounding like a cowboy, 'I simply can't wait.' He took her hand in his, kissing the back of it like the Prince Charming he was. 'I love you.'

'I love you too,' she declared to him, as she always did when it threatened to burst from her lips anyway. For a cynical woman down on romance, she was much happier than the engaged woman who'd been on that beach in Bali. She wouldn't be back there for anything. Here, in Carey Cove, right where she had laid her roots, she felt freer and more hopeful than she ever had. There was a big, wide world out there, and she couldn't wait to explore more of it with Ash, and their children. Showing Violet the world with him by her side? With their other children? That sounded like a plan worth living for.

Mrs Marnie Ellerington-to-be could not wait to get started. Christmas at Carey Cove really was magical, she decided. Looking around her at the family they had, the love and attention, the care and the shared experiences. It really was a special place, and this Christmas would be no different. It was all part of the plan.

* * * * *

COMING SOON!

We really hope you enjoyed reading this book.
If you're looking for more romance, be sure to
head to the shops when new books are
available on

Thursday 22nd December

To see which titles are coming soon, please visit

millsandboon.co.uk/nextmonth

MILLS & BOON®

Coming next month

RULES OF THEIR FAKE FLORIDA FLING
Juliette Hyland

"I wrote up that contract." Her cheeks turned bright red, and she looked everywhere but at him. "If you're willing to go along with it, I'll owe you."

He was thrilled! She'd chosen him, and he planned to spend his time with Aurora making her smile and laugh. "Have a seat, please." He knew he'd never demand repayment. "What are the rules, Aurora?"

She moved to his couch, sat down and waited for him to join her, before pulling out a sheet and handing it to him.

He raised a brow as he looked at it. "This is a real contract."

"I doubt that it would hold up in court. But one of my college roommates sent me the template they use for PR relationships."

"What?" He'd been serious about the contract, but he hadn't expected a real one.

"Oh, sometimes celebrities have a relationship just for the press...usually right before a big movie or television launch. They have specific contracts regarding how everything will go." Aurora brightened as she outlined the information.

"Do you secretly love celebrity gossip?" He almost laughed but kept it in as Aurora nodded, not wanting to make her feel bad.

"My guilty pleasure." She shrugged.

"Never understood that phrase." Asher clicked his tongue. "If it's something you enjoy then it's just a pleasure. No need to feel bad about it."

"Sometimes, I can't believe you're a neurosurgeon." Aurora clapped her hand over her mouth. "I didn't mean anything bad by that. It's just that you are so silly, happy, hot and down-to-earth…" Aurora sighed and closed her eyes. "Sorry."

"No need to apologize. All of those were adjectives I love hearing. You find me hot?" Asher reached out and tapped her knee. He pulled back almost instantly, intently aware of the tingling in his hand. The desire to leave his hand on her knee, to offer comfort…but he wouldn't deny the desire hovering in his soul either.

"You have to know you're attractive." Aurora put a hand to her cheek.

He wished there was a way to draw the embarrassment from her, but for the first time in forever no jokes came forth to lighten the moment. So he went with the truth. "You're very attractive too."

He saw her swallow. Then she pointed to the contract, "Are you okay with this?"

Asher blinked and tried to refocus. "Rule one: Remember this is a fake relationship. No falling in love."

Continue reading
RULES OF THEIR FAKE FLORIDA FLING
Juliette Hyland

Available next month
www.millsandboon.co.uk

MILLS & BOON

THE HEART OF ROMANCE

A ROMANCE FOR EVERY READER

MODERN

Prepare to be swept off your feet by sophisticated, sexy and seductive heroes, in some of the world's most glamourous and roman[tic] locations, where power and passion collide.

HISTORICAL

Escape with historical heroes from time gone by. Whether your passion for wicked Regency Rakes, muscled Vikings or rugged Highlanders, av[...] the romance of the past.

MEDICAL

Set your pulse racing with dedicated, delectable doctors in the high-pre[s]sure world of medicine, where emotions run high and passion, comfor[t...] love are the best medicine.

True Love

Celebrate true love with tender stories of heartfelt romance, from the rush of falling in love to the joy a new baby can bring, and a focus on [...] emotional heart of a relationship.

Desire

Indulge in secrets and scandal, intense drama and plenty of sizzling ho[t...] action with powerful and passionate heroes who have it all: wealth, sta[tus...] good looks…everything but the right woman.

HEROES

Experience all the excitement of a gripping thriller, with an intense ro[mance] mance at its heart. Resourceful, true-to-life women and strong, fearless [...] face danger and desire - a killer combination!

To see which titles are coming soon, please visit

millsandboon.co.uk/nextmonth

JOIN US ON SOCIAL MEDIA!

Stay up to date with our latest releases, author news and gossip, special offers and discounts, and all the behind-the-scenes action from Mills & Boon...

 @millsandboon

 @millsandboonuk

 facebook.com/millsandboon

 @millsandboonuk

It might just be true love...

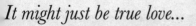

GET YOUR ROMANCE FIX!

Get the latest romance news,
exclusive author interviews, story
extracts and much more!

blog.millsandboon.co.uk